Rhodius Apollonius

The Argonautica of Apollonius Rhodius

Rhodius Apollonius

The Argonautica of Apollonius Rhodius

ISBN/EAN: 9783337399436

Printed in Europe, USA, Canada, Australia, Japan

Cover: Foto ©Andreas Hilbeck / pixelio.de

"THE ARGONAUTICA"

OF

APOLLONIUS RHODIUS.

TRANSLATED INTO ENGLISH PROSE FROM THE TEXT OF R. MERKEL

BY

EDWARD P. COLERIDGE, B.A.

E COLL. ORIEL, OXON.

LONDON:

GEORGE BELL AND SONS, YORK STREET,

COVENT GARDEN.

1889.

TABLE OF CONTENTS.

SHORT LIFE OF APOLLONIUS RHODIUS, WITH A FEW REMARKS ON HIS "ARGONAUTICA."

APOLLONIUS RHODIUS was born about B.C. 235, in the reign of Ptolemy Euergetes, either at Alexandria or at Naucratis. Strabo is in favour of the former, while Athenæus and Ælian declare for the latter place.

He appears to have given himself up at an early age to literary pursuits, and his choice is scarcely to be wondered at when we reflect upon the age in which he lived and the literary atmosphere in which he found himself. We are not expressly told whether it was choice or necessity that led him to select the career he did, but from the fact that the leading poet of that day took the young aspirant in hand and instructed him in his art, we may fairly infer that Apollonius was a man of some standing and position in life. His studies, however, under his master Callimachus were not destined to do either pupil or teacher much credit; no doubt he obtained some technical skill in his art, but the tastes of Callimachus and Apollonius were so diametrically opposed that the two poets quarrelled, and allowed their professional jealousy to go to such lengths that Apollonius lampooned the style of his teacher, while Callimachus was weak enough to retaliate in a studied retort under the title of "Ibis," the character of which poem, though lost to us, may be gathered from Ovid's poem of the same name.

Callimachus was the leading exponent of the strained and artificial poetry of his day. Apollonius, with more true artistic instinct, revolted from the want of reality characteristic of most of his contemporaries, and having a genuine admiration for the straightforward simplicity of the Epic age, set himself to imitate Homer. Naturally he made many enemies among the host of poetasters who took their cue from the animosity shown to him by the "Laureate" of the Alexandrine court. Hence, when the "Argonautica" appeared, it was at once condemned as violating the accepted canons of style and composition, and partly, perhaps, owing to certain youthful crudities which were afterwards corrected. Great was the chagrin of the young poet at the reception of his work, and fierce was his anger against Callimachus. The position of the latter, however, was unassailable, and so Apollonius, after a fruitless wordy warfare, determined to seek some new opening for his genius. Accordingly he bade farewell to ungrateful Alexandria, and retired to Rhodes, then the second great seat of literature, taking his poem with him.

Possibly experience had taught him wherein his poem was deficient. At any rate, he revised the whole of it; and now, free from the cabals of jealous rivals, he received a fair verdict, and at once rose to fame. So popular, indeed, did he become on the reading of his poem, that the Rhodians, it is said, rewarded him with extraordinary honours, and conferred their franchise upon him. From this incident in his career he came to be called "the Rhodian," a name which has clung to him for ever.

It was only natural that in his hour of triumph he should long to have his merit acknowledged in his native city—in Alexandria, the gathering place of the old world's declining literature and art. Thither, therefore, he came, with his honours upon him, and whether it was that Callimachus and his followers were out of favour, or whether the Alexandrines had relented towards their ill-used poet, certain it is that he attained to great celebrity, and was advanced to valuable posts of trust. Henceforth he could afford to rest upon his hardly-won laurels, his period of "Sturm und Drang" was over; he had passed through the fire, and it had done him no hurt—weighed in the balance he had not been found wanting.

Of his life henceforth we learn but little, beyond what Suidas tells us as to his having become librarian in the vast royal museum at Alexandria, about B.C. 194. It may well be that this was so; for the Ptolemies, in whose reigns Apollonius lived and wrote, were monarchs not unlikely to bestow such an important literary post upon a man of marked ability and studious habits. Assuming that Suidas is correct in his statement, we find plenty of internal evidence in the poem to suggest that the writer must have been a man of vast erudition, or have had at his command extensive stores of knowledge from which to draw his materials.

During this period of his life the poet was not idle. Imbued to some extent with the spirit of his age, he produced works at a great pace; epigrams, grammars, and the so-called *κτίσεις*, *i.e.* poems on the origin and foundation of towns, but all these are lost to us save a few mutilated fragments and stray lines preserved in other writers.

In the library at Alexandria he remained until his death in B.C. 181, happy enough, no doubt, amongst the endless treasures of that vast repository of art and learning.

Of his work that has come down to us, too little notice has been taken by English scholars; for though his style at times bears too evident traces of laboured study, the structure of his poem is simple and straightforward. The mind is not burdened by a multiplicity of episodes, the descriptions are singularly beautiful, and the similes, which are abundant and varied, show the hand of a master, who, if he did sometimes imitate, had at least something graceful of his own to add to what he borrowed, and not infrequently paid back his loan with interest.

The work found numerous commentators in ancient times, to whom we are indebted for the Florentine and Parisian Scholia. Moreover, Apollonius was very popular among the Romans; so much so that his poem was translated by Publius Terentius Varro Atacinus, and was imitated by Valerius Flaccus and many others.

EDITIONS.

(i.) J. Lascaris. A.D. 1496. Quarto. Florence. Contains the Scholia.

(ii.) The Aldine edition. A.D. 1581. Octavo. Venice. Little more than a reprint of the Florentine edition.

(iii.) Brunck. A.D. 1780. Quarto and octavo. Argentorat. First really critical edition.

(iv.) Beck. A.D. 1797. Octavo. Leipzig. Incomplete. Text with Latin translation and a few critical notes.

(v.) G. Schäfer. A.D. 1810-13. 2 vols. octavo. Leipzig. A better edition, and the first containing Paris Scholia.

(vi.) Wellauer. A.D. 1828. 2 vols. octavo. Leipzig. Still better. Contains readings of thirteen MSS.; also the Scholia, and notes in Latin.

(vii.) R. Merkel. A.D. 1852. Teubner, Leipzig. A careful revision of the Laurentine MS., with notes.

There are, besides these editions of the actual text, certain German essays upon Apollonius, but in England hitherto this author has received but scanty justice.

THE ARGUMENT OF THE "ARGONAUTICA," FROM THE GREEK OF THE SCHOLIASTS.

TYRO, the daughter of Salmoneus, had two sons by Poseidon, Neleus and Pelias; she afterwards wedded Cretheus, son of Æolus, and bore to him Æson, Pheres, and Amythaon. From Æson sprang Jason; from Pheres, Admetus; from Amythaon, Melampus.

Now Jason was handed over to the Centaur Chiron to be brought up and to learn the art of healing; while Æson, his father, left the kingdom to Pelias, his own brother, bidding him rule Thessaly until Jason's return from Chiron. But Pelias had received an oracle from Apollo, bidding him beware of a man who should come with only one sandal; for by him should he be slain.

So Jason grew up, and came to his uncle, for to take his share in his father's kingdom. But when he came to the river Anaurus, which is in Thessaly, wishing to ford it, there upon the bank he found Hera in the disguise of an old dame, and she would cross, but was afraid. Then did Jason take her upon his shoulders, and carry her safe over, but one sandal left he in the mud in the middle of the river. Thence he fared to the city with his one sandal, and there he found an assembly of the folk, and Pelias doing sacrifice to the gods. When Pelias saw him thus he minded him of the oracle, and being eager to be rid of him he set him this task, that he should go to Scythia in quest of the golden fleece, and then receive the kingdom. Now this he did from no wish for the fleece, but because he thought that Jason would be slain by some man in that strange land, or be shipwrecked.

This is the story of the golden fleece.

A SECOND ARGUMENT, GIVEN BY BRUNCK, FROM AN UNKNOWN ANCIENT SOURCE.

ATHAMAS, the son of Æolus, and brother of Cretheus, had to wife Nephele first, and begat two children, Phrixus and Helle. When Nephele died, he married Ino, who did plot against the children of Nephele, and persuaded her country-women to roast the seed for sowing; but the earth, receiving roasted seed, would not bear her yearly crops. So Athamas sent to Delphi to inquire about the barrenness; but Ino bribed his messengers, telling them to return and say, that the god had answered that Helle and Phrixus must be sacrificed if they wanted the barrenness to cease. Wherefore Athamas was persuaded, and placed them at the altar; but the gods in pity snatched them away through the air by means of the ram with the golden fleece; now Helle let go, and fell into the sea that bears her name, while Phrixus landed safe in Colchis. There he offered up the ram to Zeus, who helped his flight, for that he had escaped the plot of his stepmother. And having married Chalciope, daughter of Æetes, king of the Scythians, he begat four sons, Argus, Cytissorus, Melas, and Phrontis. And there he died.

GENEALOGICAL TREE TO SHOW THE RELATIONSHIP BETWEEN VARIOUS MEMBERS OF THE ÆOLID FAMILY.

ÆOLUS.

Cretheus ╤ Tyro.[1]

Æson. — Jason.

Pheres. — Admetus.

Amythaon. — Melampus.

Athamas ╤ 1. Nephele; 2. Ino.

Phrixus. Helle.

Chalciope[2] ╤ Phrixus.

Argus. Cytissorus. Melas. Phrontis.

[1] Tyro before her marriage with Cretheus had been the mother of two children, viz., Neleus and Pelias, by Poseidon. Therefore Pelias is step-uncle to Jason, whom he seeks to dispossess.

[2] Chalciope, daughter of Æetes, marries Phrixus, first cousin of Æson—so that Jason is cousin to her children.

There was a curse in the family of Æolus from the day that two members of it, Athamas and his wife Ino, ill-treated Phrixus and Helle, two other Æolids. Zeus saved the two intended victims and put a curse upon the guilty family, which could not be revoked until the golden fleece was brought from Colchis to Hellas.

THE ROUTE OF THE ARGONAUTS TO ÆA, AND THEIR RETURN THENCE TO IOLCHOS.

THERE is no particular difficulty in following Argo on her outward voyage, or in identifying the numerous places mentioned by Apollonius along the route; indeed, his knowledge of the geography up to Æa, the goal of the enterprise, is singularly accurate. It is when we attempt to follow his account of the return journey, which was made by a different route, that we find ourselves utterly perplexed, and forced to the conclusion that our author has been drawing purely from imagination, without any idea of the impossibility of the course which he assigns to the heroes.

However, we purpose to give the route as described by the poet, noticing difficulties as they occur, though we shall not attempt to correct geographical errors in an account which by no conceivable theory can be reconciled with actual fact.

The expedition starts from Iolchos in Thessaly (i. 523). The ship Argo is moored in the river Anaurus (i. 320). Leaving the harbour of Pagasæ (i. 523), the Argonauts sail through the Sinus Pelasgicus, past the promontory of Tisa (i. 568) and the headland of Sepias (i. 582); then coasting between the island of Sciathus (i. 583) and along the Thessalian coast, past the tomb of Dolops (i. 584), Melibœa (i. 592), the mouth of the river Amyrus (i. 596), Eurymenæ (i. 597), and the spurs of Ossa and Olympus (i. 598), they make right across the mouth of the Thermaic gulf to the promontory of Pallene (i. 599); thence, after sighting Mount Athos (i. 601), they steer for Lemnos (i. 608). After some stay in this island, they go out of their course to the isle of Electra or Samothrace, for the sake of certain mysteries (i. 916); then keeping Thrace on the left of the ship and Imbros on the right, they sail across the Ægean Sea (i. 923) to the mouth of the Hellespont (i. 928). Through the Hellespont they sail past Rhœteum, Ilium, Abydos, Percote, Abarnis, and so to Cyzicus, then an island, now mainland (i. 929 *sqq.*) in the Propontis. Next they pass the mouth of the river Æsepus (i. 940) and come to the harbour and bay of Chytus (i. 987), but at this point they are caught by contrary winds and driven back again to Cyzicus (i. 1110). Halting here awhile they go inland to ascend Mount Dindymus and spy out their further route; then go on again across the mouth of the river Rhyndacus in Mysia (i. 1165) until they reach the headland of Posideum (i. 1279), near to which live the savage Bebryces, whom they encounter and defeat (ii. 1 *sqq.*) at the mouth of the Bosporus. Thence, after meeting the blind prophet Phineus in Bithynia (ii. 177), they pass through the dreadful Symplegades or Cyanean Rocks, which guard the entrance to the Euxine Sea (ii. 560 *sqq.*); coasting along Bithynia (ii. 621) they pass the mouth of the river Rhebas (ii. 652), the rock of Colone, the Black Headland (ii. 658), the river Phyllis (ii. 654), the river Calpe (ii. 661), and anchor at the Thynian island (ii. 675). Next they cross the mouth of the river Sangarius (ii. 724), passing the territory of the Mariandyni (ii. 725), the river Lycus, lake Anthemous, the river Acheron and its haven (ii. 726 *sqq.*); thence past river Callichorus (ii. 906), the river Parthenius (ii. 938), Sesamus (ii. 948), Erythini, and the heights of Crobialus, Cromna, Cytorus and Carambis in Paphlagonia (ii. 945); after this they pass Sinope (ii. 948), the river Halys (ii. 965), the river Thermodon (ii. 972), the Amazons and Chalybes (ii. 987 *sqq.*), the Tibareni, Mossynœci (ii. 1012 *sqq.*), land at the isle of Ares and rescue the sons of Chalciope (ii. 1033); thence to the isle of Philyra (ii. 1234), past the territory of the Macrones, Becheiri, Sapeiræ, Byzeres, till they sight the range of Caucasus and the limit of their voyage (ii. 1245 *sqq.*); they now enter the river Phasis, the river of Colchis, wherein lies the isle of Æa (ii. 1264).

The Argonauts have thus reached Æa. Their voyage as sketched by Apollonius is singularly accurate, and it is clear that he must have been familiar with the geography to have given such an exhaustive list of places, hills, and rivers.

Briefly the voyage amounts to this. The Argonauts leave the Pelasgicus Sinus (Gulf of Volo), coast along Thessaly to Thermaicus Sinus (Gulf of Salonica), steer across Ægæum Mare (Archipelago) to the Hellespont (Dardanelles); through this strait into the Propontis (Sea of Marmara); through the Bosporus into the Euxine (Black Sea).

Except when they cross the Archipelago, their voyage is almost entirely a coasting one, and is easy to follow on a map.

The return route retraces their steps as far as the river Halys in Paphlagonia (iv. 245), but then, instead of rounding the headland of Carambis and following the coast-line (iv. 300), they strike out a new course across the open sea to the mouth of the Ister (Danube) (iv. 302). From this point very little information is afforded us by Apollonius as to the places through which the heroes passed. Certain names indeed are mentioned, but they are difficult to identify or localize, *e.g.*, Mount Anchurus (iv. 323), the rock of Cauliacus (iv. 324), the plain of Laurium (iv. 326), the Brygian isles (iv. 330). Apollonius was evidently aware of the weakness of his own geography, and avoids all details concerning this remarkable river-voyage; he eventually brings the heroes out into the Adriatic near the peninsula of Hyllis (iv. 524). It is scarcely necessary to remark on the impossibility of this route, owing to rocks, rapids, cataracts, and an impassable current; nor are we told into what river the Argonauts made their way out of the Ister in order to arrive at the Adriatic at all. After this they steer towards the Italian coast, passing the islands of Issa, Dusceladus, Pityeia, Corcyra the Black (iv. 563), Melite, Cerossus, Nymphæa, and the Ceraunian hills (iv. 570 *sqq.*); they come to the Eridanus (Po) (iv. 594), and apparently sailing right across northern Italy, gain by some unaccountable means the river Rhone (iv. 625). Here again we are not informed how they achieved this remarkable feat; the poet seems to labour under the delusion that the Eridanus and Rhone are connected, and that a continuous voyage is possible. Next the heroes are somewhat vaguely said to pass through the territory of the Celts and Ligyans (iv. 645), but no further point on their course is mentioned until they arrive at the Stœchades Insulæ (Is. d'Hières, off the southern coast of Provence) (iv. 652); thence they sail across the open sea (Mediterranean) to the isle of Æthalia, passing above Corsica (iv. 652), and so by a long coasting voyage along Italy they reach the Ææan harbour and the promontory of Circe (iv. 659); thence passing the island of the Sirens (iv. 890) they come to the Æolian isles, run the gauntlet of Scylla and Charybdis in the straits between Italy and Sicily (iv. 920 *sqq.*), coast round the bottom of Italy, and land at Drepane, *i.e.* Corcyra, where the Phæacians live (iv. 980 *sqq.*); from Drepane they coast along Epirus, Ambracia, and Acarnania, till they reach the Echinades Insulæ (iv. 1228); but here they are caught by a violent tempest and driven to the Syrtis Minor of Africa (iv. 1233). Being unable to get out of the quicksands they carry Argo overland to lake Tritonis (iv. 1389), and, launching her again, sail out to sea. Apparently they now made a very circuitous voyage along the coasts of Africa and Asia Minor until they were opposite to the island of Carpathus, which they are said to pass; from thence they came to Crete (iv. 1635); thence through the Sporades into the Ægean to Ægina (iv. 1764); then along the coast of Attica and between Eubœa and the Opuntian Locri (iv. 1779), through the Sinus Pelasgicus, to Pagasæ, whence they had started.

The return voyage teems with such insurmountable difficulties, and is altogether so hopelessly confused and mythical, that it would be a mere waste of time and patience to attempt to follow it on a modern map.

We can only indicate briefly the course the heroes are said to have taken. After crossing the Euxine (Black Sea), they rowed through river-ways right across Dacia, Mœsia, Illyria, and Dalmatia (Bulgaria, Servia, Bosnia, and Herzegovina), into the Adriatic; sailing to Italy they cross the northern part by the Eridanus (Po); sail into the Rhone, thence into the Mediterranean; right across to the west coast of Italy, along which they pass; through the Lipari islands and the strait of Messina; up the east coast of Italy to the Adriatic again; thence driven by storms they come to the African coast; being caught in the shoals of the Syrtis they carry Argo overland to lake Tritonis (Bahr Faraouni in Tunis), and finding an outlet into the Mediterranean, sail along the African coast to the coast of Asia Minor, and so into the Ægean homewards.

THE USE OF POSSESSIVE ADJECTIVES AND PERSONAL PRONOUNS IN APOLLONIUS.

EPIC poets after Homer, and perhaps none more than Apollonius, affect a singular licence in the use of possessive adjectives, and to a less extent of personal pronouns, confusing their strict meaning to such a degree, that it may be of some service to collect in a short scheme examples of Apollonius' more notable divergences from classical usage.

I. *σφωίτερος*, the possessive adj. of the 2nd person dual, does duty for—

(α) Possessive adj. of 2nd person singular. Cf. iii. 395.
(β) Possessive adj. of 3rd person singular. Cf. i. 643; iii. 335, 600, 625.
(γ) Possessive adj. of 3rd person plural. Cf. i. 1286.

II. *σφέτερος*, the possessive adj. of 3rd person plural, does duty for—

(α) Possessive adj. of 3rd person singular. Cf. iii. 186, 622.
(β) Possessive adj. of 2nd person plural. Cf. iv. 1325.

III. *ἑός*, the possessive adj. of 3rd person singular, does duty for—

(α) Possessive adj. of 2nd person singular. Cf. ii. 636; iii. 140.
(β) Possessive adj. of 3rd person plural. Cf. i. 1113; iii. 327.

IV. The personal pronoun of 3rd person singular does duty for—

(α) 1st person singular. Cf. ii. 637; iii. 99.
(β) 2nd person singular. Cf. i. 893.

BOOK I.

ARGUMENT.

Pelias, in alarm, sends Jason to Colchis to fetch the golden fleece. So Jason gathers the chieftains, and is chosen captain himself. After launching Argo they sail on without adventure as far as Lemnos, where they stay awhile, and are hospitably received by Hypsipyle the queen. Thence they come to the Doliones and their king Cyzicus, and are kindly entertained. Giants withstand them at Dindymus, but these are shot by Heracles. On the same night a storm drives the ship back to Cyzicus, and in the darkness they and the Doliones come to blows, and Cyzicus is slain. After mourning for him, they sail on to Mysia, where Hylas is lost, and Heracles, who will not be comforted, is left behind with Polyphemus.

THE ARGONAUTICA OF APOLLONIUS RHODIUS.

WITH thee, Phœbus, will I begin and record the famous deeds of those men of old time, who, at the bidding of king Pelias, rowed the good ship Argo past the mouth of the Euxine and through the rocks Cyanean[1] to fetch the golden fleece.

For Pelias had heard an oracle on this wise, that in the latter days a hateful doom awaited him, even death at the prompting of one whom he should see come forth from the people with but one sandal. And not long after, according to the sure report, came Jason on foot across the stream of a swollen torrent, and one sandal did he save from 'neath the mud, but the other left he there sticking in the river-bed. So he came to Pelias forthwith to take a part in the solemn feast, which he was offering to his father Poseidon and the other gods, but to Pelasgian Hera[2] he paid no heed. And the instant Pelias saw Jason, he was ware of him, and made ready to his hurt a grievous task of seaman-

[1] Κυανέαι πέτραι, elsewhere called Πλαγκταί and Συμπλήγαδες. These famous rocks, which are also mentioned by Homer and Euripides, were said to guard the entrance to the Pontus.

[2] The poet, whilst noticing the favour borne by Hera to Jason, gives no reason for the neglect shown to her by Pelias.

Πελασγίδος here = Θεσσαλικῆς; the Pelasgi inhabiting Phthiotis in Thessaly. Cf. Hom. Il. ii. 681.

ship, that so he might lose his return in the deep or haply among strange folk.

Now minstrels even before my day do tell how Argus by the counsels of Athene built a ship for him; but mine shall it now be to declare the lineage and name of the heroes, and their passage of the long sea, and all that they did in their wanderings; and may the Muses be the heralds of my song!

First then let us make mention of Orpheus; he it was, whom, on a day, as rumour saith, Calliope bare beside the peak of Pimpleia, her pledge of love to Thracian Œager. He, men say, did charm the stubborn rocks upon the hills and the river streams by the strains of his minstrelsy. And wild oaks, memorials yet of that his singing, which he had led right on from Pieria by the spell of his lyre, marched in ordered ranks, each behind his fellow, to range themselves, with all their leaves, upon the fringe of the Thracian shore. So mighty a man was Orpheus, whom the son of Æson, by the counsels of Chiron, did persuade and take to help him in his toils from his kingship over Bistonian Pieria.

Anon came Asterion; he it was whom Cometes did beget by the waters of swirling Apidanus, when he dwelt in Peiresia, hard by the Phylleian hill, where mighty Apidanus[1] and divine Enipeus do unite, flowing into one stream from their distant sources.

To these came Polyphemus,[2] son of Elatus, having left Larissa; who erst, what time the Lapithæ armed against

[1] The Apidanus and Enipeus, two rivers in Thessaly. The Phylleian mountain is in Macedonia. Peiresia, or Pieria, name of a Macedonian district and town.

[2] The Polyphemus here mentioned is not the same as the giant shepherd of Sicily, whom Odysseus blinded. This hero, who figures afterwards as the loyal and trusty friend of Heracles, had already distinguished himself in the famous battle between the Lapithæ and the Centaurs at the wedding feast of Pirithous.

the Centaurs, joined the fray as the youngest of the mighty Lapithæ. Now on that day were his limbs weighed down with wine, but firm abode his warlike spirit still, even as aforetime.

No long space was Iphiclus, uncle of the son of Æson, left behind in Phylace; for Æson had wedded his sister, Alcimede of Phylace; whence the claims of blood and kith bade him enrol himself in the muster.

Neither did Admetus, lord of Pheræ, rich in sheep, abide beneath the peak of the Chalcodonian mountain.

Erytus and Echion too, sons of Hermes, well skilled in craftiness, and rich in broad cornlands, lingered not in Alope; and yet a third arrived to join them as they were starting, Æthalides, their kinsman;[1] him by the stream of Myrmidonian Amphrysus did Eupolemeia, maid of Phthia, bear; but those other twain were sons of Antianeira, daughter of Menetes.

Came too Coronus, son of Cæneus,[2] leaving rich Gyrton, a goodly man, yet scarce his father's match. For minstrels tell how Cæneus, though he liveth yet, was slain by the Centaurs; what time, alone and apart from the other chiefs, he routed them; and, when they suddenly rallied again, they could not make him give way nor slay him; but he, unconquered and unflinching, passed beneath the earth, smitten by the heavy pines they hurled on him.

Next came Mopsus, sprung from Titaron; him the son of Leto had taught the augury of birds beyond all men;

[1] γνωτὸς here as elsewhere in Apollonius Rhodius means "kinsman," not "well-known."

[2] Cæneus took part in the battle between the Lapithæ and Centaurs. Ovid, Metam. xii. 171 sqq., relates how Cæneus had originally been a beautiful maiden named Cænis; this maiden Poseidon loved and changed into a man who should be invulnerable; so when in the battle the Centaurs could not kill Cæneus with sword or spear, they buried him alive beneath a mass of trees, but even so his spirit sped away in the form of a bird.

likewise came Eurydamas, son of Ctimenus, who had his dwelling in Dolopian Ctimene, nigh unto the Xunian[1] lake.

Moreover Actor sent forth his son Menœtius from Opus, to go with the chieftains.

And Eurytion followed, and valiant Eribotes; one the son of Teleon, the other of Irus, son of Actor; verily, famous Eribotes was sprung from Teleon, and Eurytion had Irus for his sire. With these went a third, Oileus, matchless for chivalry, and skilled enow in rushing on the rear of the foe, what time their ranks give way.

From Eubœa Canthus hied him forth; he it was whom Canethus, son of Abas, was sending with eager feet; yet was he never to turn again and reach Cerinthus. For his fate it was with Mopsus, that skilled diviner, to wander to his death in the utmost ends of Libya. For of evils none is too far away for man to meet therewith; seeing that men buried those twain even in Libya, as far from Colchis as the rising and the setting of the sun are seen to be from each other.

Next then gathered to the muster Clytius and Iphitus, wardens of Œchalia, sons of Eurytus the harsh—that Eurytus, to whom the far-darting god gave a bow; yet had he no joy of the gift, for of his own choice he strove with the giver himself.

After these the sons of Æacus joined the quest; they came not both together, nor from the same place; for they dwelt apart, keeping aloof from Ægina, since the day, when in their witlessness they slew their kinsman Phocus. Now Telamon had settled in Salamis, isle of Attica; while Peleus went away and builded him a home in Phthia.

Next came the warrior Butes from Cecropia, the son of

[1] The Xunian lake is in Thessaly. The Scholiast says it was so called from being on the confines of Thessaly and Bœotia, and so common (ξυνόν = κοινόν) to both; it was not far from lake Bœbe.

goodly Teleon, and Phalerus of the stout ashen spear. Alcon, his sire, had sent him forth, albeit he had no other sons to nurse the evening of his life; yet for all he was his well-beloved,[1] yea, his only-begotten, still would he send him to win renown among those heroes bold.

But Theseus, who far excelled all the sons of Erechtheus, did an unseen[2] bond keep back beneath the land of Tænarus, for thither had he gone along with Peirithous. Verily these twain might[3] have made the accomplishment of their toil lighter for them all.

And Tiphys, son of Hagnias, left his Thespian folk in Siphas; a cunning prophet he to foretell a rising tumult amid the waves of the wide sea, and cunning to divine storms of wind and the course of a ship from the sun and the stars. Him did Tritonian Athene herself rouse to the gathering of the chiefs, and he came amongst men eager for his coming; for it was Athene, too, that builded the swift ship, and with her had Argus, son of Arestor, fashioned it

[1] τηλύγετος. Whatever be the derivation of this much-disputed word, one meaning seems to cling to it throughout Apollonius Rhodius, and it is to be remembered that the Alexandrine usage of words does not necessarily correspond with that of earlier writers. The Alexandrine etymology was not unfrequently very faulty; and so in translating this doubtful Homeric word as "well-beloved," from the idea of affection naturally attaching to the last born child, we shall be following the meaning of the author, although perhaps he misunderstood the word himself.

[2] ἀίδηλος. Apollonius greatly affects the use of Homeric words, though not by any means always in their Homeric sense, which possibly was misinterpreted by the critics of Alexandria. The word ἀίδηλος is used here and elsewhere by the poet in the sense of "unseen," probably from a false etymology, though into a controversy upon Homeric words, which are still in many cases "sub judice," we cannot here attempt to enter.

Theseus, attempting to carry off Persephone from Hades, was overcome and bound by an invisible agency to a rock from which he could not rise.

[3] An ellipse of "if they had been there."

by her counsels. Wherefore was Argo far the best of all the barques that ever crossed the sea with oars.

Next came Phlias from Aræthyrea, where he dwelt in plenty by the grace of Dionysus, his father, in his home by the springs of Asopus.

From Argos came forth Talaus and Areius, two sons of Bias; and mighty Leodocus, whom Pero, daughter of Neleus, bare; for her sake Melampus, son of Æolus, endured grievous misery in the steading of Iphiclus.

Nor are we told that mighty Heracles, stout of heart, made light of the earnest prayer of the son of Æson. Nay, when he heard the report that the heroes were gathering, he changed his path anew from Arcadia and came to Lyrceian Argos, whither he was bringing alive a boar that battened in the glens of Lampeia[1] beside the vast marsh of Erymanthus; and he cast him down from off his mighty back, fast bound in chains, at the entrance to the assembly of the Mycenæans, while himself started off as he listed against the purpose of Eurystheus; and with him came Hylas, his trusty squire, in the bloom of youth, to bear his arrows and to keep his bow.

Next came the son of divine Danaus, Nauplius. Lo! he was son of Clytoneus, the child of Naubolus; and Naubolus was the son of Lernus; and of Lernus we are told that he was the son of Prœtus, whom Nauplius begat; for the maid Amymone, daughter of Danaus, in days gone by, bare, from the embraces of Poseidon, Nauplius, who far excelled all men in seamanship.

And last of those, who dwelt in Argos, came Idmon; for he would be there, although from augury he knew his fate; lest the people should grudge him a fair fame. He, of a truth, was no son of Abas, but the child of Leto himself begat him to swell the number of the famous race of

[1] A mountain in Arcadia, in which the river Erymanthus rises.

Æolus;[1] yea, and himself did teach him divination, and to heed the flight of birds, and to read signs in blazing fire.

Moreover, Ætolian Leda sent forth from Sparta strong Polydeuces and Castor, skilled to curb fleet steeds; these, her well-beloved sons, she bare at one birth in the halls of Tyndarus, and when they would go she said not nay, for her thoughts were worthy the bride of Zeus.

From Arene came the sons of Apharetus, Lynceus and Idas, of overweening pride, both too confident in their great strength; and Lynceus too excelled in the keenness of his sight, if that is really a true legend, that he could see with ease a man even beneath the earth.

And with them Periclymenus, son of Neleus, started to go, eldest of all the children that were born to divine Neleus in Pylos; him Poseidon gifted with boundless might, and granted that[2] whatsoever he should pray to be during the fray, that should he become in the stress of battle.

Again, from Arcadia came Amphidamas and Cepheus, who dwelt in Tegea, the heritage of Apheidas, the two sons of Aleus; and eke a third followed in their train, Ancæus, whom his own father Lycurgus was sending; he was elder brother to those twain, but was left behind in the city that he might care for Aleus in his old age, but he sent his own son to join his brethren. And the young man went on his way, brandishing the skin of a bear of Mænalus, and in his right hand a great two-edged axe. For his grandsire Aleus had hidden his weapons in an inner closet, if haply he might stay him even yet from setting out.

There came too Augeas, who, legend saith, is son to Helios; and over the men of Elis this prince held sway,

[1] Æolus, the son of Hellen, had two sons, Cretheus and Athamas; Æson was the son of Cretheus; Jason, the son of Æson.

[2] Periclymenus had the power of changing his shape at will during battle.

τὸ here is demonstrative = "that."

glorying in his wealth; but greatly did he long to see the land of Colchis and Æetes in person, the leader of the Colchians.

And Asterius and Amphion, sons of Hyperasius, came from Achæan Pellene, which on a day their grandsire Pelles founded on the crags by the sea-shore.

To these, again, came Euphemus, leaving Tænarus; he it was whom Europe, daughter of Tityus, of giant strength, bare, outstripping all in speed of foot. He would run upon the sea's gray swell, and never wet his swift feet; but, moistening just the soles thereof, he sped along his watery [1] path.

And there came two other sons of Poseidon; the one, to wit, Erginus, who had left the town of noble Miletus; the other, Ancæus, the proud, who had come from Parthenie, seat of Imbrasian [2] Hera; both these boasted their knowledge of seacraft and of war.

Next came valiant Meleager, son of Œneus, having started from Calydon, and Laocoon too, who was brother of Œneus; yet were they not sons of one mother, but him did a bondwoman bear; he it was whom Œneus sent, now that he was grown up, to guard his child; so while yet a youth he entered that brave band of heroes, and none, methinks, mightier than he had come, save Heracles alone, if he had stayed but one year [3] longer there and been trained

[1] *ἐιερή*. The meaning of this word in this passage at any rate is clearer than its etymology. From the context it obviously = "wet," but Homeric scholars will remember passages in which this rendering is inadmissible.

[2] *Ἰμβρασίης*, *i.e.* Samian. The Imbrasus is a river in Samos, near which, according to one legend, Hera spent her early years.

[3] *λυκάβαντα*. It is difficult on etymological grounds to account for this word. Both in Homer and in the Alexandrine imitators of his style it seems to mean "a year." One derivation connects it with *λύκη βαίνω* = the path of light, *i.e.* the sun's course, *i.e.* the year; but this is scarcely less fanciful than the Scholiast's suggestion that it is a variant form of *λυγάβαντα*, from *λύγον*, "an osier," the colour of which, he says, is black, "and with blackness the year departs."

up amongst the Ætolians. And lo! his uncle Iphiclus, the son of Thestius, bare him company on that journey, a spearman good, and skilled enow as well to match himself with any in close fight.

And with him was Palæmonius, son of Lernus, of Olenus; son of Lernus men called him, but he drew his lineage from Hephæstus, wherefore he was lame of foot; but none would have the hardihood to scorn his form and manliness, wherefore he too was numbered amongst the other chiefs, swelling the fame of Jason.

From the Phocians then came Iphitus, sprung from Naubolus, son of Ornytus; now he had been Jason's host aforetime when he came to Pytho to ask an oracle about his voyage; for there did Iphitus receive him in his halls.

Next came the sons of Boreas, Calais and Zetes, whom, on a day, Oreithyia, daughter of Erechtheus, bare to Boreas at the verge of wintry Thrace; thither it was that Thracian Boreas had snatched her away from Cecropia, as she was circling in the dance by the banks of the Ilissus. And from afar he brought her to the spot men call Sarpedon's rock, beside the stream of the river Erginus, and there he shrouded her in dark clouds, and had his will of her. These his two sons made strong pinions move on either ancle as they rose, a mighty marvel to behold, radiant with scales of gold; and about their backs, from the crown of the head and on either side the neck, dark hair was waving in the breeze.

Nor yet had Acastus, son of stalwart Pelias himself, any longing to abide within his father's house; nor Argus either, servant of the goddess Athene; nay, for they too, I ween, were to be counted in the muster.

This, then, is the tale of those who gathered to the son of Æson to aid him with their counsel; whom the neighbouring folk called Minyan chieftains, one and all, since most of them, and those the best, avowed them to be of the blood of the daughters of Minyas; even so Alcimede, the mother of Jason himself, was sprung from Clymene, a daughter of Minyas.

Now when the thralls had made all things ready, wherewith ships are furnished for their freight, whenso business calls men to make a voyage across the sea; in that hour they betook them to the ship through the city to the place men call the headland of Pagasæ,[1] in Magnesia; and around them a crowd of folk ran thronging eagerly; but they showed like bright stars amid clouds, and thus would each man say as he gazed on them flashing in their harness: "King Zeus, what is the intent of Pelias? whither is he sending such a muster of heroes from out the Panachæan[2] land? They will sack the homes of Æetes with baleful fire the very day they see them, if so be he give them not the fleece of his own accord. But the voyage may not be shunned, nor shall their toil be fruitless, if they go."

So spake they, one here, one there throughout the city; and the women lifted up their hands full oft toward heaven to the immortal gods, praying that they would grant the accomplishment of their return as their heart desired. And one to another would thus complain through her tears: "Ah, hapless Alcimede, to thee too hath sorrow come, late though it be, nor hast thou finished thy course with joy. Surely Æson is a man of sorrows, and that in no small measure. Yea, better for him had it been, if ere this he had been wrapped in his shroud[3] and were lying 'neath the earth, a stranger still to evil enterprises. Would that the black wave had engulfed Phrixus too, fleece and all,

[1] Pagasæ, the starting-point and also the landing-place on the return of the expedition, is a headland of Magnesia; there was a harbour there in the historical days of the Greek states.

[2] Thessaly is called Panachæan because it was first named Achæa, from Achæus, the son of Xuthus.

[3] *κτέρεα* generally = possessions of any kind, here = shroud. Cf. *κτέανα*.

on the day that the maiden Helle perished! But no! that prodigy of ill uttered[1] a human voice, that it might bring grief and countless woes to Alcimede, in days to come."

Thus would the women speak as the heroes went on their way forth. And many thralls, both men and maids, were already gathering, and his mother flung herself on Jason's neck. For piercing grief had entered each woman's breast; and with her his father, bowed by baleful age, made moan upon his bed, closely veiled from head to foot.

And Jason, the while, was soothing their grief with words of comfort; but he signed to the thralls to take up his weapons of war, and they in silence and with downcast[2] look took them up. But his mother, so soon as she had thrown her arms around her boy, so clung to him, while her sobs[3] came ever more thick and fast; as when a maiden in her solitude is fain to cast her arms about her gray-haired nurse and weep, one who hath none left to defend her, but she leads a cruel life under a step-mother, who ill-treats her tender years with many a flout; and as she weeps, her heart within her is held fast in misery, nor can she utter[4] half the grief she yearneth to; even thus was Alcimede weeping loud and long, as she held her son in her arms. And in her affliction she spake this word: "Ah! would that I had straight given up the ghost and so forgotten my troubles, on the day I heard king Pelias declare to my sorrow his evil hest, that thou, my child, with thine

[1] The ram which rescued Phrixus and Helle from the cruelty of their step-mother Ino had the power of human speech.

[2] *κατηφέες* literally = "with heads bowed down with woe."

[3] *κλαίουσα ἀδινώτερον.* Another Homeric phrase. *ἀδινός* = thick, close; so the meaning seems to be "with sobs coming quicker and quicker upon each other;" perhaps "choking" is an English equivalent. Homer uses the word frequently of "thronging sheep" (*ἀδινὰ μῆλα*).

[4] *ἐκφλύξαι* is literally the boiling and bubbling of water heated in a cauldron.

own dear hands mightest have buried me; since that was all I yet could wish of thee, for all else that thy nurture owed I have long enjoyed. Now shall I, who erst was so admired by the Achæan women, be left like a slave in my empty halls, miserably wasting away in longing for thee, over whom I once had much joy and glory, my only son for whom I loosed my maiden zone [1] for the first time and the last. For the goddess Eileithyia [2] exceedingly did grudge me many children. Ah me! for my blind folly! Little I recked of this, even in dreams, that Phrixus would be an evil for me to shun."

Thus was she, poor lady, sobbing and wailing, and the women her handmaids took up the wail in turn, but Jason spake to her softly with words of comfort: "Mother mine, lay not such piteous grief on me thus all too much, for by thy tears shalt thou not keep from suffering; nay, thou wilt join sorrow on to sorrow. For the gods allot to mortals woes they cannot see. Take heart to bear the lot of mortals for all thy heaviness of soul, and cheer thee with the solemn promise of Athene and with the god's answer, for very favourable was the word of Phœbus, and after these with the aid of the chieftains. But now do thou with thy handmaidens abide quietly within the house, and be not a bird of ill omen to our ship; for my clansmen and my thralls shall lead me on my way thither."

He spake, and forth from the house started on his path. Even as Apollo goes forth from his fragrant shrine through holy Delos, or Claros, or through Pytho, in his might, or wide Lycia by the streams of Xanthus; in such beauty went he through the throng of folk, and there arose a shout

[1] The poetical allusion is to the custom of young married women dedicating the μίτρα or ζώνη to Artemis after the birth of their first child.

[2] Eileithyia, *i.e.* the goddess who comes to aid women in childbirth; the Romans called her Lucina, afterwards identified with Diana.

of men giving commands all together. And there met him Iphias, the aged priestess of Artemis, protectress of the city; and she clasped him by his right hand but could not say a word for all her longing, since the crowd went hasting on; so she turned aside and left him there, as an old dame must before younger folk; and lo! he passed by and was gone far away.

Now when he had left the streets of the town with their fair buildings, and was come to the headland of Pagasæ; there did his comrades welcome him, abiding together beside the ship Argo. There she stood at the river mouth, and they were gathered over against her; when lo! they saw Acastus and with him Argus coming forth from the city to them, and they marvelled to see them hasting thither with all speed, against the will of Pelias. And the one, Argus, son of Arestor, had fastened about his shoulders a bull's hide, reaching to his feet, black, with the hair upon it; but the other had a fair mantle of double woof, which his sister Pelopeia gave to him. But Jason refrained for all that from questioning the pair on each point, but bade them seat themselves at the assembly; for there were they sitting one and all in rows on furled sails and the mast that lay upon the ground. And amongst them the son of Æson spake with good intent, "For the rest, whatsoever a ship should be furnished withal lies ready against our start, for all hath been done well and in order; therefore no long space will we hold back from our voyage on that account, when but the winds blow fair. Nay but, friends, since our return to Hellas again is for all of us, and for all is the voyage to the land of Æetes, choose ye therefore now ungrudgingly the best of you for leader, to whom each thing shall be a care, to take upon him our quarrels and our covenants with strangers."

So spake he: and the young men looked round at bold Heracles sitting in their midst; and with one shout they bade Jason declare him leader; but he forthwith, from where he sat, stretched out his right hand and uttered his voice, "Let none offer this honour to me. For I will never consent; wherefore I will even stay another from rising up. Let him who gathered us together, also lead the throng."

So spake he in the greatness of his heart; and they would have it as Heracles bade. Then arose warlike Jason himself in his gladness, and to his eager listeners thus made harangue: "If then 'tis your will that your fame be in my hands, no longer let the voyage be delayed as hitherto. Now forthwith let us appease Phœbus with sacrifice and make a feast at once; and whilst my thralls, the overseers of my steadings, go forth, whose business it is to make good choice of oxen and drive them hither from the herd; meantime will we drag the ship to sea, and do ye place all the tackling therein and allot the oars amongst the benches; and let us the while build an altar on the strand to Apollo, lord of embarkation, who in answer to my prayer hath promised to declare and show the passage o'er the sea, if haply by sacrifice to him I may begin my contest with the king."

So spake he, and was the first to turn him to the work, and they rose up obedient to him; and they piled up their garments apart in rows on a smooth ledge of rock, over which the sea burst not with its waves, but long ago the stormy brine had washed it clean. First then by the counsels of Argus they lashed the ship stoutly with a well-twisted cable from within, stretching it on either side, that the timbers might hold fast by their bolts and have strength to meet the breakers.[1] And quickly they scooped out a

[1] The account of the launching of Argo is by no means easy to understand in all its details. It seems that the heroes dug a trench in front of the bows of the ship and a little way beneath her; then, as she tilted forward of her own weight, they placed rollers under her keel, and continued their trench at a somewhat greater depth, and so on, at a

space as wide as the ship's girth encompassed, and about the prow into the deep they dug out all that she would take to run in, when they hauled her down. And ever in front of the keel they kept hollowing deeper in the ground, and in the furrow did they lay smooth rollers, and on to the first of these they tilted her forward, that she might slide along them and be carried on. And above, on this side and on that, they laid the oars across the ship, so as to project a cubit, and they bound them to the tholes; while they stood there on either side at alternate oars and pushed with hand and chest together. And amongst them went Tiphys to encourage the young men to push in time. Loudly he shouted to urge them, and they at once leant on with all their might, and thrust her with one rush right from out her place, while with their feet they strained and strove; and lo! Pelian Argo went with them very swiftly, and they darted from her sides with a cheer. Beneath her heavy keel the rollers groaned at the friction, and around them dark smoke and flame leapt[1] up beneath the weight, and into the sea she slid. Then did they check her onward course and held her with a rope. And they fitted oars on both sides to the tholes, and laid the mast and shapely sails and stores within her.

Now when they had taken careful heed to each thing, first they portioned out the benches by lot, two men being

lower and lower grade, until they eased her down to the water's edge. After this, apparently (cf. l. 278), they placed oars right across the ship from side to side, so that the blades protruded on one side, the handles on the other, alternately; then making these fast with cords to the tholes, they used them to push against, and so thrust Argo into deep water with a rush.

If this is what the poet intends, we should have to assume that the beach was naturally a sloping one; otherwise the plan of the graduated trench would have been a matter of some difficulty.

[1] κήκιε. Strictly this word means "to ooze" of juices from burnt flesh.

told off to one bench, but the midmost bench, apart from the other heroes, did they select for Heracles and Ancæus, who dwelt in the citadel of Tegea. For them alone they left the middle seat, at once, without casting lots; and with one accord they entrusted Tiphys to mind the helm of their ship with her good keel.

Next, hard by the sea, they raised a pile of shingle, and builded an altar there upon the strand to Apollo, naming it after him who holds the shore and favours those who go aboard. And quickly they laid thereon logs of dry olive; meantime, the herdsmen of the son of Æson drove before them from the herd two oxen; these the young men of his crew dragged to the altar, while others then held the lustral[1] water and meal for sprinkling nigh. And Jason called upon Apollo, the god of his fathers, and prayed, "Hearken, O king, who dwellest in Pagasæ and the city of Æson, that is called after my sire, thou who didst promise me when I sought to thee at Pytho to show me the accomplishment and end of my journey. For 'twas thou thyself that wast the cause[2] of the enterprise. Do thou then bring my ship with my comrades safe and sound hither back to Hellas. Then in thy honour will we lay hereafter on thy altar noble sacrifices of bulls for all of us who shall return, and other gifts will I bring to Pytho, and others to Ortygia in countless number. Come then and receive this sacrifice at our hands, far-darting god; which we have set before thee; a first gift, as an offering for our embarking on this ship; and may I loose my cables with a harmless destiny through

[1] *χέρνιβα* = water for washing the hands of those who offered the sacrifice.

οὐλυχύται = the bruised barley for sprinkling upon the victim and the altar as a beginning of the ceremony. Cf. the phrase *οὐλυχύτας κατάρχεσθαι*. *προχύται* in l. 425 is used in the same sense.

[2] Apollo was answerable, because he had given the oracle which frightened Pelias into sending Jason on his dangerous voyage, to get rid of him.

thy guidance, and may soft breezes blow, wherewith we may go in fair weather across the sea."

He spake, and, as he prayed, cast the barley-meal. And those twain, Ancæus the proud and Heracles, girt themselves to slay the steers. Now the one smote with his club the middle of the head about the forehead, and forthwith the ox lay fallen in a heap upon the earth. But Ancæus struck the other on his broad neck with a brazen axe and cleft the strong sinews, and down he tumbled, doubled up[1] upon his horns. Quickly then their comrades cut the oxen's throats, and flayed their hides; next broke them up and carved them, cutting out the sacred thighs, which they wrapped closely in fat all together and burnt upon firewood. Next the son of Æson poured pure libations; and Idmon was glad, when he saw the flame blaze up on every side from the sacrifice and the smoke thereof leaping up favourably in dark-gleaming wreaths; and forthwith he declared outright the will of the son of Leto.

"Lo! it is the will of heaven and your destiny to come hither again bringing the fleece with you, but countless toils meantime await you as you come and go. But for me 'tis fated to die by the hateful doom of a god, somewhere far away on Asia's strand. Even so came I forth from my fatherland, though I knew my doom a while ago from evil omens, that I might embark upon the ship, and fair fame be left me in my home for my embarking."

So spake he: and the young warriors heard his prophecy and were glad for their return, though grief seized them for the fate of Idmon. Now when the sun had passed the still hour of noon, and the plough-lands were just shadowed by the rocks, as the sun declined beneath the evening dusk; in that hour all strewed a deep couch of leaves upon the

[1] περιρρηδής. Cf. Homer, Od. xxii. 84, where one of the suitors when shot by Odysseus "falls doubled up over a table" (which he was using as a shield) περιρρηδὴς δὲ τραπέζῃ κάππεσεν.

sand and laid them down in order before the gray sea's edge, and beside them lay vast stores of food and sweet mead, which cupbearers drew forth in beakers; next they told each other tales in turn, such tales as young men oft love to tell for their pastime[1] o'er the feast and wine, what time the spirit of insatiate violence is far away. Now the son of Æson the while was lost in wonder, and was pondering each matter within himself like to one downcast, when lo! Idas noted him askance, and with loud voice railed upon him, "Thou son of Æson, what plan is this thou turnest over in thy heart? Speak out thy will here in the midst. Is it fear, that bugbear of cowards, that is coming upon thee and mastering thee? Be witness 'twixt us now, my impetuous spear, wherewith I win myself renown far beyond other men in the wars, nor is it Zeus that helpeth me the half as much as this my spear,—yea, let it witness that there shall come no deadly woe, and that no task shall remain unaccomplished while Idas is with thee, even though a god should rise up against us. Such a man am I whom thou art bringing from Arene to thy aid."

He spake; and grasping in both hands a full goblet drank off the pure sweet mead, and his lips and dark cheeks were wet with wine; but those others raised a din all together, and Idmon lifted up his voice and spake, "God help thee,[2] fool! deadly are thy thoughts, even beforehand, for thyself. Is it that the pure mead makes thy bold heart to swell within thy breast to thy undoing, and hath driven thee to slight the gods? Other are the words of comfort wherewith a man might cheer his fellow, but thou hast spoken altogether presumptuously. Such a speech, 'tis said, the

[1] *ἑψιάομαι* literally = to play with pebbles—then = to amuse oneself in any way.

[2] *δαιμόνιε* almost = my good sir, with a tone of irony and rebuke, and so always both in Homeric and Platonic Greek. A mild oath perhaps gives the force of it most nearly.

sons of Aloeus,[1] men of old time, did sputter forth against the blessed gods; and to them thou art nowise equal in manhood; yet were they both laid low by the swift arrows of the son of Leto, for all their bravery."

He ended; and Idas, son of Aphareus, laughed aloud his fill; and, with blinking[2] eyes, answered him with mocking words, "Come now, tell me this by thy divination, whether for me too the gods are fulfilling such another doom, as that father of thine gave unto the sons of Aloeus. And devise thee how thou mayest safely escape from my hands, else shalt thou die for telling a prophecy light[3] as the winds."

Thus in his wrath he upbraided him; and the quarrel would have gone further, had not their comrades and the son of Æson himself called to them with one accord and stayed them from their strife. Then too Orpheus lifted up his lyre in his left hand and made essay to sing. He sang how earth, and heaven, and sea, once all joined together in unity, were separated, each apart, after a deadly quarrel; and how, for ever in heaven, the stars, and moon, and the paths of the sea have their steadfast goal; and how the mountains rose up, and how rivers rushing noisily with their nymphs, and all creeping things came into being. Next he sang how, at the first, Ophion and Eurynome, daughter of Oceanus, held sway o'er snow-

[1] The sons of Aloeus were Otus and Ephialtes, two enormous giants, who at the age of nine were twenty-seven cubits high. They were remarkable for their strength and daring; they attempted to scale heaven by piling Pelion on Ossa, which, says Homer, they would have done had they grown to manhood, but Apollo slew them whilst yet in their childhood.

[2] *ἐπιλλίζων* = winking with the eyes—so of the blinking gaze of a drunkard.

[3] *μεταμώνιον* = *μάταιον*, "idle," "vain;" the old derivation, *μετὰ ανέμος* = "that which the wind carries away with it," is not to be credited.

capped Olympus, and how the one yielded up his honours to the mighty hands of Cronus, while she gave way to Rhea, and they plunged 'neath the waves of ocean. Awhile did these lord it over the blessed Titan gods, whilst Zeus was yet a child and thought as a child in his home beneath the Cave[1] of Dicte, for not yet had the earth-born Cyclopes made strong his hands with bolts of flashing lightning, for 'tis these that bring glory to Zeus.

He ended, and checked his lyre and voice divine; but they, as he ceased, still leant their heads towards him with eager ears, one and all hushed but hungry still by his enchantment, so strong a spell of music had he left within their hearts. But not long after did they mix libations for Zeus, as was his due, and piously poured them on the blazing tongues,[2] and so bethought them of sleep for the night.

Now when the radiant Dawn with bright eyes looked forth upon the high mountain-tops of Pelias, and the headlands of the tossing main were swept into clear view before the breeze; in that hour uprose Tiphys, and at once he bade his comrades go aboard and make ready the oars. And strangely did the harbour of Pagasæ, yea, and Pelian Argo herself cry aloud, urging them to set forth. For within Argo was laid one beam[3] divine; this it was that Athene made of oak from Dodona, and fitted all along the keel. So they went up upon the benches one after another, as before they had allotted to each in his place to row, and sat them down in order beside their gear. And in the midst sat Ancæus and Heracles, that mighty man,

[1] *Δικταῖον*, *i.e.* Cretan, from the cave Dicte in Crete, where Zeus was brought up.

[2] The tongues of the victims were burnt as a sacrifice to Hermes at the very end of the feast. Cf. Homer, Od. iii. 332.

[3] "One beam divine." This was the oaken keel cut from Dodona, home of prophetic utterance, by Athene, who gifted it with human speech.

and nigh to him he set his club, and beneath his tread the ship's keel sank deep. And now were the cables drawn in, and they poured a cup of mead upon the sea. And Jason with a tear turned his eyes away from his fatherland.

But they, like young men who range themselves to dance to Phœbus, either in Pytho, or haply in Ortygia or by the waters of Ismenus, and all together and in time they beat the ground with nimble feet to the sound of the lyre round his altar; even so they in time to the lyre of Orpheus smote with their oars the boisterous water of the deep, and the waves went dashing by, while on this side and on that the dark brine bubbled up in foam, boiling terribly 'neath the might of those strong men. And their harness flashed like flame in the sunlight as the ship sped on, while ever far behind their course was white with foam, like a track seen over a grassy plain.

On that day all the gods looked down from heaven at the ship, and those men of courage half divine, who then were sailing o'er the sea, a picked crew; and upon the tops of peaks stood the Pelian nymphs, marvelling to see the work of Itonian Athene, and the heroes too, wielding their oars in their hands. Yea, and from a mountain-top came another nigh unto the sea, Chiron,[1] son of Philyra, and he wetted his feet where the gray waves break, and with his weighty hand he waved them on full oft, chanting the while as they went a returning free from sorrow. And with him his wife, bearing on her arm Achilles, son of Peleus, sent a greeting to his dear father.

But when they had left the rounded headland of the harbour by the cunning and skill of Tiphys, wise son of Hagnias, who deftly handled the polished helm to guide the ship stedfastly, then did they set up the mighty mast in the cross-plank, and made it fast with stays, drawing

[1] Peleus had entrusted his child to Chiron to be brought up, on the day Thetis, his goddess wife, left him in anger for ever.

them taut on either side, and they spread the sails upon it, stretching them along the yard-arm. Therewith a fresh fair wind fell on them, so they fastened the ropes on the deck to polished pins, set at intervals, and quietly they sped beneath the long headland[1] of Tisa. And for them the son of Œager touched his lyre and sang in rhythmic song of Artemis, daughter of a noble sire, protectress of ships, who keepeth 'neath her care those peaks by the sea and the land of Iolchos; and the fishes darting beneath the deep sea, great and small together, followed bounding through the watery ways. As when, in the track of the shepherd, countless sheep follow to the fold filled to the full with grass, while he goeth before them gaily piping some shepherd's madrigal on his shrill pipe; even so did the fishes follow with them, and ever onward the steady wind bare Argo.

Anon the misty[2] land of the Pelasgi, with its many corn-fields, sank out of sight; and past the Pelian cliffs they went, speeding ever onward; then the Sepian[3] headland opened to them, and Sciathus[4] by the sea came in view, and in the distance were seen the Peiresian headlands and the headland of Magnesia, calm and clear upon the mainland, and the cairn of Dolops; there they beached their ship at eve, as the wind veered round, and in honour of Dolops they burnt victims at nightfall by the swell of the heaving deep. And two days they rested on the beach, but on the third they put forth the ship, stretching the wide canvas aloft; wherefore men still call that beach the loosing place of Argo.

[1] "Headland of Tisa"—a promontory either of Thessaly or Thesprotia.

[2] *ἠερία* = either "misty," or "land of the dawn." The same epithet is used of Egypt. Πελασγῶν = Θεσσαλῶν.

[3] A promontory in Iolchos, so called because Thetis changed herself into a cuttle-fish there when pursued by Peleus.

[4] An island not far from Eubœa.

Thence onward they sped past Melibœa,[1] seeing its black and stormy strand. And at dawn they saw Homole close to them lying on the deep, and past it they steered, nor was it long before they were to sail away from the streams of the river Amyrus. From thence they beheld Eurymenæ, and the sea-beat ravines of Ossa and Olympus; and then speeding on by the breath of the wind they reached at night the slopes of Pallene, beyond the headland of Canastra.[2] Now, as they fared on in the morning, the Thracian hill of Athos[3] rose before them, which overshadows with its crest Lemnos, lying as far away as a well-found merchantman could make by noon, even unto Myrine. On the self-same day the wind blew on for them till nightfall, exceeding fresh, and the sails of the ship strained to it. But at sunset, when the wind fell, they rowed, and came to Sintian Lemnos,[4] rugged isle.

There had all the men-folk together been ruthlessly slain by the women's wanton violence in the past year; for the men had rejected their wedded wives from dislike, and had had a wild passion for captive maids, whom they brought from the mainland opposite from their forays in Thrace; for the dire wrath of Cypris was upon them, for that they

[1] A city in Thessaly. Homole, a mountain in Thessaly. Amyrus, a river in Thessaly.

[2] Canastra, a promontory of Pallene.

[3] The highest point of the mountainous peninsula of Athos rises to over 6,000 feet; its shadow falls as far as Lemnos, which is half way between Mount Athos and the Hellespont.

[4] The men of Lemnos, called by Homer Thracian Sinties, had all been massacred by the women on account of their infidelity to the marriage vow; this fact, however, was concealed from the Argonauts, who remained there some time and became the fathers of a new race, called Minyæ, after their sires. Hypsipyle alone, the queen of the island, had saved her aged father, Thoas, from the massacre by sending him secretly over the sea. She now married Jason, and bore him twin sons; afterwards the other Lesbian women, discovering that she had spared her father alive, drove her from the island.

long had grudged her her honours. Ah! hapless wives, insatiate in jealousy to your own grief. Not only did they slay their husbands with those captives for their guilty love, but the whole race of men as well, that they might exact no vengeance thereafter for the pitiful murder. Alone of all the women Hypsipyle spared Thoas her aged father, who indeed was king over the people; but him she sent to drift o'er the sea in a hollow ark, if haply he might escape. Him did fisher-folk bring safe to an island, formerly called Œnoe, but afterwards Sicinus, from that Sicinus whom Œnoe, the water-nymph, bare from the embraces of Thoas. Now to these Lemnian women, one and all, the herding of cattle, and the donning of bronze harness, and ploughing the wheat-bearing tilth was an easier lot than the toils[1] of Athene, whereat ever aforetime they busied them. Yet for all that full oft would they peer across the broad sea in grievous dread against the coming of the Thracians. Wherefore when they saw Argo rowing near the island, forthwith in all speed they did on their warlike gear, and poured down to the beach from out the gates of Myrine, like to Thyades who eat raw flesh, for they thought that surely the Thracians were come; and amongst them, she, the daughter of Thoas, Hypsipyle, did on her father's harness; and they poured forth speechless with dismay; such dread was in their fluttering hearts. Meantime forth from the ship the chieftains sent Æthalides,[2] their swift herald, to whose care they entrusted their message and the wand of Hermes, his own sire, who gave to him a memory for all things, that waxed not old; for even when

[1] "The toils of Athene," *i.e.* the work of the distaff, embroidery, weaving, and other elegant arts, of which Athene was patroness.

[2] Æthalides, son of Hermes and Eupolemia, herald of the Argonauts, exemplified the doctrine of *μετεμψύχωσις*. His soul, after passing through numerous phases, at length took possession of the body of Pythagoras, in which it still recollected its former migrations.

he crossed the dreadful whirlpools of Acheron forgetfulness rushed not o'er his soul, but its portion is ever to change to and fro, now counted amongst those beneath the earth, now amongst living men in the sun-light. But why need I tell out in full the tale of Æthalides? He it was who then persuaded Hypsipyle to receive the heroes, as they came at dusk, toward the close of day; nor did they loose the cables of their ship at dawn to the breath of the north-wind.

Now the women of Lemnos went through the city and sat themselves in the assembly; for such was the bidding of Hypsipyle herself. And when they were gathered, one and all, and come together, forthwith amongst them she made eager harangue.

"My friends, come now, let us give the men gifts in plenty, all that men should have to carry on a ship, food and sweet mead, that so they may abide steadfastly outside our battlements, and may not in pursuit of their business get to know us too well, and a foul report spread far and wide; for we have wrought a great deed, which will not be wholly to their liking, if they should learn it. Let this be our plan now in this matter. But if any of you can devise better counsel, let her arise, for to this end did I call you hither."

So spake she, and sat down on her father's seat of stone. And next uprose her dear nurse Polyxo, limping on feet shrivelled with age, I trow, and leaning on a staff; and she longed exceedingly to have her say. And by her, with her white hair about her head, sat four unmarried maidens. So she stood in the midst of the assembly, and raising ever so little her bent and skinny back, she spake thus:

"Gifts let us send to the strangers, as is pleasing to Hypsipyle herself, for 'tis better to send them. But for you, what plan have ye to keep your life, if a Thracian army fall on you, or any other foe, as happeneth oft 'mongst men? since even now yon host is come unexpectedly. And if any one of the blessed gods turn this aside, yet hereafter there await us countless other woes worse than battle, when the aged women are dead, and ye younger maidens reach a cheerless old age, childless. How then will ye live, poor creatures? shall the oxen, yoked of their own accord for you, drag the plough, that cleaves the fallow, through the deep tilth, and straightway in the fulness of the year reap the harvest? Of a truth o'er me, methinks, the earth shall lie this very year that cometh, albeit the Fates have hitherto shrunk away from me, and I shall get my meed of burial even thus, as is right, or ever misfortune arrive.[1] But I bid you younger women heed these things well. For now before you open stands the door of escape, if but ye will give over to the care of strangers your homes and all your booty and your glorious town."

So spake she, and through the assembly ran a murmur of assent. For her saying pleased them well. But after her at once Hypsipyle, again uprising, took up her parable and said:

"Why, then, if unto you all this purpose is pleasing, at once will I send forth even a messenger to find their ship."

She spake, and called to Iphinoe sitting near, "Rouse thee, Iphinoe, I pray, and beg yon man who leads their company to come unto us, that I may tell to him the word that finds favour with my people, and bid his company, if they will, set foot within our land and city boldly and with a good heart."

She spake, and broke up the assembly; and then started to go to her own house. And so Iphinoe came unto the

[1] *i.e.* it matters little to me what happens, for I feel assured my end is very near, although the Fates have shrunk away so long from my hideous form. *αὔτως = οὕτως*.

Minyæ, who questioned her on what business bent she came amongst them. And forthwith she thus made answer with all haste to their questions, "Verily, 'twas the daughter of Thoas, Hypsipyle, who sent me on my journey hither to call the captain of the ship, whosoever he is, that she may tell him somewhat that hath found favour with her folk; moreover she bids you, an you list, at once now set foot within her land and city with a good heart."

So spake she; and welcome to all was her fair message. Now they imagined that Hypsipyle, the well-beloved daughter of Thoas, did reign in his stead; so quickly sent they Jason on his way, yea, and themselves made ready to go.

Now he had buckled on his shoulders a purple mantle of double woof, the handiwork of the Tritonian goddess, which Pallas gave him, on that first day she laid down the props for the ship Argo, and taught him to measure cross-planks with the rule. More easily might you gaze on the sun at his rising than on that mantle, or face the sheen thereof. For lo! the middle was red, and the top was all of purple, and on either end many cunning things were worked passing well. On it were the Cyclopes sitting at their work, that never decayeth, fashioning the thunderbolt for king Zeus; lo! it was all but made[1] in its bright splendour, but yet it lacked one single flash, which they with their hammers of iron were forging, with its breath of fierce fire.

On it were the two sons of Antiope, daughter of Asopus, Amphion and Zethus; near by lay Thebes, as yet ungirt with towers, whereof they were just laying the foundations in eager haste. Zethus was bearing shoulder-high the top

[1] *i.e.* the bolt was all but finished; it only wanted one ray of lightning to complete its composition; and so natural was the embroidery, that the Cyclopes seemed to be in the very act of adding it.

The Cyclopes were Brontes and Steropes, *i.e.* Thunder and Lightning.

of a steep mountain, like unto a man that toiled; and behind him came Amphion,[1] singing aloud to his golden lyre, while in his track twice as large a rock followed.

Next was worked thereon Cytherea, of the thick tresses, carrying the nimble shield of Ares; and from her shoulder, from beneath her bosom, hung her girdle loosely over her left arm; and there as she stood one seemed to see her sure reflection thrown upon the brazen shield. And there was a shaggy herd upon it; and the Teleboans[2] and the sons of Electryon were fighting about the cattle; these in their defence, but those others, Taphian pirates, longing to rob them; and the dewy meadow was wet with their blood, and the many had the mastery of the few, even of the herdsmen.

Two chariots racing were fashioned there. Pelops drove the one that was in front, shaking the reins, and with him was Hippodamia for his companion; while hard upon him Myrtilus urged his steeds, and with him was Œnomaus, gripping in his hand his couchèd lance, but down he fell as the axle of the wheel break sideways in the nave, in his eagerness to wound Pelops in the back.

There too was broidered Phœbus Apollo, a big boy not yet grown up, shooting at Tityos[3] as he tried, with bold hand, to snatch away his mother's veil,—great Tityos, whose mother indeed was divine Elare, but the earth gave him second birth, and brought him up.

[1] The legend was that Amphion, by playing on his lyre, drew the stones after him till they ranged themselves in order on the battlements of Thebes.

[2] The Teleboans lived in the island of Taphos, one of the Echinades group. They are notable pirates in Homer's Odyssee.

[3] The legend is given in two ways about the birth of the giant Tityos. His mother Elare, the daughter of Orchomenus, was buried alive when pregnant by Zeus, on account of the jealousy of Hera, but Earth brought the child to birth. The other legend says that Elare could not be delivered, so great was the child, and died in the effort; whereon Earth bore the babe and reared him.

Yea, and Minyan Phrixus was there, even as though he were really listening to the ram, while it was like to one that spoke. Ah! shouldst thou see them, thou wouldst be silent and deceive thy soul, expecting haply to hear their voice aloud; and long mightest thou gaze thereon in that hope.

Such then were the presents of the Tritonian goddess Athene. And in his right hand he held a spear, far-darting, which on a day Atalanta gave to him in Mænalus as a gift to a stranger, what time she met him graciously; for greatly did she long to join him on that voyage; but yet of himself and willingly he held her back, for he feared grievous quarrels for her love.

So he went on his way toward the city like a bright star, which maidens through their curtains, newly made, do see, when they awake, rising o'er their home, and through the dark mist it charms their eyes with its lovely blush; and the maiden is cheered in her longing for the youth who is amongst strange folk, for whom her parents are keeping her to be his wedded wife; like to that star the hero stepped along the path before the city. Now when they were come within the gates of the city, the maidens of the people surged behind them, glad to see the stranger; but he, with his eyes upon the ground, kept straight on, until he reached the glorious halls of Hypsipyle; and at his appearing maids threw wide the folding-doors, fitted with planks well wrought. Then did Iphinoe lead him hastily through a fair hall, and seat him on a shining couch before her mistress; but that lady cast down her eyes, and a blush stole o'er her maiden cheek; yet for all her modesty found she wheedling word to address him withal: "Strange sir, why sat ye thus so long outside our battlements? for our husbands abide not now within the city, but they are sojourners awhile upon the Thracian mainland, and do plough the wheat-bearing tilths. And I will tell thee truly all our trouble, that ye may know it surely for yourselves. When my father Thoas was king over the burghers, then did bands of our folk start forth and plunder from their ships the folds of the Thracians who dwell over against us, and hither they brought endless booty and maidens too. But Cypris, deadly goddess, schemed a scheme, which cast upon them a fatal curse. For lo! they loathed their wedded wives, and chased them from their homes, yielding to their folly, and they took for concubines the captives of their spears, luckless wights! Long time did we endure, if haply they might change their mind again at last; but ever the evil went on and doubled, for they dishonoured their true children in their halls, and there grew up a bastard race. And so maids unwed, and widowed mothers with them, went wandering in neglect through the city. Nor did a father care ever so little for his daughter, though he saw her done to death before his eyes by the hand of an insolent step-mother; nor did children ward off unseemly outrage from their mother as before, nor had brothers any thought for a sister. But only captive maidens found favour at home and in the dance, in the place of assembly, and at festivals, till some god put overweening boldness in our hearts, that we would no more receive them in our battlements on their return from the Thracians, that so they might either be minded aright, or start and go elsewhither, captive maids and all. Thereon did they demand all the male children that were left within the city, and went back again to the place where still they dwell on the snowy ploughlands of Thrace. Wherefore tarry ye here and sojourn; and if, indeed, thou wilt dwell here, and it find favour with thee, verily then shalt thou have the honour of my father Thoas. And methinks thou canst not scorn my land, for very fruitful is it beyond all other isles that lie in the Ægean sea. Nay, come now, get thee to thy ship, and tell our words unto thy crew, and abide not outside the city."

So spake she, glozing over the murderous end that had been worked upon the men; and Jason said to her in answer, "Hypsipyle, lo! so shall we gain a request that is very dear unto our hearts, which thou dost offer to our desire. But I will return again unto the city, when I have told each thing in order. But thine, and thine alone be the lordship of the island; 'tis from no scorn that I shrink therefrom, but upon me grievous toils press hard."

He spake, and took her right hand, and at once went on his way back; while about him throngs of maidens danced on every side for very joy, till he passed outside the gates. Next they went unto the shore, bearing on smoothly-running wains gifts full many for the strangers, as soon as he had told them all the message from beginning to end, even the word that Hypsipyle declared when she summoned him. Yea, and they led the heroes to their houses to entertain them, willingly. For Cypris stirred up sweet desire[1] for the sake of Hephæstus, the crafty; that so Lemnos might again be inhabited by men in time to come and get no hurt.

Then did he, the son of Æson, start for the royal home of Hypsipyle, but those others went whither chance led each, all save Heracles, for he stayed by the ship of his own free will, and with him a few chosen comrades. Anon the city made merry with dance and feast, filled with the smoke of steaming sacrifice; and beyond the rest of the immortal gods did they propitiate the famous son of Hera, yea, and Cypris too, with song and sacrifice. And ever day by day was their voyage delayed, and long time would they have tarried and rested there, had not Heracles assembled his companions, apart from the women, and thus up-

[1] Lemnos was sacred to Hephæstus, the husband of Aphrodite; so she would not allow the island to remain for ever void of males.

braided them: "God help you, sirs! is it a kinsman's murder that keeps us from our country? Was it for want of weddings that we came from that land to this, scorning the maidens of our people? or is it your pleasure to dwell here and till the fat glebes of Lemnos? No fair fame shall we win, I trow, from this our long sojourn with strange women; nor will some god of his own accord take the fleece and give it us at our prayer. Let us go each man to his own again; but leave ye that other to spend the live-long day in the arms of Hypsipyle, till he people Lemnos with male children, and so there come to him great fame."

Thus did he chide the company, and none durst look him in the face or make answer to him, but, even as they were, hasting from the assembly they made ready to be gone. But the women ran to them, when they learnt thereof. And as when bees hum round fair lilies, pouring forth from their hive in the rock, and around the dewy meadow is glad, and they the while flit from flower to flower, and gather their sweet food; even so, I ween, did those women pour forth eagerly around the men, with loud lament, while with hand and word they greeted each one, praying to the blessed gods to grant them a safe return. So too Hypsipyle prayed, taking the son of Æson by the hands, and the tears that she shed were for the loss of him departing, "Go, and heaven guide thee hither again with thy comrades all unmaimed, bearing the golden fleece to the king, even thus as thou wilt and as is thy desire. And this mine isle and my father's sceptre shall be thine, if some day hereafter thou wilt yet return and come again; and easily couldst thou gather for thyself a countless host from other cities. Nay, but thou wilt never have this eager desire, and of myself I foresee that thus it will not come to pass; still I pray thee, though thou art far away, and when thou art returning, remember Hypsipyle; and leave me now thy bidding, which I will fulfil gladly, if, as may be, the gods grant me to bear thy child."

But the son of Æson, with a look of admiration answered her: "Hypsipyle, may all these things turn out luckily by the will of the blessed gods. But do thou devise some better thought for me, for 'tis enough for me to dwell in my fatherland by the grace of Pelias; only may heaven loose me from my toils! But if it is not destined that I should come to the land of Hellas after my far journey, and thou do bear a boy, send him, when he is grown, within Pelasgian Iolchos, to my father and mother, to soothe their grief, if haply he find them yet alive, that they may sit within their halls and be cared for, though I, the king, be far away."

Therewith he went aboard before them all, and in like manner went the other chiefs, and, sitting in rows, they grasped the oars in their hands, and Argus loosed for them the stern-cables from beneath the sea-beat rock. Then did they smite the water lustily with the long oars. At eve, by the counsel of Orpheus, they beached the ship at the isle[1] of Electra, daughter of Atlas, that they might learn the secret rites through gentle initiation, and so might fare more safely over the chilling sea. Of these things will I speak no further; nay, farewell to yon isle itself, and farewell to the gods who dwell there, whose mysteries these are; of them 'tis not right for us to sing.

Hence did they row over the depths of the Black sea, speeding on, with the land of Thrace on the one side, and on the other side to starboard Imbros over against Thrace; and just at sunset they reached the promontory of Chersonese. Then did the swift south-wind blow upon them; so they set the sails to the breeze and entered the rushing

[1] "The isle of Electra," *i.e.* Samothrace. Initiation into the sacred mysteries of the Cabiri in this island was supposed to insure safety to mariners. Odysseus took this precaution, according to tradition.

stream[1] of the daughter of Athamas. At dawn the open sea to the north was left behind, and at night were they measuring their way over that which lies within the headland of Rhœteum, keeping the land of Ida on the right. Leaving Dardania they steered for Abydos, and on that night passed by Percote and the sandy beach of Abarnis and sacred Pityeia. Yea, on that night, as the ship sped on with oar and sail,[2] they passed right through the Hellespont with its dark eddies.

Now there is within Propontis a hilly isle,[3] a little from the Phrygian mainland with its rich corn-fields, sloping to the sea, and there is an isthmus in front of the mainland stretching across the sea, but the waves just wash over it. And there are there two beaches, and they lie beyond the waters of the Æsepus; and they who dwell around call the hill Arctos. On it a wild and lawless race of earth-born men ever had their home, a great wonder to their neighbours to behold; for each hath six masterful hands hanging from him, twain from his strong shoulders, and other four joined below upon his fearsome sides. About the isthmus and the plain the Doliones had their dwelling, and amongst them Cyzicus, son of Æneus, held sway, whom Ænete, daughter of divine Eusorus, bare. But these the earth-born race in no wise harried, for all their fearsomeness, for Poseidon guarded them; for from him were the Doliones first sprung. Thither Argo pressed forward, driven by the winds of Thrace, and a fair haven received the speeding ship. There too by the advice of Tiphys they loosed and left their light anchor-stone below a fountain, even the Artacian fountain; and they chose another, which suited them, a ponderous stone; but that old one did the

[1] The Hellespont, so called from Helle, the daughter of Athamas.

[2] διάνδιχα = in two ways, *i.e.* by oar and sail.

[3] Cyzicus, afterwards mainland. Apparently there was a bar of land, just covered by surf, joining Cyzicus to the mainland; eventually this bar rose clear from the water, and Cyzicus was no longer an island.

Ionians,[1] sons of Neleus, in the after time, in obedience to the oracle of Hecatus, set up as holy, as was right, in the temple of Athene, who was with Jason.

Now the Doliones, yea, and Cyzicus himself, came forth to meet them in a body, and treated them with kindness and hospitality, when they heard of their expedition and knew their lineage, and who they were, and they persuaded them to row on a space and moor the ship in the harbour of the city. There they builded an altar to Apollo, god of embarkation, and set it by the beach and busied themselves with sacrifice. And the king of his own bounty gave them in their need sweet mead and sheep as well; for lo! there came a voice from heaven which said, that when there should arrive a goodly expedition of heroes, he should straightway meet them graciously, and take no thought for war. Now he was about Jason's age; his beard was just sprouting, nor yet had he gotten children to his joy, but his bride within his house had not yet known travail, the daughter of Percosian Merops, Cleite with the fair tresses, whom he had but lately brought thither from the mainland opposite, with wondrous gifts of wooing to her father. Yet even so he left his bridal bed and chamber, and made ready a banquet amongst them,[2] casting all fear from his heart. And they questioned one another in turn; and he asked them of the end of their voyage and of the commands of Pelias, while they enquired about the cities of the folk around and about the whole gulf of wide Propontis; but he knew not how to tell them when they were anxious to know aught far ahead. So at dawn they went up to mighty Dindymus,[3] that they might spy out for themselves the passage of that sea, and they drave forth

[1] Ionian colonists led by Neleus, son of Codrus, from Attica.

[2] An oracle had warned king Cyzicus of the fate awaiting him at the hands of the Argonauts.

[3] A mountain in Cyzicus, sacred to Rhea. Chytus is the harbour of Cyzicus.

the ship from the outer basin of the harbour of Chytus; wherefore this way they went is called Jason's way.

But the earth-born men, rushing from both sides of the mountain, blocked the sea-ward mouth of boundless Chytus with rocks at the bottom, lying in wait as though for a wild beast inside. Now Heracles had been left there with the younger men; so quickly he stretched his curved bow against them and brought them to the ground one after another; and they for their part caught up jagged rocks and hurled them. For lo! Hera, goddess wife of Zeus, I wis, had raised those fearful monsters too, a labour for Heracles; and the other warlike heroes turned back anon to meet them, or ever they had mounted to their place of outlook, and joined in the slaughter of the earth-born men, receiving them with arrows and swords till they had slain them all as they rushed to meet them impetuously.

As when wood-cutters throw down in rows upon the beach long beams just hewn by their axes, that they may soak and so receive the strong bolts; even so those monsters lay stretched there[1] in the entrance to the gray haven, some with head and chest plunged all at once into the salt water, and their limbs below spread out upon the strand; others again were resting their heads upon the sand of the beach and their feet in the deep water, both alike to be a prey to birds and fishes.

But the heroes, as soon as there was nought to fear for their enterprise, at once loosed the cables of the ship to the breath of the wind, and voyaged on across the ocean-swell. And the ship sped on the live-long day under canvas; but, as night came on, the rushing wind no longer abode steadfast, but contrary blasts caught and swept them backward, till they drew nigh again to the hospitable Doliones. And they disembarked that self-same night; and that rock is

[1] *ξυνόχῃ*, *i.e.* not merely the entrance to the harbour, but also all the circumference of it.

still called the sacred rock, whereto they bound the cables of the ship in their haste. Nor did any man surely know that it was really the island, nor did the Doliones by night perceive for certain that it was the heroes again coming to them; but they supposed maybe some band of Pelasgian warriors from the Macrians[1] was landing. Wherefore they did on their harness and stretched forth their hands against them. And they drove their ashen spears and shields against each other, like a swift rush of fire, which falling on a dry thicket rears its head; and withal upon the Dolionian folk fell the din of battle, terrible and furious. Nor was he, their king, to rise above the doom of battle and come again home to his bridal chamber and bed. Nay, him did the son of Æson, with one bound, smite through the middle of the breast as he turned to face him, and the bone splintered about his spear, and he grovelling on the sand wound up his clew of fate. For mortal man may not escape his fate, but on all sides is spread a mighty snare around him. Thus upon that night it caught him in its toils, as he thought, maybe, to avoid the bitter doom dealt out by the chieftains, what time he fought with them; and many other champions were slain. Heracles slew Telecles and Megabrontes; and Acastus stript Sphodris of his arms; and Peleus laid Zelys low, and Gephyrus, that fleet warrior. And Telamon of the stout ashen spear killed Basileus. Idas slew Promeus, and Clytius Hyacinthus; and the two sons of Tyndarus slew Megalossaces and Phlogius.

Besides these the son of Œneus smote bold Itymoneus, yea, and Artaces, a leader of men; all these do the inhabitants still honour with the worship due to heroes.

But the rest gave way and fled in terror, even as doves

[1] The Macrians or Macrones were colonists from Eubœa, and neighbours of the Doliones.

"Pelasgic," because Eubœa was close to Peloponnesus, the old name of which was Pelasgia.

in flocks fly cowering from swift hawks, and they rushed headlong to the gates with loud cries; then straight was the city filled with cries and groans as the battle was turned backward. But at daybreak did both sides perceive their grievous, cureless error; and bitter anguish seized the Minyan heroes when they saw before them Cyzicus fallen mid the dust and blood. Three whole days they mourned, they and the folk of the Doliones together, tearing out their hair. And then thrice about his tomb they marched in their bronze harness and made his funeral, and instituted trial of games, as was right, on the meadow plain, where to this day is his tomb heaped up for men that shall be hereafter to see.

Nor could his bride Cleite survive her husband's death, but in her grief she wrought a deed more awful still, what time she fastened the noose about her neck. And the wood nymphs mourned her death, and all the tears they let fall to earth from their eyes for her, of these did the goddesses make a spring, which men call Cleite, the storied name of that poor maid. Yea, that was the direst day that Zeus ever sent upon the men and women of the Doliones; for none of them could bear to taste of food, and for a long time after their trouble they minded them not of the work of grinding; but they dragged on their life, eating the food, as it was, uncooked. There to this day, whenso the Ionians, that dwell in Cyzicus, pour the yearly libation to the dead, they ever grind their meal[1] at the public mill.

From thenceforth for twelve whole days and nights arose tempestuous winds, which kept them there from their voyage. But on the next night, all the other chiefs, ere this, I ween, o'ercome by sleep, were resting there for

[1] πέλανοι, literally any half-liquid mixture of various consistency. Not unfrequently a mixture of meal, honey, and oil offered to the gods, such as Circe (cf. *infra*, Bk. iv. l. 712) offers when purifying Jason and Medea. Here apparently = πέμματα, *i.e.* any kind of cooked food or sweetmeats.

the last time, while Acastus and Mopsus, son of Ampycus, guarded their sound slumbers. When lo! above the yellow head of the son of Æson there flew a king-fisher, boding by her shrill note an end of the violent winds; and Mopsus, directly he heard the lucky cry of that bird of the shore, marked it well; and the goddess brought it back again, and it darted aloft and perched above the carved stern; then did Mopsus stir Jason, where he lay upon the soft fleeces of sheep, and roused him instantly, and thus unto him spake: "Son of Æson, to yonder temple on rugged Dindymus thou must go up and seek the favour of the fair-throned queen,[1] mother of all the blessed gods; then shall cease the stormy winds. For such was the voice I heard but now of the halcyon, bird of the sea, which flew above about thy sleeping form and told me all. For this goddess hath experience of the winds and the sea and all the earth beneath and the snow-capped seat of Olympus; and before her Zeus himself, the son of Cronos, doth somewhat yield, when from her mountains she ascendeth to the wide heaven. And hence it is the other blessed deathless gods do reverence to this dread goddess."

So spake he, and welcome to Jason's ear was his word. And he roused him from his bed with joy, and hasted to awake all his crew; and, when they were risen, he declared to them the heavenly message of Mopsus, son of Ampycus. Then straight did the young men drive up oxen from the byres there to the steep mountain-top. And the rest meantime loosed the cables from the sacred rock and rowed to the Thracian[2] harbour, and themselves went forth, leaving but a few of their fellows in the ship. Now upon their

[1] Rhea was called the mother of all the gods.

[2] *i.e.* the harbour of Cyzicus, which is here called Thracian because the old inhabitants of Cyzicus had been Thracian. It is clear that the heroes did not sail across to Thrace, because Mount Dindymus is a considerable distance inland in Galatia, and it was hither they meant to come.

right hand the Macrian cliffs and all the Thracian mainland rose clear in view, and the dim entrance to the Bosporus[1] and the hills of Mysia appeared; while upon their left was the stream of the river Æsepus, and the city and plain of Nepeia, which is called Adresteia. Now there was a sturdy stump of a vine growing in a wood, an exceeding old tree; this they cut out, for to make a sacred image of the mountain goddess, and Argus polished it neatly, and there upon that rugged hill they set it up beneath a canopy of towering oaks, trees that have their roots deepest of all, I trow. Next heaped they an altar of stones, and wreathed it with oak-leaves, and busied themselves with sacrifice, calling on the name of the Dindymian mother, queen revered, that dwelleth in Phrygia, and on Titias[2] too and Cyllene, who alone are called the dispensers of destiny and assessors of the Idæan mother of all that band, who in Crete are the Dactylian priests of Ida; them on a day the nymph Anchiale brought forth in the Dictæan[3] grotto, clutching with both hands the Œaxian land. And the son of Æson besought her with many prayers to turn away the hurricane, pouring libations the while on blazing sacrifices; and therewith young men, by the bidding of Orpheus, danced a measured step in full harness,[4] smiting swords and

[1] Bosporus, the narrow part of Propontis, so called, according to legend, from Io, who in the form of a cow swam across it.

[2] Titias and Cyllenus, the Dactylian priests of Cybele in Crete. They were wizards, or, more probably, men skilled in medicine and metallurgy who lived on Mount Ida, surrounding themselves carefully, no doubt, with a certain air of mystery. They were the children of the nymph Anchiale, so called because their mother in her travail clutched the earth in her fingers (δάκτυλοι).

[3] Dictæan, *i.e.* Cretan, from Mount Dicte in Crete.

[4] The Great Mother was always worshipped in Crete with the sound of cymbals, drums, and other loud music; which custom Apollonius dates from the time of the Argonauts, who, to drown the unlucky sound of lamentation raised by the Cyzicenes for their dead king, clashed their weapons together.

bucklers, that the ill-omened cry might lose itself in wandering through the air, even the lamentation, which the folk were still raising at the funeral of their king. Whence the Phrygians do ever seek the favour of Rhea with tambourine and drum. And now, I ween, the goddess turned her ear to hearken to their pious worship; and signs, that are favourable, did appear. Trees shook down countless fruits, and around their feet the earth of herself brought forth the flowers of tender plants. Wild creatures left their lairs in the thickets and came wagging their tails. And yet another marvel she produced; for aforetime Dindymus had no running water, but now they saw it gush forth there and cease not from the thirsty hill; wherefore neighbouring folk in after time called that water Jason's spring. Then did they make a feast in honour of the goddess on Mount Arctos, singing the praise of Rhea, august queen; and at dawn the wind ceased and they rowed away from the island.

Then rivalry stirred each chieftain's heart to be the last to leave his rowing. For around them the still air had laid the tumbling waves and lulled the sea to rest. So they, trusting to the calm, drave on the ship mightily, nor would even Poseidon's steeds, that are swift as wind, have caught her as she sped through the sea. Yet as the salt waves began to rise beneath violent gusts, which toward evening were just beginning to get up from the rivers, then were they for ceasing, foredone with toil; but Heracles with mighty hands pulled those tired rowers along all together, making the joints of the ship's timbers to quiver.

But when, in their haste past the mainland of the Mysians, they had sighted and sailed by the mouth of the river Rhyndacus[1] and the great cairn of Ægæon, a little away from Phrygia; in that hour did Heracles break his

[1] A river of Phrygia.

oar in the middle as he heaved aside the furrows of the roughened surge. And backward fell he, grasping in both hands one fragment, while the sea swept the other away on its wash. And there he sat glaring round in silence, for his hands knew not to be idle.

At the hour when some delver or ploughman cometh from the field joyfully to his cottage, longing for his supper; and there on his threshold, all squalid with dust as he is, he droops his weary knees, and, gazing on his toil-worn hands, many a bitter curse he flingeth at that belly of his; in that hour, I trow, came those heroes to the abodes of the land Cianian about the Arganthonian mountain and the mouth of the river Cios. And the Mysians welcomed them with all hospitality and kindness on their coming, for they dwelt in that land, and they gave them at their need sheep and mead in plenty. So then some brought dry logs, and others mowed the plenteous herbage of the meadows for beds to strew withal, and others twirled sticks to get fire; and they mixed wine in bowls, and made ready a feast, after sacrificing to Apollo, god of embarkation, as darkness fell.

Now Heracles bade his comrades give good heed unto the feast, while he went on his way to the wood, that son of Zeus, that he might first fashion for himself an oar to suit him. And in his wandering he found a pine that was not burdened with many branches, nor had much foliage thereon, but it was like some tall poplar sapling to look at both in height and girth. Quickly then upon the ground he laid his quiver, arrows and all, and doffed his lion-skin. And when he with his heavy club of bronze had made it totter from its base, then did he grip it low down about the stump with both hands, trusting to his strength, and planting himself firmly he leant his broad shoulder against it, and so clinging to it he dragged it from the ground, deep-rooted though it was, clods of earth and all. As when a sudden squall of wind strikes aloft a ship's mast unexpectedly, just at the time of baleful Orion's winter setting, and tears it from its stays,[1] wedges and all; even thus the strong man dragged it out. And at once he caught up his bow and arrows, and his skin and club, and hasted to go back.

Meantime Hylas with a brazen pitcher went apart from the company, in quest of a sacred running spring, that he might ere his return draw for him water against supper-time, and get all else ready and in order for him at his coming. For Heracles had with his own hands brought him up in such habits from his earliest childhood, having robbed him from his father's house, goodly Theiodamas, whom he slew ruthlessly amongst the Dryopes, because he withstood him about a steer for ploughing. Now Theiodamas was ploughing up a fallow field, when the curse fell on him; and Heracles bade him give up the steer he was ploughing with, and he would not. For he longed to find some grim pretext for war against the Dryopes, for there they dwelt without regard for justice. But this would send me straying far from my story. Quickly came Hylas to the spring, which they who dwell around and near call Pegæ. Now it chanced that lately choirs of nymphs had settled there; their care it was ever to hymn Artemis with midnight song, as many of them as dwelt there round the lovely peak. All those, whose lot it is to watch o'er hill-tops and mountain-streams, and they who guard the woods, were all drawn up apart; but she, the nymph of the water, was just rising from her lovely spring, when she marked him near with the blush of his beauty and sweet grace upon him. For on him the full moon from heaven was shedding her light. And Cypris made the nymph's heart flutter, and scarce in her confusion could she collect her-

[1] σφήνεσσιν, wedges to block the mast firmly in its hole. προτόνων, stays from the top of the mast to the deck to keep it still firmer.

self. But he, so soon as he had dipped his pitcher in the stream, leaning aslant over it, and good store of water was flowing into the sounding brass and bubbling round it, lo! in that instant the nymph from below the water laid her left arm on his neck, longing to kiss his soft lips; while with her right hand she plucked him by the elbow and plunged him amid the ripple.

And as he cried out, Polyphemus, son of Elatus, alone of his comrades, heard him, as he came on along the path. For he would welcome mighty Heracles, whensoever he might come. Away rushed he towards Pegæ like some wild beast, to whom from afar hath come the bleating of sheep, and furious with hunger he goeth to find them and yet cometh not upon the flocks, for shepherds before have penned them with their own hands within the fold; but he howls and roars unceasingly till he is tired. So then did the son of Elatus cry aloud, and went to and fro about the place shouting, and piteous was his voice. Anon drew he his mighty sword and started to go forth, for fear that the boy might be a prey to beasts, or men have taken him in ambush as he was alone, and be leading him away, an easy booty. Then did he meet Heracles himself in the way, as he was brandishing his naked sword in his hand, and right well he knew him as he hasted toward the ship through the darkness. At once he told the grievous news, gasping hard for breath, "God help thee! friend, a bitter grief shall I be the first to tell thee. Hylas went unto the spring, but he cometh not again in safety; but robbers have attacked him and are leading him away, or beasts are tearing him, for I heard his loud cry."

So spake he; and, as the other listened, there broke out great beads of sweat upon his forehead, and beneath his heart the dark blood surged. Down upon the ground in wrath he cast the pine, and hasted along the path whither his feet carried him in his hurry. As when a bull somewhere, stung by the gadfly, rushes along, leaving the meadows and marsh-lands, and heedeth not the herdsmen, nor the herd, but passes on his way, at one time without stopping, and again standing still, and lifting up his broad neck he bellows aloud, 'neath the sting of that cursed fly; even so Heracles in his eagerness now made his swift knees move without a check, and now again, ceasing from his toil, he would make his loud shout peal afar.

Anon uprose the morning star above the topmost heights, and down came the breeze; quickly then did Tiphys urge them go aboard and take advantage of the wind. So they at once embarked eagerly, and they hauled in the anchor-ropes of the ship and backed her out.[1] And the sails were bellied out by the wind, and they were borne far from the beach past the headland of Posideum, glad at heart. Now when bright-eyed dawn, arising from the east, shed its light from heaven, and the paths stood out clearly, and the dew-spangled plains shone in the bright gleam, then knew they those whom they had left behind in ignorance. And there arose a fierce strife amongst them, and brawling unspeakable, to think that they had gone and left the best of all their crew. But he, the son of Æson, mazed and at a loss, had nought to say one way or the other, but there he sat, inly consuming his soul with heavy woe; but Telamon[2] was seized with wrath and thus spake he, "Sit thee then in silence thus, since it pleased thee well to leave Heracles behind; far from thee is any counsel, that so his fame may not o'ershadow thee in Hellas,[3] if haply the gods

[1] The ancient mode of landing was to beach the ship, if possible, and then fasten by cables to the land, and by anchors from the stern in the sea. Hence, to put to sea it was necessary first to haul up the anchor stones, and then back the ship out.

[2] Telamon had joined Heracles in his expedition against the Amazons, and had also sailed with him to Ilium, so that they had become close comrades.

[3] Telamon's taunt against Jason certainly gathers some weight from

grant a return home again. But what joy is there in words? for I will go even apart from thy crew, who helped thee to devise this guile."

He spake, and sprung toward Tiphys, son of Hagnias, and his two eyes were like the flash of glowing fire. And now would they have come back to the Mysian land in spite of the wide sea and the ceaseless roaring blast, had not the two sons of Thracian Boreas held back the son of Æacus with harsh words, poor wights;[1] verily upon them came a grievous vengeance in the aftertime from the hands of Heracles, for that they stayed the search for him. For he slew them in sea-girt Tenos as they returned from the games after the slaughter of Pelias, and he piled the earth about them, and set up two pillars above them, whereof the one, an exceeding marvel for men to see, is stirred by the breath of the noisy north-wind. Thus were these things to be brought to pass in days to come. But to them appeared Glaucus[2] from the depth of the sea, wise expounder of the will of godlike Nereus; and he raised aloft his shaggy head and chest from the hollow depths, and laid hold upon the ship's keel with his stalwart hand and cried to them as they hastened, "Why against the will of mighty Zeus are ye eager to take bold Heracles to the city of Æetes? His lot it is to toil in Argos for insolent

the poet's treatment of Jason's character; not enough prominence is given to him, who should be the central hero of all. Again and again Jason is overshadowed by his comrades; he fails to excite our lively interest in anything like the way that Medea's beautiful portrait stirs it.

[1] Heracles heard afterwards how the sons of Boreas had checked the proposed search for him, and, as he thought (not knowing the will of the gods), prevented his sharing the farther adventures of the Argonauts; so in his rage he slew them in Tenos as they were returning from the games held at the funeral of Pelias.

[2] Glaucus, the son of Polybus, a sea-god endowed with prophetic powers, explains the divine will in separating Polyphemus, Heracles, and Hylas from their comrades to fulfil other destinies.

Eurystheus till he complete twelve labours in all, and then to dwell amongst the deathless gods, if haply he accomplish yet a few. Wherefore let there be no regret for him. Yea, and even thus it is decreed that Polyphemus found a famous town amongst the Mysians at the mouth of the river Cios, and then wind up his clew of fate in the boundless country of the Chalybes.[1] And Hylas hath a goddess nymph taken as her husband for love of him, and this was why they wandered away and were left behind."

Therewith he dived below and wrapped the restless wave around him, and the dark water seethed and foamed in eddies about him, and he let the hollow ship go on through the sea. Then were the heroes glad; and he, Telamon, son of Æacus, made haste to come to Jason, and he grasped his hand in his own and embraced him, with these words, "Son of Æson, be not angered with me, if in my folly I was somewhat blinded, for exceeding grief urged me to speak a haughty word I could not stay. Nay, let us give our error to the winds, and be good friends even as before."

Him in answer the son of Æson cautiously addressed, "Yea, good friend, that was a grievous word enough, I trow, wherewith thou didst revile me, making me to be a sinner against a comrade kind amongst all these. Yet no long time will I nurse bitter wrath against thee, though before distressed, for it was not for flocks of sheep nor for possessions that thou wert angered into fury, but for a man that was thy comrade. Yea, fain would I have thee stand up for me too against another, if ever there come such need."

He spake, and they sat them down, united as of old; and so by the counsel of Zeus, the one was destined to found and build a city called after the river, namely

[1] The Chalybes were a Scythian race, famous for working in iron, which their country yielded in plenty.

Polyphemus, son of Elatus, while the other returned and performed the labours of Eurystheus. Now he threatened at once to ravage the Mysian land, since they could not discover for him the fate of Hylas, either alive or dead. But they chose out the noblest sons of the people, and gave them as pledges for him, and took an oath that they would never cease from the toil of seeking him. Wherefore to this day the men of Cios ask after Hylas, the son of Theiodamas, and take care of the stablished town of Trachin,[1] for there it was that Heracles did place the boys, whom they sent to him from Cios to take as hostages.

And all day long and all that night the wind bare on the ship, blowing in its strength; but as the dawn broke, never a breath stirred. So they, having marked a headland, broad enow to look upon, stretching out from a bend in the land, took to their oars and anchored there at sunrise.

[1] A city in Thessaly, where Heracles placed the boys sent to him as hostages for lost Hylas by the Mysians.

BOOK II.

ARGUMENT.

They reach Bithynia. Amycus, king of the Bebryces, having challenged any of them to box with him, is slain by Polydeuces, and in the subsequent fight many of the Bebryces fall. At Salmydessa in Thrace they find blind Phineus, whom the sons of Boreas relieve from the attacks of the Harpies. In return he tells them of their voyage. Hence they come to the Symplegades, and, after escaping through them, are received by Lycus, king of the Mariandyni. Idmon and Tiphys die there. They meet with strange adventures among the Chalybes, Tibareni, and Mossynœci. Coming to an island infested by "the birds of Ares," they pick up the shipwrecked sons of Chalciope, who henceforth serve them as guides to Colchis.

BOOK II.

HERE were the steadings and the farm of Amycus, proud king of the Bebryces, whom on a day the Bithynian nymph, Melie, bare from the embraces of Poseidon,[1] lord of birth, to be the haughtiest of men, for he laid this unseemly ordinance even on his guests, that none should go away, till he had made trial of his boxing; and many of his neighbours had he slain. So then he came to the ship, but scorned to ask the object of their voyage and who they were, in his exceeding insolence; but this word at once spake he amongst them all: "Hearken, ye rovers o'er the deep; 'tis right ye should know these things. Of stranger folk none may get him hence, whoso draweth nigh to the Bebryces, ere he have lifted up his hands to fight with me. Wherefore set the best man of your company alone and apart to do battle with me in boxing on the spot. But if ye neglect and trample on my decrees, verily some hard necessity shall follow you to your sorrow."

So spake he in his great pride. But savage anger seized them as they listened. And most of all his chiding smote Polydeuces. Quickly he stood up as champion of his fellows, and spake, "Hold thee now, and show no coward violence, whoever thou boastest to be; for we will yield to thy ordinance, as thou declarest it. I myself willingly do undertake to meet thee in this very hour."

[1] Poseidon is called "Lord of Creation" because he had power over all moisture, without which nothing could come into being.

So spake he bluntly; but the other rolled his eyes and gazed at him, as when a lion is wounded by a spear, and men encompass him upon the hills; but he, hemmed in, though he be, by the press, yet recketh no more of them, but only mindeth in his solitude that man who first did wound him and slew him not. Then did the son of Tyndarus lay aside his fine close-woven robe, that robe which one of the Lemnian maidens had given him for a stranger's gift, and he threw down his dark cloak of double woof with the brooches thereupon, and the rough shepherd's crook of wild mountain olive that he was carrying. Anon they looked about for a convenient spot near, and made their comrades all sit down in two bands upon the beach; nor were they in form or stature like each other to behold. The one was like some monstrous birth of baleful Typhoeus[1] or haply of Earth herself, such as she aforetime bare to Zeus in her displeasure;[2] while the other, the son of Tyndarus, was like a star of heaven, whose twinklings are most lovely when he shineth in the gloaming. So fair was the son of Zeus, with the young down still sprouting on his face and the glad light yet in his eyes. But his might and his spirit waxed as doth a beast's; and he swung his arms, testing them to see if they moved nimbly as of yore, or lest they might be stiff withal from toil and rowing. Amycus however made no trial of himself; there he stood apart in silence, and kept his eyes on him, and his heart beat high with eagerness to dash the other's life-blood from his breast. Betwixt them Lycoreus, henchman of Amycus, laid at their feet two pairs of thongs,[3] rough, dry, and wrinkled all about.

[1] Typhoeus, a fearful giant slain by Zeus, and buried by him in Cilicia.

[2] The legend was that when Zeus slew the Titans, children of Earth, their mother in anger and revenge produced the Giants.

[3] ἱμάντας, lit. "thongs," which were bound round the hands and arms of boxers, sometimes loaded with metal as well, to increase the effect of the blows. They were called μύρμηκες.

And Amycus with haughty words addressed the other: "Here will I freely give thee without casting lots whichever of these thou wilt, that thou mayst not find fault with me hereafter. Come, bind it about thy hand; and, when thou hast learnt, thou mayst tell another, how far I excel in cutting the hides of oxen when they are dry, and in dabbling men's cheeks with blood."

He spake; but the other answered him with never a taunt, but, lightly smiling, readily took up the thongs that lay at his own feet; and Castor came to be his squire, and mighty Talaus, the son of Bias; and quickly they bound the thongs about his arms, very earnestly exhorting him to show his prowess; while for that other Aretus and Ornytus did the like, and little they knew, poor fools, that they had bound them for the last time, with ill luck to boot.

But they then, when they were ready with their thongs, face to face, at once held out before their bodies their weighty fists, and brought their might to meet each other. Then the king of the Bebryces, like a wave of the sea that rears its rugged crest against a swift ship that only just avoids it by the skill of the crafty pilot, as the billow is eager to sweep her away within its wall of water; even so the king pressed hard the son of Tyndarus to frighten him, nor would he give him any respite. But the other, unwounded ever, kept avoiding his rush by his skill; and quickly he noted his rough boxing, to see if he were invincible in his strength or haply his inferior; so there he stood continually,[1] and gave him blow for blow. As when carpenters, urgently laying on, do strike with hammers and nail together ship-timbers with sharp mortices, while blow on blow re-echoes round unceasingly; so their cheeks and jaws on both sides resounded, and the gnashing of teeth arose incessantly, and they ceased not to smite each in turn,

[1] ἄμοτον. A word of uncertain derivation, frequently occurring in Apollonius in the sense of "insatiably."

till sore gasping o'ercame them both. Then stood they a little apart, wiping from their faces great drops of sweat, with grievous panting and hard breathing the while. Once more they roused them to the encounter, like two bulls that furiously battle for a grazing heifer. Then did Amycus, rising on tiptoe, like a butcher, strain to his full height and shot forth his heavy fist at him, but he stooped his head and went under his rush, but caught his blow just on the shoulder; then did he come up to Amycus, and advancing his knee past him dashed in and smote him above the ear, crashing the bones inward; and the other fell on his knees in agony, but the Minyan heroes cheered; and away sped his spirit at once.

But the Bebryces, I trow, left not their king thus; no, at once they caught up rough clubs and spears and made straight for Polydeuces. But his comrades drew their keen swords from the scabbards and stood up before him. 'Twas Castor first that smote a man upon the head as he rushed at him, and his skull was cleft in twain on either shoulder. Likewise he smote the giant Itymoneus and Mimas; the one he smote beneath the breast, having rushed on him with speedy foot,[1] and hurled him in the dust; the other, as he drew nigh, he struck with his right hand above the left eye-brow and tore off the lid, and the eye was left uncovered. And Oreides too, daring squire of Amycus, wounded Talaus, the son of Bias, in the loins, but he slew him not, for the bronze sped beneath his belt merely along the skin, and touched not his belly. In like manner Aretus sprang at Iphitus, steadfast son of Eurytus, and smote him with a seasoned club, not yet doomed to die miserably; Aretus indeed was soon to fall beneath the sword of Clytius.

'Twas then that Ancæus, bold son of Lycurgus, uplifted his great axe right speedily, holding his black bear skin in

[1] λάξ, an adverb, = "with the heel or foot," on the same analogy as ὀδάξ, = "with the teeth," from δάκνω, with euphon. ὀ.

his left hand, and sprang furiously into the thick of the Bebryces, and the son of Æacus charged with him, and Jason too rushed on with them.

As when, on a day in winter, grizzled wolves attack and terrify countless sheep in the fold without the knowledge of the keen-scented dogs and the shepherds themselves, and they seek how they may at once spring on them and take them, oft peering over the pens withal, while the sheep from every side huddle as they are, tumbling over one another; even so, I ween, the heroes grievously affrighted the overweening Bebryces. As shepherds or bee-keepers smoke a mighty swarm of bees in a rock, and these the while, all huddled in their hive, buzz round confusedly; and far from the rock they dart, smoked right through by the sooty fumes; so these men no longer abode steadfastly, but fled routed within Bebrycia, carrying the news of the death of Amycus; poor fools, for they knew not of another unseen woe that was very nigh to them. For their orchards and villages were wasted by the hostile spear of Lycus and the Mariandyni, now that their king was gone. For there was ever a feud twixt them about the land that yielded iron; for these at once began to pillage the farms and steadings, while the heroes forthwith plundered and carried off their countless sheep; and thus some man amongst them would say: "Bethink you what they would have brought upon themselves by their craven deeds, if haply some god had brought Heracles too hither. Very sure am I, had he been here, there would have been not so much as a trial of boxing; no, but when he came to tell his ordinances, forthwith the club would have made him forget his pride and the ordinances too which he declared. Yea, we have left him yonder on the shore without a thought and gone our way across the sea, but every man amongst us shall know that fatal mistake, now that he is far away."

Thus spake he; but all these things were wrought by

the counsels of Zeus. There they abode that night, and set to curing the wounds of those who were smitten, and they offered sacrifices to the deathless gods, and made ready a great supper; and sleep o'ertook no man beside the wine-bowls and the blazing sacrifices. And they wreathed their yellow locks with bay that groweth by the sea, whereto also were fastened the cables, and sang in sweet harmony to the lyre of Orpheus; and as they sang the headland round grew calm and still, for their song was of the son of Zeus,[1] who dwelleth in Therapnæ.

Now when the sun, rising from the east, shone upon the dewy hills, and awoke shepherds, in that hour they loosed their cables from the stem of the bay-tree, and, putting their booty on board, even all that they had need to carry, they steered with the wind along the swirling Bosporus. Then did a wave like to a steep mountain rush upon them in front, as though it were charging them, rearing itself ever above the clouds, and never wouldst thou have said they would escape a horrid fate, for it hung arching right over the middle of the ship in all its fury; but yet even this grows smooth, if but you possess a clever pilot. So then they too came forth, unscathed, though much afeard, through the skill of Tiphys. And on the next day they anchored over against the Bithynian land.

Here Phineus, son of Agenor, had his home beside the sea; he who, by reason of the divination that the son of Leto granted him aforetime, suffered most awful woes, far beyond all men; for not one jot did he regard even Zeus himself, in foretelling the sacred purpose to men unerringly. Wherefore Zeus granted him a weary length of days, but reft his eyes of the sweet light, nor suffered him to have any joy of all the countless gifts, which those, who dwelt around and sought to him for oracles, were ever bringing to

[1] "The Therapnæan son of Zeus," *i.e.* Apollo, so called from Therapnæ, a part of Sparta, which was sacred to this god.

his house. But suddenly through the clouds the Harpies darted nigh, and kept snatching them from his mouth or hands in their talons. Sometimes never a morsel of food was left him, sometimes a scrap, that he might live and suffer. And upon his food they spread a fetid stench; and none could endure to bring food to his mouth, but stood afar off; so foul a reek breathed from the remnants of his meal. At once, when he heard the sound and noise of a company, he perceived that they were the very men now passing by, at whose coming an oracle from Zeus had said that he should enjoy his food. Up from his couch he rose, as it were, a lifeless phantom, and, leaning on his staff, came to the door on his wrinkled feet, feeling his way along the walls; and, as he went, his limbs trembled from weakness and age, and his skin was dry and caked with filth, and nought but the skin held his bones together. So he came forth from his hall, and sat down with heavy knees on the threshold of the court, and a dark mantle wrapped him, and seemed to sweep the ground below all round; and there he sank with never a word, in strengthless lethargy.

But they, when they saw him, gathered round, and were astonied. And he, drawing a laboured breath from the bottom of his chest, took up his parable for them and said: "Hearken, choice sons of all the Hellenes, if 'tis you in very truth, whom now Jason, at the king's chill bidding, is leading on the ship Argo to fetch the fleece. 'Tis surely you. Still doth my mind know each thing by its divining. Wherefore to thee, my prince, thou son of Leto, do I give thanks even in my cruel sufferings. By Zeus, the god of suppliants, most awful god to sinful men, for Phœbus' sake and for the sake of Hera herself, who before all other gods hath had you in her keeping as ye came, help me, I implore; rescue a hapless wretch from misery, and do not heedlessly go hence and leave me thus. For not only hath the avenging fiend set his heel upon my eyes, not only do I drag out to the end a tedious old age, but yet another most bitter pain is added to the tale. Harpies, swooping from some unseen den of destruction, that I see not, do snatch the food from my mouth. And I have no plan to help me. But lightly would my mind forget her longing for a meal, or the thought of them, so quickly fly they through the air. But if, as happens at times, they leave me some scrap of food, a noisome stench it hath, and a smell too strong to bear, nor could any mortal man draw nigh and bear it even for a little while, no, not though his heart were forged of adamant. But me, God wot, doth necessity, cruel and insatiate, constrain to abide, and abiding to put such food in my miserable belly. Them 'tis heaven's decree that the sons of Boreas [1] shall check; and they shall ward them off, for they are my kinsmen, if indeed I am that Phineus, who in days gone by had a name amongst men for my wealth and divination, whom Agenor, my sire, begat; their sister Cleopatra [2] did I bring to my house as wife with gifts of wooing, what time I ruled among the Thracians."

So spake the son of Agenor; and deep sorrow took hold on each of the heroes, but specially on the two sons of Boreas. But they wiped away a tear and drew nigh, and thus spake Zetes, taking in his the hand of the suffering old man: "Ah! poor sufferer, methinks there is no other man more wretched than thee. Why is it that such woes have fastened on thee? Is it that thou hast sinned against the gods in deadly folly through thy skill in divination? Wherefore are they so greatly wroth against thee? Lo! our heart within us is sorely bewildered, though we yearn to help thee, if in very truth the god hath reserved for us

[1] The sons of Boreas were Zetes and Calais.

[2] Phineus in his happier days had married Cleopatra, daughter of Boreas and Orithyia; he was therefore uncle of Zetes and Calais, his destined deliverers.

twain this honour. For plain to see are the rebukes that the immortals send on us men of earth. Nor will we check the coming of the Harpies, for all our eagerness, till that thou swear that we shall not fall from heaven's favour in return for this." So spake he, and straight that aged man opened his sightless eyes and lifted them up, and thus made answer: "Hush! remind me not of those things, my son. The son of Leto be my witness, who of his kindness taught me divination; be witness that ill-omened fate, that is my lot, and this dark cloud upon my eyes, and the gods below, whose favour may I never find if I die perjured thus, that there shall come no wrath from heaven on you by reason of your aid."

Then were those twain eager to help him by reason of the oath, and quickly did the young men make ready a feast for the old man, a last booty for the Harpies; and the two stood near to strike them with their swords as they swooped down. Soon as ever that aged man did touch the food, down rushed those Harpies with whirr of wings at once, eager for the food, like grievous blasts, or like lightning darting suddenly from the clouds; but those heroes, when they saw them in mid air, shouted; and they at the noise sped off afar across the sea after they had devoured everything, but behind them was left an intolerable stench. And the two sons of Boreas started in pursuit of them with their swords drawn; for Zeus inspired them with tireless courage, and 'twas not without the will of Zeus that they followed them, for they would dart past the breath of the west wind, what time they went to and from Phineus. As when upon the hill-tops dogs skilled in the chase run on the track of horned goats or deer, and, straining at full speed just behind, in vain do gnash their teeth upon their lips; even so Zetes and Calais, darting very nigh to them, in vain grazed them with their finger-tips. And now, I trow, they would have torn them in pieces against the will of the gods on the floating islands,[1] after they had come afar, had not swift Iris seen them, and darting down from the clear heaven above stayed them with this word of rebuke: "Ye sons of Boreas, 'tis not ordained that ye should slay the Harpies, the hounds of mighty Zeus, with your swords; but I, even I, will give you an oath that they will come no more nigh him."

Therewith she sware by the stream of Styx, most dire and awful oath for all the gods, that these should never again draw near unto the house of Phineus, son of Agenor, for even so was it fated. So they yielded to her oath and turned to hasten back to the ship. And so it is that men call those isles, "the isles of turning," though aforetime they called them "the floating isles." And the Harpies and Iris parted; they entered their lair in Crete, the land of Minos, but she sped up to Olympus, soaring on her swift pinions.

Meantime the chieftains carefully washed the old man's squalid skin, and chose out and sacrificed sheep, which they had brought from the booty of Amycus. Now when they had laid a great supper in his halls, they sat them down and feasted, and with them Phineus fell afeasting ravenously, cheering his heart as in a dream. Then when they had taken their fill of food and drink, they sat up all night awaiting the sons of Boreas. And in their midst beside the hearth sat that ancient one himself, telling them of the ends of their voyage and the fulfilment of their journey: "Hearken then. All ye may not learn of a surety, but as much as is heaven's will I will not hide. Aforetime I went astray in my folly by declaring the mind of Zeus in order to the end. For he willeth himself to make plain to men oracles that need divination, to the

[1] "The Floating Isles" in the Sicilian sea. They were supposed to be capable of movement. After the flight of the Harpies here, they were called the Strophades, *i.e.* "Isles of turning."

end that they may have some need of the mind of the gods.

"First of all, when ye have gone hence from me, ye shall see the two Cyanean[1] rocks at the place where two seas meet. Through these, I trow, none can win a passage. For they are not fixed on foundations below, but oft they clash together upon each other, and much salt water boils up from beneath, rearing its crest, and loud is the roar round the bluff headland.

"Wherefore now give heed to my exhorting, if in sooth ye make this voyage with cautious mind and due regard for the blessed gods; perish not then senselessly by a death of your own choosing, nor rush on at the heels of youthful rashness. First I bid you let loose from the ship a dove, and send her forth before you to try the way. And if she fly safely on her wings through those rocks to the sea, no longer do ye delay your voyage for any time, but stoutly ply the oars in your hands and cleave through the strait of sea, for now your life will depend, not so much on your prayers, as on your stalwart arms. Wherefore leave all other things alone and exert[2] yourselves bravely to the utmost; yet ere you start, I do not forbid you to entreat the gods. But if the dove be slain right in mid passage, fare ye back again, for far better it is to yield to the deathless gods. For then could ye not escape an evil doom at the rocks, no, not if Argo were made of iron. Ah! hapless wights! dare not to go beyond my warning, although ye think me thrice as much the foe of the lords of heaven, aye and even more hateful to them than I really am; dare not to sail yet further against the omen. And these things shall be even as they may. But if ye escape the clashing

[1] πέτρας, *i.e.* the Symplegades, or "Clashers," stood at the mouth of Pontus.

[2] *i.e.* do not think prayers alone will save you, but, on the other hand, do not neglect to pray as well as to do your utmost as men.

of the rocks and come scatheless inside Pontus, forthwith keep the Bithynian[1] land upon your right, and sail cautiously amid the breakers, till that ye round the swift current of the river Rhebas and the Black headland, and be come to a haven in the Thynian isle. Thence return a short stretch across the sea, and beach your ship on the opposite shore of the Mariandyni. There is a path down to Hades, and the headland[2] of Acherusia juts out and stretches itself on high, and swirling Acheron, cutting through the foot of the cliff, pours itself forth from a mighty ravine. Very nigh to it shall ye pass by many hills of the Paphlagonians, over whom Pelops first held sway in Enete,[3] of whose blood they avow them to be. Now there is a certain cliff that fronts the circling[4] Bear, on all sides steep; men call it Carambis; above it the gusty north is parted in twain; in such wise is it turned toward the sea, towering to heaven. At once when a man hath rounded it a wide beach stretches before him, and at the end of that wide beach nigh to a jutting cliff the stream of the river Halys[5] terribly discharges, and after him, but flowing near, the Iris rolls into the sea, a lesser stream with clear ripples. Here in front a great and towering bend stands out[6]; next, Thermodon's mouth flows into a sleeping bay near the Themiscyrean headland, from its meandering through a wide continent.

[1] The Bosporus is bounded on the right by Bithynia, on the left by the Thracian land. Rhebas is a river of Bithynia.

[2] This headland was near Heraclea.

[3] Ἐνετήιος, so called from Enete, a city of Paphlagonia, the native place of Pelops.

[4] Ἑλίκη, another name for "the Bear," *i.e.* the North, so called because the Bear was supposed to be ever wheeling round so as to escape Orion, who was in pursuit.

[5] The Halys is a river of Paphlagonia, falling into the Pontus near the city Sinope.

[6] *i.e.* stands up high from the surrounding land and juts out into the sea, forming an angle. "The mouth of the Thermodon" is only a precise way of saying "the Thermodon."

There is the plain of Doias, and hard by are the triple cities of the Amazons; and after them the Chalybes [1] inhabit a rough and stubborn land, of all men most wretched, labourers they, busied with working of iron. Near them dwell the Tibareni, rich in sheep, beyond the Genetæan headland, where is a temple of Zeus, lord of hospitality. Next beyond this, but nigh thereto, the Mossynœci [2] hold the woody mainland and the foot of the mountain, men that have builded houses of timber with wooden battlements and chambers deftly finished, which they call 'Mossynæ,' and hence they have their name. Coast on past them, and anchor at a smooth isle,[3] after ye have driven off with all the skill ye may those ravening birds, which, men say, do roost upon this desert isle in countless numbers. Therein the queens of the Amazons builded a temple of stone to Ares, even Otrere and Antiope, what time they went forth to battle. Now here shall there come to you from out the bitter sea a help [4] ye looked not for, wherefore of good will I bid you there to stay. But hold; why should I once more offend by telling everything from beginning to end in my divining? In front of the island, on the mainland opposite, dwell the Philyres; [5] higher up, beyond them, are the

[1] The Chalybes, a Scythian race, so called from Chalybs, a son of Ares, great workers in iron. The Amazons, a warlike and savage race of women, living near the Doian plain in three separate cities, Lycastia, Themiscyra, and Chalybia. Their queens were Otrere and Antiope.

[2] The Mossynœci, or dwellers in wooden houses, μόσσυναι being = wooden houses. Some account of their curious customs is given infra, bk. ii. l. 1016, sqq.

[3] νησῳ, the isle of Ares, on which were the terrible Stymphalian birds with feathers which could be shot by the birds themselves like arrows.

[4] *i.e.* just when you are becoming desperate and sick of your enterprise, there shall come to you an unexpected relief from the sea in the shape of shipwrecked mariners, viz., the sons of Chalciope, who had lately left Æa, but had been wrecked on the isle of Ares; they shall serve to guide you on your voyage to Colchis. Cf. infra, bk. ii. l. 1090, sqq.

[5] The various tribes now mentioned are Scythian, then comes Sar-

Macrones; and yet beyond these, the countless tribes of the Becheiri. Next to them dwell the Sapeires, and their neighbours are the Byzeres, and right beyond them come next the warlike Colchians themselves. But cleave on your way, until ye come nigh to the inmost sea. There across the Cytæan[1] mainland, from the Amarantian hills afar, and the plain of Circe,[2] the swirling Phasis rolls his broad stream into the sea. Drive your ship into the mouth of that river, and ye shall see the towers of Cytæan Æetes and the shady grove of Ares, where a dragon, dire monster to behold, watches from his ambush round the fleece as it hangs on the top of an oak; nor night nor day doth sweet sleep o'ercome his restless eyes."

So spake he; and as they hearkened, fear fell on them forthwith. Long were they struck with speechlessness; at last spake the hero, the son of Æson, sorely at a loss, "Old man, lo! now hast thou rehearsed the end of our toilsome voyage, and the sure sign, which if we obey we shall pass through those loathèd rocks to Pontus; but whether there shall be a return again to Hellas for us, if we do escape them, this too would I fain learn of thee. How am I to act, how shall I come again over so wide a path of sea, in ignorance myself and with a crew alike ignorant? for Colchian Æa lieth at the uttermost end of Pontus and the earth."

So spake he, and to him did that old man make answer, "My child, as soon as thou hast escaped through those rocks of death, be of good cheer, for a god will guide thee on a different route from Æa; and toward Æa, there shall be plenty to guide thee. Yea, friends, bethink you of the crafty aid of the Cyprian goddess. For by her is pre-

matia about the lake Mæotis, while beyond this lies the Arctic Ocean.

[1] Colchian, Cytæa being a city in Colchis.

[2] Circe was sister of Æetes.

pared a glorious end to your toils. But question me no further of these matters."

So spake the son of Agenor, and the two sons of Thracian Boreas came glancing down from heaven, and set their rushing feet upon the threshold beside them. Up sprang the heroes from their seats, when they saw them coming near. And among the eager throng Zetes made harangue, drawing great gasps for breath after his toil, and told them how far they had journeyed, and how Iris prevented them from slaying the Harpies, and how the goddess in her favour gave them an oath, and those others slunk away in terror 'neath the vast cavern of the cliff of Dicte. Glad then were all their comrades in the house, and Phineus himself, at the news. And quickly did the son of Æson address the old man with right good will: "It seems then, Phineus, some god there was who pitied thy grievous misery, and brought us, too, hither from afar, that the sons of Boreas might help thee; if but he would grant the light unto thine eyes, methinks I would be even as glad as if I were on my homeward way."

So spake he; but the other, with downcast face, answered him: "Ah! son of Æson, that may never be recalled, nor is there any remedy for that hereafter; for blasted[1] are my sightless eyes. Instead thereof God grant me death[2] at once, and after death shall I share in all festive joys."

Thus these twain held converse together. And anon, in no long space, as they talked, the dawn appeared; and the neighbouring folk came round Phineus, they who even aforetime gathered thither day by day, ever bringing a

[1] ὑποσμύχονται literally = are smouldering away, a forcible word to express the blinding of the eyes by lightning.

[2] A wish. God grant me death; then shall I have the same chances as other men of happiness. The legend was that Phineus, being given a choice of anything he pleased, asked for long life. This was granted; but, to punish his folly, it was accompanied with blindness.

portion of food for him in spite of all. And unto all of them that aged man with good will gave oracles, whatso feeble man might come; and he loosed many of their woes by his divination; wherefore they would visit and care for him. With these came Paræbius, the man most dear to him, and glad was he to hear them in his house. For long before had he himself declared that an expedition of chieftains, on its way from Hellas to the city of Æetes, should fasten its cables to the Thynian[1] land, and they should restrain by Zeus's will the Harpies from coming to him. So then that old man sent these men forth, winning them with words of wisdom; only Paræbius he bade stay there with the chieftains; and quickly he sent him forth, bidding him bring thither the pick of all his sheep; and as he went out from the hall, Phineus made harangue graciously amongst the throng of rowers: "Friends, all men, I trow, are not overweening, nor forgetful of a kindness. Thus yonder man, brave soul as he is, came hither that he might learn his fate.[2] For when he toiled his best and worked his hardest, even then above all repeated want of food would waste him, and day on day was ever more miserable, nor was there any respite from his suffering. But he was paying a sad return for his father's sin; for he, cutting trees alone on a day in the hills, slighted the prayer of a tree-nymph, who besought him with tears and earnest entreaty not to cut the trunk of an oak that had grown up with her, whereon she had passed many a long year together, but he, in the senseless pride of youth, cut it down. Wherefore did the nymph make her death unprofitable to him and his children afterwards. Now I knew the sin, when he came to me; so I bade him build an altar to the Thynian nymph, and offer upon it sacrifice to cleanse the guilt, praying for an escape from his father's doom. Then when

[1] Thynis, a part of Thrace upon the Bosporus.

[2] μόρον here = "fate, destiny," *not* "death."

he escaped the doom sent by the goddess, he never forgat nor ceased to care for me; and scarce can I send him to the door, unwilling to depart, for he is fain to abide even here with me in my distress."

So spake the son of Agenor; and the other anon drew nigh, driving two sheep from the fold. Then up stood Jason, and up stood the sons of Boreas as the old man bade them. Quickly they called on the name of prophetic Apollo, and did sacrifice upon the hearth just as the day was waning, and the young men of the crew made ready a plenteous feast. Then when they had well feasted, some laid them to rest by the cables of the ship, and some in knots there in the house. At morn the steady summer winds[1] began to blow, which breathe o'er the whole earth equally, for such is the command of Zeus.

There runs a legend that Cyrene[2] once was herding sheep along the marsh of the Peneus amongst the men of former times, for her heart rejoiced in her maidenhood and virgin couch. But Apollo caught her up from her shepherding by the river far from Hæmonia, and set her down among the maidens of the country who dwelt in Libya beside the Myrtosian height. There she bare Aristæus unto Phœbus, whom the Hæmonians, with their rich corn-lands, call "the Hunter" and "the Shepherd." For the god, for the love of the nymph, granted her length of days and a home in the country there, and brought her infant son to be reared 'neath the cave of Chiron. And when he was grown, the divine Muses found for him a wife, and taught him the

[1] *ἐτήσιαι αὖραι.* According to the legend, a great drought prevailed once in the Cyclades, when an oracle told the people to call in to their aid Aristæus, the son of Apollo and Cyrene, from Phthia. He came to Cos, and appeased Zeus with sacrifice; whereon that god sent a cool breeze to blow upon the isle for forty days. Henceforth these winds became annual during the summer, beginning when the sun is in the last chamber of the Crab, and lasting until he enters the Lion.

[2] The mother of Aristæus just mentioned.

arts of healing and prophecy; and they made him the keeper of their flocks, all that feed along the plain of Athamas in Phthia, and around steep Othrys, and the sacred stream of the river Apidanus. Now when the Dog-star[1] from heaven scorched up the islands of Minos,[2] and for a long space the inhabitants found no relief, then by the advice of Hecatus they called him in to stay the plague. So he left Phthia at the bidding of his father, and came to dwell in Cos, having gathered thither the Parrhasian[3] folk, who are of the lineage of Lycaon; and he builded a mighty altar to Zeus, the god of rain,[4] and did fair sacrifice upon the mountains to Sirius, that baleful star, and to Zeus himself, the son of Cronos. Wherefore it is that the Etesian winds blow cool across the earth for forty days from Zeus; and even now in Cos priests offer sacrifices before the rising of the Dog.

So runs this legend; and the chiefs abode there by constraint;[5] and every day the Thynians sent forth good store of gifts for the strangers, out of favour for Phineus. After this, when they had builded an altar to the twelve blessed gods on the edge of the sea opposite, and had offered sacrifice upon it, they went aboard their swift ship to row away, nor did they forget to take with them a timorous dove, but Euphemus clutched her in his hand, cowering with terror, and carried her along, and they loosed their double cables from the shore.

Nor, I ween, had they started, ere Athene was ware of

[1] Σείριος, *i.e.* the Dogstar, "the scorching star."

[2] Μινωΐδας, *i.e.* the Cyclades, for Minos, king of Crete, held the supremacy of the sea (cf. Thuc. i.) in early times, and consequently of all the islands.

[3] Parrhasian, *i.e.* Arcadian. Parrhasia, a city of Arcadia.

[4] Ἰκμαίοιο, "Lord of rain," Zeus being appealed to as the controller of the atmosphere.

[5] ἰρυκόμενοι, *i.e.* holden there by the Etesian winds, which were not favourable to their sailing.

them, and forthwith and hastily she stepped upon a light cloud, which should bear her at once for all her weight; and she hasted on her way seaward, with kindly intent to the rowers. As when a man goes wandering from his country, as oft we men do wander in our hardihood, and there is no land too far away, for every path lies open before his eyes, when lo! he seeth in his mind his own home, and withal there appeareth a way to it over land or over sea, and keenly he pondereth this way and that, and searcheth it out with his eyes; even so the daughter of Zeus, swifty darting on, set foot upon the cheerless strand of Thynia.

Now they, when they came to the strait of the winding passage, walled in with beetling crags on either side, while an eddying current from below washed up against the ship as it went on its way; and on they went in grievous fear, and already on their ears the thud of clashing rocks smote unceasingly, and the dripping cliffs roared; in that very hour the hero Euphemus clutched the dove in his hand, and went to take his stand upon the prow, while they, at the bidding of Tiphys, son of Hagnias, rowed with a will, that they might drive right through the rocks, trusting in their might. And as they rounded a bend, they saw those rocks opening for the last time of all. And their spirit melted at the sight; but the hero Euphemus sent forth the dove to dart through on her wings, and they, one and all, lifted up their heads to see, and she sped through them, but at once the two rocks met again with a clash; and the foam leapt up in a seething mass like a cloud, and grimly roared the sea, and all around the great firmament bellowed. And the hollow caves echoed beneath the rugged rocks as the sea went surging in, and high on the cliffs was the white spray vomited as the billow dashed upon them. Then did the current spin the ship round. And the rocks cut off just the tail-feathers of the dove, but she darted away unhurt. And loudly the rowers cheered, but Tiphys himself shouted to them to row lustily, for once more the rocks were opening. Then came trembling on them as they rowed, until the wave with its returning wash came and bore the ship within the rocks. Thereon most awful fear seized on all, for above their head was death with no escape; and now on this side and on that lay broad Pontus to their view, when suddenly in front rose up a mighty arching wave, like to a steep hill, and they bowed down their heads at the sight. For it seemed as if it must indeed leap down and whelm the ship entirely. But Tiphys was quick to ease her as she laboured to the rowing, and the wave rolled with all his force beneath the keel, and lifted up the ship herself from underneath, far from the rocks, and high on the crest of the billow she was borne. Then did Euphemus go amongst all the crew, and call to them to lay on to their oars with all their might, and they smote the water at his cry. So she sprang forward twice as far as any other ship would have yielded to rowers, and the oars bent like curved bows as the heroes strained. In that instant the vaulted wave was past them, and she at once was riding over the furious billow like a roller, plunging headlong forward o'er the trough of the sea. But the eddying current stayed the ship in the midst of "the Clashers," and they quaked on either side, and thundered, and the ship-timbers throbbed. Then did Athene with her left hand hold the stubborn rock apart, while with her right she thrust them through upon their course; and the ship shot through the air like a winged arrow. Yet the rocks, ceaselessly dashing together, crushed off, in passing, the tip of the carvèd stern. And Athene sped back to Olympus, when they were escaped unhurt. But the rocks closed up together, rooted firm for ever; even so was it decreed by the blessed gods, whenso a man should have passed through alive in his ship. And they, I trow, drew breath again after their chilling fear, as they gazed out upon the sky, and the expanse of sea spreading far and wide. For verily they deemed that they were saved from Hades, and Tiphys first made harangue: "Methinks we have escaped this danger sure enough, we and the ship, and there is no other we have to thank so much as Athene, who inspired the ship with divine courage, when Argus fastened her together with bolts; and it is not right that she should be caught. Wherefore, son of Æson, no more fear at all the bidding of thy king, since God hath granted us to escape through the rocks, for Phineus, son of Agenor, declared that, after this, toils, easy to master, should be ours."

Therewith he made the ship speed past the Bithynian coast across the sea. But the other answered him with gentle words: "Ah! Tiphys, why comfort my heavy heart thus? I have sinned, and upon me has come a grievous blindness I may not cope with; for I should have refused this journey outright at once when Pelias ordained it, even though I was to have died, torn ruthlessly limb from limb; but now do I endure[1] exceeding terror, and troubles past bearing, in deadly dread to sail across the chill paths of the deep, in deadly dread whene'er we land. For on all sides are enemies. And ever as the days go by, I watch through the dreary night, and think of all, since first ye mustered for my sake; and lightly dost thou speak, caring only for thine[2] own life, while I fear never so little for myself, but for this man and for that, for thee and the rest of my comrades do I fear, if I bring you not safe and sound to Hellas."

[1] *ἄγκειμαι.* Whether this reading is what the poet originally wrote cannot now be ascertained; it has been tacitly accepted, and from the context seems to mean "I bear, sustain," but what authority there is for giving the word such a meaning it is difficult to say.

[2] *ἑῆς* for the 2nd person = *τῆς σεαυτοῦ.* *εἷο* for *ἐμεῖο*, 3rd person for 1st. *τοῖο καὶ τοῦ*, much as we might say A and B, meaning any two indefinite persons, used as instances.

So spake he, making trial of the chieftains; but they cried out with words of cheer. And his heart was glad within him at their exhorting, and once more he spake to them outright, "My friends, your bravery makes me more bold. Wherefore now no more will I let fear fasten on me, even though I must voyage across the gulf of Hades, since ye stand firm amid cruel terrors. Nay, since we have sailed from out the clashing rocks, I trow there will be no other horror in store such as this, if we surely go our way, following the counsel of Phineus."

So spake he, and forthwith they ceased from such words, and toiled in rowing unceasingly, and soon they passed by Rhebas, that swiftly-rushing river, and the rock of Colone, and, not long after, the Black headland, and, next, the mouth of the river Phyllis,[1] where aforetime Dipsacus received the son of Athamas in his house what time he was flying, together with the ram, from the city of Orchomenus; his mother was a meadow-nymph, and he loved not wanton deeds, but gladly dwelt with his mother by the waters of his father, feeding flocks upon the shore. And quickly they sighted and passed by his shrine, and the river's broad banks and the plain and Calpe with its deep stream; and day by day, the calm night through, they bent to their unresting oars. As ploughing oxen do toil in cleaving a moist fallow-field, and the sweat trickles in great drops from their flanks and neck, and they keep turning their eyes askance from under the yoke, while the parched breath from their mouths comes ever snorting forth, and they planting their hoofs firmly in the ground go toiling on the livelong day; like unto them the heroes tugged their oars through the brine.

Now when the dawn divine was not yet come, nor yet was it exceeding dark, but o'er the night was spread a

[1] A river in Bithynia.

streak of light, the hour when men arise and call it twilight;[1] in that hour they rowed into the harbour of the desert Thynian isle with laboured toil, and went ashore. And to them appeared the son of Leto, coming up from far Lycia, on his way to the countless race of the Hyperboreans; and clustering locks of gold streamed down his cheeks as he came; and in his left hand he held his silver bow, while about his back was slung his quiver from his shoulders; beneath his feet the island quaked throughout, and on the shore the waves surged up. And they were filled with wild alarm when they caught sight of him, and none dare gaze into the god's fair eyes. But there they stood with heads bowed low upon the ground, till he was far on his way to sea through the air; then at last spake Orpheus, thus declaring his word to the chieftains, "Come now, let us call this island the sacred isle of Apollo, god of dawn, for that he was seen by all passing over it at dawn, and let us sacrifice such things as we may, when we have raised an altar on the strand; but if hereafter he grant us a safe return to the land of Hæmonia, then surely will we lay upon his altar the thighs of hornèd goats. And now, as ye may, I bid you win his favour with the steam of sacrifice. Be gracious, O be gracious in thy appearing, prince!"

So spake he; and some at once made an altar of shingle,[2] while others roamed the island in quest of fawns or wild goats if haply they might see aught of either, such beasts as oft do seek their food in a wood's depths. And for them the son of Leto found a quarry; then with pious rites they wrapped the thigh bones[3] of them all in a roll of fat

[1] *ἀμφιλύκη*, an adj. agreeing with *νύξ* understood, *i.e.* the gray dawn, morning twilight.

[2] *χερμάσιν*, *i.e.* small stones or pebbles such as can be grasped in the hand (*χείρ*), *i.e.* they made the best altar they could with the materials they could find.

[3] *διπλόα μηρία*. Cf. Hom. Odyss. iii. 458, and passim. The thigh-

and burned them on the sacred altar, calling on the name of Apollo, god of dawn. And they stood in a wide ring around the burning sacrifice, chanting this hymn to Phœbus, "Hail, all hail! fair healing god;"[1] while the goodly son of Œager led for them their clear song on his Bistonian[2] lyre, telling how on a day beneath Parnassus' rocky ridge he slew the monster snake Delphine with his bow, while yet a beardless youth, proud of his long locks. "O be gracious, ever be thy hair uncut,[3] my prince, ever free from hurt, for thus 'tis right. Only Leto herself, daughter of Cœus, fondles it in her hands." And the Corycian[4] nymphs, daughters of Pleistus, oft took up the cheering strain, crying, "Hail, all hail!"[5] This then was the fair refrain they chanted to Phœbus.

Now when they had celebrated[6] him with song and dance, they took an oath by the holy drink-offering, that verily they would help one another for ever in unity of purpose, laying their hand upon the sacrifice; and still to this day there stands a temple there to cheerful Unity, the temple

bones were specially reserved for sacrifice to the gods; they were wrapped up in fat and then burnt, after which feasting began.

[1] Ἰηπαιήονα, probably connected with ἰάομαι, Apollo being the god of healing, no less than the sender of disease, as he is represented at the opening of the Iliad. Another etymology connects the word with ἵημι, *i.e.* the darting god, from his archery, like ἑκηβόλος, but not so well.

[2] Thracian, the Bistones being a Thracian tribe.

[3] With this line cf. the epithet ἀκερσεκόμης = with hair unshorn, a title of Apollo from his long, flowing locks.

[4] The Corycian cave is on Mount Parnassus. The Pleistus is a river at Delphi.

[5] Ἰήιε literally = O god saluted with the cry ἰη ἰη.

[6] μέλψαν χορείῃ ἀοιδῇ. Here we have both song and dance specifically mentioned, but frequently μολπή is used alone to express both the chant and the rhythmic dance which always accompanied it; *e.g.* in the Odyssee, Nausicaa's game at ball with her handmaids is described as μολπή, which really means "anything done in time," and so often the combination of singing and dancing.

their own hands then built to the honour of a deity most potent.

Now when the third day was come, then did they leave that steep isle with a fresh west wind. Thence they sighted over against them the mouth of the river Sangarius,[1] and the fruitful land of the Mariandyni and the streams of Lycus and the lake of Anthemoisia, and by them they passed. And as they ran before the breeze, the ropes and tackling throughout the ship were shaken; at dawn, for the wind dropped during the night, they were glad to reach the haven of the Acherusian headland, which rises up with steep beetling crags, facing the Bithynian sea; beneath it are rooted smooth sea-washed rocks, and round them the billow rolls and thunders loud, but above, upon the top, grow spreading plane trees. Further inland from this lieth a glen in the hollow, where is the cave of Hades,[2] roofed in with trees and rocks, whence an icy blast, breathing always from the chill den within, ever freezeth the sparkling rime, that thaws again beneath the noonday sun. Never spreads silence o'er that grim[3] headland, but there is a confused murmur of the booming sea, and of leaves rustling in the wind within. There too is the mouth of the river Acheron, which discharges through the headland and falleth into the sea eastward; a hollow chasm brings it down from above. The Megarians of Nisæa called it in after-times "Saviour of Mariners," when they were about to settle in the land of the Mariandyni. For lo! it saved them and their ships when they were caught by a foul tempest. So now at once the heroes passed

[1] A river of Phrygia.

[2] This description of the cave of Hades may be well compared with Vergil's account of the cavern of the Sybil.

[3] βλοσυρήν, here, in its primary sense, "grim, stern;" it also comes to mean "sturdy, strong," in which sense Plato employs it in the Republic.

through the Acherusian headland and anchored inside,[1] just as the wind was dropping.

No long time,[2] I trow, could the slayers of Amycus, as report had told, anchor without the knowledge of Lycus, lord of that mainland, or of the Mariandyni; but they made even a league with them on that account. And they welcomed Polydeuces himself as he had been a god, gathering from all sides, for long time had they warred bitterly against the overweening Bebryces. And so it was that at once within the halls of Lycus they made ready a feast that day with all good will, going to the city, and rejoiced their hearts with converse.

And the son of Æson declared his lineage and the name of each of his crew, and the commands of Pelias, and how they were entertained by the women of Lemnos, and all that they did in Cyzicus, city of the Doliones, and how they came to Mysia and Chios, where they left the hero Heracles against their will; also he declared the message of Glaucus, and told how they smote the Bebryces and Amycus, and of the prophecies and misery of Phineus, and how they escaped the Cyanean rocks, and met the son of Leto at the island. And the heart of Lycus was charmed at listening to his tale, and thus spake he amongst them all: "My friends, what a man is he whose aid ye have lost in your long, long voyage to Æetes! For well I mind seeing him here in the halls of my father Dascylus, what time he came hither afoot through the mainland of Asia, bringing the girdle of Hippolyte,[3] the warrior queen; but me he found

[1] *εἰσωποί*, *i.e.* they passed through the ravine at the mouth of the Acheron till they were behind the wall of rock, and so (*εἰσωποί* = *ἐναντίοι*) facing the back of it.

[2] *i.e.* the fame of Polydeuces and the Argonauts, as public benefactors, had preceded them, and insured them a ready welcome from Lycus and the Mariandyni, the hereditary enemies of Amycus and the Bebryces.

[3] To fetch the girdle of Hippolyte, queen of the Amazons, daughter

with the down just sprouting on my chin. Then [1] when our brother Priolaus was slain by the Mysians, whom from that day forth the people mourn in piteous elegies, he entered the lists with Titias the mighty, and vanquished him in boxing, a man who excelled all our young men in build and might; and he dashed his teeth upon the ground. Moreover he subdued to my father Phrygians and Mysians together, who inhabit the lands nigh to us, and took for his own the tribes of the Bithynians with their land, as far as the mouth of the Rhebas and the rock of Colone; next the Paphlagonians, sprung from Pelops, yielded without fight, all whom the black water of Billæus breaks around. But now the Bebryces and the violence of Amycus did separate me from Heracles, who dwells afar, for they have long cut great slices from my land, till they set their boundaries at the water-meadows of the Hypius. Yet have they paid the penalty to you, and I trow that he, the son of Tyndarus, brought not death this day upon the Bebryces without the will of heaven, what time he slew yon man. Wherefore now whatso thanks I can return, that will I right gladly. For that is right for weaklings, when others that be stronger than them begin to help them; so with you all and in your company I charge Dascylus my son to follow; [2] and if he go, verily ye shall meet with friends on your voyage as far as the mouth of Thermodon itself. Moreover I will dedicate to the sons of Tyndarus [3] a temple high upon the Acherusian hill; to it

of the giant Briareus, was the ninth of the labours laid upon Heracles by his task-master Eurystheus.

[1] ἐπὶ θανόντος, "at the time of the death," a frequent use of ἐπὶ with the genit. Cf. ἐπὶ Κύρου βασιλεύοντος = "in the reign of Cyrus."

[2] *i.e.* I will send my son Dascylus with you; his presence will insure you hospitable treatment as far as the Thermodon. νόσφι, "apart from this," *i.e.* over and above this.

[3] The sons of Tyndarus, Castor and Pollux, were the special protectors of sailors.

shall all sailors seek when they see it in the far distance o'er the sea; yea, and hereafter will I set apart for them before the city, as for gods, fat lands on the well-tilled plain."

So then, the livelong day, they took their pastime at the feast, but at dawn they went down in haste unto the ship, yea, and with them went Lycus too, bringing countless gifts to bear away, for with them was he sending from his house his son to fare.

There the doom of his fate smote Idmon, son of Abas, most excellent seer; yet could not his divining save him, for fate led him on to die. For within the water-mead beside the reedy river lay a boar, with white tusks, cooling his flanks and huge belly in the mud, a deadly monster, whereof even the nymphs that haunt the meads were afraid; and no man knew of his being there, for all alone along the broad marsh he browsed. Now he, the son of Abas, was passing by the springs of that muddy river, when lo! the boar leapt up from some unseen lair among the reeds and charged and smote him on the thigh, cutting sinews and bone right in twain. And with one bitter cry[1] down fell he upon the ground, and his comrades flocking round cried o'er their smitten fellow. But Peleus made one quick lunge with his hunting-spear at the boar as he darted in flight into the marsh, and out he rushed again to charge them, but Idas smote him, and with one grunt he fell grovelling about the sharp spear. And there they left him on the ground where he fell, and sorrowfully bare their swooning comrade to the ship, but he died in his companions' arms.

So they stayed them from all thought of sailing, and abode in bitter grief for the burial of the dead man. Three full days they mourned, and on the fourth made him a

[1] ὀξὺ κλάγξας, "with one sharp cry." Notice the true force of the aorist excellently exemplified—instantaneous action.

splendid funeral; and the people, with Lycus their king as well, joined in the funeral rites; and at the grave-side they cut the throats of countless sheep, as is the meed of the departed. So in that land this warrior's cairn was heaped, and upon it is a sign [1] for those who may yet be born to see, a log of wild olive such as ships are builded of, which putteth forth her leaf a little below the Acherusian headland. Yea, and if I must needs declare this also clearly in my song, Phœbus bade the Bœotians, who came from Nisæa, worship him, nothing doubting, as the protector of their city, and found a town about that log of ancient olive; but [2] these to-day do honour to Agamestor instead of Idmon, god-like son of Æolus.

Who next did die? that [3] must I tell; for yet again the heroes piled a barrow for a comrade dead. For verily there are yet two tombs of those two men to be seen. 'Tis said that Tiphys, son of Hagnias, died, for it was not appointed him to voyage further. Nay, a short illness closed there his eyes far from his fatherland,[4] while his company were burying the dead son of Abas. And bitter was the grief they felt at this cruel woe. For when they had buried him too beside the other there, they threw themselves down in their distress before the sea, closely wrapped from head to foot, and never a word they spake nor had they any thought for meat or drink, but sorrow made their spirit droop; for very far from their hopes was their return, and in their

[1] σῆμα, *i.e.* the monument to mark his grave.

[2] *i.e.* Phœbus commanded the Nisæans to found a city near the tomb of Idmon and pay him honour, but they in lapse of time confused Idmon with Agamestor, a native hero, and worshipped the latter instead.

[3] γὰρ δή = "you must know," introducing something new; colloquially we might say "to continue." γὰρ οὖν = "for indeed," giving a reason for what has immediately preceded, *i.e.* "I should not have mentioned this fact unless . . . ."

[4] εἰσότε = ἐν ὅσῳ χρόνῳ, "whilst."

anguish would they have stopped from going any further, had not Hera put exceeding courage in the breast of Ancæus, whom Astypalæa bare to Poseidon by the waters of Imbrasus;[1] for a right good steersman was he. So he did up anon, and spake to Peleus, "Son of Æacus, how can this be well to linger on in a strange land, neglectful of our enterprise? Jason hath in me, whom he is leading from Parthenie away to fetch the fleece, a man whose skill in war is only second to his knowledge of ships; wherefore I pray you, let this fear for the ship be short-lived. Yea, and there be others here, men of skill; and whomso of these we shall set over the helm, none shall harm our voyaging. But quickly tell all this comfort out; then boldly rouse them to a remembrance of their labour."

So spake he, and the heart of the other went out to[2] him in gladness; and anon, without delay, he made harangue in their midst, "God help us, sirs! why nurse we thus our grief in vain? The dead, I trow, have died the death that fell to their lot, but there are amongst us, methinks, helmsmen in our company, aye, plenty of them. Wherefore delay we no more our attempt, but up to your work, casting sorrow to the winds."

To him the son of Æson made answer, much perplexed: "Son of Æacus, where then be these steersmen? For they whom aforetime we boasted were men of skill, hang down their heads, more vexed at me than ever. Wherefore I foresee a sorry fate for us as well as for the dead, if indeed it be our lot neither to come to the city of baleful Æetes, nor ever again to pass the rocks and reach the land of Hellas; for here will a miserable doom hide us without fame, till we grow old for nought." So spake he; but right speedily

[1] A river in Samos, formerly called Parthenius.

[2] *ὀρέξατο—ὀρέγω*, literally "I reach out;" perhaps our phrase "went out to" may keep the meaning; in connexion with *γηθοσύνῃσιν* it means little more than "was exceeding glad, yearned for joy."

Ancæus took upon him to steer the swift ship, for verily he was turned thereto by the prompting of the goddess. And after him arose Erginus and Nauplius and Euphemus, all eager for to steer. But these did they hold therefrom, for many of the crew would have Ancæus.

So they went aboard on the twelfth day at dawn; for lo! a strong west wind did blow for them, and quickly they passed through the Acheron with rowing; and, trusting to the wind, they shook out their sails, and so sped calmly on a goodly stretch under canvas. Quickly came they past the mouth of the river Callichorus,[1] where, men say, the Nysean son of Zeus, what time he left the tribes of India and came to dwell in Thebes, held his revels and led the dance before the cave, wherein he would sleep away the gloomy[2] hours of sacred night, wherefore they who dwell around do call that river "Stream of fair dancing," and that cave "the Bedchamber,"[3] after him.

Sailing thence they saw the tomb of Sthenelus,[4] son of

[1] A river in Paphlagonia sacred to Dionysus, because he had held revels here and danced.

[2] ἀμειδήτους, "gloomy," either an ordinary epithet of the darkness of night, or possibly with an allusion to the secret mysteries of the ὄργια.

[3] Αὐλίον = "resting-place." It seems better to give an English equivalent for these Greek names; otherwise the point of the appellation is apt to be lost.

[4] The tomb of Sthenelus, the son of Actor, is in Paphlagonia; he had gone with Heracles against the Amazons, but had been wounded, and had died on the way home. His wraith now appears to the heroes, having been allowed by the queen of Hades to gaze a little space upon his fellow-men.

It is but a grim picture the ancient Greek poets draw of life in the other world. Everyone will remember the famous passage in Homer, where Achilles' spirit declares that he would sooner be a bondman to a poor man on earth than lord it over all the souls in Hades. This passage here portrays the soul of another brave man craving, with many tears, the scanty boon of seeing for a moment men in the flesh as he was once himself.

Actor, who on his way back from the bold fight with the Amazons—for thither had he gone with Heracles—died there upon the beach, of an arrow wound. So then they sailed on no further. For Persephone herself sent forth the spirit of the son of Actor, at his piteous prayer, to gaze a little on men of like passions with himself. So he took his stand on the summit of his tomb and watched for the ship, in form even as when he went to the war, and on his head shone his four-plumed helmet with the blood-red crest. And then he passed once more beneath the mighty gloom; but they marvelled at the sight, and Mopsus, son of Ampycus, did prophesy, and bade them anchor there and appease the spirit with drink-offerings. So they quickly furled the sails, and making fast the cables on the strand were busied about the tomb of Sthenelus, pouring libations to him, and offering sheep as victims. Moreover they did build, besides pouring libations, an altar to Apollo, protector of ships, and burnt sheep thereon; and there Orpheus dedicated his lyre, whence that place is called "the Lyre."

Anon, as the wind blew strong, they went aboard; and set the sail and made it taut to either sheet;[1] and Argo was carried at full speed to sea, even as when a falcon aloft through the air spreading his wings to the blast goes swiftly on his way, swerving not in his swoop, as he poises on steady pinions. And so they passed by the streams of Parthenius,[2] murmuring to the sea, gentlest of rivers, wherein the virgin child of Leto doth cool her limbs in its lovely waters, whenso she ascendeth to heaven from the chase. Then speeding ever onward through the night

[1] *πόδας*, "the sheets," *i.e.* the ropes by which the sails are tightened and slackened.

[2] *Παρθενίοιο*, *i.e.* the Maiden's stream, so called because Artemis, the virgin goddess, bathed therein, or because of the pureness of its water. It is a river in Paphlagonia, falling into the sea near the city Sesamus.

they sailed out past Sesamus and the steep Erythinian hills, Crobialus, and Cromne, and wooded Cytorus. Next after doubling Carambis, as the sun was rising, they rowed all day and all night too along a vast stretch of sand.

Anon they set foot on the soil of Assyria, where Zeus, tricked by his own promise, set down Sinope, daughter of Asopus, and granted her her virgin state. For verily he longed for her love; so the great god promised to give her whatsoever her heart desired; and she in her cunning asked her maidenhood. So too did she beguile Apollo, eager for her love, and after them the river Halys; nor did any man ever subdue her in love's embrace. There were dwelling even yet at that day the sons of noble Deimachus, prince of Triccæ, Deileon and Autolycus and Phlogius, after they had wandered away from Heracles. Now these, when they marked the expedition of the chieftains, came forth to meet them, and told them truly who they were; for they had no wish to abide there any longer, but went aboard the ship, soon as ever the clear[1] south-wind blew. So in their company they sped before the swift breeze, and left the river Halys, and Iris, that flows hard by, yea, and that part[2] of Syria that these have formed; and on that day they rounded the distant headland of the Amazons, that shutteth in their harbour.

There on a day the hero Heracles laid in ambush for Melanippe, daughter of Aretius, as she came forth; and, in ransom for her sister, Hippolyte gave him her dazzling girdle; so he set her free unhurt.

[1] *ἀργεστᾶο*, from *ἀργός*, "bright, shining," the same word that appears in the Homeric *ἀργειφοντης*. Hence the wind that clears the sky of clouds and makes it bright, *i.e.* the South-wind.

[2] *πρόχυσιν χθονός*, "alluvial deposit" such as most great rivers wash down in their course, *e.g.* the Delta of the Nile is entirely formed by the earth brought down by the stream and deposited at its mouth. In this case the Halys and Iris have formed what was called afterwards Leucosyria.

They then anchored in a bay behind the headland, at the mouth of the Thermodon, for the sea was rising against their going. This river hath no counterpart, nor is there any other that sendeth forth from itself upon the earth so many streams. If a man should count each up, there would lack but four of a hundred.[1] Yet is there only one real spring, which cometh down from high mountains unto the land. Men say these are called the Amazonian mountains. Thence it spreads straight over a somewhat hilly country far inland, wherefore it hath a winding course, and ever it twists in different directions, wheresoever it can best find a flat country; one branch far away, another near at hand; and there be many of them, of which no man knoweth, where they lose themselves in the sand; but it, mingling with a few openly, discharges its arching[2] flood of foam into cheerless Pontus. And now would they have stayed to do battle with the Amazons; nor would they, I trow, have striven without bloodshed, for the Amazons are no gentle folk, and cared not for justice in their dwellings on the plain of Doias; nay, their thoughts were set on deeds of grievous violence, and the works of Ares; for they, indeed, drew their stock from Ares and the nymph Harmonia, who bare these warrior daughters unto him, what time she won his love in the dells of the Acmonian grove; but once more, from Zeus mayhap, came the breath of the clear south-wind. And Argo left the round headland before the wind, where the Themiscyrean Amazons were doing on their harness.

These dwelt not all together in one city, but were scattered over the land by tribes in three bodies; apart

[1] A curiously roundabout way of saying that there are ninety-six distinct streams, all starting, however, from one source.

[2] *κυρτὴν ἄχνην.* If this reading be accepted, it means apparently the volume of water discharged by the river in foaming, arching billows into the sea.

were those over whom Hippolyte was then queen; and apart dwelt the Lycastiæ, and apart the Chadesiæ, who hurl the spear. On the next day, as night drew on, they came unto the land of the Chalybes. These take no thought for ploughing with oxen, nor for any planting of luscious fruit; neither do they, strange folk, herd cattle in the dewy pasture. But cleaving open the stubborn earth with her store of iron, they do take therefrom a wage to barter for food; for them dawn never riseth without toil, but mid soot and flame and smoke[1] they endure their heavy labour.

Anon, after these, they doubled the headland of Zeus, the great father, and sailed safely by the land of the Tibareni. Here it is that when the women bear children to the men, 'tis the men that throw themselves upon their beds and groan, with their heads veiled, while the women tend them carefully with food, and get ready for them the bath they use after child-birth.[2]

Next they passed the Holy mountain and land, wherein upon the hills dwell the Mossynœci in wooden houses, and hence they have their name. Strange is their justice; strange their ordinances. All that men may do openly, either among the people or in the market-place, all this they perform at home; but all that we do in our houses, that do they out of doors in the midst of the streets, with none to blame. In love is there no modesty among this people, but like swine that feed in herds, caring not a jot for the presence of any, they lie with their women upon the ground. Now their king sitteth in a house of wood, high above the rest, and declareth just judgment to the throng of folk. Poor wretch! for if haply he do err at all in his judging, they keep him shut up that day without food.

By these they passed, and, rowing all day long, cleft

[1] λιγνύς is properly smoke with flame showing through it.

[2] Travellers assert that the extraordinary customs here alluded to as practised by the Tibareni may still be witnessed amongst the Chinese.

their way, till they were almost opposite to the isle of Ares, for towards dusk the light breeze failed. Already they saw one of those birds of Ares that haunt the isle come swooping through the air from above, which did stretch his pinions o'er the speeding ship and shoot against her a sharp feather, and it fell on the left shoulder of goodly Oileus; and he let his oar fall from his hands, for he was wounded; but they marvelled to see the feathered shaft. And Eribotes from his seat hard by drew forth the feather and bound up the wound, having loosed the baldric hanging from his own scabbard; and lo! there appeared another swooping down after the former, but the hero Clytius, the son of Eurytus slew it, for he had ere this stretched his bended bow, and he shot a swift arrow at the bird, even as it flew above; and it fell with a rush hard by the swift ship; then amongst them spake Amphidamas, the son of Aleus: "Nigh to us is the isle of Ares; be sure of that from seeing these birds with your own eyes. And I think that arrows will not help us much to disembark; but let us provide some other counsel for our help, if haply ye mean to anchor here, mindful of the bidding of Phineus. For not even Heracles, when he came to Arcadia, was able to drive away with his arrows the birds that swam [1] on the Stymphalian mere; that saw I with mine own eyes. But he, shaking his rattling bronze armour in his hands, did raise a din upon a lofty height, and they were scared afar, screaming in frightful terror. Wherefore now let us too devise some such plan, and I will tell you myself, since I have ere this thought upon it. Put on your heads your high-crested helmets, and half of you take turns at rowing, and the other half guard [2] the ship with polished spears and

[1] *πλωίδας*, so called because they swam about the Stymphalian lake in Arcadia, whence Heracles had chased them.

[2] *ἄρσετε*, Ionic future from *ἀραρίσκω*, *i.e.* from the notion of joining comes that of roofing in the ship, as it were, with a penthouse of shields.

bucklers. And at once raise a mighty shout all together, that they may be scared by the uproar, from being unused thereto, and the nodding plumes and uplifted spears. And if we reach the island itself, then shout and raise a hideous din by smiting on your shields."

So spake he; and his helpful counsel pleased them all; so about their heads they put their brazen helmets, dreadfully flashing, and upon them waved the blood-red plumes. And part took turns at rowing, while the rest with sword and shield did guard the ship. As when a man doth roof a house with tiles, an ornament to his house and a defence against the rain, as one tile is fitted firmly on another; so they covered in the ship with a pent-house of shields. And as the clash that goeth up from a warlike throng of men in motion, what time the lines of battle meet, even such was the sound that rose into the air on high from the ship. Nor could they see any of the birds the while, but when they drew nigh the island and smote upon their bucklers, forthwith those birds rose in thousands, flying this way and that. As when the son of Cronos sends a heavy hailstorm from the clouds on city and houses, and they who dwell beneath them hear the rattle on their roofs and sit in silence, for the wintry season is not come upon them unawares, but ere its coming have they made fast the roof; even so the birds let loose on them a thick shower of shafts, as they darted high o'er the sea to the hills on the farther shore.

What did Phineus mean, (that must I tell,) in bidding the divine company of heroes anchor here? or what help was to come to them at their desire? The sons of Phrixus had gone on board a Colchian ship, and were faring to the city of Orchomenus from Æa, at the direction of Cytæan Æetes, that they might take unto themselves the boundless wealth of their father, for he, as he lay a-dying, laid this journey on them. And very nigh were they to the island on that day. But Zeus stirred up the mighty north-wind to blow, marking the wet path of Arcturus in the waves; so all day long he shook the leaves upon the mountains a little, blowing lightly on the topmost branches, but at night came he seaward in his giant strength, roaring and stirring the billow with his breath; and a dark mist veiled the sky, nor were the bright stars to be seen from the clouds, but a curtain of gloom settled over all. And they, the sons of Phrixus, dripping and in terror of a fearsome death, were drifting thus before the waves. And the furious wind rent their sails, yea, and brake their ship in pieces, shaken as it was by the breakers. Then by heaven's guidance those four men seized hold upon a mighty beam, such as were scattered in plenty, after the wreck, held together by sharp bolts. And them did the waves and the breath of the wind drive in sore distress unto the island, within a little of death. Anon there burst on them a wondrous[1] storm of rain, and it rained over the sea and the island, and all the coast over against the island, where dwelt the haughty Mossynœci. And the onset of the wave hurled them, the sons of Phrixus, together with the stout beam, upon the beach of the island in the gloom of night; but at sunrise it ceased, that heaven-sent torrent, and quickly they drew nigh and met one another, and Argus first made harangue:—

"By Zeus, who seeth all, we do entreat you, whosoever ye be, to be favourable and help us at our need. For rough tempests, grievously buffeting the sea, have scattered piecemeal the timbers of our shameful barque,[2] wherein we were

[1] *ἀθέσφατος.* Etymol. *ἀ* negat., *θεός*, *φάναι*, *i.e.* impossible for even gods to tell, *i.e.* marvellously great.

[2] *ἀεικελίης νηὸς* = "that sorry ship of ours." Æetes, wishing to get rid of the sons of Phrixus, had encouraged them to undertake their voyage to Orchomenus, but had purposely given them an unseaworthy ship that they might be wrecked. He was afraid of them, because an oracle had warned him of dangers to come from his own family. He failed to guess that Medea, not Chalciope and her sons, was the real cause of danger.

cleaving our way, on business bent. Wherefore now we implore you, if ye will hearken, give us some rag to wrap around our skin and take us hence, in pity for companions in adversity. Yea, reverence suppliant strangers for the sake of Zeus, the god of strangers and suppliants; for we are both suppliants of Zeus and strangers. And, I trow, he hath his eye even upon us."

Him in answer did the son of Æson question carefully, for he thought that the prophecies of Phineus were being accomplished, "Anon will we provide all these things with good will. But come now, tell me truly, in what country ye dwell, and the business that bids you fare across the sea, and your own famous name and lineage."

And Argus answered him in helpless misery, "Haply ye have heard yourselves even aforetime, I deem, and of a surety, how one Phrixus, son of Æolus, came from Hellas unto Æa,—that Phrixus, who came to the town of Æetes, sitting astride a ram, the ram that Hermes made of gold; yea, and even now might ye see the fleece fluttering on the rough branches of an oak. For afterwards, by the ram's own counsel, Phrixus sacrificed him to Zeus, the son of Cronos, who helpeth fugitives,[1] before all other gods. Him did Æetes receive into his house and gave to him his daughter Chalciope without gifts of wooing in the gladness of his heart. From these twain are we sprung. But he, even Phrixus, died long ago, full of years, in the halls of Æetes; and we, obeying our father's command, set out at once to Orchomenus to take the possessions of Athamas. And if, as thou sayest, thou hast a mind to learn our name, lo! this man is called Cytisorus, and this Phrontis, and that Melas, and me myself shall ye call Argus."

So spake he; and the chieftains were glad at the meeting, and they crowded round them in wonder. But Jason

[1] Φύξιος. Zeus was worshipped under this title amongst the Thessalians.

again made answer thus, as was fitting: "Why, lo! ye come as kinsmen[1] of my father and beg our kindly aid in your wretchedness. For Cretheus and Athamas were brothers; and I, the grandson of Cretheus, am on my way with these my comrades from Hellas itself into the city of Æetes. But we will speak of these matters yet again to each other; but first put on raiment; for by heaven's guidance, I ween, have ye come to my hands in your need."

Therewith he gave them raiment from the ship to put on. And at once thereafter made they for the temple of Ares, to offer sacrifice of sheep, and right eagerly they set themselves about the altar, which stood outside the roofless temple, built of pebbles; within is a black stone planted, the holy stone whereto in days gone by all the Amazons did pray, nor was it lawful, when these did come from the mainland opposite, to burn sacrifices of oxen and sheep upon this altar, but they kept great herds of horses and sacrificed them. Now when the heroes had done sacrifice and eaten the feast they had prepared, then did the son of Æson take up his parable and begin to speak: "Zeus hath still his eye on all things, I trow; and of a surety we men escape not his ken, those of us who be god-fearing, nor yet those who be just; for even so he rescued your father from a murderous step-mother,[2] and gave him boundless wealth away from her; and even so hath he also rescued you unhurt from the destroying storm. And ye may fare upon this ship this way or that, whither ye list, either to Æa, or to the rich city of goodly Orchomenus. For 'twas Athene

[1] γνωτοί = συγγενεῖς. The relationship comes thus: Cretheus and Athamas were brothers. Æson was the son of Cretheus, Jason the son of Æson. Phrixus was the son of Athamas, Argus the son of Phrixus. Jason and Argus were therefore cousins.

[2] φόνοιο μητρυιῆς, "murder by a stepmother," *i.e.* Ino, who was jealous of her step-children.

that built this ship and cut with brazen axe her timbers about the peak of Pelion; and with the goddess worked Argus. But that ship of yours hath the angry wave riven asunder, or ever she came nigh to the rocks which clash together the livelong day in the sea's narrow channel. But come now, even ye, and help us in our struggle to bring the fleece of gold to Hellas, and be our pilots, for I am sent to make full atonement for the attempted sacrifice[1] of Phrixus, that stirred the wrath of Zeus against the sons of Æolus."

So spake he to comfort them, but they would none of it when they heard; for they thought they would find Æetes no gentle host, if they desired to take the ram's fleece. Thus spake Argus, sore vexed that they were bent on such a quest, "My friends, the strength that is in us shall never be withheld from helping you, no, not one jot, when any need arise. But terribly is Æetes furnished with deadly cruelty. Wherefore I do greatly fear to voyage thither. He avows him[2] to be the son of Helios, and around him dwell countless tribes of Colchians, and he might match even with Ares his dread war cry and mighty strength. Yea, and 'twere no easy task to take the fleece away from Æetes; so huge a serpent keepeth guard around and about it, a deathless, sleepless snake, which earth herself did rear in the wolds of Caucasus, by the rock of Typhon, where they say Typhon, smitten by the bolt of Zeus, the son of Cronos, what time he stretched out his strong hands against him, did drop warm gore from his head; and he came with this wound to the mountains and plain of Nysa; where to this day he lies, deep beneath the waters of the Serbonian[3] mere."

[1] *i.e.* Pelias had sent Jason ostensibly to fetch the golden fleece, for an oracle had said that there should be no peace for the sons of Æolus until the fleece was brought to Iolchos, for Zeus was wroth at the treatment Phrixus had received; *θυηλὰς Φρίξοιο* is therefore = the attempted sacrifice of Phrixus.

[2] *στεῦται*, Lat. jactare, "avows himself, boasts."

[3] "The Serbonian lake" is near Pelusium in Egypt.

So spake he; and o'er the cheek of many did paleness spread at once, when they heard the greatness of their labour. But Peleus quickly answered and said, with brave words, "Be not so exceeding fearful at heart, my trusty friend.[1] For we are not so wanting in valiancy, as to be no match for a bout in arms with Æetes; nay, methinks we too came hither knowing somewhat of war, for we are near in blood to the blessed gods. Wherefore if he give us not the fleece of gold for love, I trow his tribes of Colchians shall not much avail him."

Thus did they hold converse together, until, satisfied with food, they fell asleep. And when they woke at dawn, a gentle breeze was blowing; so they set the sails, which did strain before the rushing wind; and swiftly they left the isle of Ares on the lee.

On the following night they passed the isle of Philyra,[2] where Cronos, son of Uranus, lay with Philyra, having deceived Rhea, when he ruled the Titans on Olympus, and that other, Zeus, was yet being reared in a cave in Crete by the Idæan Curetes; but the goddess caught them in the midst of their dalliance; and he sprang up and sped away in the semblance of a horse with flowing mane, but she, that child of Oceanus, Philyra, left that country and those haunts in shame, and came to the distant hills of the Pelasgi, where she bare to him in return for his love huge Chiron, half horse, half god in appearance.

Thence they sailed on past the Macrones and the boundless coast of the Becheiri, and the lawless Sapeiræ, and the Byzeræ next to them; for ever onward they cleft their way

[1] ἠθεῖε, mostly an address of respect by a younger man to an elder, though often, as here, the address of one friend to another.

[2] So called from Philyra, the daughter of Oceanus, who lived there. Cronos, when he ruled over the Titans, formed a connexion with Philyra, but being discovered by his wife Rhea, he changed himself into a stallion and fled, while Philyra retired to Thessaly and there gave birth to Chiron the Centaur, who was half man, half horse.

in haste, borne forward by the gentle wind. And as they sailed, there came in sight a bay of the sea, and before them rose up the steep cliffs of the Caucasian mountains, where Prometheus was feeding with his liver an eagle, swooping back again and again, his limbs fast bound to the hard rocks with bands of brass, unbreakable; that eagle did they see at eve skimming right above the ship with loud rush of wings nigh to the clouds, and yet he made all the sails to shake as he flapped his pinions. For he had not the form of a bird of the air, but, when he moved his swift feathers, they were like to polished oars. And no long time after, they heard a bitter cry, as the liver of Prometheus was torn, and the welkin rang with his screams, until again they marked the savage eagle soaring on his way from the mountain; and at night, by the skill of Argus, came they to the broad stream of the Phasis, and the uttermost ends of the sea.

Anon they furled and put away the sails and the yard-arm within the hollow mast-hold, and they let down the mast too along the deck, and quickly rowed into the river's broad current; and he dashed all round them, yet gave way. Upon their left hand they kept steep Caucasus and the Cytæan town of Æa, and next the plain of Ares and that god's sacred grove, where the serpent keepeth watch and ward o'er the fleece as it hangs on the oak's rough branches. Then did the son of Æson with his own hand pour a libation sweet as honey, of unmixed wine, from a golden chalice into the river to Earth and the gods of that land,[1] and the spirits of heroes dead and gone; and he besought them to be his kindly helpers graciously, and to allow a fair anchoring of the ship. And forthwith Ancæus

[1] ἐνναέταις = ἐγχωρίοις, "gods of the country;" a precaution usual amongst Greeks to sacrifice to the gods and heroes of any new country in which they might find themselves. In the same way Alexander of Macedon went out of his way to sacrifice to Zeus Ammon.

spake this word amongst them. "Lo! we are come to the Colchian land and the stream of Phasis; 'tis high time to make plans for ourselves, whether indeed we will try Æetes with gentleness, or whether haply some different attempt shall win the day."

So spake he; and Jason, by the advice of Argus, bade them row the ship into a shaded backwater[1] and let her ride at anchor in deep water, and that they found close by; so there they bivouacked for the night; and no long time after appeared the dawn to their longing eyes.

[1] ἕλος = properly "a marsh, water meadow," but this scarcely fits the context; possibly "a backwater" is meant. Here they would run less risk of being observed.

BOOK III.

ARGUMENT.

Hera and Athene persuade Aphrodite to send Eros to Medea. Meantime Jason comes to Æetes, king of Colchis, and begs the fleece; but the king was exceeding wroth, and set him great labours to perform, namely, to yoke two fire-breathing bulls, and sow the dragon's teeth upon Ares' acre, and then to slay the earth-born giants who should rise o'er the lea.

But Medea is in love with Jason, and gives him drugs to tame those bulls, telling him how to accomplish all. Wherefore Jason finished the appointed task, to the grief and wonder of Æetes.

BOOK III.

COME now, Erato,[1] stand at my side and tell, how Jason brought the fleece hence to Iolchos by the love of Medea. For thou too hast a share in all that the Cyprian queen decrees, and by thy cares dost charm maidens yet unwed; wherefore is joined to thee a name that tells of love.

Thus those chieftains abode in their ambush, unseen among the thick reeds, and the goddesses, Hera and Athene, were ware of them; so they came unto a chamber, apart from Zeus himself and the other immortal gods, and took counsel together; and first did Hera make trial of Athene: "Do thou now first begin with thy plan, daughter of Zeus. What is to be done? wilt thou devise some crafty wile, whereby they shall take the golden fleece from Æetes and carry it to Hellas, or shall they haply persuade him with gentle words and so prevail? For surely he is terribly haughty. And yet it is not right that any attempt of ours should be turned aside."

So spake she; and Athene answered her at once: "I was even pondering these very things myself, Hera, when thou didst question me outright; but not yet, methinks, have I

[1] Ἐρατώ, the Muse of dancing. The name of this Muse at first sight seems introduced here merely to bring in a weak play upon words—ἔρως, Ἐρατώ, ἐπήρατον. But as this third book is to relate Jason's wooing and winning of Medea, there is a certain appropriateness in an address to the Muse who presided over such festivities as were customary at weddings. Ἐρατώ vocat. = Ἐρατοῖ Attice.

devised a plan to help those chieftains brave, though many are the schemes my mind revolves."

Therewith those goddesses fixed their eyes upon the ground before them, pondering separately in their hearts. Anon, when she had thought thus awhile, Hera broke the silence: "Let us hence to Cypris; and, when we are come, let us both urge her to speak unto her boy, if haply he can be persuaded to shoot an arrow at the daughter of Æetes, mighty sorceress, and bewitch her with love of Jason. For, methinks, he would by her helping counsel bear the fleece to Hellas."

So spake she; and her sage plan pleased Athene, and once more she answered her with winning words: "Ah! Hera, my sire begat me to know nought of the darts of love, nor wot I of any magic spell of desire. But if this word pleaseth thee thyself, surely I will follow; but thou must speak when thou comest before her."

Therewith went they darting to the great house of Cypris, the house which her lord of the strong arms had builded for her, when first he brought her from Zeus to be his bride. So they entered the courtyard and stood beneath the corridor that led to her chamber, where the goddess used to make ready the couch of Hephæstus. But he had gone to his smithy[1] and anvils at dawn, a cavern vast within a floating island, wherein he would forge all manner of cunning work with the blast of fire; so she was sitting alone in her house on her rounded chair, facing the door, and she was combing her hair with a golden comb, letting it cover her white shoulders on either side, and she was in the act of plaiting her long tresses when she saw them before her, and stopped; and she bade them enter, and arose from her throne and made them sit on seats; then sat she down herself and bound up her uncombed hair

[1] Hephæstus' forge was said to be in Lipara, one of the isles of Æolus, not far from Sicily.

with her two hands. And thus with a smile she spake to them in wheedling words, "Fair ladies, what purpose or business doth bring you hither after so long a time? and why are ye twain come that came not very often aforetime to visit me? for ye are far above all other goddesses."

Thus then did Hera answer her in turn: "Thou dost mock us; but the heart of us twain is stirred by sore mischance. For even now in the river Phasis the son of Æson stays his ship, and those others who come with him to fetch the fleece. Verily for them all do we fear exceedingly, since their work is nigh, but most of all for the son of Æson. Him will I save, though he sail even to Hades, to free Ixion[1] there below from his fetters of brass, so far as there is any strength in my limbs, that Pelias may not mock if he escape his evil doom; he who in his haughtiness left me without my meed of sacrifice. Yea, and, beyond all that, Jason was ever dear to me aforetime, from that day when he met me at the mouth of the swollen Anaurus, as he came up from hunting, and I did test the righteousness of men; and all the hills and towering crags were coated with snow, and their torrents came rushing down from them with loud roar. But he had compassion on me in the likeness of an old hag, and took me up upon his shoulders and bore me through the headlong flood. Wherefore he hath honour of me unceasingly, nor shall Pelias work outrage upon him, even though thou grant him not his return."

So spake she; but speechlessness seized Cypris. For she

[1] Ixion was bound to an ever-turning wheel by Zeus because he had insulted Hera. "Even him," says Hera, "I would release if Jason required it, for I remember how he showed kindness to me on the day I made trial of men's hearts." Hera had assumed the form of an old woman, in which guise Jason had found her on the banks of the swollen torrent Anaurus; and when she would go over but dare not, Jason carried her across upon his shoulders, and knew not that it was the goddess.

was awe-struck at seeing Hera ask a favour of her, and she answered her with kindly words, "Dread goddess, may nought worse than Cypris[1] ever come to thee, if I neglect thy desire in word or deed, so far as these weak hands can effect aught; and let me have no thanks in return."

So spake she; and Hera once again made prudent speech: "We come not to thee through lack of might or strength at all. But, as thou canst, softly bid thy boy bewitch the daughter of Æetes[2] with passion for the son of Æson. For if she do help him with friendly counsel, lightly, I trow, will he take the golden fleece and return to Iolchos; for she is very crafty."

So spake she; and Cypris said unto them both, "Hera, and Athene, he will obey you rather than me. For shameless as he is, haply will he have some little reverence at sight of you, but me he regardeth not, but ever and aye he slighteth me, and striveth with me. And lo! overcome by his naughtiness, I have a mind to break his bow and ill-sounding arrows before his eyes; for in a burst of anger he threatened me on this wise, that if I would not keep my hands off him, whilst he was mastering his temper, I would have only myself to blame hereafter."

So spake she; and the goddesses smiled, and looked at one another; but Cypris answered with a sigh, "Others can laugh at my sorrows, nor ought I to tell them to every one; enough that my own heart knows them. But now since this is the will of both of you, I will try and coax him, nor will he disobey."

So spake she; and Hera stroked her dainty hand, and with a soft smile spake to her in answer, "Yes, even so accomplish this business now at once, as thou sayest, O

[1] *i.e.* may all of whom you make requests be as easy to persuade as Aphrodite, then will you ever gain your point. Merely a rhetorical way of saying that she will do all she can.

[2] *i.e.* Medea.

Cytherea, and distress not thyself at all, nor wrathfully strive with thy child, for he shall cease tormenting thee hereafter."

Therewith she left her seat, and Athene went with her. So they twain went back again, and Cypris too went on her way through the wolds of Olympus, to see if she could find her son. And she found him far away in a blooming orchard of Zeus, not alone, but Ganymede was with him; he it was whom Zeus on a day brought to dwell in heaven with the immortals, eager for his beauty. And those twain were sporting with golden dice, as youths alike in habits will. Now the one, even greedy Eros, held the palm of his left hand quite full already beneath his breast as he stood there upright; and a sweet blush was mantling on the skin of his cheeks; but the other sat crouching near in moody silence, and he held two dice, casting one forth upon the other, where he sat, and he was angered at the loud laughter of Eros. Now when he had lost these at once as well as the first, away he went with empty hands, helpless, and he was not ware of Cypris as she drew nigh; so she stood facing her child, and at once, laying her hand upon his mouth, she spake to him: "Thou monstrous rogue, why laughest thou? surely thou didst cheat him, poor dupe, at that game, and thou didst not fairly get the better of him. But come now, accomplish readily the business I shall tell thee of, and verily I will give thee that fair plaything, which his fond nurse, Adresteia, made for Zeus, in the cave of Ida, while he was yet a little child, a ball well-rounded, than which thou canst get no fairer toy from the hands of Hephæstus. Of gold are his circles fashioned,[1]

[1] The description of the ball is rather puzzling on account of the numerous allusions to the seams in it. κύκλα = the pieces of which the ball was made; ἀψῖδες are the fastenings which hold it together; ῥαφαί are the stitches of these fastenings; while over and around all the fastenings runs a spiral (ἕλιξ) of blue, not as a fastening, but as an ornament to the whole work.

and round each runneth a double fastening, holding them together, but the seams thereof are hidden, for a blue spiral runneth over them all. And if thou toss it in thy hands, it sends a track of flame through the air, like a star. Yea, this will I give thee, but do thou shoot at the daughter of Æetes and bewitch her with love for Jason, and let there be no delay, for then would the gratitude be fainter."

So spake she; and 'twas a welcome word to him when he heard. Down he threw all his toys, and caught hold of the goddess's robe with both hands eagerly on either side. And he besought her instantly to give it him at once; but she met him with gentle words, and drew his cheek to hers and put her arms round him and kissed him, answering: "Be witness[1] now thine own darling head and mine, that I will surely give it thee, and will not deceive thee, if thou fix thy shaft in the heart of the daughter of Æetes."

Thus she; and he gathered his dice together, and, after counting them all carefully, cast them into the fold of his mother's bright robe. Next he slung about him with a belt of gold his quiver, which was hanging on a tree-trunk, and he took up his bended bow, and went on his way from the halls of Zeus through the fruitful orchard. Then came he forth from the heavenly gates of Olympus, where is a path down from heaven; for the world's two poles, the highest points on earth, whereon the sun at his rising rests with his earliest rays, uphold steep mountain-tops; while below, on the one side, Earth, the life-giver, and the cities of men, and sacred river-streams, and, on the other, hills and sea all round appeared to him, as he passed through the wide upper air.

Now the heroes sat in council on the ship's benches, in their ambush apart, in a backwater of the river. And

[1] *i.e.* I swear by myself and by the love I bear you.

amongst them the son of Æson himself was speaking, while they, sitting quietly in their place in order, did listen: "My friends, surely I will tell you what seems good to me myself; but 'tis for you to bring it to pass. For all alike share this quest, and all alike can speak; and he who silently withholds his purpose and counsel, let him know, that 'tis he and he alone who robbeth this expedition of its return. Do ye others abide here quietly in the ship with your arms; but I will go to the halls of Æetes, taking the sons of Phrixus and two comrades as well. And when I meet him, I will first see what words may do, whether he be willing to give us the golden fleece for love, or, if[1] he will not, but, trusting to his might, will not heed our quest. For thus of himself shall we learn his ill-will afore and devise, whether to meet him in the field, or whether there shall be some other plan to help us, if we restrain our battle-cry. But let us not deprive him of his possession thus by force, till we have tried what words can do. Nay, 'twere better first to go and conciliate him with words. Full oft, I wis, hath a word easily accomplished at need, what might would scarce have won, in that it seemed soothing. Yea, and this man too once welcomed gallant[2] Phrixus as he fled from the wiles of a step-mother and the sacrifice[3] his father had prepared. For all men in all lands, even the most shameless, do reverence and regard the ordinance of Zeus, the god of strangers."

So spake he; and forthwith the young men agreed to the word of the son of Æson, and there was not one who could bid him do otherwise. So then he roused the sons of

[1] ἠὲ καὶ οὔ. The καὶ shows that the speaker does not anticipate that Æetes will give up the fleece for love.

[2] ἀμύμονα, purely an "epitheton ornans," without any reference to the man's moral character or attributes, much as we say "my honourable friend," "the noble lord," &c.

[3] *i.e.* the sacrifice of his own son and daughter.

Phrixus and Telamon and Augeas to go with him; and in his hand he took the wand of Hermes;[1] and anon forth they went from the ship, beyond the reeds and water, toward the country over a rising plain. This, they say, is called the plain of Circe, and on it were growing in rows many willows and osiers,[2] on whose branches hang dead men, bound with cords. For to this day 'tis an abomination to Colchians to burn the corpses of men with fire; nor is it lawful to lay them in the earth, and heap a cairn above them; but two[3] men must roll them up in hides untanned, and fasten them to trees afar from the town. And yet the earth getteth an equal share with the air, for they bury their women folk in the ground; for such is the custom they have ordained.

Now as the heroes went through the city, Hera, with friendly intent, shed a thick mist on them, that they might reach the house of Æetes, unseen by the countless Colchian folk; but straight when they were come from the plain to the city and house of Æetes, then again did Hera disperse the cloud. And they stood at the entrance, astonied at the king's fenced walls and wide gates and columns, which stood in rows upholding the walls; and above the house

[1] *σκῆπτρον Ἑρμείαο.* This wand had been entrusted in the outset to the herald Æthalides as the badge of his sacred office—its presence would insure the safety of the bearer.

[2] Curious customs of the Colchians, who do not bury men, but hang their corpses on trees. However, not to cheat the earth of its due, they resign to it the dead bodies of women; by which means they consider that earth and air are both satisfied.

[3] *κατειλύσαντε.* If this reading is the true one, it seems an extraordinary introduction of an unusual number, viz., the dual. This number has not been previously used in this connexion, and the only possible explanation of its meaning (" that *two* men wrap up each corpse ") seems exceedingly strained, to say the least of it. Many editions, previous to Wellauer, read *κατειλύσαντες*, with an absolute disregard of metre; the dual has now been substituted for the plural by subsequent editors, but it is difficult to believe that Apollonius wrote it so.

was a coping of stone resting upon triglyphs[1] of bronze. Then went they quietly over the threshold. And nigh thereto were garden-vines in full blossom, shooting on high, and covered with green young foliage. Beneath them flowed those four eternal springs, which Hephæstus digged, whereof the one did gush with milk, another with wine, while a third flowed with fragrant unguents, and the last gave a stream of water, which was warm at the setting of the Pleiads, and in turn at their rising spouted up cold as ice from the hollow rock. These were the wondrous works that crafty Hephæstus did devise in the halls of Cytæan Æetes. And he fashioned for him bulls with brazen feet, and mouths of brass, wherefrom they breathed the fearful blaze of fire; yea, and he forged for him besides a plough of stout adamant, all of one piece, in return for the kindness of Helios,[2] for he had taken him up in his chariot, when he was weary at the battle on Phlegra's plain.

Next was builded the inner court; and in the walls thereof on either side were close-folding doors and rooms; and all along both walls ran a corridor of carved work; and across at either end stood higher buildings; in one of these, which towered over all, dwelt king Æetes with his wife, and in the other lived Absyrtus,[3] son of Æetes, whom Asterodia, nymph of Caucasus, bare, ere that Eidyia became his wedded wife, last-born child of Tethys and Oceanus; him the sons of the Colchians did call by the name of Phaethon, for he outshone all the young men.

[1] γλύφιδες, properly "the notch of an arrow" which fits on the string, here = τρίγλυφοι, which in Doric architecture is the three-grooved tablet placed at equal distances along the frieze.

[2] Helios, the Sun-god, father of Æetes and Circe, took up Hephæstus, who owing to his lameness was tired, and carried him in his chariot away from the plain of Phlegra in Thrace, where the giants had done battle with the gods.

[3] Also called Phaethon.

But the servants and the two daughters of Æetes, Chalciope[1] and Medea, had the other rooms. Now they found Medea going from chamber to chamber in quest of her sister; for Hera had kept her at home, though aforetime she came not very often into the house, but all day long was busied at the temple of Hecate, for 'twas she that was priestess of the goddess. And when she saw them near, she cried out, and quickly did Chalciope hear, and the maid-servants threw down at their feet their yarn and thread, and came running out all together. But Chalciope, when she saw her sons with those others, lifted up her hands for joy, and so too did they greet their mother, and embraced her for joy when they saw her. And thus spake she through her sobs: "So then, after all, ye were not to wander very far, leaving me in my anguish[2]; but fate hath turned you back. Ah! woe is me! what a desire for Hellas did ye feel, prompted by some pitiful infatuation, at the bidding of your father Phrixus! who dying did ordain bitter sorrow for my heart. Why should ye go to the city of Orchomenus, whoever this Orchomenus is,[3] for the sake of the goods of Athamas, leaving your mother behind in her sorrow?"

So spake she; and last of all came Æetes forth to the door, and forth came Eidyia in person, wife of Æetes, when she heard Chalciope; and anon that whole courtyard was filled with a throng. Thralls in crowds were busy now,

[1] Elder daughter of Æetes, sister of Medea; she had been married to Phrixus, now dead, and had several sons, who were now in the company of Jason.

[2] *ἀκηδείῃ* here, as infra, iii. 298, *ἀκηδείῃσι νόοιο*, is capable of two meanings, (1) = *ἀφροντίστως*, "carelessly, without a thought," (2) = *πολυκηδείαις*, "in anguish." In the first case it would refer to the sons of Chalciope; in the second, which is rather favoured by the position of the words, to Chalciope herself.

[3] "Whoever this Orchomenus is." In her bitterness she purposely assumes that Orchomenus is a man, not a city.

some about a mighty bull, while others were cleaving dry wood with the axe, and others were heating at the fire water for baths, and there was none who ceased from toil, in obedience to the king.

Meantime Eros went through the clear air unseen, confusing them, as when the gad-fly ariseth against grazing heifers, the fly which herdsmen call the goad of cattle. Quickly within the porch, beneath the lintel, he stretched his bow and drew from his quiver a shaft of sorrow never yet used. Then did he pass unseen across the threshold with hasty steps, glancing quickly round, and gliding close past the son of Æson himself, he laid the notch of the arrow on the middle of the bow-string, and drawing[1] it to the head with both hands he let it fly straight against Medea; and speechless amaze took hold upon her. But he sped away again from the high-roofed hall, laughing loudly. And the shaft burnt beneath the maiden's heart, like a flame, and ever she kept darting glances toward the son of Æson, and her heart was wildly beating in her breast in distress, and she remembered nought but him, and her soul was melting with sweet sorrow. As when some poor workwoman hath strewn dry chips about a blazing brand—one whose business is to spin wool—that she may make a blaze at night beneath her roof, waking exceeding early; which darting up wondrously from the tiny brand doth consume all the chips with itself; even so love in his might,[2] couched beneath her heart, was burning secretly; and her soft cheeks would pale and blush by turns, in the anguish of her soul.

Now when the thralls had made ready food for them,

[1] *i.e.* drawing it to the full, when the arms would be wide apart.

[2] *οὖλος*, by some said to be a variant form in poets of *ὅλος*, = Lat. totus, *i.e.* "the god in all his might," which meaning it certainly bears in some contexts. Others make it = *ὀλοος*, as *οὐλόμενος*, Epic for *ὀλόμενος*, *i.e.* "destructive, baleful."

and they had washed themselves in warm baths, gladly did they take their fill of food and drink. Then did Æetes question the sons of his daughter, addressing them with these words: "Sons of my daughter and of Phrixus, whom I honoured above all strangers in our halls, how came ye back again to Æa? did some misfortune come betwixt you and your safety, preventing you? Ye hearkened not to me when I set before you the measure of the voyage. For I knew it that day I whirled along in the car of Helios, my father, when he was bringing my sister Circe into the land of the west,[1] and we came to a headland of the Tyrsenian mainland, where she dwelleth even now, very far from the Colchian land. What pleasure, though, have I in telling hereof? Come tell me plainly what befell you, or who these are who bear you company, and whence ye have come from your hollow ship."

Somewhat afeard was Argus for the expedition of the son of Æson when he questioned so straitly, but he before his brethren made a gentle answer, for he was the eldest: "Æetes, that ship of ours did raging winds soon wreck; but the wave cast us up, as we crouched on timbers, on the dry land of the isle of Enyalius, in the dead of night, for some god saved us. For not even were the birds of Ares roosting on that desert isle, which were there aforetime, nor did we find them any more. But these men had driven them away, when they came forth from their ship on the previous day, and the mind of Zeus or some chance kept them there, in pity for us; for at once they gave us food and raiment in plenty, after hearing the famous name of Phrixus and of thee thyself, for to thy city were they faring. If thou wouldst surely know their business, I will not hide it from thee. A certain king, eager to drive yonder man far from his

[1] *i.e.* Italy.

country and his goods, for that he excelled very greatly in his might all the sons of Æolus, is sending him hither on a difficult voyage; for it is ordained that the race of Æolus shall not escape the grievous wrath and fury of implacable Zeus, nor the awful pollution and the punishment for the sake of Phrixus, until the fleece come to Hellas. And Pallas Athene hath builded his ship, in no wise like the ships amongst the Colchian folk, whereof we chanced upon the vilest;[1] for furious winds and waves tore it in pieces enow. But that other holds fast unto her bolts, even though all the winds fall heavy on her. And swift as the wind she speeds, whenso her crew bend to their oars with a will. And Jason hath gathered together in her the chosen heroes from all Achæa, and is come to thy city, after wandering to many towns, and over the face of the loathly sea, to see if thou wilt give him the fleece. And as it is pleasing to thee, so shall it be; for he is not come to use violence, but 'tis his desire to pay thee fair quittance for the gift; for he heareth from me that the Sauromatæ are thy grievous foes; so he will subdue these to thy rule. And if, as thou sayest, thou art anxious to know too their name and lineage, who they be, verily let me tell thee all. Him, for sake of whom the rest mustered from Hellas, men call Jason, son of Æson, whom Cretheus begat. Now if he is really of the stock of Cretheus himself, so must he be a kinsman on his father's side to us. For both Cretheus and Athamas were sons of Æolus; and Phrixus again was son of Athamas, who was son of Æolus. Lo! here dost thou see Augeas, if ever thou dost hear of this son of Helios, and this is Telamon, sprung from famous Æacus, whom Zeus himself begat. So too all the rest, who follow in his crew, are sons or scions of immortal gods."

This was the tale that Argus told. And the king was

[1] Æetes had given the sons of Chalciope a bad ship in the hope of their being wrecked.

angered at his word, as he listened. And his heart swelled high with rage, and he spake with a troubled mind, but most of all was he wroth with the sons of Chalciope, for he thought that Jason had come on this quest by reason of them; and his eyes flashed beneath his brows in his fury: "Away, ye caitiff wretches, at once from my sight; depart from my land with your trickery, ere some of you see the fleece and Phrixus to your sorrow. 'Twas not to fetch the fleece, but to take my sceptre and my kingly power, that ye banded together and came hither at once from Hellas. But if ye had not tasted first of my board, of a truth I would have cut out your tongues and chopped off both your hands and sent you forth with feet alone, that ye might be stayed from setting forth thereafter; what lies too have ye told about the blessed gods!"

So spake he in his fury; and mightily was the heart of the son of Æacus swelling in his breast; and his spirit within him longed to give him back a fatal answer,[1] but the son of Æson checked him; and, before he could speak, himself made gentle answer: "Æetes, bear with me anent this my coming. For we are in no wise come unto thy town and home, as thou belike dost think, nor with any such desire. For who would willingly venture to cross so wide a gulf for the goods of another? Nay, 'twas a god and the chilling hest of a presumptuous king that sent us forth. Grant thy favour to our prayer; and I will carry throughout Hellas a wondrous report of thee; yea, and we are ready even now to make thee quick recompense in thy wars, if haply thou desirest to bring beneath thy sway even the Sauromatæ or some other folk."

So spake he, trying to win him with gentle speech. But that other's heart was pondering a double design, either to set upon them and slay them out of hand, or, strong king as

[1] ὀλοὸν ἔπος, *i.e.* an answer that would have had deadly consequences to someone.

he was, to make trial of their might. And as he thought thereon, this seemed the better plan; and so he caught him up and said, "Stranger, why shouldst thou tell me all to the end? For if ye are really of the race of gods, or have set foot upon a foreign shore no ways my inferiors, I will give thee the golden fleece to carry hence, if so thou wilt, after trying thee. For in the case of good men I grudge it noways, as yourselves declare he doth who is king in Hellas. But to test your spirit and strength there shall be a task, which I myself can compass with my hands, hard though it be. Two bulls with brazen hoofs, breathing flame from their mouths, do browse upon yon plain of Ares; these do I yoke and drive over the rough fallow of Ares of four plough-gates, and when I have speedily turned it up with the plough to the end I sow for seed in the furrows, not the corn of Demeter, but the teeth of a dread serpent, which grow into the form[1] of armed men. These do I next utterly destroy with my spear as they stand round to meet me. At early dawn I yoke my oxen, and at eventide I cease from my harvesting.

"Now, if thou wilt accomplish the like, thou shalt bear away to the king's palace the fleece upon the self-same day. Ere that I will not give it thee; so hope not so. For it were shameful indeed for a good man born to yield unto a worse."

So spake he; but Jason fixed his eyes in front of him and sat speechless, as he was, at a sore loss. Long time turned he the plan over, and no way could he find to accept the challenge courageously, for the task seemed a great one; but at last he made answer with crafty words: "Æetes, very straitly dost thou shut me up within thy right. Wherefore I will even endure that toil, passing hard though it be; yea, though it be my lot to die. For there is nothing worse that cometh on men than dire neces-

[1] δέμας used adverbially = "in form, appearance."

sity, and 'twas it that forced me to come hither at the king's command."

So spake he, smitten with dismay; and the other answered him in his distress with grim words: "Come now unto the gathering,[1] since thou art even eager for the toil; but if thou art afraid to put the yoke upon the oxen's neck, or if haply thou shrink from the deadly harvesting, these things severally shall be my care, that so any other may fear to come to a man that is better than he."[2]

So spake he bluntly; but the other, even Jason, leapt up from his seat, and Augeas and Telamon by his side, but only Argus[3] went with him, for he signed to his brothers, whilst they were yet there, that they should stay behind. But they went forth from the hall. And the son of Æson shone out wondrously amongst them all for beauty and grace, and the maiden cast shy glances at him, holding her bright veil aside, consuming her heart with woe; and her thoughts stole after him like a dream,[4] and flitted in his footsteps as he went. So they went forth from the house, sore at heart. And Chalciope, avoiding the wrath of Æetes, had gone swiftly to her chamber with her sons. And in like manner came Medea after her; and much she brooded in her heart, even all the cares that love doth

[1] μεθ' ὅμιλον, "to the place of gathering," μετα = προς. This usage is very common in Apollonius. The phrase might also mean "come after the crowd," but that suits the context less well, for the crowd would naturally follow rather than precede men who were about to hazard so dangerous an enterprise.

[2] *i.e.* a dark threat of punishment for Jason's presumption in preferring such a request, = "I will take good care that for the future adventurers like you think twice before they come with such impudent proposals to me."

[3] οἶος Ἄργος, *i.e.* Argus signed to his brothers to stay behind and make what way they could with their mother Chalciope.

[4] νόος ἠΰτ' ὄνειρος, a curiously bold expression, identifying the mind of the dreamer with the vision dreamt. We should have to say "as in a dream."

urge. For before her eyes everything yet seemed to be, her lover's very form, the raiment that he wore, the words he said, the way he sat upon his seat, and how he went unto the door; and, as she thought thereon, she dreamed there never was such another man; and ever in her ears his voice was ringing and the sweet words he spake. And she feared for him, that the oxen or haply Æetes with his own hands might slay him; and she mourned for him as though he were already slain outright, and the tears ran softly down her cheeks in her affliction from her exceeding pity; and, softly weeping, she uttered her voice aloud:— "Why doth this sorrow come o'er me to my grief? Whether he be the best or worst of heroes that is now to perish, let him die. Ah! would that he might escape unhurt. Yea, let that even come to pass, O dread goddess, daughter of Perses[1]; let him escape death and return home. But if 'tis fated that he be slain by the oxen, let him learn ere his doom, that I at least exult not in his cruel fate."

Even thus was that maiden weighed down with care. Now when those others had gone outside the crowd and the city along the path, which aforetime they had taken from the plain; in that hour did Argus speak to Jason with these words, "Son of Æson, thou wilt scorn the counsel I shall tell thee[2]; and yet it is not right at all to desist from any attempt in trouble. Haply thou too hast somewhat heard before that one of my sisters useth sorcery by the prompting of Hecate, daughter of Perses; if we can persuade her, no longer, methinks, shall there be any fear

[1] Περσηΐ, another name of Hecate, the goddess to whom Medea as a sorceress naturally prays; she was so called as being a daughter of Perses, or Persæus, though other legends declare her to have sprung from Zeus.

[2] *i.e.* you may not think much of my counsel in this particular case, but I give it all the same, for one ought to neglect no precaution in difficult circumstances.

that thou be foiled in thy emprise; but terribly I fear,[1] that my mother will not undertake this for me. Yet will I go to her again to entreat her; for o'er the heads of all of us hangeth joint destruction."

So spake he in kindliness, and the other thus made answer: "Good friend, if now this finds favour in thine own eyes, I have nought against it. Speed thee then and hasten to implore thy mother with words of wisdom. Yet wretched indeed is our hope, when we have entrusted our return to women."

So spake he; and quickly they came unto the backwater. And their comrades questioned them with joy when they saw them drawing near. But sorrowfully did the son of Æson tell out his tale to them, "Friends, the heart of cruel Æetes is angered at us outright. For never will the goal be reached by me, nor yet by you who question me on every point. Now he saith there are two bulls, with hoofs of bronze, that range the plain of Ares, breathing flame from their mouths. And he hath bidden me plough with these a fallow-field of four plough-gates; then, he says he will give me seed of the jaws of a serpent, which maketh earth-born men to rise in their bronze harness, and on that very day must I slay them. Which thing I did promise him outright, for no better plan could I devise."

So spake he, and it seemed to them all a toil not to be accomplished; long time looked they on one another in speechless silence, bowed down with anguish and dismay; but at the last spake Peleus bravely amongst all the chieftains: "'Tis time to devise what we are to do. I deem there is not so much help in counsel as in strong arms. If then, hero son of Æson, thou art minded thyself to yoke

[1] *δείδω μὴ ὀυ* = Lat. vereor ne non = vereor ut. *τόγε*, the service in question, *i.e.* the enlistment of the sympathies of Medea for the enterprise by Chalciope.

the oxen of Æetes, and art eager for the labour, lo! keep now thy promise and make thee ready; but if thy spirit hath no sure trust in thy valiancy, hasten not thyself, nor sitting here look round for some other amongst these men. For I myself will not hold back, for the worst grief that can come will be but death."

So spake the son of Æacus; and the spirit of Telamon was stirred; and he sprang up in hot haste, and with him uprose Idas in his pride, and the two sons of Tyndarus as well; and with them the son of Œneus, ranked among men of prowess,[1] albeit the soft down scarce showed upon his face; so high rose the courage of his heart. But those others gave way and kept silence. And anon spake Argus this word to them in their eagerness for the enterprise, "My friends, lo! this is left us at the last.[2] But, methinks, there shall come to us from my mother a very present help. Wherefore, for all your eagerness, restrain yourselves a little space in the ship, as heretofore; for 'tis better to hold back withal than recklessly to choose an evil doom. There dwells a maid in Æetes' halls, whom Hecate hath taught exceeding skill in all simples, that the land and flowing water do produce. By them is quenched even the blast of tireless flame; and in a moment she stays the rush of roaring streams, and she can bind the stars and the courses of the holy moon. Of her we bethought us as we came hither along the path from the house, if haply our mother, own sister to her, can persuade her to aid our labour. Now if this finds favour in your sight too,

[1] ἀίζηος literally = "a vigorous, lusty man," then any man who has come to his full strength, in which latter sense it is often employed by Homer, though probably the idea of "manliness" ought in every case to be kept prominent.

[2] "This is left us at the last," *i.e.* if we can find no better way, we will do and die in the attempt if necessary; but, ere that, let us employ all the means that offer, and despise no plan of escape, even if it do proceed from a woman.

verily I will go this very day back to the house of Æetes to make essay; and perhaps some god will be with me in my attempt."

So spake he; and the gods of their good will gave unto them a sign. A trembling dove, flying from a strong hawk, came down and settled in her terror in the bosom of the son of Æson; but the hawk transfixed[1] himself upon the pointed stern. At once Mopsus took up his parable and spake this word amongst them all, "My friends, here is a sign for you by the will of the gods; no otherwise could they more clearly bid us go speak with the maiden and seek to her with all our skill. And methinks she will not slight us, if, that is, Phineus said truly, that our return should depend on the Cyprian goddess. Yon gentle bird just 'scaped her fate; and even as my heart within me foresees according to this omen, so shall it surely be. But come, friends, call on Cytherea to help you, and in this very hour hearken to the persuasion of Argus."

So spake he; and the young men approved his words, for they remembered the bidding of Phineus; only Idas, son of Aphareus, sprang up; sore troubled was he, and he cried aloud, "How now, pray, did we come hither in company with women, that our men call on Cypris to come and help us, and no longer on the great War-god? Will ye, for the sight of doves and hawks, stay you from your enterprise? get you gone, and take no thought for deeds of war, but how to cajole weak girls by prayers."

So cried he in his hot anger; and many of his comrades muttered low, but there was none, I trow, that gave him answer back. So down he sat much in wrath; but Jason forthwith cheered them, and declared his mind thus, "Let Argus go forth from the ship, since this finds favour with

[1] *περικάππεσεν*, literally "fell about it," *i.e.* fell on it and was pierced by it. Cf. Soph. Aias, *περιπτυχὴς φασγάνῳ*, literally "folded about his sword," *i.e.* fallen upon it and pierced by it.

all, while we will now fasten our cables openly ashore out from the river. For assuredly 'tis well to lie hid no longer, crouching in fear from the battle-cry."

Therewith, sent he Argus forth at once to go swiftly a second time unto the city; but they hauled their anchors aboard at the bidding of the son of Æson, and rowed the ship a little space from out the backwater, and moored her to the shore.

Anon Æetes held a gathering of the Colchians apart from his house, where they sat aforetime, devising against the Minyæ treachery intolerable and troubles. For he threatened[1] that, so soon as the oxen should have torn that fellow in pieces, who had taken upon him the performance of the grievous labour, he would then cut down an oak-thicket upon the wooded hill-top and burn their ship, men and all, that they, with their over-weening schemes, may splutter out[2] their grievous insolence. For he would never have received Phrixus, son of Æolus, as a guest within his halls, for all his craving,—Phrixus who exceeded all strangers in gentleness and holiness,—had not Zeus sent to him his own messenger Hermes, that so Phrixus might meet with a kindly host. Verily were pirates to come to his land, they would not long be without sorrows of their own, folk who make it their business to stretch out their hand upon the goods of strangers, and to weave secret

[1] στεῦτο, "he threatened." From the sense of boasting that one is so and so, or will do so and so, the transition to that of threatening is not difficult. We find the word in three different significations: cf. ii. 1204, "he avows himself to be;" iii. 337, "is it destined;" iii. 579, "he threatened."

[2] ἀποφλύξωσιν, a grim jest on the part of Æetes. The word means "to boil up, splutter;" then "to babble idly," used by the king in scorn of the words Jason had spoken, and also with an allusion to the effect the fire would have on the heroes—"fire makes water boil away, perhaps it may make these babblers splutter out all their presumption." Cf. φλυαρία = "nonsense."

plots, and to harry the steadings of herdsmen in forays, heralded by their dreaded shout. Moreover he said that the sons of Phrixus, apart from this, should pay him a proper penalty[1] for returning in the company of evil-doers as their guides, that they might drive him from his honour and his kingdom heedlessly; for once on a time he had heard a dismal warning from his father Helios, that he must avoid the deep guile and plotting and the wily mischief of his own race. Wherefore he sent them, according to their father's bidding, eager as they were, to the land of Achæa, a long journey. But small fear had he of his daughters, or of his son Absyrtus, that they would ever devise any baleful plan; but he thought these fell deeds were to be accomplished among the race of Chalciope; and so it was that terrible things did he pronounce[2] in his wrath against those other folk; and he made a mighty threat that he would keep them from the ship and their comrades, that none might escape destruction.

Meantime Argus came unto the house of Æetes, and strove to win his mother with every argument he knew, that she might entreat Medea's aid; but she pondered the matter first herself. For fear held her back, lest haply he should win her over in vain, and contrary to fate; so fearful was she of her father's deadly anger, or lest, if she consented to his prayer, her deed might get abroad and be clearly known.

Now deep sleep relieved the maid Medea from her troubles, as she lay upon her bed. But anon fearsome cheating

[1] *μείλια* = anything that pleases; then a marriage portion; here equivalent to *ποιναί*, which, however, viewed from Æetes' point of view, would be distinctly pleasing. The word is used above, iii. 135, for "a toy, plaything."

[2] *πιφαύσκετο*, "he declared" that he would bring to pass. *δημοτέροισιν* literally = "common, vulgar." It is not quite clear who is meant; possibly the rest of the heroes, as distinct from the sons of Phrixus and Chalciope, who were to receive special punishment.

dreams assailed her, as they will a maiden in her woe. She thought yon stranger had taken that toil upon him, not because he greatly desired to carry off the ram's fleece, nor at all, for its sake, had he come to the city of Æetes, but that he might lead her to his home to be his own true wife; and she dreamed that she herself strove with the oxen, and did the toil right easily; but her parents made light of their promise; for they had set the yoking of the oxen, not before their daughter, but before the stranger. Then arose a strife of doubtful issue betwixt her father and the strangers; and both did entrust it unto her to be even as she should direct. At once she chose that stranger, and forgat her parents, and grievous was their anguish, and they cried out in anger; then did sleep forsake her, and she awoke with a cry. And she arose quivering with terror, and peered all round the walls of her chamber, and scarce could she regain her courage as before in her breast, and she uttered her voice aloud, "Ah! woe is me! how have fearful dreams affrighted me! I fear that this voyage of the heroes is bringing some awful calamity. My heart is in suspense[1] for the stranger. Let him woo some Achæan maiden, far away among his own people, and let my virgin state and my parents' home be my care. Verily, though I have cast shame out of my heart, I will not yet make any attempt without the advice of my sister, if haply she entreat me to help their enterprise, in sorrow for her sons; that would assuage the bitter grief in my heart."

Therewith she rose and opened the door of her chamber, barefoot, in her shift alone; and lo! she longed to go to her sister, and she passed over the threshold of her room. And long time she waited there at the entrance of her chamber, held back by shame, and she turned her back once more; and yet again she went from her room, and

[1] *ἠερέθονται*, a lengthened form of *ἀείρομαι*, = "to hang floating in the air." Hence metaph. "to waver."

again stole back; for her feet bore her in vain this way and that; yea, and oft as she was going straight on, modesty kept her within; then would bold desire urge her against the curb of modesty. Thrice she tried, and thrice she held back; the fourth time she turned and threw herself face down upon the bed. As when a bride doth mourn within her chamber a strong young husband, to whom her brethren and parents have given her, and she holds no converse with all her attendants for very shame and thinking of him; but sitteth in a corner lamenting, but him hath some doom destroyed, ere they twain have had any joy each of the other's counsels; while she, with burning heart, looks on her widowed bed and sheds the silent tear, that the women may not mock and scoff at her; like to her was Medea in her lamentation. Now on a sudden, while she wept, a maid-servant coming forth did hear her, one that had waited on her in her girlhood; and forthwith she told Chalciope; now she was sitting amongst her sons, devising how to win her sister to their side. Yet not even so did she make light of it, when she heard the maid's strange story, but she hasted in amaze from room to room throughout the house to the chamber wherein the maiden lay in her anguish, and tore her cheeks;. and when she saw her eyes all dimmed with tears, she said to her, "Ah, woe is me! Medea, and wherefore dost thou shed these tears? What has happened to thee? what awful grief hath come into thy heart? Has some disease of heaven's sending fastened on thy limbs, or hast thou learnt some deadly threat of my father concerning me and my sons? Would that I no longer beheld this house of my parents, nor their city, but dwelt in the uttermost parts of the earth, where is not so much as heard the name of Colchians."

So spake she, but a blush rose to her sister's cheeks, and long time maiden modesty stayed her from answering, fain as she was. At one moment the word would rise to the tip of her tongue, at another it would speed back deep within her breast. Oft her eager lips yearned to tell their tale, but the words came no farther. At the last she made this subtle speech, for love's bold hand was heavy on her, "Chalciope, my heart is in sore suspense for thy sons, for fear lest our father slay them outright with the strangers. For as I fell asleep just now and slumbered for a little space, I saw a fearful vision. May some god make it of none effect, and mayest thou get no bitter grief for thy sons!"

So spake she, making trial of her sister; and the other thus answered: "Lo! I came to thee myself bent upon this business entirely, to see if thou couldst help me with counsel and devise some aid. Come, swear by heaven and earth that thou wilt keep in thy heart what I shall say to thee, and will help me in the work. I pray thee by the blessed gods, by thyself, and by our parents, do not see them piteously destroyed by some evil fate; or else will I die with my dear sons and be to thee hereafter a fearful spirit of vengeance from Hades."

So spake she, and forthwith her tears gushed forth in streams, and she clasped her hands below her knees, and let her head sink on her bosom. Then did the two sisters make piteous lament over each other, and there arose through the house a faint[1] sound of women weeping in their sorrow.

But Medea first addressed the other, sore distressed: "God help us, sister! what cure can I work for thee? what a word is thine, with thy dread curses and spirits of vengeance! Would that it were surely in my power to save thy sons! Witness now that awful oath of the Colchians,

[1] λεπταλέῃ ἰωῇ, properly "fine, delicate." In this connexion it would seem to mean "subdued," so that their grief might not be noticed and cause suspicion.

which thyself wouldst have me swear; great heaven and earth beneath, mother of gods! as far as in me lies I will not fail thee, so thou ask aught I can perform."

So spake she, and Chalciope thus made answer: "Canst thou then devise no trick, no help for the enterprise of the stranger, even if his own lips ask it, for the sake of my children? lo! Argus is come from him, urging me to try and gain thy help; him did I leave within the house the while I came hither."

So she; and the other's heart within her leapt for joy, and a deep blush withal mantled o'er her fair skin, and a mist came o'er her eyes as her heart melted, and thus she answered: "Chalciope, I will do even as is dear and pleasing to you. May the dawn shine no more upon mine eyes; mayst thou no longer see me in the land of the living, if I hold aught before thy soul, or before thy sons, who verily are my cousins, my kinsmen dear, and of mine own age. Even so I do declare I am thy sister and thy daughter too, for thou didst hold me to thy breast while yet a babe, equally with those thy sons, as ever I heard in days gone by from my mother. But go now, hide my service in silence that I may make good my promise without the knowledge of my parents, and at dawn will I carry to the temple of Hecate drugs to charm the bulls."

So Chalciope went back again from the chamber; while she set to devising some help for her sister's sons. But once more did shame and an horrible dread seize her when she was alone, to think that she was devising such things for a man, without her father's knowledge.

Then did night spread darkness o'er the earth, and they who were at sea, the mariners, looked forth from their ships toward the Bear and the stars of Orion; and now did every wayfarer and gatekeeper long for sleep; and o'er every mother, weeping for children dead, fell the pall of deep slumber; no more did dogs howl through the town;

no more was heard the noise of men, but silence wrapped the darkling gloom. Yet not at all did sleep shed its sweetness o'er Medea; for in her love for the son of Æson many a care kept her awake, terrified at the mighty strength of the bulls, before whom he was to die a shameful death on Ares' acre. And her heart was wildly stirred within her breast; as when a sun-beam reflected from water plays upon the wall of a house, water just poured into a basin or a pail maybe; hither and thither it darts and dances on the quick eddy; even so the maiden's heart was fluttering in her breast, and tears of pity flowed from her eyes; and, ever within, the pain was wasting her, smouldering through her body, and about her weakened nerves, and right beneath the back of her head,[1] where the keenest pain doth enter in, when the tireless love-god lets loose[2] his tortures on the heart. At one time she thought she would give him drugs to charm the bulls, at another she thought nay, but that she would die herself; anon she would not die herself, nor would she give him the drugs, but quietly even so would endure her sorrow. So she sat halting between two opinions, then spake, "Ah, woe is me! am I now to toss hither and thither in woe? my mind is wholly at a loss; there is no help for my suffering, but it burneth ever thus. Oh! would that I had died by the swift arrows of Artemis, or ever I had seen him, or ever the sons of Chalciope started for the Achæan land; some god or some spirit of vengeance hath brought them hither from thence to cause us tears and woe enow. Well, let him perish in his attempt, if 'tis his lot to die upon the fallow. For how can I contrive the drugs, and my parents know it not? what tale am I to tell about them? What cunning, what crafty scheme shall there be for their aid? Shall I greet him kindly if I see him alone apart from his comrades?

[1] *ἰνίον* strictly is "the nape of the neck."

[2] *ἐνισκίμψωσιν*, literally "to dash in or upon" (trans.).

Unhappy maid am I; methinks I would not be quit of sorrow even though he were dead and gone. For sorrow will come upon me in the hour that he is bereft of life. Away with shame, perish beauty! he shall be saved, unhurt, and by my help; then let him go whithersoever his heart listeth. But may I die the self-same day that he fulfilleth his enterprise, either hanging by my neck from the roof-tree, or tasting of drugs that rive body and soul asunder. But, if I die thus, every eye will wink[1] and mock at me, and every city far away will ring with the tale of my death, and the Colchian women will make a byword of me for their unseemly gibes; the maid who cared so dearly for a stranger that she died for him, who shamed her home and parents by yielding to her mad passion. What disgrace is there that will not be mine? Ah me! for my infatuation! Far better will it be this very night to leave life behind in my chamber by an unseen fate, avoiding all ill reproaches, or ever I complete this infamous disgrace!"

Therewith she went to fetch a casket, wherein were laid many drugs for her use, some healing, others very deadly. And she laid it on her lap, and wept. And her bosom was wet with her ceaseless weeping, for the tears flowed in streams as she sat there, making piteous lament for her fate. Then she hasted to choose a deadly drug, that she might taste thereof. And lo! she was just loosing the fastenings of the casket, eager to draw them forth, poor unhappy lady, when in an instant passed across her mind an awful horror of loathly Hades; and long time she stayed her hand in speechless fear, and life with all its cares seemed sweet to her. For she thought of all the joyous things there are amongst the living, and of her happy band of companions, as a maiden will; and the sun

[1] ἐπιλλίζουσι = "to wink with the eye" in mockery. Cf. supra, i. 486, where it is used of the unsteady gaze of a drunken man.

grew sweeter to her than before to look upon, just to see[1] if really in her heart of hearts she longed for each of them. So she laid the casket down again from off her knees, changing her mind by the prompting of Hera, and no more did her purpose waver otherwhither; but she longed for the dawn to rise and come at once, that she might give Jason her magic drugs as she had covenanted,[2] and meet him face to face. And oft would she loose the bolts of her door, as she watched for the daylight; and welcome to her was the light, when Dawn sent it forth, and each man went on his way through the city.

Now Argus bade his brethren abide there yet, that they might learn the mind and plans of the maiden, but himself went forth and came unto the ship again.

But the maid Medea, soon as ever she saw the light of dawn, caught up her golden tresses in her hands, which she had let hang about her in careless disarray, and wiped clean her tear-stained cheeks; and she cleansed her skin with ointment of heavenly fragrance, and put on a fair robe, fastened with brooches deftly turned; and upon her head, divinely fair, she cast a shining veil. Then she passed forth from her chamber there, treading the ground firmly, in forgetfulness of her sorrows, which were close upon her in their countless legions, while others were yet to follow afterward. And she bade her handmaids, who passed the night in the entering in of her fragrant bower, —twelve maids in all of her own age who had not yet found a mate,—quickly to yoke mules to the wain, to bear her to the lovely shrine of Hecate. Then did the maidens make ready the wain; but she, the while, chose from the depth of her casket a drug, which men say is called the

1 "Just to see," &c., *i.e.* to see if she did not really long for them in spite of her belief that they were nothing to her any more.

2 *συνθεσίῃσι*, "according to her covenant." Medea had promised her sister Chalciope that she would give Jason the necessary drugs.

drug of Prometheus. If a man should anoint his body therewith, after appeasing Persephone, that maiden only-begotten, with midnight sacrifice; verily that man could not be wounded by the blows of bronze weapons, nor would he yield to blazing fire, but on that day [1] should his valiancy and might master theirs. This first had its birth, when the ravening eagle let drip to earth upon the wolds of Caucasus the bleeding life-stream [2] of hapless Prometheus. The flower thereof, as it were a cubit high, appeareth in colour like the saffron of Corycus, growing upon a double stalk, but its root within the ground resembleth flesh just cut. Now she had gathered for her drugs the dark juice thereof, like to the sap of a mountain oak, in a Caspian shell, after she had washed herself in seven eternal springs, and seven times had called on Brimo,[3] good nursing-mother, who roams by night, goddess of the nether world, and queen of the dead, in the murk of night, in sable raiment clad. And, from beneath, the dark earth quaked and bellowed, as the Titan root [4] was cut, and the son of Iapetus too did groan, frantic with pain. That simple drew she forth and placed within her fragrant girdle, that was fastened about her fair waist. And forth to the door she came and mounted the swift car, and with her on either side went two handmaids; so she took the reins and the shapely whip in her right hand, and drove through the town; while those others, her handmaids, holding to the body of the wain behind, ran along the broad high-road, having kilted their fine robes up to their white knees. Fair as the daughter of Leto,[5] when she mounts her golden car, and drives her fleet fawns o'er the downs across the

[1] κεῖν' ἦμαρ, *i.e.* that day only.

[2] ἰχῶρα = the blood of a god.

[3] Hecate.

[4] The root sprang from the blood of Prometheus, who was a Titan, that is, a primeval god.

[5] Artemis, the chaste huntress.

calm waters of Parthenius, or haply from her bath in Amnisus' stream, as she cometh from far to the rich steam of a hetacomb; and with her come the nymphs, that bear her company, some gathering by the brink of the Amnisian spring, others about the groves and rocks with their countless rills; and around her wild creatures fawn and whimper, trembling at her approach. Even so the maidens hasted through the city, and the people made way on either side, shunning the eye of the princess. Now when she had left the streets of the town, with their fair buildings, and had come in her driving across the plain unto the temple, then she lighted down quickly from the smooth-running wain and spake thus amongst her maidens: "Friends, verily I have sinned an awful sin, for I find no cause to be wroth with yon strangers, who are roaming about our land. The whole city is smitten with dismay; wherefore also none of the women hath come hither, who aforetime did gather here day by day. Yet since we are here, and none other comes forth against us, let us with soothing song and dance satisfy our souls without stint, and after we have plucked these fair blossoms of the tender field, then in that very hour will we return. Yea, and ye this day shall go unto your homes with many a rich gift, an ye will grant me this my desire; for Argus is urgent[1] with me, and so too is Chalciope;—keep what ye hear of me silent in your hearts, lest my words come to my father's ears;—lo! they bid me take yon stranger's gifts, who hath taken on him to strive with the oxen, and save him from his fell emprise. So I agreed unto their words, and I bade him meet me here alone, apart from his comrades, that we may divide amongst ourselves those gifts, if haply he bring them with him, and we may give him in return a drug

[1] *παρατρέπει, not* in its usual sense of "turning a person away from a thing," but = *προτρέπει*, "urge on to."

more baleful [1] than he knows. But do ye stand aloof from me against his coming."

So spake she, and her cunning counsel pleased them all. Anon Argus drew the son of Æson apart from the crew, as soon as he heard from his brothers, that she had gone at daybreak to the holy temple of Hecate, and across the plain he led him; and with them went Mopsus, son of Ampycus, skilled in interpreting omens from birds when they appeared, and skilled in giving the right advice when they were gone.

Never was there such a man amongst the men of bygone days, neither among all the heroes who sprang from Zeus himself, nor among those who were of the blood of other immortal gods, as the wife of Zeus made Jason on that day, either to see face to face or to talk with.[2] Even his comrades marvelled, as they gazed at him resplendent with grace; and the son of Ampycus was glad as they went, for already, I trow, he boded, how each thing would be.

Now there is by the path along the plain, nigh to the temple, a black poplar with a crown of countless leaves, whereon, full oft, chattering crows would roost. And one of these, as she flapped her wings aloft on the branches, declared the will of Hera: "Here is a sorry seer, that hath not so much knowing as children have; for no sweet word of love will the maid speak to yon youth, so long as there be other strangers with him. Begone, thou sorry prophet, dull-witted seer, for 'tis not thou, whom Cypris and her gentle Loves inspire, in their kindness."

So spake the chiding crow, and Mopsus smiled to hear the bird's inspired utterance, and thus spake he: "Son of Æson, get thee now to the temple of the goddess, wherein thou wilt find the maiden; very kindly shall her greeting

[1] More deadly than anyone else could give.

[2] *i.e.* he was not only noble to look upon, but he had also a shrewd understanding.

be to thee, thanks to Cypris, who will help thee in thy labours, even as Phineus, son of Agenor, did say before. But we twain, Argus and I, will stand in this very spot aloof, awaiting thy coming; and do thou thyself alone entreat her, turning her heart by words of wisdom."

So spake he very sagely; and nigh at hand they both agreed to wait. Nor, I trow, had Medea any thought but this, for all her play; for none of all the games she played would serve for her amusement long. But she kept changing them in confusion, nor could she keep her eyes at rest towards her group of maids, but earnestly she would gaze o'er the paths afar, turning her cheeks aside. Oft her heart sank broken within her breast, whenever she fancied a footfall or a breath of wind was hurrying by. But very soon came Jason in sight before her longing eyes, striding high o'er the plain, like Sirius when he rises from ocean, very fair and clear to see, but bringing woe unspeakable to flocks; so fair was the son of Æson to see as he came nigh, but the sight of him brought hateful faintness upon her. Her heart sank within her breast, and her eyes grew dim withal, and o'er her cheeks rushed the hot blush; and her knees had no strength to move backward or forward, but her feet were rooted to the ground under her. Now her handmaids, the while, had withdrawn from them, one and all; so they twain stood facing one another without word or sound, like oaks or lofty pines, which stand rooted side by side in peace upon the mountains, when winds are still; but lo! there comes a breath of wind to rustle them, and sighs, that none can number, steal therefrom; even so those twain were soon to tell out all their tale before the breath of Love. But the son of Æson perceived that she was scared by some bewilderment from heaven, and with a kindly smile he thus hailed her, "Why, maiden, art thou so fearful of me when I come alone? Verily I was never aforetime, not even when I dwelt in mine own country, one of those braggart fellows. Wherefore fear not exceedingly, maiden, either to question me or say what is in thine heart. Nay, but since we are met together as friends in this most holy place, where to sin were wrong, speak openly and tell me all; and deceive me not with comfortable words,[1] for at first thou didst promise thine own sister to give me the drugs my heart desired. By Hecate herself, by thy parents, and by Zeus, whose hand is over strangers and suppliants, I entreat thee. As stranger and as suppliant both, am I come hither to thee to implore thee in my sore need. For without thee never shall I achieve my dismal task. And I will make thee recompense hereafter for thy help, as is right, making thy name and fame glorious, as becometh those who dwell apart[2]; yea, and in like manner shall the other heroes spread thy fame through Hellas on their return; and so shall the heroes' wives and mothers, who now belike are sitting on the shore and mourning for us, whose grievous sufferings thou wilt scatter to the winds. In days gone by, Ariadne,[3] daughter of Minos, did, of her good heart, free Theseus from his evil task; she it was whom Pasiphae, daughter of the Sun-god, bore. Yea,[4] and she went aboard his ship with him and left

[1] Smooth words which will not offend the ear, but yet will cause trouble in the end from their being found untrue.

[2] *i.e.* I will make every return which a man in a far country can to a benefactor, viz., speak well of you, and make others do the like.

[3] Ariadne, daughter of Minos, king of Crete, helped Theseus to slay the Minotaur and find his way out of a pathless maze; so Theseus took her away on his ship to sail to Athens, but abandoned her cruelly in Naxos, where, however, the god Dionysus found her, and set her as a star in heaven.

[4] *καὶ*, emphatic. Ariadne *even* went aboard the ship of Theseus at his request; I only ask for your aid without any further sacrifice.

εὔνασε χόλον. Either she fled because Minos had only lulled his anger for a time, and would make her suffer for her share in the success of Theseus later on, or else the expression might mean that Minos having swallowed his vexation, allowed Ariadne to sail away with the

her country, since Minos did lull his rage; and the immortal gods showed their love as well, for there in mid sky is her sign, a crown of stars, which men call Ariadne's crown, wheeling by night amid the heavenly constellations. Such thanks shalt thou too have from the gods, if thou wilt save this famous host of chieftains. For surely from thy form, methinks, thou shouldst excel in gentle acts of kindness."

So spake he praising her; and she cast down her eyes with a sweet smile,[1] and her heart within her melted, as he extolled her. And she looked straight into his eyes, and had no word to answer him withal at first, but longed to tell him all at once together. And forth from her fragrant girdle she drew the drug ungrudgingly, and he with joy took it in his hands at once. And now would she have drawn her whole soul forth from her breast and given it him at his desire eagerly; so mightily did love light up his sweet torch from the son of Æson's yellow locks, and snatched bright glances from her eyes; and her heart wasted and melted within her, as the dew upon roses melts and wastes away in the sun's beams at morn. But they would fix their eyes one time upon the ground in modesty, and then again would cast a glance at each other, with a smile of love in their glad eyes. At the last, and scarcely then, the maiden thus did greet him:

"Take heed now, that I may devise some help for thee. When my father hath given thee, at thy coming for them,

adventurer. This view is favoured, if not confirmed, by a remark of Jason's (infra, 1099), where he speaks of the aid lent by Minos to Theseus for the sake of his daughter. Homer styles him ὀλοόφρων, "the man of baleful thoughts." Also, it would tend to increase the confidence of Medea if she could be persuaded that her father would forgive her in the end, and let her marry her lover as Ariadne had married Theseus.

[1] "A smile divinely sweet." νεκτάρεον is mostly used of sweet smells, then anything sweet that surpasses man's power.

the fell teeth from the snake's jaws to sow withal, then watch for the hour when the night is evenly divided in twain, and after washing thyself in the stream of the tireless river, dig a round hole, alone apart from the others, in sable garb; there slay a ewe and sacrifice her whole, having heaped high the fire above the hole itself. And propitiate Hecate, daughter of Perses, the only-begotten, pouring libations of honey from a chalice. Then when thou hast taken heed to appease the goddess, draw back again from the fire; and let no sound of feet or howling of dogs drive thee to turn round, lest haply thou cut all short and come not thyself back duly to thy companions. At dawn soak this drug; then strip and with it anoint thy body as it were with oil; and there shall be in it boundless valiancy and great strength, and thou wilt think thyself a match for deathless gods, not for men. Moreover, let thy shield and sword and spear be sprinkled therewith. Then shall not the keen swords of the earth-born men cut thee, nor shall the flame of those deadly bulls dart forth resistlessly against thee. Yet shalt thou not be thus mighty for a long space, but for that day only; yet never shrink thou from thy enterprise. And I will supply thee yet another help. So soon as thou hast yoked the strong oxen, and by thy might and manhood hast quickly ploughed the hard fallow, and they, the giants, at once spring up along the furrows when the teeth of the snake are sown over the dark soil, if thou but watch them rising in crowds from the lea, then cast secretly at them a heavy rock; and they will destroy one another upon it, like fierce dogs about their food; but be not thyself eager for the fray. Hereby shalt thou carry yon fleece to Hellas, far from Æa, I trow. Yet go, whither thou listest, when thou art gone hence."

So spake she, and dropping her eyes in silence before her did wet her cheek, divinely fair, with warm tears, mourning the day when he would wander far from her across the main. And once again she spake to him with sad words, taking hold on his right hand, for lo! shame had left her gaze: "Remember the name of Medea, if haply thou return one day to thy home; so will I remember thee when thou art gone. And tell me this in kindness, where is thy home, where wilt thou fare from hence in thy ship across the sea? Wilt thou go haply nigh to rich Orchomenus, or may-be toward the Ææan isle? And tell me of the maid thou didst speak of, the far-famed daughter of Pasiphae,[1] who is of my father's kindred."

So spake she, and, as the maiden wept, love in his might stole o'er him as well, and thus he answered her, "Yea, verily, if I escape my fate, methinks I will never forget thee by night, nor yet by day, if indeed I shall escape scatheless to Achæa, and Æetes set not before us some other toil yet worse than this. But if it please thee to learn of my country, I will tell thee, for much doth my heart bid me myself as well. There is a land, ringed round with steep hills, rich withal in sheep and pasture, where Prometheus, son of Iapetus, begat goodly Deucalion,[2] who was the first to found cities and build temples for the immortal gods, and the first too to lord it over men. Hæmonia, the folk who dwell around, do call that land. Therein is Iolchos itself, my city, and in it too are many other cities, where men have not so much as heard the name of the Ææan isle[3]; there is, indeed a legend that Minyas, of the race of Æolus, once started from thence and founded the town of Orchomenus, that borders on

[1] Pasiphae was a daughter of Helios, and Æetes was a son of the same god; so that Ariadne and Medea were first cousins.

[2] Deucalion was the son of Prometheus and Pandora; he was king of Thessaly, and with his wife Pyrrha was supposed to be the only survivor of a great deluge which flooded the earth in early times. Horace alludes to the story in Odes I. ii. 5.

[3] "The isle of Æa" was a small island in the river Phasis, in which the golden fleece was kept.

the Cadmeans. But why do I tell thee all these idle tales, and of our home and of famous Ariadne, daughter of Minos, for that was the glorious name men gave the lovely maiden, of whom thou askest me? Would that, as Minos was then well pleased with Theseus for her sake, so too thy father might be at one with us!"

So spake he, caressing her with fond and tender words. But grief, most bitter, stirred her heart, and in her distress she hailed him with earnest speech: "It may be that in Hellas these things are fair, to heed the ties of kin; but Æetes is not such another amongst men, as thou sayest Minos, the husband of Pasiphae, was; nor can I compare with Ariadne; wherefore tell me nought of hospitality. Only do thou, when thou comest to Iolchos, remember me; and I will remember thee even in spite of my parents. And may there come to me from a far-off land some voice, or some bird with tidings, when thou hast forgotten me; or may the swift winds catch me up and bear me hence across the sea to Iolchos, that I may remind thee that thou didst escape by my aid, reproaching thee to thy face! Would I might then sit me down openly[1] in thy halls!"

So spake she, shedding piteous tears adown her cheeks, but Jason caught her up[2] there and said: "God help thee, lady! leave the winds to wander emptily, and that bird too to bring thee tidings, for thy words are light as wind. For if thou ever come to those abodes and the land of Hellas, thou shalt have honour and respect amongst men and women, and they shall reverence thee even as a goddess, since their sons did return home again by thy counsel, yea, and many a brother of theirs and kinsman, and strong young husband was saved. And in our bridal

[1] *i.e.* "would that I might come openly and of right as thy wedded wife."

[2] *i.e.* cutting her short, taking her up.

bower shalt thou make ready our couch, and nought shall come 'twixt love and us, ere the doom of death o'ershadow us."

So spake he, and her heart within her melted as she heard, and yet she shuddered at the thought of that dark[1] enterprise, poor maiden; but she was not long to refuse a home in Hellas. For such was the mind of Hera, that Ææan Medea should come to sacred Iolchos, to the bane of Pelias, leaving her own country. But now were her handmaidens looking about for her silently at a distance, much distressed, for the time of day demanded the maiden's return home to her mother. But she thought not yet of going, for her heart rejoiced both in his beauty and his flattering words; but the son of Æson, seeing that it was now late, did say, "'Tis time to depart, lest the sun sink before we know it, and some stranger get to know all; yet will we meet again at this tryst."

Thus far those twain made trial of each other with gentle words; and then again they parted; Jason hasting back in joy to his comrades and the ship, and she to her handmaids; and they came nigh to meet her in a body, but she heeded them not as they gathered about her, for her soul had winged its flight to soar amid the clouds. With random steps she mounted the swift wain, and in one hand took the reins and in the other the carven whip to drive the mules withal, and they dashed swiftly cityward to her home. Now when she was come thither, Chalciope, in agony for her sons, did question her; but she, at a loss through fear and doubt, heard never a word, and made no haste to answer her questions. But she sat her down on a low stool at the foot of the couch, leaning her cheek on her left hand, and her eyes were wet with tears, as she darkly pondered what an evil work she was sharing by her counsels.

[1] ἔργ' ἀΐδηλα, "works whose issue she could not see."

But when the son of Æson was again come among his comrades in the place where he had left them when he went away, he started to go with them unto the gathering of the heroes, telling them each thing; and together they drew nigh the ship. And the others did warmly greet him, when they saw him, and questioned him. And he amongst them all did tell the maiden's counsels, showing them the awful drug; only one sat alone apart from his comrades, nursing his rage, even Idas; but the rest in gladness, with peaceful hearts, were busying themselves the while about their beds, for dark night had stayed their hands. But at dawn sent they to Æetes two men, to ask him for the seed, first of all Telamon, great warrior, and with him Æthalides, Hermes' famous child. Forth on their way went they, nor was their journey in vain, for Æetes, the prince, gave them, at their coming, the fell teeth for the task of that Aonian[1] dragon, which Cadmus slew in Ogygian Thebes at its post by the Aretian spring, what time he came thither in quest of Europa; there he dwelt, guided thither by a cow,[2] which Apollo vouchsafed to go before him on his way according to his oracle. These teeth the goddess Tritonis[3] had drawn from the serpent's jaws, and given equally to Æetes and to Cadmus, who himself slew the monster. Now he, even Cadmus, son of Agenor, sowed his share upon the plains of Bœotia, and founded a race of earth-born men from the remnant left after the harvesting of Ares' spear; but the rest Æetes at that time readily gave them to bear unto the ship, for he

[1] *i.e.* Bœotian. Bœotia originally was called Aonia. Thebes was called Ogygian from a king Ogygus.

[2] Apollo told Cadmus to found a city where the cow, which guided him, should halt. Cadmus founded Thebes.

[3] Athene. The goddess gave half the serpent's teeth to Cadmus and half to Æetes. Cadmus sowed his share, and raised a nation from the residue who remained after the deadly conflict which ensued.

never thought that Jason would make an end of his toil, even if he should cast the yoke upon the oxen.

Far in the west the sun was sinking beneath the dark earth, beyond the farthest hills of the Æthiopians; and night was yoking his steeds; so those heroes made ready their beds upon the ground by the hawsers. But Jason, soon as ever the stars of Helice, the bright Bear, did set, and all the firmament of heaven grew still, gat him to the wilderness, like some stealthy thief, with all that was needful, for by day had he taken thought for everything; and Argus went with him bringiug a ewe and milk from the flock, which things he took from the ship itself. But when he saw a spot, far from the tread of man, in a clear[1] water-mead beneath the open sky, then first of all he washed his tender body devoutly in the sacred river, and then put on a sable robe, which Hypsipyle of Lemnos erst gave him, in memory of many a night of love. Next he dug a hole in the ground, a cubit deep, and piled therein cleft wood, and cut the throat of the sheep and laid it carefully thereupon; then did he kindle the logs by putting fire under, and he poured upon the sacrifice mixed libations, calling Hecate by her name Brimo to help him in his toil. So then he called upon her and then stept back, and she, that awful goddess, heard him and came to the sacrifice of the son of Æson from the nethermost hell, and about her on the branches of the oaks twined gruesome snakes, and there was the flash of countless torches, and the dogs of hell howled loudly round her. About her path all the meadows quaked, and those nymphs, that haunt marshes and rivers, and flit about that water-meadow of the Amarantian Phasis,[2] cried out. Yea, and fear took hold upon the son of Æson, but his feet brought him for all that

[1] *καθαρῇσιν*, *i.e.* an open space.

[2] The Amarantians were a race of barbarians further inland beyond the Colchians, in whose land the Phasis rises.

without one glance backward, till he was amongst his comrades; and already Dawn, the child of morning, was rising above snow-capped Caucasus and shedding his light abroad.

In that hour Æetes buckled on his stiff[1] breast-plate, which Ares gave him, after he had slain with his own hand Phlegræan Mimas; and on his head he put a golden helmet, with four plumes, blazing like the sun's round ball of light, when he first rises from ocean. In one hand he wielded a buckler of many hides, in the other a sword, dreadful, irresistible; that blade could none of the heroes have withstood, now that they had left Heracles far behind; he alone could have stood up to battle against it. And Phaethon[2] held his shapely chariot with the fleet steeds nigh for him to mount; so he went up thereon and took the reins in his hands. Forth from the town he drave along the broad high-road, to take his station in the lists, and with him a countless throng hasted forth. Like as when Poseidon, mounted on his car, goeth to the Isthmian games, or to Tænarus,[3] or cometh in his might to the waters of Lerna[4] or through the grove of Hyantian Onchestus, and with his steeds he cometh even to Calaurea, and the Hæmonian rock, or to wooded Geræstum; such was Æetes, captain of the Colchians, for to behold.

Meantime Jason, by the advice of Medea, soaked the

[1] στάδιον, "standing fast, firm, unyielding," so as epithet of ὑσμίνη, or alone (cf. i. 200) it means "close, hand-to-hand fight," Lat. pugna stataria.

[2] The other name of Absyrtus, son of Æetes.

[3] Tænarus, a promontory of Laconia, sacred to Poseidon.

[4] Lerna, a fountain in Argos. Ὑαντίου, i.e. Bœotian. The Hyantes were a Bœotian race, and Onchestus is a city in Bœotia. Calaurea is an island near Trœzen. Hæmonia, i.e. Thessaly; Pindar uses the epithet Πετραῖος of Poseidon. Geræstus, a promontory of Eubœa. All the places here mentioned were sacred to the worship of Poseidon, and several had temples in the god's honour.

drug, and sprinkled his shield and weighty spear and his sword all over; and his comrades around him tested his harness with might and main; but they were not able to bend that spear ever so little, but it remained hard and unbroken as before in their stalwart hands. Then did Idas, that son of Aphareus, in furious anger, hack the butt end thereof with his mighty sword, but the edge leapt from it like a hammer from an anvil, beaten back, and the others, the heroes, cheered in their joy, with good hope for his emprise. Next did he sprinkle himself as well, and into him there entered fearful valiancy, marvellous, dauntless, and his hands on either side grew stronger, swelling[1] with might. As when a war-horse, eager for the battle, leaps and neighs and paws the ground, and in his pride pricks up his ears and rears his neck; in like manner the son of Æson exulted in the strength of his limbs. And oft he sprang into the air, hither and thither, brandishing his shield of bronze and his ashen spear in his hands. Thou wouldst have thought 'twas lightning in winter-time, darting from the gloomy sky, and leaping, flash on flash, from out the clouds, what time they hurry in their wake the blackest storm.

Now would they hold back no longer from their enterprise, but, sitting them in rows upon the benches, very quickly they rowed to yon plain of Ares. Now it lay over against the entrance to the town, as far therefrom as is the turning-post, which a chariot must win, from the starting-place, when at a prince's death his friends appoint contests[2]

[1] *σφριγόωσαι.* The word literally = "to be full to bursting, to be plump and full," Lat. turgere; then "to be in full health and strength," Lat. vigere; lastly, "to swell with pride," *e.g.* *σφριγῶν μῦθος* = "an arrogant speech." It is an easy transition from one meaning to the other.

[2] Funeral games were a regular custom in ancient times. Cf. the account, in Homer's Iliad ad fin., of the games instituted by Achilles in

for footmen and horsemen. There found they Æetes and hosts of other Colchians; these were stationed on the Caucasian rocks, but he beside the river's winding bank.

Forth leapt the son of Æson from the ship, with spear and shield, unto his task, so soon as his crew had fastened the cables; and with him he took a gleaming bronze helmet, full of the sharp teeth, and his sword slung about his shoulders, with naked[1] body, somewhat resembling Ares, and haply somewhat Apollo with his sword of gold. One glance he took along the lea, and saw the bulls' brazen yoke and the plough, made of one piece of ponderous adamant, upon it. So he drew nigh, and fixed his strong sword upright to the hilt[2] hard by, and set the helmet down resting against it. Then he set forward with shield alone, tracking the countless traces of the bulls, and they from some unseen den beneath the ground, where were their strong stalls, all wrapt in smoke and flame, rushed forth together, breathing flaming fire. Sore afraid were the heroes at that sight; but he, firmly planting himself,[3] awaited their onset, as a reef of rock awaits the billows driven against it by the countless blasts. And in front he held his shield to meet them; and they together bellowing, smote thereon with their strong horns; yet they heft him up never a jot by their attack. As when the good leathern

honour of his dead friend Patroclus, and Vergil's account of games at the death of Anchises.

[1] γυμνὸς. Ares was represented in ancient art as a naked old man. As far as his nakedness went, Jason resembled him, but in manly beauty he was like Apollo. γυμνὸς here probably means "with only a light undergarment," *i.e.* without his cloak, a common usage in Greek.

[2] *i.e.* he stuck his sword into the earth far enough to rest the helmet against the hilt.

[3] *i.e.* planting himself firmly to meet the onset of the bulls. *Cf.* i. 1199, where the same expression is used of Heracles when he sets himself to pull up the tree by its roots.

bellows of braziers now send forth a jet of flame through the holes in the smelting pot,[1] kindling a consuming fire, and now again do cease their blast, while an awful roar goeth up therefrom, when it darts up from below; even so those two bulls did bellow as they breathed from their mouths the rushing fire, and all about Jason ran the consuming flame, striking him like lightning; but the maiden's spells protected him. Then did he catch the ox on his right hand by the top of his horn, and dragged him with all his might and main, till he was near the brazen yoke, and then he threw him down upon the ground on his knees with one quick kick[2] against his brazen hoof. In like manner he tripped the other on his knees as he charged, smitten with one stroke. And he cast from him his broad shield on the earth, and kept those oxen twain where they were fallen on their knees, stepping from side to side, now here, now there, rushing headlong through the flame. But Æetes marvelled at the might of the man. Meantime those sons of Tyndarus,—for so had it been long before ordained for them,—came near, and gave him the yoke from off the ground to cast about them. And he bound it carefully upon their necks, and lifting the brazen pole between them, made fast its pointed tip unto the yoke. Then those twain started back from the fire toward the ship; but he once more took up his shield, and slung it on his back behind, and grasped the weighty helmet, full of sharp teeth, and his resistless spear, wherewith, like some labourer with a Pelasgian goad, he pricked them, thrusting beneath their flanks; and with a firm hand he guided the shapely plough-handle, fashioned of adamant. But the bulls, the while,

[1] *ὅτε μὲν*, answered by *ὅτ' αὖ*. *τρητοῖς χοάνοις*, the *χοάνος* (*χέω*) is the mould into which the liquid metal is poured for casting. Apparently it had holes at the top (*τρητοῖς*, *i.e.* bored through), through which jets of flame leapt up at each blast of the bellows.

[2] *i.e.* Jason kicked the bull's legs from under it.

were exceeding wroth, breathing against him furious flaming fire; and their breath was as the roar of blustering winds, in fear of which sea-faring folk do mostly furl their wide sail.

But yet a little while, and they started in obedience to the spear, and the grim fallow was cleft behind them, broken up by the might of the bulls and the strong ploughman. Terribly groaned the clods withal along the furrows of the plough as they were broken, each a man's burden; and he followed, pressing down the left stilt with heavy tread, while far from him he was casting the teeth along the clods as each was tilled, with many a backward glance, lest the fell crop of earth-born men should rise against him ere he was done; and on toiled those oxen, treading with their brazen hoofs. Now when the third part of day, as it waned from dawn, was still left, when swinked labourers call the sweet unyoking hour to come to them at once, in that hour the lea was finished ploughing by the tireless ploughman, for all it was four plough-gates; and he loosed the plough from the oxen, and scared them in flight o'er the plain. Then went he again unto the ship, while yet he saw the furrows free of the earth-born men. And he drew of the river's stream in his helmet, and quenched his thirst with water; and he bent his knees to supple[1] them, and filled his mighty soul with courage, eager as a wild boar, that whets his tusks against the hunters, while from his angry mouth the foam runs in great flakes to the ground. Lo! now were those earth-born men springing up o'er all the tilth, and the acre of Ares the death-dealer was all bristling with mighty shields and twy-pointed[2] spears and gleaming helmets; and the sheen thereof went flashing through the air from earth beneath

[1] *γνάμψε ἐλαφρά.* The adjective is probably here a predicate, "bent them into suppleness."

[2] *i.e.* spears pointed at both ends.

to Olympus. As when, in the murk of night, after a heavy storm of snow hath fallen on the earth, the winds do scatter the wintry clouds once more, and all the heavenly signs at once are seen shining through the gloom: even so those warriors shone as they grew up above the earth. But Jason remembered the counsel of crafty Medea, and caught up from the plain a great round rock, a fearful quoit for Ares[1] the War-god; four strong men could not have stirred it ever so little from the ground. This did he take in his hand, and threw it very far into their midst with one swing, while himself did boldly couch beneath his shield. And the Colchians gave a mighty cry, like the cry of the sea when it roars on jagged rocks, but on the king Æetes came dumb dismay at the hurtling of that mighty quoit. Then did they like sharp-toothed[2] dogs leap upon it, and with loud yells did rend each other; and they were falling on their mother earth 'neath their own spears, like pines or oaks, which sudden gusts of wind do shake. Like as when a fiery meteor shoots from heaven, with a trail of light behind, a marvel to mankind, whoso see it dart and flash through the darkling air; in such wise rushed the son of Æson on the earth-born men, and he bared his sword from the scabbard, and smote them, mowing them down one upon another, many in the belly and flanks as they were but half risen to the air, and some in the legs as they were rising, others just standing upright, and some as they were even now hastening to the fray. As when some yeoman, when a war hath broken out upon his boundaries, fearful lest men will ravage his fields, seizes in his hand a curved sickle, newly-sharpened, and hastes to cut his crop

[1] *σόλον Ἄρεος, i.e.* a stone big enough to serve Ares for a quoit. Enyalius, or the War-god, a Homeric epithet of Ares; so Enyo is the goddess of war, Lat. Bellona.

[2] *θοοί* = (1) quick, swift, active; (2) sharp, pointed. It occurs in both senses frequently in Apollonius.

unripe, nor waiteth for it to ripen in its season by the beams of the sun; even so did he then cut the crop of earth-born men, and the furrows were filled with blood, as the channels of a spring are filled with water. There they fell; some on their faces, biting with their teeth the rough clods; some upon their backs; others on the palms of their hands and sides; like sea-monsters in shape to behold. And many wounded, or ever they had stept forth from the earth, bowed their damp brows to the ground and rested there, as much of them as had emerged to the air above. Even so shoots newly-planted in an orchard do droop to the ground, snapped from their roots, when Zeus sendeth a torrent of rain, a toil to gardening folk; and heavy grief and bitter sorrow cometh on him who owns the plot of ground and tends the plants. So then o'er the heart of king Æetes stole heavy grief. And he gat him homeward to his town together with his Colchians, musing darkly how he might most quickly meet them.[1]

And daylight died, and Jason's toil was ended.

[1] *i.e.* devising some plan to overreach the heroes, and anticipate their action. *θοώτερον*, *i.e.* more quickly than they expected.

BOOK IV.

ARGUMENT.

Æetes discovers all; but meantime Medea has fled to the Argonauts; and by her aid they have taken the fleece and gone. Absyrtus, son of Æetes, gives chase; but coming up with them is treacherously slain, at the mouth of the Ister, by Jason and Medea; whereat Zeus is angry, but Hera ever befriends them. Thence they come to Circe to be purified of the murder; and they pass through "the Wandering Rocks," and through Scylla and Charybdis, and past the Sirens, all save Butes; and come unto Corcyra, where Medea is saved by Alcinous from the pursuit of the Colchians, and is wedded to Jason. Next they are driven to the Syrtis off Libya, and suffer greatly from thirst. Here Canthus and Mopsus meet their doom; and the rest are saved by Triton and sent upon their way to Crete, where Talus withstands them, only to fall before Medea's magic.

After this they make a straight run to Ægina, and so without further adventure to their home in Thessaly.

BOOK IV.

NOW tell, O Muse, child of Zeus, in thine own words, the toil and plans of the Colchian maiden. For verily my mind within me is swayed perplexedly, as I ponder thereon, whether I am to say, 'twas the sad outcome of bitter infatuation or unseemly panic, that made her leave the tribes of the Colchians.

Æetes, of a truth, amongst the chosen captains of his people was devising sheer [1] treachery against the heroes all night in his halls, in wild fury at the sorry ending of the contest; and he was very sure, that angry sire, that these things were not being accomplished without the aid of his own daughters.

But upon Medea's heart Hera cast most grievous fear, and she trembled, like some nimble fawn, which the barking of hounds hath frighted in the thickets of a deep woodland. For anon she thought, that of a surety her help would never escape her father's eye, and right soon would she fill up her cup of bitterness. And she terrified her handmaids, who were privy thereto; and her eyes were full of fire, and in her ears there rang a fearful sound; and oft would she clutch at her throat, and oft tear the hair upon her head and groan in sore anguish. Yea, and in that hour would the maid have overleapt her doom and died of a poisoned cup, bringing to nought the plans of Hera; but the goddess drove her in panic to fly with the sons of

[1] *αἰπὺν*, strictly = steep, but metaphorically as here, "sheer, utter." Cf. the expressions *αἰπὺς ὄλεθρος*, *αἰπὺς χόλος*.

Phrixus. And her fluttering heart was comforted within her. So she in eager haste poured from the casket all her drugs at once into the folds of her bosom. And she kissed her bed and the posts of the doors on either side, and stroked the walls fondly, and with her hand cut off one long tress and left it in her chamber, a memorial of her girlish days for her mother; then with a voice all choked with sobs she wept aloud, "Ah, mother mine! I leave thee here this one long tress instead of me, and go; so take this last farewell as I go far from hence; farewell Chalciope, farewell to all my home! Would that the sea had dashed thee, stranger, in pieces, or ever thou didst reach the Colchian land!"

So spake she, and from her eyes poured forth a flood of tears. Even as a captive maid stealeth forth from a wealthy house, one whom fate hath lately reft from her country, and as yet knoweth she nought of grievous toil, but a stranger to misery and slavish tasks, she cometh in terror 'neath the cruel hands of a mistress; like her the lovely maiden stole forth swiftly from her home. And the bolts of the doors yielded of their own accord to her touch, springing back at her hurried spells. With bare feet she sped along the narrow paths, drawing her robe with her left hand over her brows to veil her face and fair cheeks, while with her right hand she lifted up the hem of her garment. Swiftly along the unseen track she came in her terror outside the towers of the spacious town, and none of the guard marked her, for she sped on and they knew it not. Then marked she well her way unto the temple, for she was not ignorant of the paths, having wandered thither oft aforetime in quest of corpses and the noxious roots of the earth, as a sorceress must; yet did her heart quake with fear and trembling. Now Titania, goddess of the moon,[1] as she sailed up the distant sky, caught sight of that

[1] The Moon was the child of Hyperion the Titan and Theia.

maid distraught, and savagely she exulted o'er her in words like these, "So I am not the only one to wander to the cave on Latmos; not I alone burn with love for fair Endymion! How oft have I gone hence before thy cunning spells, with thoughts of love, that thou mightest work in peace, in the pitchy night, the sorceries so dear to thee. And now, I trow, hast thou too found a like sad fate, and some god of sorrow hath given thee thy Jason for a very troublous grief. Well, go thy way; yet steel thy heart to take up her load of bitter woe, for all thy understanding."

So spake she; but her feet bare that other hasting on her way. Right glad was she to climb the river's high banks, and see before her the blazing fire, which all night long the heroes kept up in joy for the issue of the enterprise. Then through the gloom, with piercing voice, she called aloud to Phrontis, youngest of the sons of Phrixus, from the further bank; and he, with his brethren and the son of Æson too, deemed it was his sister's voice, and the crew marvelled silently, when they knew what it really was. Thrice she lifted up her voice, and thrice at the bidding of his company cried Phrontis in answer to her; and those heroes the while rowed swiftly over to fetch her. Not yet would they cast the ship's hawsers on the mainland, but the hero Jason leapt quickly ashore from the deck above, and with him Phrontis and Argus, two sons of Phrixus, also sprang to land; then did she clasp them by the knees with both her hands, and spake: "Save me, friends, me most miserable, aye, and yourselves as well from Æetes. For ere now all is discovered, and no remedy cometh. Nay, let us fly aboard the ship, before he mount his swift

[1] Latmos is a hill in Caria, where Endymion dwelt in a cave. He had incurred the anger of Zeus by becoming enamoured of Hera, wherefore he was condemned to sleep for ever; and the Moon saw him asleep and was struck by his beauty, so that she came often to the cavern on Latmos.

horses. And I will give you the golden fleece, when I have lulled the guardian snake to rest; but thou, stranger, now amongst thy comrades take heaven to witness to the promises thou didst make me, and make me not to go away from hence in scorn and shame, for want of friends."

So spake she in her sore distress, and the heart of the son of Æson was very glad; at once he gently raised her up, where she was fallen at his knees, and took her in his arms and comforted her, "God help thee, lady! Be Zeus of Olympus himself witness of mine oath, and Hera, queen of marriage, bride of Zeus, that I will of a truth establish thee as my wedded wife in my house, when we are come on our return to the land of Hellas."

So spake he, and therewith clasped her right hand in his own. Then bade she them row the swift ship with all speed unto the sacred grove, that they might take the fleece and bear it away against the will of Æetes, while yet it was night. Without delay deeds followed words; for they made her embark, and at once thrust out the ship from the shore; and loud was the din, as the heroes strained at their oars. But she, starting back, stretched her hands wildly to the shore; but Jason cheered her with words, and stayed her in her sore grief.

In the hour when huntsmen[1] were shaking sleep from their eyes, men who trust unto their hounds and never sleep away the end part of the night, but shun the light of dawn, lest it smite them too soon with its clear beams, and efface the track and scent of the game; in that hour the son of Æson and the maiden stept from the ship into a grassy spot, called "the Ram's couch," the spot where first he rested his weary knees from bearing on his back the Minyan son of Athamas. Nigh thereto are the foundations of an altar, smirched with soot, which on a day

[1] ἀγρόται is here = ἀγρευται, "huntsmen," *not* "countrymen," as the word properly means.

Phrixus, son of Æolus, did build to Zeus, who aideth fugitives, offering that strange creature with his fleece of gold, even as Hermes had bidden, when of his good will he met him. There it was that the heroes set them down by the counsel of Argus. So they twain went along the path to the sacred grove, in quest of the wondrous oak, whereon the fleece was hung, resting there like a cloud that turns to red in the fiery beams of the rising sun. But right in their way that serpent with his keen sleepless eyes, stretched out his long neck, when he saw them coming, and horribly he hissed, so that the long banks of the river and the grove echoed strangely all around. Even they heard it, who dwelt in the Colchian land very far from Titanian[1] Æa by the mouth of the Lycus, that stream that parteth from the roaring river Araxes, and brings his sacred flood to join the Phasis; and they twain flow on together and pour into the Caucasian[2] sea. And women in their travail arose in terror, and cast their arms in agony about their new-born babes, who cried in their mothers' arms, trembling at the serpent's hiss. As when, above smouldering wood, countless sooty eddies of smoke do whirl, and one upon another rises ever upward from below, hovering aloft in wreaths; so then that monster writhed his endless coils, covered with hard dry scales. But, as he writhed, the maiden came in sight, calling with sweet voice Sleep, highest[3] of gods, to her aid, to charm the fearsome beast; and she called on the queen of the nether world, who roams by night, to grant her a favourable enterprise. And the son of Æson followed in fear. But lo! that snake, charmed by her voice, loosened the giant coil of his long spine, and

[1] The land was so called from the river Titan.

[2] *i.e.* the Euxine, into which the Phasis falls, so called from its vicinity to the Caucasus.

[3] Sleep is first or highest of gods, inasmuch as all must obey its dictates.

stretched out his countless folds, like a dark wave, dumb and noiseless, rolling o'er a sluggish sea; but yet he held his gruesome head on high, eager to seize them both in his deadly jaws; but the maiden dipt a spray of juniper just cut in her thick broth,[1] and sprinkled charms unmixed upon his eyes, chanting the while; and all around him the potent smell of the drug shed slumber, and he let his jaw sink down upon that spot, and far behind him through the trunks of the wood his endless coils were stretched. Then did Jason take the golden fleece from the oak, at the maiden's bidding; while she stood staunchly by him and rubbed the beast's head with her drug, until the voice of Jason bade her turn and come unto the ship, for he was leaving the dusky grove of Ares. As a maiden catches on her fine-wrought robe the rays of the moon at her full,[2] when she soareth above the high-roofed chamber, and her heart within her rejoices at the sight of the lovely light; so then was Jason glad, as he lifted the great fleece in his hands, and o'er his sun-burnt cheeks and brow there settled a flush as of flame from the flashing of the fleece; as is the hide of a yearling ox, or of a hind which hunters call a brocket, even such was the skin of the fleece,[3] all covered with gold and heavy with wool; and the ground sparkled exceedingly before his feet as he went. On strode he with it thrown now over his left shoulder, and hanging from his neck above down to his feet, and now again would he gather it up in his hands; for he feared exceedingly, lest some god or man should meet him and take it from him.

Dawn was spreading o'er the earth, when they came

[1] A thick hell-broth of magical drugs, such as the witches in "Macbeth" are represented as brewing.

[2] To see the moon at her full was a lucky omen for a young bride.

[3] ἄωτον is strictly the best or choicest of its kind, the pick of the whole. Here it is used of the finest wool. Homer employs it in the same sense, and also of the finest linen, λίνοιο λεπτὸν ἄωτον.

unto their company; and the young men were astonied at sight of the great fleece, flashing like the lightning of Zeus. And each man was eager to touch it and take it in his hands. But the son of Æson checked them all, and o'er it cast a new-made robe; then he took and set the maiden on the stern, and thus spake amongst them all: "No longer, friends, shrink now from faring homeward. For now is the need accomplished easily by the plans of the maiden, for which we dared this grievous voyage in toil and sorrow. Her of her own free will I will bear to my home to be my wedded wife; and do ye protect her, for that she was a ready champion of all Achæa and of you. For surely, an I think aright, Æetes will come to stop us with an armèd throng from getting sea-ward from out the river. So one half of you throughout the ship row at the oars, seated man by man, while the other half hold up your oxhide shields before them, a ready defence against the darts of the enemy, and fight ye for our return. For now, my friends, we hold in our hands our children and our country and our aged parents; and the fate of Hellas hangeth on our enterprise, to win deep shame or haply great renown."

So spake he, and did on his harness of war; and they cried aloud, filled with a strange desire. But he drew his sword from the scabbard and cut the stern-cables of the ship, and nigh to the maiden he set himself to fight by[1] the pilot Ancæus, with his helmet on his head; then on sped the ship, as they hasted to row her ever onward and clear of the river.

But now was Medea's love and her work known to proud Æetes and to all the Colchians, and they gathered to the assembly in their harness. Countless as the waves, that raise their crests before the wind on a stormy sea, or as the

[1] *παρεβασκε*, "set himself to fight by" = *ἦν παραβάτης*. The *παραβάτης* was the warrior who stood beside the charioteer. Cf. Homer, Iliad, ii. 104.

leaves, that fall to earth through the wood with its thick branches in the month when leaves are shed, and who shall tell their number? in such countless throngs they flocked along the river-banks, with eager cries; but their king Æetes towered o'er all with his steeds in his shapely car, those steeds which Helios did give him, swift as the breath of the wind; in his left hand he held his round shield, and in the other a long pine-torch,[1] and his huge sword was ready drawn before him, and Absyrtus grasped the reins of the horses. But the ship was cleaving her way out to sea already, driven on by the stout rowers and the downward current of the mighty river. Then the king in sore distress raised his hands and called on Helios and Zeus to witness their evil deeds; and forthwith uttered he fearful threats against all his people, if they should not bring the maiden with their own hands, either upon shore or finding the ship on the swell of the open sea, that he might sate his eager soul with vengeance for all these things, while they should know and endure in their own persons all his fury and all his revenge.

So spake Æetes, and on the self-same day the Colchians launched their ships and put the tackling in them, and the self-same day sailed out to sea; thou wouldst not have thought it was a fleet of ships so much as a vast flight of birds, screaming o'er the sea in flocks.

Swift blew the wind by the counsels of the goddess Hera, that so Ææan Medea might come most quickly to the Pelasgian land to plague the house of Pelias; and on the third day at dawn they bound the cables of the ship to the cliffs of the Paphlagones, at the mouth of the river Halys; for Medea bade them go ashore and appease Hecate with sacrifice. Now that which the maiden did prepare

[1] πεύκη strictly = the fir-tree; then anything made of it, as here "a torch." Æetes intended to fire Argo first of all, and cut off all escape.

and offer in sacrifice, let no man know, nor let my heart urge me to sing thereof. I shudder to utter it. Verily that altar which the heroes builded on the strand unto the goddess, abideth from that day forth until now, for men of later days to see.

Anon the son of Æson minded him of Phineus, and likewise did the other heroes, how that he told them they should find a different course from Æa, but his meaning was hidden from them all. But to their eager ears did Argus made harangue: "Let us now to Orchomenus, whither that unerring seer, whom ye met aforetime, foretold that ye would come. For there is another course, well known unto the priests of the immortal gods, who are sprung from Tritonian Thebe.[1] While as yet the stars, which wheel in the firmament, were not; nor yet was any sacred race of Danai to be heard of, but only Apidanean Arcadians, those Arcadians who are said to have lived before ever the moon was, feeding on acorns in the hills; nor as yet was the Pelasgian land ruled by the famed sons of Deucalion;[2] in the days when Egypt, mother of primeval men, was called the rich land of the morning, with that Tritonian river[3] of seven streams, whereby all that land of the morning is watered; for no rain[4] from Zeus doth wet the soil, and yet do crops spring up abundantly at the river's mouth. Yea, and they tell how a man[5] went forth from

[1] Thebe in Egypt. The Egyptian priests were the great repository of all occult knowledge in ancient times.

[2] "The sons of Deucalion" were said to have founded a dynasty in Thessaly, anciently called Pelasgia, from Pelasgus, one of its kings.

[3] Is the Nile.

[4] The theory that rain never falls in Egypt is not authenticated; it does fall occasionally and heavily, though it is true that the rising of the Nile is more to be depended on than the occasional showers.

[5] The king Sesonchosis, sometimes called Sesostris. Herodotus in his account of Egypt gives interesting details respecting this Egyptian monarch.

thence upon his travels through all Europe and Asia, trusting in the might and strength of his people and in his own courage; and, as he went, he founded many a town, some whereof men haply still inhabit, and some maybe no longer; for many a long age hath passed since then.

But Æa still abides steadfast, and the children of those men, whom that king did plant therein to dwell there; these men preserve writings of their fathers, graved upon pillars, whereon are all the ways and limits of sea and dry land, far and wide, for those who come thither. Now there is a river, farthest branch of Ocean, broad and very deep for e'en a merchant ship to pass thereon; they call it Ister,[1] and far away they have traced it on their chart; for a while it cleaveth through the boundless tilth in one solitary stream, for its springs roar and seethe far away beyond the north wind's breath in the Rhipæan mountains.

But when it enters the boundaries of Thrace and Scythia, thenceforth in two streams it pours one half its waters by one channel into the Ionian sea, while the residue it sends, after the division, through a deep bay that openeth into the Trinacrian[2] sea, which lieth along your coast, if[3] in very truth the Achelous flows forth from your land."

So spake he; and the goddess vouchsafed them a lucky sign, at sight whereof all gave glory to her, that this was their appointed path. For before them went a trail of heavenly radiance, where they might pass. So there they left the son of Lycus, and sailed in gladness of heart across the sea, with canvas set, their eyes upon the hills of the

[1] The Ister (modern Danube), according to Apollonius, passing through Scythia and Thrace, becomes two streams, one of which falls into the Euxine, the other into the Tyrrhenian sea.

[2] Τριvακρίου, *i.e.* Sicilian, so called from the three headlands of Sicily, Pachynus, Lilybæum, and Pelorus (*τρι-ἄκραι*).

[3] *εἰ ἐτεὸν δή*. Argus only knew of Hellas by hearsay; he is not therefore certain if he has heard aright about the river Achelous.

Paphlagones. But they did not round Carambis, for the winds and the blaze of heavenly fire abode with them, till they entered Ister's mighty stream.

Now some of the Colchians, after a vain search, had sailed through the Cyanean rocks into Pontus, while others had made for the river under the command of Absyrtus, and he had withdrawn a space and entered the "fair mouth." So he had just anchored before them beyond a neck of land inside the furthest bay of the Ionian sea; for Ister floweth round an island by name Peuce, triangular in shape, with its base unto the sea shore, and a narrow angle toward the river's stream; around it the river branches into two channels. One they call the mouth of Narex, the other below the bottom of the island, call they the "fair mouth"; and here it was that Absyrtus and his Colchians put in and anchored in haste; while the heroes sailed further up-stream to the top of the island. And in the water-meads the shepherds of the country left good store of sheep, in fear of the ships, for they thought them monsters coming forth from the teeming deep. For they had never seen sea-faring ships anywhere before, nor yet had the Scythians, who are mixed with the Thracians, nor the Sigynni, nor yet the Graucenii, nor the Lindi who dwell next to these on the great Laurian steppes.

Now when they had passed by the mountain of Anchurus and the rock of Cauliacus, a little space from that mountain, round which the Ister parts in twain and rolls his full tide this way and that, and past that Laurian plain; then did the Colchians go forth into the Cronian [1] sea, and cut off all the routes that they might not escape them. But the heroes reached the river after them, and passed close to the two Brygean [2] isles of Artemis, where on the

[1] The Adriatic, so called because Cronos had lived upon its shores.

[2] Βρυγηίδας. The Brygians were a savage Thracian tribe, worshipping Artemis.

one was a sacred building, and on the other they did land, being ware of the host of Absyrtus; for the Colchians had left those islands within the river void of cities as they were, in awe of the daughter of Zeus; though the others, which guarded the passages to the sea, were crowded with their folk; and so it was that Absyrtus left his host upon the headlands, nigh to the isles, between the river Salangon and the Thracian [1] land.

There would the handful of Minyæ have yielded then in pitiful fray to their more numerous foes; but ere that they made a treaty and covenant, avoiding the dire quarrel; they were still to keep fairly the golden fleece, since Æetes himself had so promised them, if they should fulfil their tasks, whether they did wrest it from him by guile or haply in the open, against his will; but for Medea,—for there was the quarrel,—they were to deliver her to the virgin child of Leto apart from their company, until one of the kings, that defend justice, should decide whether she must go again unto her father's house, or follow the chieftains to the land of Hellas.

Now when the maiden inly mused on each thing, verily sharp anguish shook her heart unceasingly, and she called Jason apart from his crew and led him aside, till they were far withdrawn; then to his face she told her piteous tale, "Son of Æson, what is this purpose ye design together about me? hath thy triumph cast such exceeding forgetfulness on thee, and dost thou pay no heed to all that thou didst promise in thine hour of need? where are thy oaths by Zeus, the god of suppliants? where are all thy honied promises fled? for which, in shameful wise, with shameless will, I have put far from me my country, my glorious home, my parents too, all that I held most dear; and all alone am I being carried far over the sea with the sad

[1] Νέστιδος, *i.e.* Thracian. The Nestus is a small river in Thrace, dividing it from Macedonia.

king-fishers, for the sake of thy troubles, that by mine aid thou mightest accomplish in safety thy toils with the bulls and the earth-born warriors. Lastly, 'twas by my foolish help thou didst take the fleece when it was found. But I have spread a foul reproach on the race of women. Lo! I thought I should come with thee to the land of Hellas as thy bride, thy wife, and sister dear. Oh! save me with all good will! leave me not apart from thee, whilst thou goest to the kings. Nay, save me as I am, and let that just and sacred bond, that we twain made, be firmly tied; else do thou here at once cleave through this throat with thy sword, that I may receive the gift my mad passion has deserved. Ah! woe is me! if yon king, whose judgment ye await in this your bitter covenant, should decide that I am my brother's. How shall I come before my father? Will not my fame be passing fair? what vengeance, what grievous torture shall I not endure in agony for the awful deeds that I have done? and thou, shalt thou find the return thou longest for? No, that may the bride of Zeus, queen of the world, in whom is thy joy, never bring to pass! And some day mayest thou remember even me, when thou art racked with anguish; and may the fleece, like a dream, float away from thee into darkness on the wings of the wind. Yea, and may my avenging spirit chase thee anon from thy fatherland; so terrible is my fate through thy cruelty. Nor is it ordained that these curses fall fruitless to the ground, for thou hast sinned indeed against a mighty oath, without pity; nay, ye shall not long at your ease wink the eye in mockery of me hereafter, for all your covenant."

So spake she, in the heat of her vehement rage; for she was longing to fire the ship, and tear it all asunder, and then to throw herself upon the devouring flame. But Jason, though somewhat afraid, made answer thus with soothing words: "God help thee, lady! stay thine hand. These things are not after mine own heart. But we seek some delay from the conflict, so thick is the cloud of furious foes around us for thy sake. For all who dwell in this land are eager to help Absyrtus, that they may bring thee home again unto thy father, like some captive maid. And we, if we meet them in battle, shall all be slain ourselves by a hateful doom; and that surely will be a grief yet more bitter, if we die and leave thee a prey in their hands. Now this our covenant shall accomplish a cunning wile, whereby we will bring Absyrtus to destruction. And they who dwell around will never come against us for thy sake after all, to pleasure the Colchians, without their prince, who is both thy champion and thy brother; nor will I shrink from fighting them face to face, if so be they will not let us sail forth."

So spake he, soothing her; but she let fall a deadly[1] speech: "Hearken now. Needs must one in sorry case devise a sorry plan; for at the first was I led astray by a mistake, and evil were the desires I had from heaven. Do thou in the turmoil ward off from me the spears of the Colchians, and I will entice him[2] to come into your hands, and do thou welcome him with gladdening gifts, if haply I can persuade the heralds to depart and bring him all by himself to agree to my proposals. Then, if this deed is to thy mind, slay him and join in fray with the Colchians; 'tis nought to me."

So they twain agreed and planned great treachery against Absyrtus, and they gave him many a gift for stranger's welcome, and amongst them that dark robe divine of Hypsipyle; the robe which the goddess Graces had made with their own hands for Dionysus in sea-girt Naxos, and he gave it afterwards to his son Thoas, who left it in turn

[1] *i.e.* a speech that would bring death to someone—in this case to Absyrtus—so that it comes to be predicative or prolative.

[2] *i.e.* Absyrtus.

to Hypsipyle, and she gave that robe too, a fair-wrought stranger's gift with many another wonder, unto the son of Æson for to take with him. Never wouldst thou satisfy thy sweet longing in stroking it or gazing thereupon. And the smell thereof was likewise wondrous sweet, from the day on which the prince of Nysa[1] himself lay down thereon, flushed with wine and nectar, with the fair form of Minos' daughter in his arms, whom on a day Theseus had left in the isle of Naxos, when she followed him from Crete.

Now when Medea had declared her meaning to the heralds, so as to persuade them to depart, as soon as Absyrtus came by agreement to the temple of the goddess and night's black pall was over all, that so she might devise with him a cunning plan whereby to take the fleece of gold, and come again unto the house of Æetes; for, said she, the sons of Phrixus gave her by force unto the strangers to bear away. Thus did she persuade them, sprinkling the air and the breeze with magic drugs, such as can draw the wild beast from the pathless hill, be he never so far away.

O cruel Love, man's chiefest bane and curse! from thee proceed deadly feuds and mourning and lamentation; yea, and countless sorrows beside all these are by thee stirred up. Up, and arm thee against the foemen's sons, thou deity, as in the day thou didst inspire Medea, with her fell murderous thoughts. But how did she slay Absyrtus by an evil doom when he came to her? For that must our song tell next.

When they had left her in the isle of Artemis, as had been agreed, then did these anchor their ships apart from one another; but that prince, Jason, went unto an ambush to await Absyrtus and his company. But he, tricked by their promises so dire for him, rowed quickly in his ship

[1] Dionysus, who found Ariadne on the island of Naxos, after her desertion by Theseus.

across the gulf of sea, as the night grew dark, and landed on the sacred isle. Straight on his way he went alone, and made trial of his sister with words, even as a tender child tries a torrent in winter, which not even strong men can pass; if haply she would devise some guile against the strangers. So they twain agreed together on all points, when on a sudden the son of Æson leapt from the thick ambush, clutching in his hand a naked sword; quickly the maiden turned away her eyes, covering them with her veil, that she might not see the blood of her brother when he was smitten. Him did Jason strike from his ambuscade, as a butcher strikes a mighty bull with strong horns, hard by the temple, which the Brygians, who dwell on the mainland opposite, once had built for Artemis. There at its threshold he fell upon his knees, but as the hero breathed out his soul with his dying breath, he caught up in his hands black blood from the wound, and dyed with crimson his sister's silvery veil and robe, as she shrunk from him. But a pitiless spirit of vengeance, irresistible, gave one quick look askance at the murderous deed they wrought. Then the hero, the son of Æson, first cut off some limbs[1] of the murdered man, and thrice licked up some blood, and thrice spat the pollution from his mouth, for so must they make expiation who have murdered a man by treachery. Then he buried the clammy corpse in the ground, where to this day lie his bones amongst the Absyrtians.[2]

In the same hour the heroes, seeing before them a blazing torch, the signal which the maiden raised for them

[1] Those who had committed murder cut off certain extremities of the murdered one, by way of averting the curse of bloodshed. These they hung as charms about their necks, and also performed certain other ceremonies as here mentioned.

[2] Ἀψυρτεῦσιν. The followers of Absyrtus were afraid to return to Æetes after the murder of his son, so they settled in Illyria, near the Ceraunian mountains, under the name of Absyrtians.

to cross, laid their ship alongside the Colchian barque, and slew the crew thereof, as hawks drive flocks of doves in confusion, or fierce lions a great flock of sheep, when they have leapt upon the fold. Not one of them escaped death, but they fell on the whole crew, destroying them as fire doth; at the last came Jason up, eager to help them, but they had no need of his succour; but were already anxious on his account. Then they sat them down and took sage counsel about the voyage; and as they mused thereon came the maiden to join them, and Peleus first made harangue: "Lo! I bid you embark now, while it is yet night, upon the ship, and take the passage opposite to that which the enemy hold; for at dawn, as soon as they perceive all, methinks there is no argument which will urge them to pursue us further, so as to prevail with them; but they will part asunder in grievous quarrels, as men do who have lost their king. And when once the folk are divided, 'twill be an easy route for us, or indeed for any who come hither hereafter."

So spake he, and the young men approved the word of the son of Æacus. So they went quickly aboard and bent to their oars unceasingly, until they came to the sacred isle of Electra, chiefest of isles, nigh to the river Eridanus.

Now the Colchians when they learnt the death of their prince, were right eager to search the Cronian sea throughout for Argo and the Minyæ. But Hera restrained them by fearful thunderings and lightnings from the sky. And they ended by being afraid of their own homes in the Cytæan land for fear of Æetes' savage fury. So they came to land in different places and settled there securely. Some landed on those very islands, on which the heroes had halted; and there they dwell, called after Absyrtus; others built a fenced city by the deep black stream of the Illyrian river, where is the tomb of Harmonia and Cadmus, settling amongst the Encheleans; and others dwell upon the mountains, which are called "the Thunderers," from the day that the thunder of Zeus the son of Cronos stayed them from going to the island over against them.

But the heroes, when now their return seemed assured them, did then bind their cables on the shore of the Hylleans and go forth. For there be groups of islands scattered there, making the passage through them hard for sailors. But the Hylleans no more devised enmity against them, as before; but of themselves did further their voyage, getting as their guerdon Apollo's mighty tripod. For Phœbus gave to the son of Æson tripods twain, to carry to that far country, when he journeyed thither in obedience to an oracle, on the day when he came to sacred Pytho to enquire about this very voyage; and it was ordained that wheresoever these were set up, that land should never be ravaged by the attack of foemen. Wherefore to this day that tripod is buried in yon land near the pleasant city of Hyllus, deep beneath the soil, that it may ever be hidden from mortal ken.

But they found not king Hyllus still living there, whom comely Melite bare to Heracles in the land of the Phæacians. For Heracles came hither to the house of Nausithous and to Macris, the nurse of Dionysus, to wash away the awful murder of his children; there did that hero vanquish in love's warfare the daughter of the river Ægæus, Melite, the water-nymph, and she bare strong Hyllus. But he, when he grew up, cared not to abide in the island itself, under the eye of Nausithous, its prince, but went o'er the Cronian sea, having gathered to him the people of the Phæacians who dwelt there; for the hero Nausithous helped him on his way; there did he settle, and was slain by the Mentores, as he stood up to do battle for the oxen of his field.

But, ye goddesses, how came Argo's wondrous pennon in

clear view outside the sea, about the Ausonian[1] land and the Ligystian islands, which are called "the line of isles?" what need, what business brought her so far away? what breezes bare them hither?

Zeus, I trow, the king of gods, was seized with fury at their deed, when Absyrtus was mightily o'erthrown; but yet he ordained that they should wash away the guilt of blood by the counsels of Ææan Circe, and after first enduring countless woes should return. Now none of the chieftains was ware thereof; but starting from the land of Hyllus they hasted far on their way, and they left on the lee those islands of the Liburni that lie in order on the sea, peopled formerly by Colchians, Issa and Dusceladus and lovely Pityeia. And, next to them, they came unto Corcyra, where Poseidon had settled the daughter of Asopus, Corcyra of the fair tresses, far from the land of Phlius, whence he had snatched her in his love; and sailors, seeing it rise darkly from the main with black woodland all around, do call it Corcyra the Black. Next passed they Melite, rejoicing greatly at the gentle breeze, and steep Cerossus, and Nymphæa on the far horizon, where queen Calypso, daughter of Atlas, had her home; and lo! they deemed they saw the shadowy "hills of thunder." Then was Hera ware of the angry counsels and the heavy wrath of Zeus for their sake; and forasmuch as she was planning the fulfilment of that voyage, she did stir up head-winds,[2] whereby they were caught and carried back upon the rocky isle of Electra.

[1] Ἀυσονίην, *i.e.* Italy. As a matter of fact, Apollonius is guilty of an anachronism in using this name for Italy in the time of the Argonauts, for it took the title in later times from Auson, the son of Odysseus and Calypso.

Λιγυστίδας. These islands are three in number, and lie in a row off the coast of Italy.

[2] Hera brought them by contrary winds to the island of Electra, in order that Jason and Medea might there be purified by Circe of the blood of Absyrtus.

Anon from out the hollow ship, in mid course, the oaken beam from Dodona, which Athene had fitted down the middle of the keel, found a tongue and cried out in human voice. And deadly fear came on them as they heard the voice, that told of Zeus's grievous wrath. For it said they should not escape a passage o'er a lengthy sea, nor troublous tempests, unless Circe purged them of the ruthless murder of Absyrtus; and it bade Polydeuces and Castor pray to the deathless gods to grant a passage first across the Ausonian sea, wherein they should find Circe, daughter of Perse and Helios.

So cried Argo in the gloom; and they, the sons of Tyndarus, arose, and raised their hands to the immortals, praying for each and all; for deep dismay was come upon the other Minyan heroes. But the ship sped on apace; and they entered far into the stream of Eridanus, where on a day Phaethon, smitten through the breast with a blazing bolt, fell scorched from the chariot of Helios into the mouth of that deep sheet of water, and it belches forth heavy clouds of steam from his wound that still is smouldering. No bird can spread his light pinions and cross that water, but half-way it flutters and then plunges in the flame. Round about the daughters of the Sun[1] sadly raise their dirge of woe, as they dance round the tall poplars; and from their eyes they shed upon the ground bright drops of amber, which dry up on the sand beneath the sun's heat; but when the swollen billows of the dark mere do dash against the rocks before the blast of the noisy wind, then are they rolled all together along the billowy tide into the Eridanus. And the Celts have set this legend to them, how that they

[1] The daughters of the Sun are represented as ever weeping for the death of their brother Phaethon, who was slain by the thunderbolt of Zeus, for Phaethon had persuaded his father Helios to let him drive his chariot for one day, but he had proved unable to manage the steeds, and had endangered the safety of the universe.

are the tears of Apollo, son of Leto, hurried away in the swirling stream, all those many tears he shed the day he came to the sacred race of the Hyperboreans,[1] leaving radiant heaven at the chiding of his father, wroth at the slaying of his son, whom divine Coronis bare in rich Lacereia by the mouth of the Amyrus. So runs the legend 'mongst those folk. But these felt no desire for meat or drink, nor did their spirit turn to mirth. But all day, I trow, were they worn out and grievously weakened by the foul stench, which the streams of Eridanus sent up unceasingly from smouldering Phaethon; and all night too they heard the shrill lament of the daughters of the Sun, loudly wailing; and as they mourned their tears were borne along the waters, as it were drops of oil.

Thence they entered the deep stream of Rhodanus, which comes to join the Eridanus; and at their meeting doth the water roar in wild commotion. Now that river, rising in a land very far away, where are the portals and the habitation of Night, doth pour himself on one side upon the ocean's cliffs, on another doth he fall into the Ionian sea, while by yet a third channel he casts his stream through seven mouths into the Sardinian sea and its boundless bay. Thence they sailed into stormy lakes, which open out along the vast mainland of the Celts, and there would they have met with a foul mishap. For a certain off-stream was bearing them into the ocean-gulf, and they not knowing were about to sail thereinto; whence they would never have won a safe return. But Hera sped forth from heaven and shouted from the Hercynian rock; and one and all did quake with fear at her shout, for terribly rumbled the wide firmament. So

[1] Apollo left Olympus and went to live among the Hyperboreans, the most remote of men, when Zeus had slain his son Æsculapius, because he, *i.e.* Æsculapius, by his physician's art had raised men to life after death.

they turned back before the goddess, noting now the way along which they must go for their return. At last they reached the sea-coast by the counsels of Hera, passing through the coasts of countless Celtic and Ligyan tribes, without being attacked. For about them the goddess shed a thick mist all day as they went. So they sailed through the river's midmost mouth and came unto "the line of islands," saved through the intercession of the sons of Zeus; wherefore are altars and temples builded there for ever, for it was not that voyage alone they did attend to succour; but to them Zeus vouchsafed to aid the ships also of future mariners. After leaving "the line of islands" they sailed to the isle of Æthalia, and there[1] upon its shingly beach they wiped off in the lists much sweat; and the pebbles on the strand were strewn as it were with skin; and there lie their quoits and tattered raiment, wondrous many; so that the harbour therein is called Argo's haven after them.

Quickly they sailed thence across the ocean swell with their eyes upon the Tyrsenian cliffs of Ausonia, and came unto the famous harbour of Ææa, and they drew nigh and fastened the ship's hawsers on the rocks. There they found Circe washing her head in the sea-water, for greatly was she scared by the visions of the night. Her chamber and the walls of her house seemed to be all running with blood, and fire was devouring her store of drugs, wherewith afore she bewitched strangers, whoso came hither; and she did quench the fire's bright blaze with blood of

[1] It is far from clear what the meaning of these lines is. If we suppose that the Argonauts held a contest of games, though this is not definitely stated, it is possible to extract a meaning; *i.e.* *καμόντες* = as they strove in the lists, while the next line might refer to the practice of using the strigil or body-scraper by athletes to remove dirt and sweat after hard exercise. Lastly, the mention of *σόλοι*, "quoits," then becomes intelligible, and the allusion to *τρύχεα*, "tattered garments," is natural enough in the same connection.

murdered men, scooping it up in her hands; and so she ceased from deadly fear.[1] Wherefore so soon as dawn was come, she arose and would wash her hair and raiment in the waters of the sea. And beasts, that resembled not ravening brutes of prey, nor yet had the form of men, but each wore his fellow's limbs in medley strange, came trooping forth, like sheep when they throng from the fold at the heels of the shepherd. Such creatures earth herself produced from the primeval mud,[2] compact of divers kinds of limbs, when as yet she was not made solid by the thirsty air, nor yet had gotten one drop of moisture from the rays of the scorching sun; but time put these forms together and led them forth in rows; e'en such were the shapeless things that followed her. And exceeding wonder seized the heroes; and anon, as each man gazed upon the form and face of Circe, easily he guessed she was a sister of Æetes.

Now when she had sent from her the terror of her dream by night, at once she started back again, and she bade them follow her in her subtlety, caressing them with her hand. Now his company abode there steadfastly at the bidding of the son of Æson, but he took with him the Colchian maiden; and they twain went with her along the road, until they came to the hall of Circe; then that lady bade them sit on fair seats, in great amaze at their coming. But those twain without a word or sound darted to her hearth and sat them down, as is the custom of sad sup-

[1] λῆξεν ὀλοοῖο φόβοιο. λήγω is here intransitive, "she ceased from deadly fear." But whether it means that her efforts to quench the flame were successful and so she ceased to be afraid, or whether her terror was so acute that she stopped from what she was doing in consequence, is hard to determine. The Greek is in favour of the first rendering, but the context points the other way, otherwise why did she purify herself in the morning?

[2] προτέρης ἐξ ἰλύος, the primeval mud from which all things were made in the beginning. Cf. "princeps limum" of Horace.

pliants, and Medea buried her face in her hands, but Jason fixed his great hilted sword in the ground, wherewith he slew the son of Æetes, but his eye would never look her full in the face. In that moment Circe knew, 'twas murder and blood-guiltiness from which they fled. Wherefore in reverence for the ordinance of Zeus, the suppliants' god, who is a very jealous god, yet mightily succoureth murderers, she offered the sacrifice, wherewith ruthless suppliants purify themselves when they come to the altar. First, to release them from the unatoned bloodshed, she held above their heads the young of a sow, whose dugs were still full of milk after her litter, and wetted their hands in the blood when she had cut its skin; next made she atonement with other libations, calling on Zeus the while to purify them; for he is the champion of blood-guilty suppliants. And all that she used in the cleansing did attendant nymphs, who brought each thing to her, bear forth from the house. But she within stood by the hearth and burned thereon, praying the while, a soothing sop of honey, oil, and meal with nought of wine[1] therein, that she might stay the grim spirits of vengeance from their fury, and that Zeus might be propitious and favourable to them both, whether they sought atonement for hands defiled with a stranger's blood or haply for a kinsman, themselves his kith and kin.

Now when all her task was duly done, then did she raise them up, and seated them on polished chairs, and herself sat near facing them. And straightway she questioned them straitly of their business and their voyage, and whence they came to her land and house, to sit them down as suppliants in such wise. For lo! a hideous re-

[1] Offerings to the Eumenides must contain no wine, being composed of water, milk, and honey. The Erinnys of the murdered man had to be appeased.

membrance of her dream came o'er her, as her heart mused thereon; and she yearned to hear the voice of the maiden, her kinswoman, soon as ever she saw her lift her eyes from the ground. For all the race of Helios was manifest at sight, for they shot far in front of them a gleam, as it had been of gold, from the twinkling of their eyes. Then did she, the daughter of grave Æetes, make soft answer in the Colchian tongue to all her questioning, telling of the expedition and the journey of the heroes, and all their suffering in their hurried toils, and how she had sinned at the bidding of her sorrowing sister, and how she fled with the sons of Phrixus from the awful horrors her father might inflict; but of the murder of Absyrtus she was careful not to speak. But nowise did it escape the ken of Circe; yet for all that she pitied the weeping maiden, and thus unto her said, "Unhappy girl! verily an evil and a shameful return thou hast devised. No long time, I trow, shalt thou escape Æetes' fearful wrath; for soon will he go even to the homes in the land of Hellas, to take vengeance for the murder of his son; seeing that thou hast wrought a terrible deed. But, forasmuch as thou art my suppliant and of my race, I will devise no further evil against thee at thy coming hither; but get thee from my house in company with this stranger, this fellow whom thou hast taken unbeknown to thy father; entreat me not, sitting at my hearth, for I will not consent to thy counsels and thy shameful flight."

So spake she; and grievous sorrow laid hold upon Medea, and she wrapt her robe about her eyes and wept; till the hero took her by the hand and led her forth to the door of the hall, quivering with terror; so they left the house of Circe.

But they escaped not the knowledge of the wife of Zeus, the son of Cronos; but Iris told her, when she marked them going from the hall. For Hera bade her watch them closely, until they came unto the ship, and again she spake and hailed her, " Dear Iris, now, if ever thou hast accomplished my bidding, come, speed thee on swift wings and bid Thetis arise from out the deep, and come hither to me. For need of her aid is come upon me; and next get thee to the cliffs, where the brazen anvils of Hephæstus clang to the blows of his heavy hammers, and bid him lull his fiery blasts to rest, until Argo has sailed by those cliffs. Then go to Æolus, Æolus who rules the wind, children of the upper air,[1] and tell him this my mind, that he make all wind to cease under heaven, and suffer no breeze to roughen the sea; only let a favouring west-wind blow, that the heroes may come to the Phæacian isle of Alcinous."

So spake she; and forthwith Iris darted from Olympus, cleaving her way, with her light wings outspread. And she plunged into the Ægean sea, just where the home of Nereus is. And she came to Thetis first, and told her tale as Hera bade, and roused her to go to her. Next went she to Hephæstus; and quickly stayed him from his iron hammers, and his sooty bellows ceased from their blast. Lastly came she to Æolus, famous son of Hippotas. And even while she was telling him her message, and resting her swift knees from her course, did Thetis leave Nereus and her sisters and go from the sea to Olympus, unto the goddess Hera, who made her sit beside her, and declared her speech; "Hearken now, lady Thetis, to that which I fain would tell thee. Thou knowest how dear to my heart is the hero son of Æson, and those others that do help him in his toil; for 'twas I alone, that saved them in their passage through the wandering rocks, where erst dire tempests roared and the billows boiled round the rugged rocks. But now awaits them a journey past the mighty

[1] αἰθρηγενέεσσιν either = "born in the clear air," or "making the air clear."

rock of Scylla, and Charybdis, horribly belching. Nay, hear me; for lo! 'twas I that with mine own hands tended and caressed thee from thine infancy above all others, who dwell within the sea, because thou wouldst not yield to the importunities of Zeus. For he is ever bent on such deeds, to lie with women, be they mortal or immortal. But thou, from reverence of me and from fear, didst avoid him; wherefore he then did swear a mighty oath, that thou shouldst never be called the wife of an immortal god. Yet did he lie in wait for thee an unwilling mate, and would not give thee up, until aged Themis told him all, how that of a surety it was ordained that thou shouldst bear a son better than his father; wherefore he gave thee up, for all his strong desire, in fear that another should be his rival and rule the deathless gods, yea, and for ever wrest away his power. But I gave thee the best[1] of mortal men to be thy husband, that thou mightest find the joys of wedlock and bear children; and to thy marriage-feast I bade the gods, one and all, and with mine own hand raised the wedding torch,[2] to repay that thy generous respect. But come now, I will tell thee a tale that lieth not; whenso thy son cometh to the Elysian plain, he, I mean, whom water-nymphs now do tend in the home of the Centaur Chiron, though he longeth for thy milk; needs must[3] he be the husband of Medea, daughter of Æetes; do thou, then, as a mother, help thy future daughter, and Peleus as well. Why is thy wrath so firmly rooted? 'Tis blindness; for even to gods will blindness come. Verily I do think that

[1] *i.e.* Peleus, the father of Achilles.

[2] I performed for you the most sacred rite of bearing the nuptial torch at your marriage, a custom usually performed by the mother of the bride.

[3] An oracle had declared that in the after-world Achilles should wed Medea, so Thetis, if she now lends her aid to them, will only be helping her future daughter-in-law.

at my bidding Hephæstus will cease to make his furious fire burn, and Æolus, son of Hippotas, will check the winds' swift flight, all save the steady west, until they come to the havens of the Phæacians; so do thou devise for them a painless return. My only fear is for thy rocks and mountainous billows, which, with the aid of thy other sisters, thou canst turn aside. Oh! leave them not to drift helplessly into Charybdis, lest with one gulp she take them all down, nor let them come to Scylla's foul lair, murderous Scylla of Ausonia, whom Hecate that roameth by night, bare to Phorcus, whom men call 'the Mighty One,' lest haply she dart upon them with her fearful jaws and slay the chosen heroes. But keep thou the ship just in the course where there shall be a hair-breadth escape from destruction."

So spake she; and Thetis answered her thus; "If, of a truth, the furious raging fire and the stormy winds shall cease, verily I too will with confidence promise to save the ship from the wave's attack too, while the west wind is piping. But 'tis time to set out upon my long weary way, till I shall come unto my sisters, who shall help me, and to the place where the ship's cables are fastened, that at dawn they may bethink them of winning their return."

Therewith she shot down from the sky and plunged amid the eddies of the deep blue sea, and she called other Nereids, her own sisters, to her aid, and they heard her voice and came together. Then Thetis rehearsed the bidding of Hera, and sent them all at once to the Ausonian sea. But herself, swifter than the twinkling of an eye, or the rays of the sun, when he riseth high above the horizon, sped quickly on her way through the water, till she reached the Ææan cliff of the Tyrsenian mainland. There she found the heroes by the ship, taking their pastime with quoits and archery, and she drew near and took Peleus, son of Æacus, by the hand, for he was her husband, but no man might see her at all; only to his eye did she appear, and thus spake she: "Abide no longer now sitting on the Tyrsenian strand, but at dawn loose the hawsers of the swift ship, in obedience to Hera, your champion. For at her command my Nereid maids are met, to send your ship in safety, and with all speed through the rocks which are called 'the Wanderers.' For that is your proper route. But do thou point me out to no man, what time thou seest me present with these; lay that to heart, lest thou anger me in more downright earnest than ever thou hast afore."

Therewith she plunged unseen into the depths of the sea, and sore grief smote Peleus, for he had never seen her come, since first she left her bridal chamber in anger, when noble Achilles was yet a babe. For the goddess ever used to wrap about his mortal body fiery flame through the night, and by day she would anoint his tender skin with ambrosia, that he might become immortal, and that she might ward off hateful old age from his body. But Peleus saw his dear son gasping in the flame, and he sprang from his bed with a cry of horror at the sight, fond fool! but she, when she heard him, cast the screaming babe headlong to the ground, and herself passed forth from the house in haste, like to a breath of wind or as a dream, and leapt into the sea in anger; and she never came back again. So blank dismay tied up his heart; yet, for all that, he told to his comrades all the bidding of Thetis. And they hurriedly broke off in the midst and ceased their contests, and busied themselves about supper and their pallet beds, whereon, when they had eaten, they slept through the night, as aforetime.

But when Dawn, giver of light, was touching the edge of heaven, in that hour they went from the land to sit upon the rowing benches, as the swift west-wind came down; and from the deep they hauled up the anchors, glad at heart; and made all the rest of the tackling taut as was needful; and they set the sail, stretching it on the sheets of the yardarm. And a gentle wind carried the ship along. Anon they beheld an island, fair and full of flowers, where the Sirens, clear-voiced daughters of Achelous, used to charm with their sweet singing whoso cast anchor there, and then destroy him. These are the children that comely Terpsichore, one of the Muses, bare to Achelous for his love; once they had the charge of Demeter's noble daughter,[1] while she was yet unwed, singing to her in chorus; at that time were they part bird, part maiden to behold. Ever they keep watch from their outlook, with its fair haven; and many a one have they reft of his joyous return, making him waste away slowly; forthwith then to the heroes they wafted their delicate voice. And these would at once have cast their cables on the rocks, had not Thracian Orpheus, son of Æager, forthwith strung his lyre in his hands, and let a hasty snatch of quick music ring out loudly, that their ears might be dinned as he at the same time swept the twanging chords; and his lyre did drown the voice of the maidens. And the west-wind and the roaring wave, rushing astern, together bore on the ship, while the Sirens raised their ceaseless[2] song. Yet even thus Teleon's goodly son, Butes, did alone elude his fellows and leapt from the polished bench into the sea, for his heart was melted by the clear singing of the Sirens; and he swum through the darkling swell to reach that shore, unhappy mortal! Quickly would they rob him of his return then and there; but the goddess Cypris, who watcheth o'er Eryx,[3] did pity him, and

[1] Proserpine, the daughter of Demeter, who was guarded in her youth by the Sirens on the plains of Enna in Sicily, until Hades carried her away to be his bride.

[2] ἄκριτον either = "unceasing" or "unarranged." Cf. the Latin "incompositum," as applied to natural melody.

[3] In Sicily. Aphrodite had a temple there.

caught him up, while he was yet in the eddying wave, and with kindly aid brought him to a safe dwelling-place on the headland of Lilybeum. So they left the Sirens, holden with grief withal; but other perils of shipwreck, direr still, did await them in the strait, where two seas meet. For on one side arose Scylla's sheer wall of cliff, and on the other Charybdis did spout and roar unceasingly; while in another place "the Wandering rocks" thundered at the buffet of mighty waves, there where in front of them a blazing flame vomited from the top of the crags, high o'er a red-hot rock. And the air was murky with smoke; nor couldst thou have seen the rays of the sun. Moreover, though Hephæstus had ceased from his work, the sea still sent up warm steam. Here the Nereids flocked from all sides to meet them; while the goddess, lady Thetis, took hold of the rudder-blade behind to drag the ship inside "the Wandering rocks." As when dolphins come forth from the sea in fair weather, and gambol in flocks round a speeding ship, now seen in front, and now behind, and yet again alongside, to the joy of the sailors; even so the Nereids darted up and circled in their ranks about the good ship Argo, while Thetis steered her course. Now when they were just coming nigh unto the Wandering rocks, in a moment they drew the edge of their robes up above their white knees, and darting up to the very top of the cliffs and on to the beach, ranged themselves in rows on either side. And the stream smote upon the ship's side, and the wave, rising furiously about them, broke over the rocks. And these at one moment had their sharp points covered as it were with mist, and at another their base was seen far down beneath the nether depth, while that wild surf poured in floods over them. But they, like maids, who play at ball hard by a sandy beach, with the folds of their dress rolled up to their waists out of their way; and one catcheth the ball from another and sends it soaring high into the air, and it never reaches the ground; even so they sent the ship on her way from hand to hand o'er the crests of the waves, ever clear of the rocks, while the water belched and seethed around them. There on the top of a smooth rock stood king Hephæstus in person, resting his heavy shoulder on the handle of his hammer, and watching them; and above the dazzling firmament stood the wife of Zeus, with her arm about Athene's waist, so mightily was she frightened at the sight. Long as is a day's allotted space in spring-time, so long they toiled, heaving the ship through the echoing rocks; and the heroes, catching the wind once more, sped onward, and quickly they passed the meadow of Trinacria, where graze the kine of Helios. Then did the Nereids plunge beneath the depths like water-fowl, for they had performed the commands of the wife of Zeus. Now did the bleating of sheep come to them confusedly through the air, and a lowing of kine smote upon their ears nigh at hand. The sheep was Phaethusa, youngest of the daughters of Helios, shepherding adown the dewy thickets, with a crook of silver in her hand; but Lampetie herded the kine, brandishing a herdsman's staff of gleaming orichalcum. These kine the heroes saw grazing by the waters of the river along the plain and the water meadow; there was not one among them of dark colour, but all, white as milk, with horns of gold, moved proudly on their way. By these they passed in the day-time; and in the coming night they cleft their path o'er a wide gulf of sea, rejoicing; till once again Dawn, child of morning, shed his light upon their path.

Now there is in front[1] of the Ionian gulf a rich island,

[1] *παροιτέρη* = *ἔμπροσθεν*. *ἀμφιλαφής* either = thickly covered with shrubs and trees, or with a harbour on either side (Schol.). The word is perhaps derived from *ἀμφι λαβεῖν*. Apollonius uses it three times: (1) in ii. 733, as epithet of "plane-trees;" (2) here of an island; (3) iv. 1366, of a horse. Possibly it means little more than "large," in which

thickly o'ergrown, in the Ceraunian sea, beneath which, legend saith, there lies a sickle—be gracious, ye Muses, for I tell not willingly this tale of olden times—wherewith Cronos reft his sire of his manhood ruthlessly; but others say it is the reaping-hook of Demeter, goddess of the nether world. For Demeter, they say, once dwelt in that land, and taught the Titans to reap the corn-crop for her love of Macris; whence it was called "the Hook"[1] by name, and became the sacred nursing-mother of the Phæacians, and so it is that the Phæacians really are by lineage of the blood of Uranus. To them came Argo, after stress of many toils, driven by the wind from the Trinacrian sea; and these, Alcinous and his people, received them gladly at their coming with gracious sacrifice; and the whole city made merry in their honour; thou wouldst have said, 'twas their own sons they were rejoicing over. And the heroes likewise rejoiced among the folk, even as if they had set foot in the heart of Hæmonia. But soon were they to arm and raise the battle-cry, so close behind them hove in sight a

sense it is used elsewhere, *e.g.* in Herodotus, of elephants. From Homer's account we learn that this island, Corcyra, had a harbour on both sides, so that it is not unlikely that Alexandrine grammarians made use of this fact to account for the meaning of a difficult and unexplained Homeric word.

[1] Drepane, *i.e.* Corcyra, had had a variety of names, viz., Macris, Drepane, Scheria, and lastly Corcyra. As the Phæacians, its early inhabitants, had been, next to the Phœnicians, the earliest and most enterprising of sailors and colonists, it is not surprising to find it made the centre of a mass of legend and myth, at a time when communication, especially by sea, was difficult and dangerous. Drepane, otherwise Corcyra, mentioned l. 988 and 1221, is the modern Corfu, an island off the coast of Epirus, famous in the history of Thucydides. It is only called Drepane in Apollonius. It must not be confounded with Corcyra Nigra (Κέρκυρα μέλαινα), modern Corzola, an island off the coast of Dalmatia, passed by the Argonauts soon after they emerged from the Rhone. The latter is several degrees further north. Cf. iv. 564-569.

countless host of Colchians, who had passed through the mouth of Pontus and the rocks Cyanean in search of the chieftains. Above all, they were eager to carry Medea, without excuse, unto her father's home; or else they threatened to raise their dire war-cry both then and thereafter with savage cruelty, after the fashion of Æetes.[1]

But king Alcinous restrained their eagerness for war, for he would fain end their lawless quarrel for both sides without going to battle. And the maiden, in deadly fear, earnestly implored the companions of the son of Æson by their names, and with suppliant hands she touched the knees of Arete, wife of Alcinous: "I entreat thee, queen, and be thou gracious; give me not up to the Colchians to take unto my father, if haply thou too art[2] only of the race of mortals, whose heart rusheth headlong to their doom from trifling slips. For I did lose my senses; 'twas not mad passion led me on. Witness the sacred light of Helios, witness the rites of the maiden, who flieth by night, the daughter of Perses;[3] never of my own accord would I have started from Æa with strange folk, but grievous terror urged me to plan this flight, in the hour of my sin, for there was no other remedy. Still is my honour pure and chaste, as in my father's house. Oh! pity me, great lady, and implore thy

[1] *σὺν 'Αιήταο κελεύθῳ*, *i.e.* not only would they do all they threatened, but they would do it after the fashion of Æetes (if this is what this extraordinary expression means). κελευθος certainly is occasionally used in much the same way as *τρόπος*. Æetes has the reputation of being cruel and relentless, so it is as much as to say "relentlessly." *αὖθί τε καὶ μετέπειτα*—*αὖθι* = *αὐτόθι*—"at once on the spot and afterwards as well," *i.e.* they would give them no peace from their vengeance, like true followers of Æetes.

[2] *φέρβεαι*, lit. "thou art fed," here = *εἶ*, "thou art."

[3] Hecate, the daughter of Perses and Asteria. As one who dealt in sorcery and witchcraft, Medea would naturally swear by the queen of darkness, who was supposed to have all black arts in her special keeping.

lord; and may the gods grant thee a perfect life, and joy, and children, and the glory of a town unsacked."[1]

Thus did she implore Arete through her tears, and thus each man of the chieftains in turn: "For you, ye peerless princes, and for your toils wherein I have helped you, am I sore afflicted; for by my help ye yoked the bulls, and reaped the deadly harvest of earth-born warriors, and by my means will ye return to Hæmonia anon, and bear with you the golden fleece. Lo! here am I, a maid who hath lost country, parents, home, aye, all the joy in life; while for you I have contrived a return unto your country and your homes; and ye will yet see your parents with glad eyes; but from me god's heavy hand hath reft all joy, and I wander accursed with strangers. Fear your covenant and your oaths; fear the spirit who avengeth suppliants, and the resentment of the gods, if I fall into the hands of Æetes to be slain with grievous outrage. I have no temple, no tower of defence, no protection else, but on you, and you alone, I cast myself. Woe to your cruelty, ye pitiless men! ye have no reverence in you for me, though ye saw me helplessly stretch out my hands to supplicate the stranger queen; yet would ye, in your eagerness to get the fleece, have met the whole Colchian nation and proud Æetes too in battle; but now have ye forgotten your chivalry, when there be but these, and they severed from their people."

So prayed she; and each of those she did entreat, encouraged her, striving to stay her anguish. And they brandished well-pointed lances in their hands, and swords drawn from their sheaths; for they declared they would not hold their hands from her succour, if they should meet with unrighteous judgment. But on the weary warriors, thronging there, came down the night, that puts an end to

[1] Not an unusual wish in heroic times, when life and property were anything but safe. To become the prey of a conquering invader must have been the constant dread of women in these disturbed times.

toil, and shed calm o'er all the earth together; but to the maiden's couch came no sleep, no, never so little; but her heart within her breast was wrung with anguish. As when a toiling woman winds her thread the livelong night, and about her moan her orphan babes, now she is widowed; and the tear-drop courses down her cheek, as she weepeth for the piteous lot that hath fallen to her; even so Medea's cheeks were wet, and her heart within her was throbbing, pierced with sharp agony.

Now those twain, the lord Alcinous, and Arete, his wife revered, were in their house within the city, as aforetime, pondering the maiden's case, upon their bed by night; and thus the wife addressed her lord and husband with persuasive[1] words: "Dear husband, come, rescue this poor maiden, I pray thee, from the Colchians, doing a favour to the Minyæ. For Argos and the men of Hæmonia are very nigh unto our island, but Æetes neither dwelleth near us, nor know we aught of him save by hearsay; and this poor suffering maid hath broken my heart by her entreaties. Give her not over to the Colchians to take to her father's home, O king. 'Twas blindly done, when she did give him at the first her drugs to charm the oxen; and now, to cure one evil by another close upon it, as oft we do through our mistakes, she hath fled from the awful fury of her proud father. Moreover Jason, as I hear, is bound by a mighty oath of his own taking to make her his wedded wife within his halls. Wherefore, dear husband, make not the son of Æson to perjure himself, at least if thou canst help it; nor let the father in his fury do his child some terrible injury, when thou canst stay it. For parents are exceeding jealous of their children; such punishment did Nycteus

[1] θαλεροῖσι, etym. θαλεῖν, so = (1) blooming, fresh; vigorous, active; (2) luxuriant, abundant. Apollonius uses it twice elsewhere, in iii. 114, as epithet of an orchard; in iii. 1127, of young married men. The transition from "vigorous" to "persuasive" is not difficult.

devise for Antiope,[1] fair of face; so grievous were the woes, again, that Danae[2] endured upon the deep, all through her father's infatuate folly; yea, and but lately, and not so far away, did Echetus[3] in wanton cruelty thrust bronze spikes into his daughter's eyeballs; and now she wastes away by a piteous fate, grinding bronze[4] for corn within a gloomy hut."

Thus spake she in entreaty; and his heart melted at the words of his wife, and thus he answered, "Arete, I would even drive out the Colchians with their harness for the maiden's sake, doing a favour to the heroes. But I do fear to slight the just ordinance of Zeus. Nor is it well to treat Æetes lightly, as thou sayest; for there is no mightier prince than he. And if he will, he will carry his quarrel against Hellas, though he come from far. Wherefore it behoveth me to give the judgment that shall seem best amongst all men, and I will not hide it from thee. If she

[1] Antiope, the daughter of Nycteus, was ravished by Zeus, who had changed himself into a satyr for the purpose. Her father was so enraged that she had to fly for her life, and came to Sicyon, where she bore Zethus and Amphion, and suffered many hardships for her secret love.

[2] Danaë was the daughter of Acrisius. Her father had been told by an oracle of Apollo that, if his daughter bore a son, this son would cause his death. So Acrisius went to Argos, and there shut his daughter up straitly in a tower of brass, but Zeus was enamoured of her beauty, and introduced himself to her in a shower of gold, despite her keepers. Perseus was the issue of their love. Acrisius, in his anger, set mother and child adrift on the sea, but fishermen saved them. In after years, when Perseus grew up, he engaged in some games at Larissa; and there, by accident, threw a quoit upon the foot of Acrisius and slew him, and so the oracle was fulfilled.

[3] Echetus is also mentioned by Homer as the most savage of men, as one who delighted in mutilating and torturing all who came within his power.

[4] Apparently the barbarous Echetus had *κριθαι* made of bronze for his daughter to grind, in order to render her toil harder and more thankless.

be yet a maid, my decision is, that they carry her back to her father; but, if she share a husband's bed, I will not separate her from her lord; nor, if she carry a child within her womb, do I give her up unto her enemies."

So spake he; and forthwith fell asleep. But she laid up in her heart his wise words, and at once arose from her bed, and went about the house; and the women, her handmaids, hastened together, bustling about their mistress. Quietly she had her herald called, and told him her commands, in her shrewdness eager that the son of Æson should at once wed the maiden, and so avoid entreating king Alcinous; for this was the decision he would carry with his own lips to the Colchians, that, if she were yet a maid, he would deliver her to her father's house; but, if she were already some man's wife, he would sever her no more from honourable love.

So spake Arete, and quickly his feet bare him from the hall, that he might announce to Jason the fair speech of Arete, and the plan of godlike Alcinous. And he found them keeping watch by the ship in harness in the Hyllic harbour, near to the town; so he told them all his message, and the heart of each hero was glad, for he spake a word that pleased them right well.

At once they mixed a bowl for the blessed gods, as was right, and dragged sheep to the altar with pious hands, and made ready that very night for the maiden her bridal bed in the holy cave, where Macris once did dwell, the daughter of Aristæus, the bee-keeper, who discovered the use of honey and the fatness of the olive, prize of toil. She it was, that at the first took to her breast the Nysean son of Zeus in Eubœa, home of the Abantes,[1] and with honey she moistened his parched lips, when Hermes brought him

[1] Εὐβοίης Ἀβαντίδος. Eubœa was anciently called Abantis, from the Abantes who came from Phocis and settled there.

from out the fire;[1] but Hera saw her, and in her rage drove her right away from the island. So then she came to dwell far away in the holy cavern of the Phæacians, and she granted to the folk around wondrous prosperity. There then they strewed a great couch, and upon it did throw the glistering fleece of gold, that the marriage might have honour and renown. And the nymphs plucked every kind of blossom and brought them in their white bosoms, and a blaze as of fire played round them all; so bright was the radiance gleaming from the golden tufts. And it kindled in their eyes a sweet desire, yet reverence prevented each one from laying hands thereon, for all her longing. Of these some were called the daughters of the river Ægæus; others dwelt about the peaks of the hill of Melite, and some came from the plains, woodland nymphs. For Hera herself, the wife of Zeus, had sent them, in honour of Jason. And that cave, to this day, is called Medea's sacred grotto, where they spread fine linen, very fragrant, and wedded those twain together. Meantime the heroes brandished in their hands their warlike spears, that no unseen host of foes might fall upon them to fight withal, ere the deed was done; and wreathing their heads with leafy boughs, they sung in tune to the clear music of Orpheus a marriage hymn at the entrance to the bridal bower. Now the hero, the son of Æson, was not minded to complete his marriage now, but in the halls of his father, on his return to Iolchos; and Medea, too, was of like mind with him. But needs must they wed

[1] ἐκ πυρός. Dionysus, the son of Zeus and Semele, was saved when his mother perished through her own folly in desiring to see Zeus appear in all his majesty. The mother was killed by the blaze of the lightning (cf. the opening of Euripides' "Bacchæ"), but Hermes snatched the untimely babe from her womb and carried it to Zeus, in whose side it was sewn up until the proper time for its birth arrived. Zeus then handed it over to the nymph Macris to rear, but Hera's jealousy persecuted Macris relentlessly in consequence.

then and there. Yea, for never do we tribes of suffering mortals embark on happiness without alloy; but ever there cometh with our gladness some bitter grief. Wherefore they too, for all their joy of sweet love, were holden with fear, whether the decision of Alcinous would be fulfilled.

Then came Dawn again with his light divine, and broke up the gloom of night throughout the sky; and the island beach and the dewy paths across the plains laughed out afar; and in the streets was the noise of men; for through the city the inhabitants were astir, and the Colchians far away at the end of the Macridian peninsula. Anon went Alcinous to them, as he had agreed, to declare his purpose concerning the maiden, and in his hand he held his golden wand of judgment; whereby the folk had righteous judgment dealt them throughout the city. And with him came the chiefs of the Phæacians in their warlike gear, drawn up in ranks. And forth from the towers came the women in crowds to see the heroes, and with them came the country folk when they heard thereof, for Hera had sent forth a sure report. One brought the chosen ram of his flock, and another a heifer that never yet had worked, and others set jars of wine nigh at hand for mixing; and the smoke and flame of sacrifice leapt up in the distance. But the women brought fine linen, fruit of honest toil, as women will, and toys of gold, and divers ornaments beside, such as couples newly-wed are furnished with; and they were astonied to see the form and beauty of the noble heroes, and the son of Æager in their midst oft beating the ground with his rich sandal in time to his ringing lyre and song. And all the nymphs in chorus, whenever he made mention of marriage, raised a joyous wedding hymn; and yet again would others sing alone, as they circled round in the dance in thy honour, O Hera; for 'twas thou, who didst put it in the heart of Arete to speak her word of wisdom to Alcinous. But he, so soon as he had declared the issue of his judgment, and when already the marriage was declared complete, took good care that so it should abide for ever; for no deadly fear, nor the grievous threats of Æetes touched him, but he held fast bound by the oath he would not break.

So when the Colchians learnt that they were come to him in vain, and he bade them either hold his ordinances in honour or withdraw their ships far from the harbours of his land; then but not before were they afraid of the threats of their own king, and besought Alcinous to receive them among his people; so for a very long time afterward they dwelt among the Phæacians, until the Bacchiadæ,[1] a race of men that came from Corinth, settled among them after a while; then they crossed to the island over against them, and from thence they were soon to go to the Ceraunian hills of the Abantes and the Nestæans[2] and to Oricum; but these things happened after a long lapse of years. Yet still do the altars, which Medea builded there to the Fates and the Nymphs in the holy place of Apollo, god of shepherds, receive their yearly sacrifice. Now when the Minyæ went away, Alcinous gave them many a stranger's gift, and Arete did the like; moreover she gave to Medea twelve Phæacian slave-girls from her house, to bear her company. 'Twas on the seventh day they left Drepane; and a fresh breeze came forth from Zeus at dawn, and they went hasting onward before the breath of the wind. Still it was not ordained for the heroes yet to set foot in Achæa, till they

[1] Βακχιάδαι. Bacchius, a son of Dionysus, founded a dynasty at Corinth, called the Bacchiadæ, who held sway until an act of cruelty roused the Corinthians to expel them. So they came to Corcyra, and colonized it, driving out the Colchians, who were there already. Ἐφύρηθεν, *i.e.* from Corinth, Ephyra being its old name.

[2] Another name for the Thracians, from the river Nestus in Thrace.

had toiled somewhat further, even in Libya's utmost bounds.

Lo! they had even now left the bay behind, that is named after the Ambracians; even now had they left, with all sail set, the land of Ætolia [1] and next thereto the isles of the Echinades with their narrow passage, and the land of Pelops just hove in sight, when the baleful blast of the north-wind caught them in mid course and swept them nine whole nights and as many days towards the Libyan sea, till they came right within the Syrtis,[2] whence cometh no ship forth again, when once 'tis forced inside that gulf. For all around are shoals, and masses of sea-weed on every side, and thereon are bubbles of noiseless foam, while on the dim horizon stretches a plain of sand. No creeping thing nor winged creature moveth thereupon. 'Twas here that the flood-tide thrust them far up the beach on a sudden, and only a little of the keel was left in the water, for yon tide full oft recoils from the land, and then again with furious onset discharges itself over the beach.

But they leapt forth from the ship, and sorrow seized them, when they beheld the great wide stretch of misty land, reaching on and on into the distance like a haze; nor could they see any place to water in, nor path, nor herdsmen's steading far away; but all was wrapt in deathless calm. And one would ask his neighbour sorrowfully, "What land doth this call itself? whither have the tempests thrust us forth? Would that we, setting deadly fear aside, had dared to try the way even betwixt the rocks! Far better had it been to go even beyond the will of Zeus and die, venturing some high resolve! For now what can we do, if we be forced here to abide holden by the winds,

[1] Κουρῆτιν, *i.e.* Ætolia, from the Curetes who inhabited Pleuron in Ætolia.

[2] Σύρτιν, a dangerous sandbank on the coast of Africa. There were two of this name, called the Syrtis Major and Minor.

be it never so short a while? so desolate is the strand of this vast land, that looms before us."

Thus would he say; and amongst them Ancæus, the helmsman, made harangue, sore grieved himself at the hopelessness of their evil case: "We are undone, it seems, by a most grievous fate, and there is no escaping from our trouble, but now must we suffer ghastly woes where we have fallen on this wilderness, if haply the winds blow steadily from the land, for I see on all sides a sea of shoals after a wide look-out, and the water is fretted into long lines of foam as it washes just the surface of the gray sand. Yea, and long, long ago would yon sacred ship have been miserably shattered far from the shore, unless the tide itself had borne her high ashore from out the deep. But now hath it rushed back sea-ward, and nought but spray and spray alone, that covereth but the top of the ground, breaks about us. Wherefore I deem that all hope of our voyage and our return is utterly cut off. So let some other shew his skill, for he may sit at the helm striving to win our escape. But Zeus hath no great wish to bring about the day of return, after all our toil."

So spake he through his tears; and all they that knew aught of ships spake with him in his distress; but the heart of all, I trow, was cold and stiff, and paleness spread o'er their cheeks. As when men move like lifeless spectres, about a town, awaiting the end that war or famine bring, or the issue of some fearful storm, which hath washed away acres of the oxen's toil;[1] or when images do sweat and of themselves run down with blood, and bellowing is heard in sacred shrines, or the sun maybe at noon brings night from the sky, while through the gloom the stars shine bright; even so the chieftains wandered now, groping their way along the weary strand. Anon dark eve

[1] *i.e.* the tilled lands.

came down upon them; and they, piteously embracing each other, were fain to weep, that thereafter they might lie down, each man apart, to die upon the sand. Hither and thither they went their way to find a resting-place further off; and then they wrapped their heads in their cloaks and laid them down without meat[1] or drink the whole night and the dawn, waiting a death most miserable. Apart from them beside the daughter of Æetes her maidens moaned, huddled all together. As when in the wilderness young birds unfledged fall from a hole in the rock and loudly do they twitter; or as when on the banks of fair-flowing Pactolus[2] swans lift up their melody, and the dewy meadow echoes around, and the river's fair streams; even so those maidens, casting their golden tresses in the dust, wailed the livelong night a piteous lament. And all, then and there, would have vanished from among the living, out of the ken of mortal men, yea, those chosen heroes on their aimless quest, had not the heroines,[3] who watch o'er Libya, pitied them hopelessly wasting away; these be the goddesses, who erst, when Athene sprang in bright armour from her father's head,[4] met her at the waters of Triton and bathed her. 'Twas noon, and terribly the sun's piercing rays were scorching Libya; when lo! they stood beside the son of Æson, and lightly drew his

[1] *ἄκμηνοι*, with accent proparoxytone = fasting, must be carefully distinguished from *ἀκμηνοί* = full-grown. The derivation of the first is uncertain; the latter is from *ἀκμή*.

[2] A river in Lydia whose waters were said to flow with gold, from the large amount of it washed down in the sand.

[3] Apparently these are demi-goddesses or tutelary deities of the country, who watch over Libya, and are honoured there with divine rites.

[4] *ἐκ πατρὸς κεφαλῆς*. The legend was that Zeus, being troubled with severe pains in his head, sent for Hephæstus, who with a blow of his hammer cleft open the skull of Zeus, whence issued Athene, full-grown and in full armour.

mantle from his head. But he cast down his eyes and looked aside, in reverence for the goddesses. And they with gentle words spake unto him alone openly in his affliction, "Poor wretch! why art thou so cast down? We know ye went in quest of the golden fleece; we know each toil of yours, all the wondrous things that ye have done in your wanderings o'er land and sea. We are the goddesses of this land; here tend we sheep,[1] and speak the speech of men; heroines we, daughters of Libya and warders of her land. Up now; no longer be so disquieted with grief, and rouse thy comrades. But mark, when Amphitrite doth loose anon the smooth-running car of Poseidon; in that very hour make recompense to your mother[2] for all her travail in bearing you so long time in her womb; and so shall ye yet return to holy Achæa."

So spake they, and forthwith vanished from their place, as their words died away. But Jason sat up on the ground and looked about him, and thus spake he: "Be gracious, noble goddesses, who dwell in this wilderness, but I understand not very clearly what ye said about our return. Verily I will gather my crew together and tell them all, if haply we can find somewhat that points to our escape; for the wisdom of many is better than the wisdom of one."

Therewith he sprang up and cried aloud to his comrades, all squalid with dust, like a lion, who roars as he seeks his mate through the woodland; and the glens in the mountains far away tremble at his deep voice; and oxen in the field and they that herd them shudder horribly

[1] *οἰοπόλοι*, probably derived from *ὄις*, *πολεῖν*, *i.e.* tenders of sheep, cf. l. 1411, infra. Another derivation is from *οἶος*, *πέλομαι* = being alone, solitary. The word is found in both significations, but the first meaning suits the context of Apollonius best.

[2] The ship which had carried them so long like a mother in her womb.

with fear. Yet had his voice nought to make them shudder, friend calling unto friends. So they gathered near him with downcast looks, and he made them sit down in their sorrow nigh to where the ship lay, together with the women,[1] and made harangue, declaring each thing: "Friends, hearken; there stood above my head, very nigh to me, as I lay grieving, three goddesses, girt in goatskins from the neck above about the back and waist, like maidens; and with light hand they drew aside my robe and uncovered my head, bidding me rise up myself, and go rouse you; and they bid us pay bounteous recompense unto our mother for all her travail in carrying us this long time in her womb, whenso Amphitrite shall loose the smooth-running car of Poseidon. Now I cannot wholly understand this message divine. They said, indeed, that they were heroines, daughters of Libya and warders of her land. Yea, and they declared that full well they knew everything that we ourselves had endured ere this on land and sea. Then I saw them no more in their place, but some mist or cloud came betwixt us and veiled their brightness."

So spake he, and they were all astonied as they listened. Then came unto the Minyæ this wonder passing strange: From out the sea toward the land leapt forth a monster horse; a mighty[2] steed was he, with mane of gold floating in the wind; lightly he spurned the salt foam from his legs and started on his course with legs that matched the wind. Then up spake Peleus with a cry of joy among his comrades gathered there: "Verily I do

[1] *i.e.* Medea and her twelve Phæacian handmaids, given her by Arete.

[2] ἀμφιλαφής either = "vast, huge," its usual meaning in Herodotus, or "having hair on both sides," *i.e.* "shaggy." Probably the former, as the mane of the horse is also definitely mentioned, and to add another similar epithet would be redundant.

think that Poseidon's chariot hath already been loosed by the hands of his dear wife, and I deem that our mother is no other than the ship herself; for surely she doth bear us in her womb and groaneth unceasingly in hard travail. Come, we will lift her up with unshaken might and tireless shoulders and carry her within this sandy country, whither yon swift steed is gone before us. For he, brave beast, will not plunge beneath the dry ground, and I trow his tracks will show us some bay of the sea far inland."

So spake he; and his ready counsel pleased them all. This is the tale the Muses told; and I, the servant of the Pierian maidens, do sing it; and this is what I heard in all honesty, that ye, brave sons of kings, exceeding bold, did lift your ship and all ye took therein high upon your shoulders and carried her in your might and manhood o'er the desert sandhills of Libya twelve whole days and as many nights. Yet who can tell the pain and anguish these men endured in that toil? Surely they were of the blood of the immortals, so great was the work they took upon them under the stress of need. Now when they had carried her right gladly far to the waters of the lake Tritonis,[1] straightway they waded in and set her down from their stalwart shoulders.

Then like hounds, mad with thirst, they darted forth to find a spring; for to their misery and suffering was added parching drought. But not in vain did they wander; and they came to the sacred plain, where but yesterday Ladon,[2]

[1] A lake in Libya.

[2] Ladon was the huge serpent which guarded the apples of the Hesperides, and was slain by Heracles a few days before the arrival of the Argonauts in Libya. The Hesperides were nymphs, daughters of Phorcus and Ceto, who ministered to the wants of the guardian snake. On the appearance of the Argonauts they changed into dust and ashes, until Orpheus besought their aid, when they resumed their original forms under the names Hespere, Erytheis, and Ægle, and showed the Argonauts where to find water.

a serpent of that land, did guard the golden apples in the place of Atlas, while about him the Hesperides used to busy themselves, singing their lovely song. But now, lo! he was fallen against the trunk of the apple-tree from the wound that Heracles had given him; only with the tip of his tail was he still writhing, but from his head unto the end of his dark spine lifeless he lay; and where the arrows had left their bitter gall in the blood of the Lernæan snake flies were busy at his festering wounds. And near him the Hesperides raised their loud lament, their fair white arms clasped about their golden hair; when on a sudden came the heroes nigh to them, and lo! at once those maidens turned, as they stood, to dust and ashes, even while the men came hasting on. But Orpheus was ware of the divine marvel, and for his comrades' sake he lifted up a prayer to the maidens: "Ye queens divine, so fair and kind, be gracious, whether ye are counted amongst the goddesses of heaven, or those of earth, or are called the nymphs that tend the sheep-fold; come, maidens, holy race of Oceanus, appear to us face to face, and show us at our desire some fount of water gushing from the rock, or some holy stream bubbling up from the earth, whereat, O goddesses, to quench the thirst, that parches us unceasingly. And if we come again some day o'er the sea to the land of Achæa, then will we offer you gladly countless gifts amongst the first of goddesses, with drink-offerings and rich feasts."

So prayed he aloud; and the goddesses from their station nigh had pity on their suffering, and first of all they made grass spring up from the earth, and above the grass tall shoots sprang up; and next young trees in bloom shot high o'er the ground and stood upright. Hespere became a poplar, Erytheis an elm, and Ægle a willow with sacred trunk. And from these trees their forms looked out, even as they were before, a wonder passing strange; then spake

Ægle to their longing ears a gentle answer, "Yea, verily there hath come hither one that can succour your troubles full well, that man accursed,[1] who robbed our guardian snake of life, and is gone taking with him the golden apples of the goddesses; and grievous woe is left to us. Yestreen there came a man, a very fiend in form and wanton violence; his eyes gleamed from under his grim[2] forehead; a ruthless wretch; and he was girt about with the skin of a huge lion, rough and untanned, and he bare a heavy bough of olive, and a bow, wherewith he shot to death yon monster-snake. And he too came all parched with thirst, as a wayfarer might; and wildly he rushed about this place in quest of water, but none was he likely to see, I trow. Now here stood a rock nigh to the lake Tritonis, which he, strong giant, smote with his foot below, on purpose or mayhap by some god's prompting; and yonder spring gushed out at once. Then did he, sprawling with hands and chest upon the ground, drink a mighty draught from the cleft in the rock, till, like a beast with head thrown forward, he had filled his deep belly."

So spake she; and gladly they hasted with joyful steps, until they found the spot where Ægle had told them of the spring. As when burrowing ants crawl in swarms about a narrow hole, or as when flies, lighting about a tiny drop of sweet honey, do throng there in terrible eagerness; even so the Minyæ then were thronging around the spring in the rock; and thus would one say in his gladness as he moistened his lips, "Lo! you now; in very sooth, Heracles, though far away, hath saved his comrades dying of thirst. Aye, would that we might find him on his way, as we pass through the mainland!"

Therewith, when such as were ready for this work,

[1] *i.e.* Heracles, who had slain the snake.

[2] *βλοσυρός*, a word of uncertain etymology with two meanings, (1) grim, stern, (2) burly, manly.

had answered; they started up and parted, hither and thither, to search; for on the night-wind a sound of steps had come rolling to their ears, as the sand was stirred. Forth sped the two sons of Boreas, trusting to their wings; and Euphemus, relying on his fleetness of foot; and Lynceus too, to cast his keen glance far and wide; and yet a fifth hurried to their side, even Canthus. Him, I trow, did heaven's high will and his brave soul send forth upon that journey, that he might learn for certain from Heracles, where he had left Polyphemus, son of Elatus; for he was minded to question him on every point about his comrade. But Polyphemus had founded a famous town among the Mysians, and then, anxious to return, had gone in quest of Argo afar across the mainland; and he came meantime to the land of the Chalybes, that live beside the sea; there did his fate o'ertake him. And his tomb lieth beneath a tall poplar, facing the sea, a little space therefrom. But now Lynceus thought he saw Heracles alone, far away over the boundless shore, just as a man seeth, or thinks he seeth, the new moon through a mist. So he came, and told his companions, that no one could ever track him further and o'ertake [1] him on his way; and back those others also came, Euphemus, fleet of foot, and the two sons of Thracian Boreas, after fruitless toil.

But on thee, Canthus, fate laid her deadly hold. Thou didst come upon flocks at pasture; but the man that did shepherd them slew thee with the blow of a stone for sake of his sheep to prevent thee from carrying them off to thy needy comrades; for Caphaurus was no feeble foe, that grandson of Lycorean [2] Phœbus, and of the chaste maid Acacallis, the daughter whom Minos on a day did bring to

[1] *μὴ . . . κιχησέμεν*, *i.e.* no one would overtake him now at that distance.

[2] Λυκωρείοιο = Δελφικοῦ, for the Delphians were originally called Lycorians, from Lycoreia, a town in the neighbourhood of Delphi.

dwell in Libya, bearing in her womb a heavy load[1] from the god; and she bare a noble son to Phœbus, whom men call Amphithemis, or Garamas. And Amphithemis in his turn lay with a Tritonian nymph, who bare to him Nasamon and strong Caphaurus; he it was, who now slew Canthus, in defence of his sheep. Yet was not he, strong warrior, to escape the stern hands of the heroes, when they learnt what he had done. For the Minyæ, when they knew it, took up his corpse and brought it back and buried him; but those sheep the heroes took unto themselves, mourning the while.

There too upon the self-same day relentless Fate laid her hand upon Mopsus, son of Ampycus, nor could his divination save him from his bitter doom. For there is no way to hinder death. Now there was lying on the sand a fearsome snake, seeking to avoid the noontide heat, too sluggish indeed purposely to wound an unwitting foe, nor yet would it have darted at one who shrunk from meeting it. But on whomsoever it once should dart its black venom of all living creatures that have breath, whom Earth the life-giver doth nurture, for him is his road to Hades not so much as a span long; no, not even if the healing god[2] should be his leech (if I may speak openly), when that snake hath but grazed him with its fangs. For when god-like Perseus, whom his mother also called Eurymedon, flew over Libya, carrying to king Polydectes the Gorgon's head just severed,[3] all the drops of dark blood, that fell to

[1] κῦμα, by syncope for κύημα.

[2] Παιήων, Ionic for Παιάν, the physician of the gods. Later the name was transferred to Apollo, who was invoked by the cry ἰήιε Παιάν.

[3] Perseus, called also Eurymedon, was commanded by Polydectes, king of Seriphos, to bring to him the head of Medusa the Gorgon, which had the power of turning all who gazed on it into stone. Perseus, however, by the aid of Hermes and Athene, who gave him winged sandals, a cap to render him invisible, and a bright shield in which he

the ground, did breed a race of those serpents. Now Mopsus trod upon the reptile's back with the sole of his left foot; but the snake, writhing round in pain, bit and tore the flesh 'twixt his shin and calf. And Medea and the other women, her handmaids, fled in terror; but he bravely handled the bleeding wound, for it did not vex him very much, poor wretch! Verily even now beneath the skin a lethargy, that looseth the limbs, was spreading, and o'er his eyes fell a thick mist. Anon his heavy limbs sank upon the ground, and he grew cold and helpless; and his comrades gathered round him, and the hero son of Æson, sore dismayed at this chain of disasters. Not even, when dead, might he lie ever so short a time in the sun; for the venom at once began to rot the flesh within, and the hair decayed and fell from the skin. So, quickly and in haste, they dug a deep grave with brazen picks; and themselves and the maidens likewise tore their hair, bewailing the dead man's piteous fate; and thrice, in harness clad, they marched round him, when he had gotten his fair meed of burial; and then heaped up the earth above him.

But when they were gone aboard,—for the south wind blew across the sea,—and were determined to go on their way across the lake Tritonis, no longer had they any plan, and so were driven at random the livelong day. As a serpent creeps along his crooked path, when the sun's piercing heat doth scorch him, and twists his head from side to side, hissing the while, and his eyes withal flash like sparks of fire in his fury, till he hath crept to his

might see the Gorgon's reflection without meeting the monster face to face and so being turned into stone, accomplished his quest. Then he brought the head to Polydectes, and turned him and his people into stone, because they had formerly refused him hospitality. After this, Athene took the head, and placed it as a blazon on her shield. Legend said that as Perseus flew over Libya with his spoil, the blood which fell from the freshly-severed head turned into the most venomous serpents.

hole through a cleft; even so Argo long time was busy seeking an outlet for ships from the lake. Anon Orpheus bade bring out from the hold Apollo's mighty tripod, and set it up before the gods of that land to be a propitiation for their return. So they went and set up on the shore the gift of Phœbus, and mighty Triton met them in the semblance of a young man, and taking up a clod of earth he offered it unto the chieftains as a stranger's gift with these words, "Take this, good friends; for no great gift have I here by me to give to strangers at their request. But if ye desire to know aught of the ways of this sea, as men oft crave, when voyaging over strange waters, I will tell you. For lo! my father Poseidon made me very knowing in this sea, and I am king of the sea-coast, if haply in your distant home ye ever hear of Eurypylus,[1] born in Libya, home of wild beasts."

So spake he; and gladly Euphemus held out his hands for the clod, and thus addressed him in reply, "Hero, if haply thou knowest aught of Apis[2] and the sea of Minos, tell us truly at our asking. For hither we are come, not of our own will; but, brought nigh to the bounds of this land by tempestuous winds, we did carry our ship shoulder-high to the waters of this lake across the mainland, groaning 'neath the weight; but we know not at all, where lies the route for coming to the land of Pelops."

So spake he; and the other stretched out his hand and showed them far away the sea and the lake's deep mouth, and thus he said, "Lo! yonder is the outlet to the sea, just where the deep water lies black and still, and on either side white breakers seethe[3] with crests transparent; betwixt the

[1] Son of Poseidon and Celæno, king of Cyrene in Libya.

[2] An island off Crete, *i.e.* Mare Creticum, so called from Minos, a legendary king of Crete, who had put down piracy and organized a naval supremacy.

[3] φρίσσουσι, etym. φρίξ, *i.e.* the ruffling of a smooth surface—the

breakers there is[1] your course, a narrow one to sail outside. And yonder sea, that spreads to the horizon,[2] reaches above Crete to the sacred land of Pelops; but steer[3] toward the right hand when ye enter the gulf of sea from the lake, keeping close the while along the shore, till it extends inland; but when the coast-line bends the other way, then your course lies safe and straight before you, starting from that projecting angle. Now go in joy; and as for toil let none repine that limbs, still in their youthful vigour, have to toil."

So spake he with good will; and they went aboard quickly, eager to row out from the lake. And on they sped in their haste; but he meantime, even Triton, took up the mighty tripod and was seen to enter the lake, but after that no man saw him, how he vanished so near them, tripod and all. And their heart was cheered, for that one of the blessed gods had met them in kindly mood. And they bade the son of Æson offer in his honour the choicest of their remaining sheep, and raise the song of praise, when he had taken him. Quickly that hero chose him out with haste, and, having taken him up to the stern, there sacrificed him, and prayed, "God, who didst appear upon the bounds of this lake, whether the daughters of

ruffling or ripple caused by a gust of wind sweeping over a smooth sea. *φρίσσειν* is also used of any rough appearance (cf. Lat. horrescere), *e.g.* of corn-fields, of a body of spearmen. Hence the meaning "to shudder with fear, to dread a person," also "to thrill" with strong emotion, *e.g.* *ἔφριξ' ἔρωτι.*

[1] *τελέθει* merely = *ἐστί.*

[2] *ὑπηέριον*, *i.e.* with nothing but sky around; you lose sight of the land altogether.

[3] After leaving the Tritonian lake and making the sea, they are to coast closely along the shore till they come to a gulf; then sail across its mouth to a headland opposite; after which they can make a straight course across the Ægæan. (A glance at a map will best explain the directions here given; they seem fairly accurate, and are not difficult to identify.)

ocean[1] call thee Triton, wonder of the deep, or Phorcys, or Nereus, be favourable and grant the accomplishment of our return, as we desire."

Therewith and as he prayed, he cut the throat of the sheep and cast him from the stern into the water. And lo! the god appeared from out the deep in his own true form. As when a man will train a fleet horse for the wide race-course, holding the obedient creature by his bushy mane, and running the while beside him, and the horse, with proud arching neck, follows his guide, and in his mouth the bright bit rattles in answer as he champs it this way and that; even so that strong god laid his hand on the keel of hollow Argo and guided her seaward. Now from the top of his head and about his back and waist as far as the belly, he was wondrous like the blessed gods in form; but below the loins stretched the tail of a sea-monster, forked this way and that, and with the spines thereof he cleft the surface of the water, for these parted below into two curved fins, like to the horns of the moon. On he led the ship, till he brought her on her way into the sea, and then suddenly he plunged beneath the mighty depths; and those heroes cried out, when they saw the strange marvel with their eyes. There is the harbour of Argo, and signs[2] left by the ship, and altars to Poseidon and Triton; for they stopped there that day. But at dawn they set sail, keeping that desert land upon the right; and

[1] *ἁλοσύδναι*, "children of the sea," a name mostly applied to Thetis and Amphitrite. Etym. *ἅλς ὕδνης*.

[2] It is not clear what these signs were, possibly a pictorial design, or a model of the ship, or some ship implement such as an oar, set up to commemorate the coming of Argo to the place. We have frequent mention made of *σήματα* placed on the barrows of heroes' tombs, generally their weapons, or something that they prized in life, which should tell their story to future ages. The phrase *σήματα νηός* occurs supra, l. 552, where possibly it means either the flag of Argo or her figure-head.

on they sped before the breath of the west wind. And on the next morning they saw a projecting tongue of land and an inland sea lying beyond it. Anon the west wind ceased, and the breath of the clear south came on, and they were glad at heart for the wind. But when the sun sank, and rose the star, that bids the shepherd fold[1] and stays the ploughman from his toil; in that hour of pitchy night the wind fell; so they furled the sails and stooped the tall mast, and took to their polished oars lustily all night and day and the next night as well. And in the distance craggy Carpathus[2] welcomed them; thence were they, strong rowers, soon to cross to Crete, which standeth out above all other isles upon the sea.

But brazen Talos prevented them from mooring, when they came to the roadstead of the Dictæan haven, by breaking off rocks from the hard cliff. He was a descendant of the brazen stock of men, who sprung from ash trees,[3] ranking among demi-gods; him the son of Cronos gave to Europa, to be the warder of the island of Crete, whereabouts he roameth with those brazen feet. Now truly he is made of brass, unbreakable, in his limbs and all the rest of his body; only beneath the tendon by the ancle was a vein[4] of blood, and thin was the skin that

[1] *ἀστὴρ αὔλιος*, *i.e.* Hesperus, the evening star. *ἀνέπαυσεν διζυρούς*. The adjective is perhaps predicative, so that the expression means "stays the ploughman from being wretched," *i.e.* by ending his toil.

[2] *Κάρπαθος*, one of the Sporades, not far from Cos.

[3] After the golden age and the silver age came the brazen age. The race of men then born were so hard, says Hesiod, that they were said to have sprung from ash-trees (*μελία γίγνομαι*). To this age belonged Talos, the brazen giant who kept guard over Crete, and was absolutely invulnerable save in one spot, where a vein of blood near the ancle held all that was mortal in him.

[4] *σύριγξ* is anything shaped like a pipe; here a vein. ὃ, Ionic for ὅς, demonstr. pronoun. The ὃ *λεπτὸς ὑμὴν* is only an expansion of *σύριγξ*, *i.e.* that one vein with its thin covering of skin held the issues of life and death.

covered it with its issues of life and death. So the heroes, though sore foredone with toil, quickly backed from the land in grievous fear. And now would they have got them far from Crete sorrowfully, suffering both from thirst and pain, had not Medea hailed them as they drew away: "Hearken to me. For methinks I can by myself master yon man for you, whoever he is, even though he hath his body all of brass, seeing that his life is not to last for ever. But keep the ship here, nothing loth, out of stone-throw,[1] till he yield himself my victim."

Thus spake she, and they held the ship out of range, waiting to see what plan she would bring to work unexpectedly. Then did she wrap the folds of a dark cloak about both her cheeks and went upon the deck; and the son of Æson, taking her hand in his, guided her steps along the benches. Then did she make use of witching spells, invoking the goddesses of death,[2] that gnaw the heart, the fleet hounds of Hades, who hover all through the air and settle on living men. Thrice with spells she invoked their aid with suppliant voice, and thrice with prayers; and, having framed her mind to evil, she bewitched[3] the sight of brazen Talos with her hostile glance, and against him she gnashed[4] grievous fury and sent forth fearful phantoms in the hotness of her rage.

O father Zeus, verily my heart within me is moved with amaze to see, how death o'ertakes us not merely by disease

[1] ἰρωῆς. ἰρωή = any quick violent motion, *e.g.* the flight of a spear, and, as here, the rush of a missile stone.

[2] Κῆρας. Κήρ is the goddess of fate or death, usually employed in the plural, for there were three Κῆρες in ancient mythology, who appeared to men on the eve of their death.

[3] ἐμέγηρεν ὀπωπάς literally = grudged him the sight of his eyes, so that he was unable to see where he was going.

[4] πρῖεν χόλον, *i.e.* gnashed her teeth in her fury against Talos. Cf. Lat. "stridere (or) frendere dentibus." πρίω literally = "I saw, cut in twain."

and wounds, but lo! even from a distance a man may harass us; just as that giant, for all his brazen frame, yielded himself a victim to the might of Medea, the sorceress; for, as he did heave great heavy stones to prevent their coming to the haven, he scratched his ancle against a sharp point of rock, and forth gushed the stream of life like molten lead, nor could he stand any longer on his pinnacle of jutting rock. But like some towering pine, high on the hills, which wood-cutters have left half-cleft by their sharp axes, when they came down from the wood; at first it quivers in the blast at night, then at last it snaps at the bottom and falls; even so that mighty giant stood towering there awhile upright on his tireless feet, then fell at last with mighty crash, a strengthless mass. So then the heroes spent that night after all in Crete; and after that, just as dawn was growing bright, they built a temple to Minoan Athene, and drew water and embarked, that they might row as soon as possible beyond the headland of Salmoneus.[1]

Anon, as they were hasting o'er the wide gulf of Crete, night scared them, that night men call "the shroud of gloom." No stars nor any ray of the moon pierced through its horror; but it was black chaos come from heaven, or haply thick gloom rising from the nethermost abyss. And they knew not so much as whether they were drifting into Hades or along the water, but to the sea they committed their return, not knowing whither it would carry them. Then Jason, with uplifted hands, cried aloud to Phœbus, calling on him to save, and his tears ran down in his distress; and he promised he would bring great store of gifts to Pytho[2] and to Amyclæ, and likewise to Ortygia. Lightly didst thou come, son of Latona, from heaven, in ready response, unto the rocks of Melas, which lie there in the sea,

[1] A promontory of Crete.

[2] Pytho, Amyclæ, and Ortygia are various seats of Apollo's worship.

and on the top of one of the twin peaks thou didst settle, holding thy golden bow on high in thy right hand; and the bow flashed a dazzling radiance all around. Then a little island[1] of the Sporades appeared in sight of them, fronting the tiny isle of Hippuris; and there they cast anchor and waited. Anon the dawn arose and showed his light, and they made for Apollo a noble enclosure and an altar, with trees above, in a shady grove, calling Phœbus "radiant god" because of his far-seen radiance; and the bare isle called they "isle of appearing," for that Phœbus did there appear to them at their sore need. And they offered all that men can find to offer on a barren strand; and so it was that when Medea's Phæacian damsels saw them pouring libations of water on the blazing brands, they could no longer keep back their laughter in their breasts, for they had ever seen oxen in plenty slain in the halls of Alcinous. But the heroes, glad at their jesting, scoffed at them with words of abuse; and among them rose the merry sound of taunting gibe and raillery; and from that sport of the heroes the women do strive on this wise with the men in the island, when they will appease with sacrifice Apollo, "god of radiance," champion of his "isle of appearing."

But when they had loosed their cables thence in calm weather, then did Euphemus remember a vision he saw in the night, in awe of the famous son of Maia;[2] for it seemed to him that that strange clod, held in the palm of his hand, was being suckled at his breast with white streams of milk; and out of the clod, little though it was, grew a woman, like to a virgin; and he, o'ercome by strong desire, lay with her in love's embrace; but in the act he pitied her as though she were a maiden, whom himself was feeding with his milk; but she comforted him with soothing

[1] A little island called Anaphe, near Thera.

[2] Hermes was the god who sent visions to men.

words: "Dear husband, I am the daughter of Triton, thy children's nurse, no maiden I; for Triton and Libya are my parents. But give me back to the maidens of Nereus, to dwell within the deep nigh to 'the isle of appearing'; and I will come back again to the sun-light, ready to help thy children."[1]

Of this vision Euphemus now minded him, and he told it to the son of Æson; and he, when he had pondered awhile the oracles of Hecatus, uttered his voice, and said: "Lo! you now; verily there hath fallen to thee a great and glorious fame. For of yon clod the gods will make an island for thee, when thou hast cast it into the sea, where thy children's children in days to come shall dwell; for Triton did vouchsafe to thee this clod of the Libyan mainland as a stranger's gift; 'twas none other than he of the immortals, who met us and gave thee this."

So spake he, and Euphemus made not light of the answer of the son of Æson, but flung the clod into the deep, cheered at the word of prophecy. Therefrom rose the isle Calliste,[2] holy nurse of the children of Euphemus, who at first dwelt some time in Sintean Lemnos, but, being driven from Lemnos by Tyrsenians, they came to Sparta as suppliants; and, when they left Sparta, Theras, goodly son of Autesion, brought them to the isle of Calliste, and it took the name of Thera from him in exchange for its own. But these things happened after the time of Euphemus.

And when they were gone hence, they sailed steadily through the boundless swell, and stopped at the beach of Ægina. Here on a sudden arose an innocent strife among them about the drawing of water, who should be first to

[1] νεπόδεσσιν = τέκνοις, in which sense this word is always used by Alexandrine writers.

[2] The isle of Calliste, afterwards called Thera, from Theras, son of Autesion, who colonized it from Sparta.

draw his jar, and get him to the ship again; for need and the ceaseless breeze hurried them alike. There, to this day,[1] the young men of the Myrmidons take up full jars upon their shoulders, and at once dart off to race striving for the victory.

Be gracious, O race of blessed chieftains! and from year to year may these songs be sweeter to sing to men! For now am I come unto the end of your glorious toils; for there was no further adventure ordained you as ye came from Ægina, nor did hurricanes rise against you, but calmly ye coasted by the land of Cecrops and past Aulis, in under Eubœa and the towns of the Opuntian Locri, till with gladness ye stept forth upon the strand of Pagasæ.

[1] ἔνθ' ἔτι νῦν, *i.e.* the custom is still observed amongst their descendants.

Chiswick Press
CHARLES WHITTINGHAM AND CO.
TOOKS COURT, CHANCERY LANE.

CATALOGUE OF

BOHN'S LIBRARIES.

718 Volumes, £158 8s. 6d.

N.B.—It is requested that all orders be accompanied by payment. Books are sent carriage free on the receipt of the published price in stamps or otherwise.

The Works to which the letters 'N. S.' (denoting New Style) are appended are kept in neat cloth bindings of various colours, as well as in the regular Library style. All Orders are executed in the New binding, unless the contrary is expressly stated.

Complete Sets or Separate Volumes can be had at short notice, half-bound in calf or morocco.

New Volumes of Standard Works in the various branches of Literature are constantly being added to this Series, which is already unsurpassed in respect to the number, variety, and cheapness of the Works contained in it. The Publishers beg to announce the following Volumes as recently issued or now in preparation :—

Seneca's Minor Essays and On Clemency. Translated by A. Stewart, M.A. [*Ready. See p.* 16.

Schopenhauer on the Fourfold Root and on the Will in Nature. Translated from the German. [*Ready. See p.* 9.

Schumann's Early Letters. [*Ready. See p.* 8.

Bond's Handy Book of Rules and Tables for Verifying Dates WITH THE CHRISTIAN ERA, &c. [*Ready. See p.* 19.

Chess Congress, 1862. *Second and Cheaper Edition.* [*Ready. See p.* 18.

Arthur Young's Travels in France. Edited by Miss Betham Edwards. With a Portrait. [*Ready. See p.* 8.

Johnson's Lives of the Poets. Edited by Robina Napier. [*In the press.*

The Works of Flavius Josephus. Whiston's Translation. Revised by Rev. A. R. Shilleto, M.A. With Topographical and Geographical Notes by Sir C. W. Wilson, K.C.M.G. [*In the press.*

Hoffmann's Works. Translated by Lieut.-Colonel Ewing. Vol. II. [*In the press.*

North's Lives of the Norths.

Pascal's Thoughts. Translated by C. Kegan Paul. [*In the press.*

Björnsen's Arne and the Fisher Lassie. Translated by W. H. Low. [*In the press.*

Apollonius Rhodius. The Argonautica. Trans. by E. P. Coleridge.

Racine's Plays. Translated by R. B. Boswell.

For forthcoming Volumes in the SELECT LIBRARY, see p. 24.

BOHN'S LIBRARIES.

STANDARD LIBRARY.

322 *Vols. at 3s. 6d. each, excepting those marked otherwise.* (57*l.* 1*s.* 6*d.*)

ADDISON'S Works. Notes of Bishop Hurd. Short Memoir, Portrait, and 8 Plates of Medals. 6 vols. *N. S.*
This is the most complete edition of Addison's Works issued.

ALFIERI'S Tragedies. In English Verse. With Notes, Arguments, and Introduction, by E. A. Bowring, C.B. 2 vols. *N. S.*

AMERICAN POETRY. — *See Poetry of America.*

BACON'S Moral and Historical Works, including Essays, Apophthegms, Wisdom of the Ancients, New Atlantis, Henry VII., Henry VIII., Elizabeth, Henry Prince of Wales, History of Great Britain, Julius Cæsar, and Augustus Cæsar. With Critical and Biographical Introduction and Notes by J. Devey, M.A. Portrait. *N. S.*
— *See also Philosophical Library.*

BALLADS AND SONGS of the Peasantry of England, from Oral Recitation, private MSS., Broadsides, &c. Edit. by R. Bell. *N. S.*

BEAUMONT AND FLETCHER. Selections. With Notes and Introduction by Leigh Hunt.

BECKMANN (J.) History of Inventions, Discoveries, and Origins. With Portraits of Beckmann and James Watt. 2 vols. *N. S.*

BELL (Robert).—*See Ballads, Chaucer, Green.*

BOSWELL'S Life of Johnson, with the TOUR in the HEBRIDES and JOHNSONIANA. New Edition, with Notes and Appendices, by the Rev. A. Napier, M.A., Trinity College, Cambridge, Vicar of Holkham, Editor of the Cambridge Edition of the 'Theological Works of Barrow.' With Frontispiece to each vol. 6 vols. *N.S.*

BREMER'S (Frederika) Works. Trans. by M. Howitt. Portrait. 4 vols. *N.S.*

BRINK (B. T.) Early English Literature (to Wiclif). By Bernhard Ten Brink. Trans. by Prof. H. M. Kennedy. *N. S.*

BRITISH POETS, from Milton to Kirke White. Cabinet Edition. With Frontispiece. 4 vols. *N. S.*

BROWNE'S (Sir Thomas) Works. Edit. by S. Wilkin, with Dr. Johnson's Life of Browne. Portrait. 3 vols.

BURKE'S Works. 6 vols. *N. S.*

— **Speeches on the Impeachment** of Warren Hastings; and Letters. 2 vols. *N. S.*

— **Life.** By J. Prior. Portrait. *N. S.*

BURNS (Robert). Life of. By J. G. Lockhart, D.C.L. A new and enlarged edition. With Notes and Appendices by W. S. Douglas. Portrait. *N. S.*

BUTLER'S (Bp.) Analogy of Religion; Natural and Revealed, to the Constitution and Course of Nature; with Two Dissertations on Identity and Virtue, and Fifteen Sermons. With Introductions, Notes, and Memoir. Portrait. *N. S.*

CAMÖEN'S Lusiad, or the Discovery of India. An Epic Poem. Trans. from the Portuguese, with Dissertation, Historical Sketch, and Life, by W. J. Mickle. 5th edition. *N. S.*

CARAFAS (The) of Maddaloni. Naples under Spanish Dominion. Trans. by Alfred de Reumont. Portrait of Massaniello.

CARREL. The Counter-Revolution in England for the Re-establishment of Popery under Charles II. and James II., by Armand Carrel; with Fox's History of James II. and Lord Lonsdale's Memoir of James II. Portrait of Carrel.

CARRUTHERS. — *See Pope, in Illustrated Library.*

CARY'S Dante. The Vision of Hell, Purgatory, and Paradise. Trans. by Rev. H. F. Cary, M.A. With Life, Chronological View of his Age, Notes, and Index of Proper Names. Portrait. *N. S.*
This is the authentic edition, containing Mr. Cary's last corrections, with additional notes.

CELLINI (Benvenuto). Memoirs of, by himself. With Notes of G. P. Carpani. Trans. by T. Roscoe. Portrait. *N. S.*

CERVANTES' Galatea. A Pastoral Romance. Trans. by G. W. J. Gyll. *N. S.*

— **Exemplary Novels.** Trans. by W. K. Kelly. *N. S.*

— **Don Quixote de la Mancha.** Motteux's Translation revised. With Lockhart's Life and Notes. 2 vols. *N. S.*

CHAUCER'S Poetical Works. With Poems formerly attributed to him. With a Memoir, Introduction, Notes, and a Glossary, by R. Bell. Improved edition, with Preliminary Essay by Rev. W. W. Skeat, M.A. Portrait. 4 vols. *N. S.*

CLASSIC TALES, containing Rasselas, Vicar of Wakefield, Gulliver's Travels, and The Sentimental Journey. *N. S.*

COLERIDGE'S (S. T.) Friend. A Series of Essays on Morals, Politics, and Religion Portrait. *N. S.*

— **Aids to Reflection. Confessions** of an Inquiring Spirit; and Essays on Faith and the Common Prayer-book. New Edition, revised. *N. S.*

— **Table-Talk and Omniana.** By T. Ashe, B.A. *N.S.*

— **Lectures on Shakspere and** other Poets. Edit. by T. Ashe, B.A. *N.S.*
Containing the lectures taken down in 1811-12 by J. P. Collier, and those delivered at Bristol in 1813.

— **Biographia Literaria; or, Bio**graphical Sketches of my Literary Life and Opinions; with Two Lay Sermons. *N. S.*

— **Miscellanies, Æsthetic and** Literary; to which is added, THE THEORY OF LIFE. Collected and arranged by T. Ashe, B.A. *N.S.*

COMMINES.—*See Philip.*

CONDÉ'S History of the Dominion of the Arabs in Spain. Trans. by Mrs. Foster. Portrait of Abderahmen ben Moavia. 3 vols.

COWPER'S Complete Works, Poems, Correspondence, and Translations. Edit. with Memoir by R. Southey. 45 Engravings. 8 vols.

COXE'S Memoirs of the Duke of Marlborough. With his original Correspondence, from family records at Blenheim. Revised edition. Portraits. 3 vols.
. An Atlas of the plans of Marlborough's campaigns, 4to. 10*s.* 6*d.*

— **History of the House of Austria.** From the Foundation of the Monarchy by Rhodolph of Hapsburgh to the Death of Leopold II., 1218-1792. By Archdn. Coxe. With Continuation from the Accession of Francis I. to the Revolution of 1848. 4 Portraits. 4 vols.

CUNNINGHAM'S Lives of the most Eminent British Painters. With Notes and 16 fresh Lives by Mrs. Heaton. 3 vols. *N. S.*

DEFOE'S Novels and Miscellaneous Works. With Prefaces and Notes, including those attributed to Sir W. Scott. Portrait. 7 vols. *N. S.*

DE LOLME'S Constitution of England, in which it is compared both with the Republican form of Government and the other Monarchies of Europe. Edit., with Life and Notes, by J. Macgregor, M.P.

DUNLOP'S History of Fiction. With Introduction and Supplement adapting the work to present requirements. By Henry Wilson. 2 vols., 5*s.* each.

EMERSON'S Works. 3 vols. Most complete edition published. *N. S.*
Vol. I.—Essays, Lectures, and Poems.
Vol. II.—English Traits, Nature, and Conduct of Life.
Vol. III.—Society and Solitude—Letters and Social Aims—Miscellaneous Papers (hitherto uncollected)—May-Day, &c.

FOSTER'S (John) Life and Correspondence. Edit. by J. E. Ryland. Portrait. 2 vols. *N. S.*

— **Lectures at Broadmead Chapel.** Edit. by J. E. Ryland. 2 vols. *N. S.*

— **Critical Essays contributed to** the 'Eclectic Review.' Edit. by J. E. Ryland. 2 vols. *N. S.*

— **Essays: On Decision of Charac**ter; on a Man's writing Memoirs of Himself; on the epithet Romantic; on the aversion of Men of Taste to Evangelical Religion. *N. S.*

— **Essays on the Evils of Popular** Ignorance, and a Discourse on the Propagation of Christianity in India. *N. S.*

— **Essay on the Improvement of** Time, with Notes of Sermons and other Pieces. *N. S.*

— **Fosteriana:** selected from periodical papers, edit. by H. G. Bohn. *N. S.*

FOX (Rt. Hon. C. J.)—*See Carrel.*

GIBBON'S Decline and Fall of the Roman Empire. Complete and unabridged, with variorum Notes; including those of Guizot, Wenck, Niebuhr, Hugo, Neander, and others. 7 vols. 2 Maps and Portrait. *N. S.*

GOETHE'S Works. Trans. into English by E. A. Bowring, C.B., Anna Swanwick, Sir Walter Scott, &c. &c. 13 vols *N. S.*

Vols. I. and II.—Autobiography and Annals. Portrait.

Vol. III.—Faust. Complete.

Vol. IV.—Novels and Tales: containing Elective Affinities, Sorrows of Werther, The German Emigrants, The Good Women, and a Nouvelette.

Vol. V.—Wilhelm Meister's Apprenticeship.

Vol. VI.—Conversations with Eckerman and Soret.

Vol. VII.—Poems and Ballads in the original Metres, including Hermann and Dorothea.

Vol. VIII.—Götz von Berlichingen, Torquato Tasso, Egmont, Iphigenia, Clavigo, Wayward Lover, and Fellow Culprits.

Vol. IX.—Wilhelm Meister's Travels. Complete Edition.

Vol. X.—Tour in Italy. Two Parts. And Second Residence in Rome.

Vol. XI.—Miscellaneous Travels, Letters from Switzerland, Campaign in France, Siege of Mainz, and Rhine Tour.

Vol. XII.—Early and Miscellaneous Letters, including Letters to his Mother, with Biography and Notes.

Vol. XIII.—Correspondence with Zelter.

—— Correspondence with Schiller. 2 vols.—*See Schiller.*

GOLDSMITH'S Works. 5 vols. *N.S.*

Vol. I.—Life, Vicar of Wakefield, Essays, and Letters.

Vol. II.—Poems, Plays, Bee, Cock Lane Ghost.

Vol. III.—The Citizen of the World, Polite Learning in Europe.

Vol. IV.—Biographies, Criticisms, Later Essays.

Vol. V.—Prefaces, Natural History, Letters, Goody Two-Shoes, Index.

GREENE, MARLOW, and BEN JONSON (Poems of). With Notes and Memoirs by R. Bell. *N. S.*

GREGORY'S (Dr.) The Evidences, Doctrines, and Duties of the Christian Religion.

GRIMM'S Household Tales. With the Original Notes. Trans. by Mrs. A. Hunt. Introduction by Andrew Lang, M.A. 2 vols. *N. S.*

GUIZOT'S History of Representative Government in Europe. Trans. by A. R. Scoble.

—— English Revolution of 1640. From the Accession of Charles I. to his Death. Trans. by W. Hazlitt. Portrait.

—— History of Civilisation. From the Roman Empire to the French Revolution. Trans. by W. Hazlitt. Portraits. 3 vols

HALL'S (Rev. Robert) Works and Remains. Memoir by Dr. Gregory and Essay by J. Foster. Portrait.

HAUFF'S Tales. The Caravan—The Sheikh of Alexandria—The Inn in the Spessart. Translated by Prof. S. Mendel. *N. S.*

HAWTHORNE'S Tales. 3 vols. *N. S.*

Vol. I.—Twice-told Tales, and the Snow Image.

Vol. II.—Scarlet Letter, and the House with Seven Gables.

Vol. III.—Transformation, and Blithedale Romance.

HAZLITT'S (W.) Works. 7 vols. *N.S.*

—— Table-Talk.

—— The Literature of the Age of Elizabeth and Characters of Shakespeare's Plays. *N. S.*

—— English Poets and English Comic Writers. *N. S.*

—— The Plain Speaker. Opinions on Books, Men, and Things. *N. S.*

—— Round Table. Conversations of James Northcote, R.A.; Characteristics. *N. S.*

—— Sketches and Essays, and Winterslow. *N. S.*

—— Spirit of the Age; or, Contemporary Portraits. To which are added Free Thoughts on Public Affairs, and a Letter to William Gifford. New Edition by W. Carew Hazlitt. *N. S.*

HEINE'S Poems. Translated in the original Metres, with Life by E. A. Bowring, C.B. *N. S.*

—— Travel-Pictures. The Tour in the Harz, Norderney, and Book of Ideas, together with the Romantic School. Trans. by F. Storr. With Maps and Appendices. *N. S.*

HOFFMANN'S Works. The Serapion Brethren. Vol. I. Trans. by Lt.-Col. Ewing. *N. S.* [*Vol. II. in the press.*

HUGO'S (Victor) Dramatic Works: Hernani—Ruy Blas—The King's Diversion. Translated by Mrs. Newton Crosland and F. L. Slous. *N. S.*

—— **Poems,** chiefly Lyrical. Collected by H. L. Williams. *N. S.*
This volume contains contributions from F. S. Mahoney, G. W. M. Reynolds, Andrew Lang, Edwin Arnold, Mrs. Newton Crosland, Miss Fanny Kemble, Bishop Alexander, Prof. Dowden, &c.

HUNGARY: its History and Revolution, with Memoir of Kossuth. Portrait.

HUTCHINSON (Colonel). Memoirs of. By his Widow, with her Autobiography, and the Siege of Lathom House. Portrait. *N. S.*

IRVING'S (Washington) Complete Works. 15 vols. *N. S.*

—— **Life and Letters.** By his Nephew, Pierre E. Irving. With Index and a Portrait. 2 vols. *N. S.*

JAMES'S (G. P. R.) Life of Richard Cœur de Lion. Portraits of Richard and Philip Augustus. 2 vols.

—— **Louis XIV.** Portraits. 2 vols.

JAMESON (Mrs.) Shakespeare's Heroines. Characteristics of Women. By Mrs. Jameson. *N. S.*

JEAN PAUL.—*See Richter.*

JONSON (Ben). Poems of.—*See Greene.*

JUNIUS'S Letters. With Woodfall's Notes. An Essay on the Authorship. Facsimiles of Handwriting. 2 vols. *N. S.*

LA FONTAINE'S Fables. In English Verse, with Essay on the Fabulists. By Elizur Wright. *N. S.*

LAMARTINE'S The Girondists, or Personal Memoirs of the Patriots of the French Revolution. Trans. by H. T. Ryde. Portraits of Robespierre, Madame Roland, and Charlotte Corday. 3 vols.

—— **The Restoration of Monarchy** in France (a Sequel to The Girondists). 5 Portraits. 4 vols.

—— **The French Revolution of 1848.** 6 Portraits.

LAMB'S (Charles) Elia and Eliana. Complete Edition. Portrait. *N. S.*

—— **Specimens of English Dramatic** Poets of the time of Elizabeth. Notes, with the Extracts from the Garrick Plays. *N. S.*

—— **Talfourd's Letters of Charles** Lamb. New Edition, by W. Carew Hazlitt. 2 vols. *N. S.*

LANZI'S History of Painting in Italy, from the Period of the Revival of the Fine Arts to the End of the 18th Century. With Memoir of the Author. Portraits of Raffaelle, Titian, and Correggio, after the Artists themselves. Trans. by T. Roscoe. 3 vols.

LAPPENBERG'S England under the Anglo-Saxon Kings. Trans. by B. Thorpe, F.S.A. 2 vols. *N. S.*

LESSING'S Dramatic Works. Complete. By E. Bell, M.A. With Memoir by H. Zimmern. Portrait. 2 vols. *N. S.*

—— **Laokoon, Dramatic Notes, and** Representation of Death by the Ancients. Frontispiece. *N. S.*

LOCKE'S Philosophical Works, containing Human Understanding, with Bishop of Worcester, Malebranche's Opinions, Natural Philosophy, Reading and Study. With Preliminary Discourse, Analysis, and Notes, by J. A. St. John. Portrait. 2 vols. *N. S.*

—— **Life and Letters,** with Extracts from his Common-place Books. By Lord King.

LOCKHART (J. G.)—*See Burns.*

LONSDALE (Lord).—*See Carrel.*

LUTHER'S Table-Talk. Trans. by W. Hazlitt. With Life by A. Chalmers, and LUTHER'S CATECHISM. Portrait after Cranach. *N. S.*

—— **Autobiography.**—*See Michelet.*

MACHIAVELLI'S History of Florence, THE PRINCE, Savonarola, Historical Tracts, and Memoir. Portrait. *N. S.*

MARLOWE. Poems of.—*See Greene.*

MARTINEAU'S (Harriet) History of England (including History of the Peace) from 1800-1846. 5 vols. *N. S.*

MENZEL'S History of Germany, from he Earliest Period to the Crimean War. Portraits. 3 vols.

MICHELET'S Autobiography of Luther. Trans. by W. Hazlitt. With Notes. *N. S.*

—— **The French Revolution** to the Flight of the King in 1791. *N. S.*

MIGNET'S The French Revolution, from 1789 to 1814. Portrait of Napoleon. *N. S.*

MILTON'S Prose Works. With Preface, Preliminary Remarks by J. A. St. John, and Index. 5 vols.

MITFORD'S (Miss) Our Village. Sketches of Rural Character and Scenery. 2 Engravings. 2 vols. *N. S.*

MOLIÈRE'S Dramatic Works. In English Prose, by C. H. Wall. With a Life and a Portrait. 3 vols. *N. S.*

'It is not too much to say that we have here probably as good a translation of Molière as can be given.'—*Academy.*

MONTAGU. Letters and Works of Lady Mary Wortley Montagu. Lord Wharncliffe's Third Edition. Edited by W. Moy Thomas. With steel plates. 2 vols. 5*s.* each. *N. S.*

MONTESQUIEU'S Spirit of Laws. Revised Edition, with D'Alembert's Analysis, Notes, and Memoir. 2 vols. *N. S.*

NEANDER (Dr. A.) History of the Christian Religion and Church. Trans. by J. Torrey. With Short Memoir. 10 vols.

—— **Life of Jesus Christ, in its Historical** Connexion and Development. *N. S.*

—— **The Planting and Training of** the Christian Church by the Apostles. With the Antignosticus, or Spirit of Tertullian. Trans. by J. E. Ryland. 2 vols.

—— **Lectures on the History of** Christian Dogmas. Trans. by J. E. Ryland. 2 vols.

—— **Memorials of Christian Life in** the Early and Middle Ages; including Light in Dark Places. Trans. by J. E. Ryland.

OCKLEY (S.) History of the Saracens and their Conquests in Syria, Persia, and Egypt. Comprising the Lives of Mohammed and his Successors to the Death of Abdalmelik, the Eleventh Caliph. By Simon Ockley, B.D., Prof. of Arabic in Univ. of Cambridge. Portrait of Mohammed.

PERCY'S Reliques of Ancient English Poetry, consisting of Ballads, Songs, and other Pieces of our earlier Poets, with some few of later date. With Essay on Ancient Minstrels, and Glossary. 2 vols. *N. S.*

PHILIP DE COMMINES. Memoirs of. Containing the Histories of Louis XI. and Charles VIII., and Charles the Bold, Duke of Burgundy. With the History of Louis XI., by J. de Troyes. With a Life and Notes by A. R. Scoble. Portraits. 2 vols.

PLUTARCH'S LIVES. Newly Translated, with Notes and Life, by A Stewart, M.A., late Fellow of Trinity College, Cambridge, and G. Long, M.A. 4 vols. *N. S.*

POETRY OF AMERICA. Selections from One Hundred Poets, from 1776 to 1876. With Introductory Review, and Specimens of Negro Melody, by W. J. Linton. Portrait of W. Whitman. *N. S.*

RANKE (L.) History of the Popes, **their Church and State, and their Conflicts** with Protestantism in the 16th and 17th Centuries. Trans. by E. Foster. Portraits of Julius II. (after Raphael), Innocent X. (after Velasquez), and Clement VII. (after Titian). 3 vols. *N. S.*

—— **History of Servia.** Trans. by Mrs. Kerr. To which is added, The Slave Provinces of Turkey, by Cyprien Robert. *N. S.*

—— **History of the Latin and Teutonic** Nations. 1494-1514. Trans. by P. A. Ashworth, translator of Dr. Gneist's 'History of the English Constitution.' *N. S.*

REUMONT (Alfred de).—*See Carafas.*

REYNOLDS' (Sir J.) Literary Works. With Memoir and Remarks by H. W. Beechy. 2 vols. *N. S.*

RICHTER (Jean Paul). Levana, a Treatise on Education; together with the Autobiography, and a short Memoir. *N. S.*

—— **Flower, Fruit, and Thorn Pieces,** or the Wedded Life, Death, and Marriage of Siebenkaes. Translated by Alex. Ewing. *N. S.*

The only complete English translation.

ROSCOE'S (W.) Life of Leo X., with Notes, Historical Documents, and Dissertation on Lucretia Borgia. 3 Portraits. 2 vols.

—— **Lorenzo de' Medici,** called 'The Magnificent,' with Copyright Notes, Poems, Letters, &c. With Memoir of Roscoe and Portrait of Lorenzo.

RUSSIA, History of, from the earliest Period to the Crimean War. By W. K. Kelly. 3 Portraits. 2 vols.

SCHILLER'S Works. 7 vols. *N. S.*

Vol. I.—History of the Thirty Years' War. Rev. A. J. W. Morrison, M.A. Portrait.

Vol. II.—History of the Revolt in the Netherlands, the Trials of Counts Egmont and Horn, the Siege of Antwerp, and the Disturbance of France preceding the Reign of Henry IV. Translated by Rev. A. J. W. Morrison and L. Dora Schmitz.

Vol. III.—Don Carlos. R. D. Boylan —Mary Stuart. Mellish—Maid of Orleans. Anna Swanwick—Bride of Messina. A. Lodge, M.A. Together with the Use of the Chorus in Tragedy (a short Essay). Engravings.

These Dramas are all translated in metre.

Vol. IV.—Robbers—Fiesco—Love and Intrigue—Demetrius—Ghost Seer—Sport of Divinity.

The Dramas in this volume are in prose.

Vol. V.—Poems. E. A. Bowring, C.B.

Vol. VI.—Essays, Æsthetical and Philosophical, including the Dissertation on the Connexion between the Animal and Spiritual in Man.

Vol. VII.—Wallenstein's Camp. J. Churchill.—Piccolomini and Death of Wallenstein. S. T. Coleridge.—William Tell. Sir Theodore Martin, K.C.B., LL.D.

SCHILLER and GOETHE. Correspondence between, from A.D. 1794-1805. With Short Notes by L. Dora Schmitz. 2 vols. *N. S.*

SCHLEGEL'S (F.) Lectures on the Philosophy of Life and the Philosophy of Language. By A. J. W. Morrison.

—— **The History of Literature,** Ancient and Modern.

—— **The Philosophy of History.** With Memoir and Portrait.

—— **Modern History,** with the Lectures entitled Cæsar and Alexander, and The Beginning of our History. By L. Purcel and R. H. Whitelock.

—— **Æsthetic and Miscellaneous** Works, containing Letters on Christian Art, Essay on Gothic Architecture, Remarks on the Romance Poetry of the Middle Ages, on Shakspeare, the Limits of the Beautiful, and on the Language and Wisdom of the Indians. By E. J. Millington.

SCHLEGEL (A. W.) Dramatic Art and Literature. By J. Black. With Memoir by A. J. W. Morrison. Portrait.

SCHUMANN (Robert), His Life and Works. By A. Reissmann. Trans. by A. L. Alger. *N. S.*

—— **Early Letters.** Translated by May Herbert. *N.S.*

SHAKESPEARE'S Dramatic Art. The History and Character of Shakspeare's Plays. By Dr. H. Ulrici. Trans. by L. Dora Schmitz. 2 vols. *N. S.*

SHERIDAN'S Dramatic Works. With Memoir. Portrait (after Reynolds). *N. S.*

SKEAT (Rev. W. W.)—*See Chaucer.*

SISMONDI'S History of the Literature of the South of Europe. With Notes and Memoir by T. Roscoe. Portraits of Sismondi and Dante. 2 vols.

The specimens of early French, Italian, Spanish, and Portugese Poetry, in English Verse, by Cary and others.

SMITH'S (Adam) The Wealth of Nations. An Inquiry into the Nature and Causes of. Reprinted from the Sixth Edition. With an Introduction by Ernest Belfort Bax. 2 vols. *N. S.*

SMITH'S (Adam) Theory of Moral Sentiments; with Essay on the First Formation of Languages, and Critical Memoir by Dugald Stewart.

SMYTH'S (Professor) Lectures on Modern History; from the Irruption of the Northern Nations to the close of the American Revolution. 2 vols.

—— **Lectures on the French Revolu**tion. With Index. 2 vols.

SOUTHEY.—*See Cowper, Wesley, and (Illustrated Library) Nelson.*

STURM'S Morning Communings with God, or Devotional Meditations for Every Day. Trans. by W. Johnstone, M.A.

SULLY. Memoirs of the Duke of, Prime Minister to Henry the Great. With Notes and Historical Introduction. 4 Portraits. 4 vols.

TAYLOR'S (Bishop Jeremy) Holy Living and Dying, with Prayers, containing the Whole Duty of a Christian and the parts of Devotion fitted to all Occasions. Portrait. *N. S.*

THIERRY'S Conquest of England by the Normans; its Causes, and its Consequences in England and the Continent. By W. Hazlitt. With short Memoir. 2 Portraits. 2 vols. *N. S.*

TROYE'S (Jean de).—*See Philip de Commines.*

ULRICI (Dr.)—*See Shakespeare.*

VASARI. Lives of the most Eminent Painters, Sculptors, and Architects. By Mrs. J. Foster, with selected Notes. Portrait. 6 vols., Vol. VI. being an additional Volume of Notes by J. P. Richter. *N. S.*

WERNER'S Templars in Cyprus. Trans. by E. A. M. Lewis. *N. S.*

WESLEY, the Life of, and the Rise and Progress of Methodism. By Robert Southey. Portrait. 5*s*. *N. S.*

WHEATLEY. A Rational Illustration of the Book of Common Prayer, being the Substance of everything Liturgical in all former Ritualist Commentators upon the subject. Frontispiece. *N. S.*

YOUNG (Arthur) Travels in France. Edited by Miss Betham Edwards. With a Portrait. *N. S.*

HISTORICAL LIBRARY.

22 *Volumes at 5s. each.* (5*l.* 10*s. per set.*)

EVELYN'S Diary and Correspondence, with the Private Correspondence of Charles I. and Sir Edward Nicholas, and between Sir Edward Hyde (Earl of Clarendon) and Sir Richard Browne. Edited from the Original MSS. by W. Bray, F.A.S. 4 vols. *N. S.* 45 Engravings (after Vandyke, Lely, Kneller, and Jamieson, &c.).

N.B.—This edition contains 130 letters from Evelyn and his wife, contained in no other edition.

PEPYS' Diary and Correspondence. With Life and Notes, by Lord Braybrooke. 4 vols. *N. S.* With Appendix containing additional Letters, an Index, and 31 Engravings (after Vandyke, Sir P. Lely, Holbein Kneller, &c.).

JESSE'S Memoirs of the Court of England under the Stuarts, including the Protectorate. 3 vols. With Index and 42 Portraits (after Vandyke, Lely, &c.).

— Memoirs of the Pretenders and their Adherents. 7 Portraits.

NUGENT'S (Lord) Memorials of Hampden, his Party and Times. With Memoir. 12 Portraits (after Vandyke and others). *N. S.*

STRICKLAND'S (Agnes) Lives of the Queens of England from the Norman Conquest. From authentic Documents, public and private. 6 Portraits. 6 vols. *N. S.*

— Life of Mary Queen of Scots. 2 Portraits. 2 vols. *N. S.*

— Lives of the Tudor and Stuart Princesses. With 2 Portraits. *N. S.*

PHILOSOPHICAL LIBRARY.

17 *Vols. at 5s. each, excepting those marked otherwise.* (3*l.* 19*s. per set.*)

BACON'S Novum Organum and Advancement of Learning. With Notes by J. Devey, M.A.

BAX. A Handbook of the History of Philosophy, for the use of Students. By E. Belfort Bax, Editor of Kant's 'Prolegomena.' 5*s.* *N. S.*

COMTE'S Philosophy of the Sciences. An Exposition of the Principles of the *Cours de Philosophie Positive.* By G. H. Lewes, Author of 'The Life of Goethe.'

DRAPER (Dr. J. W.) A History of the Intellectual Development of Europe. 2 vols. *N. S.*

HEGEL'S Philosophy of History. By J. Sibree, M.A.

KANT'S Critique of Pure Reason. By J. M. D. Meiklejohn. *N. S.*

— Prolegomena and Metaphysical Foundations of Natural Science, with Biography and Memoir by E. Belfort Bax. Portrait. *N. S.*

LOGIC, or the Science of Inference. A Popular Manual. By J. Devey.

MILLER (Professor). History Philosophically Illustrated, from the Fall of the Roman Empire to the French Revolution. With Memoir. 4 vols. 3*s.* 6*d.* each.

SCHOPENHAUER on the Fourfold Root of the Principle of Sufficient Reason, and on the Will in Nature. Trans. from the German.

SPINOZA'S Chief Works. Trans. with Introduction by R. H. M. Elwes. 2 vols. *N.S.*

Vol. I.—Tractatus Theologico-Politicus —Political Treatise.

Vol. II.—Improvement of the Understanding—Ethics—Letters.

TENNEMANN'S Manual of the History of Philosophy. Trans. by Rev. A. Johnson, M.A.

THEOLOGICAL LIBRARY.

15 *Vols. at 5s. each, excepting those marked otherwise.* (3*l.* 13*s.* 6*d. per set.*)

BLEEK. Introduction to the Old Testament. By Friedrich Bleek. Trans. under the supervision of Rev. E. Venables, Residentiary Canon of Lincoln. 2 vols. *N. S.*

CHILLINGWORTH'S Religion of Protestants. 3*s.* 6*d.*

EUSEBIUS. Ecclesiastical History of Eusebius Pamphilius, Bishop of Cæsarea. Trans. by Rev. C. F. Cruse, M.A. With Notes, Life, and Chronological Tables.

EVAGRIUS. History of the Church. —*See Theodoret.*

HARDWICK. History of the Articles of Religion; to which is added a Series of Documents from A.D. 1536 to A.D. 1615. Ed. by Rev. F. Proctor. *N. S.*

HENRY'S (Matthew) Exposition of the Book of Psalms. Numerous Woodcuts.

PEARSON (John, D.D.) Exposition of the Creed. Edit. by E. Walford, M.A. With Notes, Analysis, and Indexes. *N. S.*

PHILO-JUDÆUS, Works of. The Contemporary of Josephus. Trans. by C. D. Yonge. 4 vols.

PHILOSTORGIUS. Ecclesiastical History of.—*See Sozomen.*

SOCRATES' Ecclesiastical History. Comprising a History of the Church from Constantine, A.D. 305, to the 38th year of Theodosius II. With Short Account of the Author, and selected Notes.

SOZOMEN'S Ecclesiastical History. A.D. 324-440. With Notes, Prefatory Remarks by Valesius, and Short Memoir. Together with the ECCLESIASTICAL HISTORY OF PHILOSTORGIUS, as epitomised by Photius. Trans. by Rev. E. Walford, M.A. With Notes and brief Life.

THEODORET and EVAGRIUS. Histories of the Church from A.D. 332 to the Death of Theodore of Mopsuestia, A.D. 427; and from A.D. 431 to A.D. 544. With Memoirs.

WIESELER'S (Karl) Chronological Synopsis of the Four Gospels. Trans. by Rev. Canon Venables. *N. S.*

ANTIQUARIAN LIBRARY.

35 *Vols. at 5s. each.* (8*l.* 15*s. per set.*)

ANGLO-SAXON CHRONICLE. —*See Bede.*

ASSER'S Life of Alfred.—*See Six O. E. Chronicles.*

BEDE'S (Venerable) Ecclesiastical History of England. Together with the ANGLO-SAXON CHRONICLE. With Notes, Short Life, Analysis, and Map. Edit. by J. A. Giles, D.C.L.

BOETHIUS'S Consolation of Philosophy. King Alfred's Anglo-Saxon Version of. With an English Translation on opposite pages, Notes, Introduction, and Glossary, by Rev. S. Fox, M.A. To which is added the Anglo-Saxon Version of the METRES OF BOETHIUS, with a free Translation by Martin F. Tupper, D.C.L.

BRAND'S Popular Antiquities of England, Scotland, and Ireland. Illustrating the Origin of our Vulgar and Provincial Customs, Ceremonies, and Superstitions. By Sir Henry Ellis, K.H., F.R.S. Frontispiece. 3 vols.

CHRONICLES of the CRUSADES. Contemporary Narratives of Richard Cœur de Lion, by Richard of Devizes and Geoffrey de Vinsauf; and of the Crusade at Saint Louis, by Lord John de Joinville. With Short Notes. Illuminated Frontispiece from an old MS.

DYER'S (T. F. T.) British Popular Customs, Present and Past. An Account of the various Games and Customs associated with different Days of the Year in the British Isles, arranged according to the Calendar. By the Rev. T. F. Thiselton Dyer, M.A.

EARLY TRAVELS IN PALESTINE. Comprising the Narratives of Arculf, Willibald, Bernard, Sæwulf, Sigurd, Benjamin of Tudela, Sir John Maundeville, De la Brocquière, and Maundrell; all unabridged. With Introduction and Notes by Thomas Wright. Map of Jerusalem.

ELLIS (G.) Specimens of Early English Metrical Romances, relating to Arthur, Merlin, Guy of Warwick, Richard Cœur de Lion, Charlemagne, Roland, &c. &c. With Historical Introduction by J. O. Halliwell, F.R.S. Illuminated Frontispiece from an old MS.

ETHELWERD. Chronicle of.—*See Six O. E. Chronicles.*

FLORENCE OF WORCESTER'S Chronicle, with the Two Continuations: comprising Annals of English History from the Departure of the Romans to the Reign of Edward I. Trans., with Notes, by Thomas Forester, M.A.

GEOFFREY OF MONMOUTH. Chronicle of.—*See Six O. E. Chronicles.*

GESTA ROMANORUM, or Entertaining Moral Stories invented by the Monks. Trans. with Notes by the Rev. Charles Swan. Edit. by W. Hooper, M.A.

GILDAS. Chronicle of.—*See Six O. E. Chronicles.*

GIRALDUS CAMBRENSIS' Historical Works. Containing Topography of Ireland, and History of the Conquest of Ireland, by Th. Forester, M.A. Itinerary through Wales, and Description of Wales, by Sir R. Colt Hoare.

HENRY OF HUNTINGDON'S History of the English, from the Roman Invasion to the Accession of Henry II.; with the Acts of King Stephen, and the Letter to Walter. By T. Forester, M.A. Frontispiece from au old MS.

INGULPH'S Chronicles of the Abbey of Croyland, with the CONTINUATION by Peter of Blois and others. Trans. with Notes by H. T. Riley, B.A.

KEIGHTLEY'S (Thomas) Fairy Mythology, illustrative of the Romance and Superstition of Various Countries. Frontispiece by Cruikshank. *N. S.*

LEPSIUS'S Letters from Egypt, Ethiopia, and the Peninsula of Sinai; to which are added, Extracts from his Chronology of the Egyptians, with reference to the Exodus of the Israelites. By L. and J. B. Horner. Maps and Coloured View of Mount Barkal.

MALLET'S Northern Antiquities, or an Historical Account of the Manners, Customs, Religions, and Literature of the Ancient Scandinavians. Trans. by Bishop Percy. With Translation of the PROSE EDDA, and Notes by J. A. Blackwell. Also an Abstract of the 'Eyrbyggia Saga' by Sir Walter Scott. With Glossary and Coloured Frontispiece.

MARCO POLO'S Travels; with Notes and Introduction. Edit. by T. Wright.

MATTHEW PARIS'S English History, from 1235 to 1273. By Rev. J. A. Giles, D.C.L. With Frontispiece. 3 vols.—*See also Roger of Wendover.*

MATTHEW OF WESTMINSTER'S Flowers of History, especially such as relate to the affairs of Britain, from the beginning of the World to A.D. 1307. By C. D. Yonge. 2 vols.

NENNIUS. Chronicle of.—*See Six O. E. Chronicles.*

ORDERICUS VITALIS' Ecclesiastical History of England and Normandy. With Notes, Introduction of Guizot, and the Critical Notice of M. Delille, by T. Forester, M.A. To which is added the CHRONICLE OF St. EVROULT. With General and Chronological Indexes. 4 vols.

PAULI'S (Dr. R.) Life of Alfred the Great. To which is appended Alfred's ANGLO-SAXON VERSION OF OROSIUS. With literal Translation interpaged, Notes, and an ANGLO-SAXON GRAMMAR and Glossary, by B. Thorpe, Esq. Frontispiece.

RICHARD OF CIRENCESTER. Chronicle of.—*See Six O. E. Chronicles.*

ROGER DE HOVEDEN'S Annals of English History, comprising the History of England and of other Countries of Europe from A.D. 732 to A.D. 1201. With Notes by H. T. Riley, B.A. 2 vols.

ROGER OF WENDOVER'S Flowers of History, comprising the History of England from the Descent of the Saxons to A.D. 1235, formerly ascribed to Matthew Paris. With Notes and Index by J. A. Giles, D.C.L. 2 vols.

SIX OLD ENGLISH CHRONICLES: viz., Asser's Life of Alfred and the Chronicles of Ethelwerd, Gildas, Nennius, Geoffrey of Monmouth, and Richard of Cirencester. Edit., with Notes, by J. A. Giles, D.C.L. Portrait of Alfred.

WILLIAM OF MALMESBURY'S Chronicle of the Kings of England, from the Earliest Period to King Stephen. By Rev. J. Sharpe. With Notes by J. A. Giles, D.C.L. Frontispiece.

YULE-TIDE STORIES. A Collection of Scandinavian and North-German Popular Tales and Traditions, from the Swedish, Danish, and German. Edit. by B. Thorpe.

ILLUSTRATED LIBRARY.

87 *Vols. at 5s. each, excepting those marked otherwise.* (23*l.* 3*s.* 6*d. per set.*)

ALLEN'S (Joseph, R.N.) Battles of the British Navy. Revised edition, with Indexes of Names and Events, and 57 Portraits and Plans. 2 vols.

ANDERSEN'S Danish Fairy Tales. By Caroline Peachey. With Short Life and 120 Wood Engravings.

ARIOSTO'S Orlando Furioso. In English Verse by W. S. Rose. With Notes and Short Memoir. Portrait after Titian, and 24 Steel Engravings. 2 vols.

BECHSTEIN'S Cage and Chamber Birds: their Natural History, Habits, &c. Together with SWEET'S BRITISH WARBLERS. 43 Plates and Woodcuts. *N. S.*

—— or with the Plates Coloured, 7*s.* 6*d.*

BONOMI'S Nineveh and its Palaces. The Discoveries of Botta and Layard applied to the Elucidation of Holy Writ. 7 Plates and 294 Woodcuts. *N. S.*

BUTLER'S Hudibras, with Variorum Notes and Biography. Portrait and 28 Illustrations.

CATTERMOLE'S Evenings at Haddon Hall. Romantic Tales of the Olden Times. With 24 Steel Engravings after Cattermole.

CHINA, Pictorial, Descriptive, and Historical, with some account of Ava and the Burmese, Siam, and Anam. Map, and nearly 100 Illustrations.

CRAIK'S (G. L.) Pursuit of Knowledge under Difficulties. Illustrated by Anecdotes and Memoirs. Numerous Woodcut Portraits. *N. S.*

CRUIKSHANK'S Three Courses and a Dessert; comprising three Sets of Tales, West Country, Irish, and Legal; and a Mélange. With 50 Illustrations by Cruikshank. *N. S.*

—— **Punch and Judy.** The Dialogue of the Puppet Show; an Account of its Origin, &c. 24 Illustrations by Cruikshank. *N. S.*

—— With Coloured Plates. 7*s.* 6*d.*

DIDRON'S Christian Iconography; a History of Christian Art in the Middle Ages. By the late A. N. Didron. Trans. by E. J. Millington, and completed, with Additions and Appendices, by Margaret Stokes. 2 vols. With numerous Illustrations.

Vol. I. The History of the Nimbus, the Aureole, and the Glory; Representations of the Persons of the Trinity.

Vol. II. The Trinity; Angels; Devils; The Soul; The Christian Scheme. Appendices.

DANTE, in English Verse, by I. C. Wright, M.A. With Introduction and Memoir. Portrait and 34 Steel Engravings after Flaxman. *N. S.*

DYER (Dr. T. H.) Pompeii: its Buildings and Antiquities. An Account of the City, with full Description of the Remains and Recent Excavations, and an Itinerary for Visitors. By T. H. Dyer, LL.D. Nearly 300 Wood Engravings, Map, and Plan. 7*s.* 6*d.* *N. S.*

—— **Rome:** History of the City, with Introduction on recent Excavations. 8 Engravings, Frontispiece, and 2 Maps.

GIL BLAS. The Adventures of. From the French of Lesage by Smollett. 24 Engravings after Smirke, and 10 Etchings by Cruikshank. 612 pages. 6*s.*

GRIMM'S Gammer Grethel; or, German Fairy Tales and Popular Stories, containing 42 Fairy Tales. By Edgar Taylor. Numerous Woodcuts after Cruikshank and Ludwig Grimm. 3*s.* 6*d.*

HOLBEIN'S Dance of Death and Bible Cuts. Upwards of 150 Subjects, engraved in facsimile, with Introduction and Descriptions by the late Francis Douce and Dr. Dibdin. 7*s.* 6*d.*

HOWITT'S (Mary) Pictorial Calendar of the Seasons; embodying AIKIN'S CALENDAR OF NATURE. Upwards of 100 Woodcuts.

INDIA, Pictorial, Descriptive, and Historical, from the Earliest Times. 100 Engravings on Wood and Map.

JESSE'S Anecdotes of Dogs. With 40 Woodcuts after Harvey, Bewick, and others. *N. S.*

—— With 34 additional Steel Engravings after Cooper, Landseer, &c. 7*s.* 6*d.* *N. S.*

KING'S (C. W.) Natural History of Gems or Decorative Stones. Illustrations. 6*s.*

—— **Natural History of Precious** Stones and Metals. Illustrations. 6*s.*

KITTO'S Scripture Lands. Described in a series of Historical, Geographical, and Topographical Sketches. 42 Maps.

—— With the Maps coloured, 7*s.* 6*d.*

KRUMMACHER'S Parables. 40 Illustrations.

LINDSAY'S (Lord) Letters on Egypt, Edom, and the Holy Land. 36 Wood Engravings and 2 Maps.

LODGE'S Portraits of Illustrious Personages of Great Britain, with Biographical and Historical Memoirs. 240 Portraits engraved on Steel, with the respective Biographies unabridged. Complete in 8 vols.

LONGFELLOW'S Poetical Works, including his Translations and Notes. 24 full-page Woodcuts by Birket Foster and others, and a Portrait. *N. S.*

—— Without the Illustrations, 3*s*. 6*d*. *N. S.*

—— **Prose Works.** With 16 full-page Woodcuts by Birket Foster and others.

LOUDON'S (Mrs.) Entertaining Naturalist. Popular Descriptions, Tales, and Anecdotes, of more than 500 Animals. Numerous Woodcuts. *N. S.*

MARRYAT'S (Capt., R.N.) Masterman Ready; or, the Wreck of the *Pacific*. (Written for Young People.) With 93 Woodcuts. 3*s*. 6*d*. *N. S.*

—— **Mission; or, Scenes in Africa.** (Written for Young People.) Illustrated by Gilbert and Dalziel. 3*s*. 6*d*. *N. S.*

—— **Pirate and Three Cutters.** (Written for Young People.) With a Memoir. 8 Steel Engravings after Clarkson Stanfield, R.A. 3*s*. 6*d*. *N. S.*

—— **Privateersman.** Adventures by Sea and Land One Hundred Years Ago. (Written for Young People.) 8 Steel Engravings. 3*s*. 6*d*. *N. S.*

—— **Settlers in Canada.** (Written for Young People.) 10 Engravings by Gilbert and Dalziel. 3*s*. 6*d*. *N. S.*

—— **Poor Jack.** (Written for Young People.) With 16 Illustrations after Clarkson Stanfield, R.A. 3*s*. 6*d*. *N. S.*

—— **Midshipman Easy.** With 8 full-page Illustrations. Small post 8vo. 3*s*. 6*d*. *N.S.*

—— **Peter Simple.** With 8 full-page Illustrations. Small post 8vo. 3*s*. 6*d*. *N.S.*

MAXWELL'S Victories of Wellington and the British Armies. Frontispiece and 4 Portraits.

MICHAEL ANGELO and RAPHAEL, Their Lives and Works. By Duppa and Quatremère de Quincy. Portraits and Engravings, including the Last Judgment, and Cartoons. *N. S.*

MILLER'S History of the Anglo-Saxons, from the Earliest Period to the Norman Conquest. Portrait of Alfred, Map of Saxon Britain, and 12 Steel Engravings.

MILTON'S Poetical Works, with a Memoir and Notes by J. Montgomery, an Index to Paradise Lost, Todd's Verbal Index to all the Poems, and Notes. 120 Wood Engravings. 2 vols. *N. S.*

MUDIE'S History of British Birds. Revised by W. C. L. Martin. 52 Figures of Birds and 7 Plates of Eggs. 2 vols. *N.S.*

—— With the Plates coloured, 7*s*. 6*d*. per vol.

NAVAL and MILITARY HEROES of Great Britain; a Record of British Valour on every Day in the year, from William the Conqueror to the Battle of Inkermann. By Major Johns, R.M., and Lieut. P. H. Nicolas, R.M. Indexes. 24 Portraits after Holbein, Reynolds, &c. 6*s*.

NICOLINI'S History of the Jesuits: their Origin, Progress, Doctrines, and Designs. 8 Portraits.

PETRARCH'S Sonnets, Triumphs, and other Poems, in English Verse. With Life by Thomas Campbell. Portrait and 15 Steel Engravings.

PICKERING'S History of the Races of Man, and their Geographical Distribution; with AN ANALYTICAL SYNOPSIS OF THE NATURAL HISTORY OF MAN. By Dr. Hall. Map of the World and 12 Plates.

—— With the Plates coloured, 7*s*. 6*d*.

PICTORIAL HANDBOOK OF Modern Geography on a Popular Plan. Compiled from the best Authorities, English and Foreign, by H. G. Bohn. 150 Woodcuts and 51 Maps. 6*s*.

—— With the Maps coloured, 7*s*. 6*d*.

—— Without the Maps, 3*s*. 6*d*.

POPE'S Poetical Works, including Translations. Edit., with Notes, by R. Carruthers. 2 vols.

—— **Homer's Iliad,** with Introduction and Notes by Rev. J. S. Watson, M.A. With Flaxman's Designs. *N. S.*

—— **Homer's Odyssey,** with the BATTLE OF FROGS AND MICE, Hymns, &c., by other translators, including Chapman. Introduction and Notes by J. S. Watson, M.A. With Flaxman's Designs. *N. S.*

—— **Life,** including many of his Letters. By R. Carruthers. Numerous Illustrations.

POTTERY AND PORCELAIN, and other objects of Vertu. Comprising an Illustrated Catalogue of the Bernal Collection, with the prices and names of the Possessors. Also an Introductory Lecture on Pottery and Porcelain, and an Engraved List of all Marks and Monograms. By H. G. Bohn. Numerous Woodcuts.

—— With coloured Illustrations, 10*s*. 6*d*.

PROUT'S (Father) Reliques. Edited by Rev. F. Mahony. Copyright edition, with the Author's last corrections and additions. 21 Etchings by D. Maclise, R.A. Nearly 600 pages. 5*s*. *N. S.*

RECREATIONS IN SHOOTING. With some Account of the Game found in the British Isles, and Directions for the Management of Dog and Gun. By 'Craven.' 62 Woodcuts and 9 Steel Engravings after A. Cooper, R.A.

RENNIE. Insect Architecture. Revised by Rev. J. G. Wood, M.A. 186 Woodcuts. *N. S.*

ROBINSON CRUSOE. With Memoir of Defoe, 12 Steel Engravings and 74 Woodcuts after Stothard and Harvey.

—— Without the Engravings, 3*s.* 6*d.*

ROME IN THE NINETEENTH CENTURY. An Account in 1817 of the Ruins of the Ancient City, and Monuments of Modern Times. By C. A. Eaton. 34 Steel Engravings. 2 vols.

SHARPE (S.) The History of Egypt, from the Earliest Times till the Conquest by the Arabs, A.D. 640. 2 Maps and upwards of 400 Woodcuts. 2 vols. *N. S.*

SOUTHEY'S Life of Nelson. With Additional Notes, Facsimiles of Nelson's Writing, Portraits, Plans, and 50 Engravings, after Birket Foster, &c. *N. S.*

STARLING'S (Miss) Noble Deeds of Women; or, Examples of Female Courage, Fortitude, and Virtue. With 14 Steel Portraits. *N. S.*

STUART and REVETT'S Antiquities of Athens, and other Monuments of Greece; with Glossary of Terms used in Grecian Architecture. 71 Steel Plates and numerous Woodcuts.

SWEET'S British Warblers. 5*s.*—*See Bechstein.*

TALES OF THE GENII; or, the Delightful Lessons of Horam, the Son of Asmar. Trans. by Sir C. Morrell. Numerous Woodcuts.

TASSO'S Jerusalem Delivered. In English Spenserian Verse, with Life, by J. H. Wiffen. With 8 Engravings and 24 Woodcuts. *N. S.*

WALKER'S Manly Exercises; containing Skating, Riding, Driving, Hunting, Shooting, Sailing, Rowing, Swimming, &c. 44 Engravings and numerous Woodcuts.

WALTON'S Complete Angler, or the Contemplative Man's Recreation, by Izaak Walton and Charles Cotton. With Memoirs and Notes by E. Jesse. Also an Account of Fishing Stations, Tackle, &c., by H. G. Bohn. Portrait and 203 Woodcuts. *N. S.*

—— With 26 additional Engravings on Steel, 7*s.* 6*d.*

—— **Lives of Donne, Wotton, Hooker,** &c., with Notes. A New Edition, revised by A. H. Bullen, with a Memoir of Izaak Walton by William Dowling. 6 Portraits, 6 Autograph Signatures, &c. *N. S.*

WELLINGTON, Life of. From the Materials of Maxwell. 18 Steel Engravings.

—— **Victories of.**—*See Maxwell.*

WESTROPP (H. M.) A Handbook of Archæology, Egyptian, Greek, Etruscan, Roman. By H. M. Westropp. Numerous Illustrations. 7*s.* 6*d.* *N. S.*

WHITE'S Natural History of Selborne, with Observations on various Parts of Nature, and the Naturalists' Calendar. Sir W. Jardine. Edit., with Notes and Memoir, by E. Jesse. 40 Portraits. *N. S.*

—— With the Plates coloured, 7*s.* 6*d.* *N. S.*

YOUNG LADY'S BOOK, The. A Manual of Recreations, Arts, Sciences, and Accomplishments. 1200 Woodcut Illustrations. 7*s.* 6*d.*

—— cloth gilt, gilt edges, 9*s.*

CLASSICAL LIBRARY.

TRANSLATIONS FROM THE GREEK AND LATIN.

102 *Vols. at* 5*s. each, excepting those marked otherwise.* (25*l.* 0*s.* 6*d. per set.*)

ÆSCHYLUS, The Dramas of. In English Verse by Anna Swanwick. 4th edition. *N. S.*

—— **The Tragedies of.** In Prose, with Notes and Introduction, by T. A. Buckley, B.A. Portrait. 3*s.* 6*d.*

AMMIANUS MARCELLINUS. History of Rome during the Reigns of Constantius, Julian, Jovianus, Valentinian, and Valens, by C. D. Yonge, B.A. Double volume. 7*s.* 6*d.*

ANTONINUS (M. Aurelius), The Thoughts of. Translated literally, with Notes, Biographical Sketch, and Essay on the Philosophy, by George Long, M.A. 3*s.* 6*d.* *N. S.*

APULEIUS, The Works of. Comprising the Golden Ass, God of Socrates, Florida, and Discourse of Magic. With a Metrical Version of Cupid and Psyche, and Mrs. Tighe's Psyche. Frontispiece.

ARISTOPHANES' Comedies. Trans., with Notes and Extracts from Frere's and other Metrical Versions, by W. J. Hickie. Portrait. 2 vols.

ARISTOTLE'S Nicomachean Ethics. Trans., with Notes, Analytical Introduction, and Questions for Students, by Ven. Archdn. Browne.

— Politics and Economics. Trans., with Notes, Analyses, and Index, by E. Walford, M.A., and an Essay and Life by Dr. Gillies.

— Metaphysics. Trans., with Notes, Analysis, and Examination Questions, by Rev. John H. M'Mahon, M.A.

— History of Animals. In Ten Books. Trans., with Notes and Index, by R. Cresswell, M.A.

— Organon; or, Logical Treatises, and the Introduction of Porphyry. With Notes, Analysis, and Introduction, by Rev. O. F. Owen, M.A. 2 vols. 3*s*. 6*d*. each.

— Rhetoric and Poetics. Trans., with Hobbes' Analysis, Exam. Questions, and Notes, by T. Buckley, B.A. Portrait.

ATHENÆUS. The Deipnosophists; or, the Banquet of the Learned. By C. D. Yonge, B.A. With an Appendix of Poetical Fragments. 3 vols.

ATLAS of Classical Geography. 22 large Coloured Maps. With a complete Index. Imp. 8vo. 7*s*. 6*d*.

BION.—*See Theocritus.*

CÆSAR. Commentaries on the Gallic and Civil Wars, with the Supplementary Books attributed to Hirtius, including the complete Alexandrian, African, and Spanish Wars. Trans. with Notes. Portrait.

CATULLUS, Tibullus, and the Vigil of Venus. Trans. with Notes and Biographical Introduction. To which are added, Metrical Versions by Lamb, Grainger, and others. Frontispiece.

CICERO'S Orations. Trans. by C. D. Yonge, B.A. 4 vols.

— On Oratory and Orators. With Letters to Quintus and Brutus. Trans., with Notes, by Rev. J. S. Watson, M.A.

— On the Nature of the Gods, Divination, Fate, Laws, a Republic, Consulship. Trans., with Notes, by C. D. Yonge, B.A.

— Academics, De Finibus, and Tusculan Questions. By C. D. Yonge, B.A. With Sketch of the Greek Philosophers mentioned by Cicero.

CICERO'S Orations.—*Continued.*

— Offices; or, Moral Duties. Cato Major, an Essay on Old Age; Lælius, an Essay on Friendship; Scipio's Dream; Paradoxes; Letter to Quintus on Magistrates. Trans., with Notes, by C. R. Edmonds. Portrait. 3*s*. 6*d*.

DEMOSTHENES' Orations. Trans., with Notes, Arguments, a Chronological Abstract, and Appendices, by C. Rann Kennedy. 5 vols.

DICTIONARY of LATIN and GREEK Quotations; including Proverbs, Maxims, Mottoes, Law Terms and Phrases. With the Quantities marked, and English Translations.

— With Index Verborum (622 pages). 6*s*.

— Index Verborum to the above, with the *Quantities* and Accents marked (56 pages), limp cloth. 1*s*.

DIOGENES LAERTIUS. Lives and Opinions of the Ancient Philosophers. Trans., with Notes, by C. D. Yonge, B.A.

EPICTETUS. The Discourses of. With the Encheiridion and Fragments. With Notes, Life, and View of his Philosophy, by George Long, M.A. *N. S.*

EURIPIDES. Trans., with Notes and Introduction, by T. A. Buckley, B.A. Portrait. 2 vols.

GREEK ANTHOLOGY. In English Prose by G. Burges, M.A. With Metrical Versions by Bland, Merivale, Lord Denman, &c.

GREEK ROMANCES of Heliodorus, Longus, and Achilles Tatius; viz., The Adventures of Theagenes and Chariclea; Amours of Daphnis and Chloe; and Loves of Clitopho and Leucippe. Trans., with Notes, by Rev. R. Smith, M.A.

HERODOTUS. Literally trans. by Rev. Henry Cary, M.A. Portrait.

HESIOD, CALLIMACHUS, and Theognis. In Prose, with Notes and Biographical Notices by Rev. J. Banks, M.A. Together with the Metrical Versions of Hesiod, by Elton; Callimachus, by Tytler; and Theognis, by Frere.

HOMER'S Iliad. In English Prose, with Notes by T. A. Buckley, B.A. Portrait.

— Odyssey, Hymns, Epigrams, and Battle of the Frogs and Mice. In English Prose, with Notes and Memoir by T. A. Buckley, B.A.

HORACE. In Prose by Smart, with Notes selected by T. A. Buckley, B.A. Portrait. 3*s*. 6*d*.

JULIAN THE EMPEROR. By the Rev. C. W. King, M.A.

JUSTIN, CORNELIUS NEPOS, and Eutropius. Trans., with Notes, by Rev. J. S. Watson, M.A.

JUVENAL, PERSIUS, SULPICIA, and Lucilius. In Prose, with Notes, Chronological Tables, Arguments, by L. Evans, M.A. To which is added the Metrical Version of Juvenal and Persius by Gifford. Frontispiece.

LIVY. The History of Rome. Trans. by Dr. Spillan and others. 4 vols. Portrait.

LUCAN'S Pharsalia. In Prose, with Notes by H. T. Riley.

LUCIAN'S Dialogues of the Gods, of the Sea Gods, and of the Dead. Trans. by Howard Williams, M.A.

LUCRETIUS. In Prose, with Notes and Biographical Introduction by Rev. J. S. Watson, M.A. To which is added the Metrical Version by J. M. Good.

MARTIAL'S Epigrams, complete. In Prose, with Verse Translations selected from English Poets, and other sources. Dble. vol. (670 pages). *7s. 6d.*

MOSCHUS.—*See Theocritus.*

OVID'S Works, complete. In Prose, with Notes and Introduction. 3 vols.

PAUSANIAS' Description of Greece. Translated into English, with Notes and Index. By Arthur Richard Shilleto, M.A., sometime Scholar of Trinity College, Cambridge. 2 vols.

PHALARIS. Bentley's Dissertations upon the Epistles of Phalaris, Themistocles, Socrates, Euripides, and the Fables of Æsop. With Introduction and Notes by Prof. W. Wagner, Ph.D.

PINDAR. In Prose, with Introduction and Notes by Dawson W. Turner. Together with the Metrical Version by Abraham Moore. Portrait.

PLATO'S Works. Trans., with Introduction and Notes. 6 vols.

—— Dialogues. A Summary and Analysis of. With Analytical Index to the Greek text of modern editions and to the above translations, by A. Day, LL.D.

PLAUTUS'S Comedies. In Prose, with Notes and Index by H. T. Riley, B.A. 2 vols.

PLINY'S Natural History. Trans., with Notes, by J. Bostock, M.D., F.R.S., and H. T. Riley, B.A. 6 vols.

PLINY. The Letters of Pliny the Younger. Melmoth's Translation, revised, with Notes and short Life, by Rev. F. C. T. Bosanquet, M.A.

PLUTARCH'S Morals. Theosophical Essays. Trans. by C. W. King, M.A. *N. S.*

—— Ethical Essays. Trans. by A. R. Shilleto, M.A. *N.S.*

—— Lives. *See page 7.*

PROPERTIUS, The Elegies of. With Notes, Literally translated by the Rev. P. J. F. Gantillon, M.A., with metrical versions of Select Elegies by Nott and Elton. *3s. 6d.*

QUINTILIAN'S Institutes of Oratory. Trans., with Notes and Biographical Notice, by Rev. J. S. Watson, M.A. 2 vols.

SALLUST, FLORUS, and VELLEIUS Paterculus. Trans., with Notes and Biographical Notices, by J. S. Watson, M.A.

SENECA DE BENEFICIIS. Newly translated by Aubrey Stewart, M.A. *3s. 6d. N. S.*

SENECA'S Minor Works. Translated by A. Stewart, M.A. *N.S.*

SOPHOCLES. The Tragedies of. In Prose, with Notes, Arguments, and Introduction. Portrait.

STRABO'S Geography. Trans., with Notes, by W. Falconer, M.A., and H. C. Hamilton. Copious Index, giving Ancient and Modern Names. 3 vols.

SUETONIUS' Lives of the Twelve Cæsars and Lives of the Grammarians. The Translation of Thomson, revised, with Notes, by T. Forester.

TACITUS. The Works of. Trans., with Notes. 2 vols.

TERENCE and PHÆDRUS. In English Prose, with Notes and Arguments, by H. T. Riley, B.A. To which is added Smart's Metrical Version of Phædrus. With Frontispiece.

THEOCRITUS, BION, MOSCHUS, and Tyrtæus. In Prose, with Notes and Arguments, by Rev. J. Banks, M.A. To which are appended the METRICAL VERSIONS of Chapman. Portrait of Theocritus.

THUCYDIDES. The Peloponnesian War. Trans., with Notes, by Rev. H. Dale. Portrait. 2 vols. *3s. 6d.* each.

TYRTÆUS.—*See Theocritus.*

VIRGIL. The Works of. In Prose, with Notes by Davidson. Revised, with additional Notes and Biographical Notice, by T. A. Buckley, B.A. Portrait. *3s. 6d.*

XENOPHON'S Works. Trans., with Notes, by J. S. Watson, M.A., and others. Portrait. In 3 vols.

COLLEGIATE SERIES.

10 *Vols. at 5s. each.* (2*l.* 10*s. per set.*)

DANTE. The Inferno. Prose Trans., with the Text of the Original on the same page, and Explanatory Notes, by John A. Carlyle, M.D. Portrait. *N. S.*

— **The Purgatorio.** Prose Trans., with the Original on the same page, and Explanatory Notes, by W. S. Dugdale. *N. S.*

NEW TESTAMENT (The) in Greek. Griesbach's Text, with the Readings of Mill and Scholz at the foot of the page, and Parallel References in the margin. Also a Critical Introduction and Chronological Tables. Two Fac-similes of Greek Manuscripts. 650 pages. 3*s.* 6*d.*

— or bound up with a Greek and English Lexicon to the New Testament (250 pages additional, making in all 900). 5*s.*

The Lexicon may be had separately, price 2*s.*

DOBREE'S Adversaria. (Notes on the Greek and Latin Classics.) Edited by the late Prof. Wagner. 2 vols.

DONALDSON (Dr.) The Theatre of the Greeks. With Supplementary Treatise on the Language, Metres, and Prosody of the Greek Dramatists. Numerous Illustrations and 3 Plans. By J. W. Donaldson, D.D. *N. S.*

KEIGHTLEY'S (Thomas) Mythology of Ancient Greece and Italy. Revised by Leonhard Schmitz, Ph.D., LL.D. 12 Plates. *N. S.*

HERODOTUS, Notes on. Original and Selected from the best Commentators. By D. W. Turner, M.A. Coloured Map.

— **Analysis and Summary of,** with a Synchronistical Table of Events—Tables of Weights, Measures, Money, and Distances—an Outline of the History and Geography—and the Dates completed from Gaisford, Baehr, &c. By J. T. Wheeler.

THUCYDIDES. An Analysis and Summary of. With Chronological Table of Events, &c., by J. T. Wheeler.

SCIENTIFIC LIBRARY.

57 *Vols. at 5s. each, excepting those marked otherwise.* (14*l.* 17*s. per set.*)

AGASSIZ and GOULD. Outline of Comparative Physiology touching the Structure and Development of the Races of Animals living and extinct. For Schools and Colleges. Enlarged by Dr. Wright. With Index and 300 Illustrative Woodcuts.

BOLLEY'S Manual of Technical Analysis; a Guide for the Testing and Valuation of the various Natural and Artificial Substances employed in the Arts and Domestic Economy, founded on the work of Dr. Bolley. Edit. by Dr. Paul. 100 Woodcuts.

BRIDGEWATER TREATISES.

— **Bell (Sir Charles) on the Hand;** its Mechanism and Vital Endowments, as evincing Design. Preceded by an Account of the Author's Discoveries in the Nervous System by A. Shaw. Numerous Woodcuts.

— **Kirby on the History, Habits,** and Instincts of Animals. With Notes by T. Rymer Jones. 100 Woodcuts. 2 vols.

— **Whewell's Astronomy and** General Physics, considered with reference to Natural Theology. Portrait of the Earl of Bridgewater. 3*s.* 6*d.*

BRIDGEWATER TREATISES.—*Continued.*

— **Chalmers on the Adaptation of** External Nature to the Moral and Intellectual Constitution of Man. With Memoir by Rev. Dr. Cumming. Portrait.

— **Prout's Treatise on Chemistry,** Meteorology, and the Function of Digestion, with reference to Natural Theology. Edit. by Dr. J. W. Griffith. 2 Maps.

— **Buckland's Geology and Mineralogy.** With Additions by Prof. Owen, Prof. Phillips, and R. Brown. Memoir of Buckland. Portrait. 2 vols. 15*s.* Vol. I. Text. Vol. II. 90 large plates with letterpress.

— **Roget's Animal and Vegetable** Physiology. 463 Woodcuts. 2 vols. 6*s.* each.

— **Kidd on the Adaptation of External** Nature to the Physical Condition of Man. 3*s.* 6*d.*

CARPENTER'S (Dr. W. B.) Zoology. A Systematic View of the Structure, Habits, Instincts, and Uses of the principal Families of the Animal Kingdom, and of the chief Forms of Fossil Remains. Revised by W. S. Dallas, F.L.S. Numerous Woodcuts. 2 vols. 6*s.* each.

CARPENTER'S Works.—*Continued.*
— **Mechanical Philosophy, Astronomy,** and Horology. A Popular Exposition. 181 Woodcuts.

— **Vegetable Physiology and Systematic** Botany. A complete Introduction to the Knowledge of Plants. Revised by E. Lankester, M.D., &c. Numerous Woodcuts. 6*s.*

— **Animal Physiology.** Revised Edition. 300 Woodcuts. 6*s.*

CHESS CONGRESS of 1862. A collection of the games played. Edited by J. Löwenthal. New edition, 5*s.*

CHEVREUL on Colour. Containing the Principles of Harmony and Contrast of Colours, and their Application to the Arts; including Painting, Decoration, Tapestries, Carpets, Mosaics, Glazing, Staining, Calico Printing, Letterpress Printing, Map Colouring, Dress, Landscape and Flower Gardening, &c. Trans. by C. Martel. Several Plates.

— With an additional series of 16 Plates in Colours, 7*s.* 6*d.*

ENNEMOSER'S History of Magic. Trans. by W. Howitt. With an Appendix of the most remarkable and best authenticated Stories of Apparitions, Dreams, Second Sight, Table-Turning, and Spirit-Rapping, &c. 2 vols.

HIND'S Introduction to Astronomy. With Vocabulary of the Terms in present use. Numerous Woodcuts. 3*s.* 6*d.* *N.S.*

HOGG'S (Jabez) Elements of Experimental and Natural Philosophy. Being an Easy Introduction to the Study of Mechanics, Pneumatics, Hydrostatics, Hydraulics, Acoustics, Optics, Caloric, Electricity, Voltaism, and Magnetism. 400 Woodcuts.

HUMBOLDT'S Cosmos; or, Sketch of a Physical Description of the Universe. Trans. by E. C. Otté, B. H. Paul, and W. S. Dallas, F.L.S. Portrait. 5 vols. 3*s.* 6*d.* each, excepting vol. v., 5*s.*

— **Personal Narrative of his Travels** in America during the years 1799–1804. Trans., with Notes, by T. Ross. 3 vols.

— **Views of Nature; or, Contemplations** of the Sublime Phenomena of Creation, with Scientific Illustrations. Trans. by E. C. Otté.

HUNT'S (Robert) Poetry of Science; or, Studies of the Physical Phenomena of Nature. By Robert Hunt, Professor at the School of Mines.

JOYCE'S Scientific Dialogues. A Familiar Introduction to the Arts and Sciences. For Schools and Young People. Numerous Woodcuts.

JOYCE'S Introduction to the Arts and Sciences, for Schools and Young People. Divided into Lessons with Examination Questions. Woodcuts. 3*s.* 6*d.*

JUKES-BROWNE'S Student's Handbook of Physical Geology. By A. J. Jukes-Browne, of the Geological Survey of England. With numerous Diagrams and Illustrations, 6*s.* *N.S.*

— **The Student's Handbook of** Historical Geology. By A. J. Jukes-Brown, B.A., F.G.S., of the Geological Survey of England and Wales. With numerous Diagrams and Illustrations. 6*s.* *N.S.*

— **The Building of the British** Islands. A Study in Geographical Evolution. By A. J. Jukes-Browne, F.G.S. 7*s.* 6*d.* *N.S.*

KNIGHT'S (Charles) Knowledge is Power. A Popular Manual of Political Economy.

LILLY. Introduction to Astrology. With a Grammar of Astrology and Tables for calculating Nativities, by Zadkiel.

MANTELL'S (Dr.) Geological Excursions through the Isle of Wight and along the Dorset Coast. Numerous Woodcuts and Geological Map.

— **Petrifactions and their Teachings.** Handbook to the Organic Remains in the British Museum. Numerous Woodcuts. 6*s.*

— **Wonders of Geology; or, a** Familiar Exposition of Geological Phenomena. A coloured Geological Map of England, Plates, and 200 Woodcuts. 2 vols. 7*s.* 6*d.* each.

MORPHY'S Games of Chess, being the Matches and best Games played by the American Champion, with explanatory and analytical Notes by J. Löwenthal. With short Memoir and Portrait of Morphy.

SCHOUW'S Earth, Plants, and Man. Popular Pictures of Nature. And Kobell's Sketches from the Mineral Kingdom. Trans. by A. Henfrey, F.R.S. Coloured Map of the Geography of Plants.

SMITH'S (Pye) Geology and Scripture; or, the Relation between the Scriptures and Geological Science. With Memoir.

STANLEY'S Classified Synopsis of the Principal Painters of the Dutch and Flemish Schools, including an Account of some of the early German Masters. By George Stanley.

STAUNTON'S Chess-Player's Handbook. A Popular and Scientific Introduction to the Game, with numerous Diagrams and Coloured Frontispiece. *N.S.*

STAUNTON.—*Continued.*
— **Chess Praxis.** A Supplement to the Chess-player's Handbook. Containing the most important modern Improvements in the Openings; Code of Chess Laws; and a Selection of Morphy's Games. Annotated. 636 pages. Diagrams. 6*s.*

— **Chess-Player's Companion.** Comprising a Treatise on Odds, Collection of Match Games, including the French Match with M. St. Amant, and a Selection of Original Problems. Diagrams and Coloured Frontispiece.

— **Chess Tournament of 1851.** A Collection of Games played at this celebrated assemblage. With Introduction and Notes. Numerous Diagrams.

STOCKHARDT'S Experimental Chemistry. A Handbook for the Study of the Science by simple Experiments. Edit. by C. W. Heaton, F.C.S. Numerous Woodcuts. *N. S.*

URE'S (Dr. A.) Cotton Manufacture of Great Britain, systematically investigated; with an Introductory View of its Comparative State in Foreign Countries. Revised by P. L. Simmonds. 150 Illustrations. 2 vols.

— **Philosophy of Manufactures,** or an Exposition of the Scientific, Moral, and Commercial Economy of the Factory System of Great Britain. Revised by P. L. Simmonds. Numerous Figures. 800 pages. 7*s.* 6*d.*

ECONOMICS AND FINANCE.

GILBART'S History, Principles, and Practice of Banking. Revised to 1881 by A. S. Michie, of the Royal Bank of Scotland. Portrait of Gilbart. 2 vols. 10*s.* *N. S.*

REFERENCE LIBRARY.

28 *Volumes at Various Prices.* (8*l.* 15*s.* *per set.*)

BLAIR'S Chronological Tables. Comprehending the Chronology and History of the World, from the Earliest Times to the Russian Treaty of Peace, April 1856. By J. W. Rosse. 800 pages. 10*s.*

— **Index of Dates.** Comprehending the principal Facts in the Chronology and History of the World, from the Earliest to the Present, alphabetically arranged; being a complete Index to the foregoing. By J. W. Rosse. 2 vols. 5*s.* each.

BOHN'S Dictionary of Quotations from the English Poets. 4th and cheaper Edition. 6*s.*

BOND'S Handy-book of Rules and Tables for Verifying Dates with the Christian Era. 4th Edition. *N. S.*

BUCHANAN'S Dictionary of Science and Technical Terms used in Philosophy, Literature, Professions, Commerce, Arts, and Trades. By W. H. Buchanan, with Supplement. Edited by Jas. A. Smith. 6*s.*

CHRONICLES OF THE TOMBS. A Select Collection of Epitaphs, with Essay on Epitaphs and Observations on Sepulchral Antiquities. By T. J. Pettigrew, F.R.S., F.S.A. 5*s.*

CLARK'S (Hugh) Introduction to Heraldry. Revised by J. R. Planché. 5*s.* 950 Illustrations.

— *With the Illustrations coloured,* 15*s.* *N. S.*

COINS, Manual of.—*See Humphreys.*

DATES, Index of.—*See Blair.*

DICTIONARY of Obsolete and Provincial English. Containing Words from English Writers previous to the 19th Century. By Thomas Wright, M.A., F.S.A., &c. 2 vols. 5*s.* each.

EPIGRAMMATISTS (The). A Selection from the Epigrammatic Literature of Ancient, Mediæval, and Modern Times. With Introduction, Notes, Observations, Illustrations, an Appendix on Works connected with Epigrammatic Literature, by Rev. H. Dodd, M.A. 6*s.* *N. S.*

GAMES, Handbook of. Comprising Treatises on above 40 Games of Chance, Skill, and Manual Dexterity, including Whist, Billiards, &c. Edit. by Henry G. Bohn. Numerous Diagrams. 5*s.* *N. S.*

HENFREY'S Guide to English Coins. Revised Edition, by C. F. Keary, M.A., F.S.A. With an Historical Introduction. 6*s.* *N. S.*

HUMPHREYS' Coin Collectors' Manual. An Historical Account of the Progress of Coinage from the Earliest Time, by H. N. Humphreys. 140 Illustrations. 2 vols. 5*s.* each. *N. S.*

LOWNDES' Bibliographer's Manual of English Literature. Containing an Account of Rare and Curious Books published in or relating to Great Britain and Ireland, from the Invention of Printing, with Biographical Notices and Prices, by W. T. Lowndes. Parts I.-X. (A to Z), 3*s*. 6*d*. each. Part XI. (Appendix Vol.), 5*s*. Or the 11 parts in 4 vols., half morocco, 2*l*. 2*s*.

MEDICINE, Handbook of Domestic, Popularly Arranged. By Dr. H. Davies. 700 pages. 5*s*.

NOTED NAMES OF FICTION. Dictionary of. Including also Familiar Pseudonyms, Surnames bestowed on Eminent Men, &c. By W. A. Wheeler, M.A. 5*s*. *N. S.*

POLITICAL CYCLOPÆDIA. A Dictionary of Political, Constitutional, Statistical, and Forensic Knowledge; forming a Work of Reference on subjects of Civil Administration, Political Economy, Finance, Commerce, Laws, and Social Relations. 4 vols. 3*s*. 6*d*. each.

PROVERBS, Handbook of. Containing an entire Republication of Ray's Collection, with Additions from Foreign Languages and Sayings, Sentences, Maxims, and Phrases. 5*s*.

— **A Polyglot of Foreign.** Comprising French, Italian, German, Dutch, Spanish, Portuguese, and Danish. With English Translations. 5*s*.

SYNONYMS and ANTONYMS; or, Kindred Words and their Opposites, Collected and Contrasted by Ven. C. J. Smith, M.A. 5*s*. *N. S.*

WRIGHT (Th.)—*See Dictionary.*

NOVELISTS' LIBRARY.

12 *Volumes at* 3*s*. 6*d*. *each, excepting those marked otherwise.* (2*l*. 5*s*. *per set.*)

BURNEY'S Evelina; or, a Young Lady's Entrance into the World. By F. Burney (Mme. D'Arblay). With Introduction and Notes by A. R. Ellis, Author of 'Sylvestra,' &c. *N. S.*

— **Cecilia.** With Introduction and Notes by A. R. Ellis. 2 vols. *N. S.*

DE STAËL. Corinne or Italy. By Madame de Staël. Translated by Emily Baldwin and Paulina Driver.

EBERS' Egyptian Princess. Trans. by Emma Buchheim. *N. S.*

FIELDING'S Joseph Andrews and his Friend Mr. Abraham Adams. With Roscoe's Biography. *Cruikshank's Illustrations.* *N. S.*

FIELDING.—*Continued.*

— **Amelia.** Roscoe's Edition, revised. *Cruikshank's Illustrations.* 5*s*. *N. S.*

— **History of Tom Jones, a Foundling.** Roscoe's Edition. *Cruikshank's Illustrations.* 2 vols. *N. S.*

GROSSI'S Marco Visconti. Trans. by A. F. D. *N. S.*

MANZONI. The Betrothed: being a Translation of 'I Promessi Sposi.' Numerous Woodcuts. 1 vol. (732 pages). 5*s*. *N. S.*

STOWE (Mrs. H. B.) Uncle Tom's Cabin; or, Life among the Lowly. 8 full-page Illustrations. *N. S.*

ARTISTS' LIBRARY.

9 *Volumes at Various Prices.* (2*l*. 8*s*. 6*d*. *per set.*)

BELL (Sir Charles). The Anatomy and Philosophy of Expression, as Connected with the Fine Arts. 5*s*. *N. S.*

DEMMIN. History of Arms and Armour from the Earliest Period. By Auguste Demmin. Trans. by C. C. Black, M.A., Assistant Keeper, S. K. Museum. 1900 Illustrations. 7*s*. 6*d*. *N. S.*

FAIRHOLT'S Costume in England. Third Edition. Enlarged and Revised by the Hon. H. A. Dillon, F.S.A. With more than 700 Engravings. 2 vols. 5*s*. each. *N. S.*

Vol. I. History. Vol. I. Glossary.

FLAXMAN. Lectures on Sculpture. With Three Addresses to the R.A. by Sir R. Westmacott, R.A., and Memoir o Flaxman. Portrait and 53 Plates. 6*s*. *N.S.*

HEATON'S Concise History of Painting. New Edition, revised by W. Cosmo Monkhouse. 5*s*. *N.S.*

LECTURES ON PAINTING by the Royal Academicians, Barry, Opie, Fuseli. With Introductory Essay and Notes by R. Wornum. Portrait of Fuseli.

LEONARDO DA VINCI'S Treatise on Painting. Trans. by J. F. Rigaud, R.A. With a Life and an Account of his Works by J. W. Brown. Numerous Plates. 5*s*. *N.S.*

PLANCHÉ'S History of British Costume, from the Earliest Time to the 19th Century. By J. R. Planché. 400 Illustrations. 5*s*. *N. S.*

BOHN'S CHEAP SERIES.

PRICE ONE SHILLING EACH.

A Series of Complete Stories or Essays, mostly reprinted from Vols. in Bohn's Libraries, and neatly bound in stiff paper cover, with cut edges, suitable for Railway Reading.

ASCHAM (*ROGER*).—

SCHOLEMASTER. By PROFESSOR MAYOR.

CARPENTER (*DR. W. B.*).—

PHYSIOLOGY OF TEMPERANCE AND TOTAL ABSTINENCE.

EMERSON.—

ENGLAND AND ENGLISH CHARACTERISTICS. Lectures on the Race, Ability, Manners, Truth, Character, Wealth, Religion, &c. &c.

NATURE: An Essay. To which are added Orations, Lectures and Addresses.

REPRESENTATIVE MEN: Seven Lectures on PLATO, SWEDENBORG, MONTAIGNE, SHAKESPEARE, NAPOLEON, and GOETHE.

TWENTY ESSAYS on Various Subjects.

THE CONDUCT OF LIFE.

FRANKLIN (*BENJAMIN*).—

AUTOBIOGRAPHY. Edited by J. SPARKS.

HAWTHORNE (*NATHANIEL*).—

TWICE-TOLD TALES. Two Vols. in One

SNOW IMAGE, and other Tales.

SCARLET LETTER.

HOUSE WITH THE SEVEN GABLES.

TRANSFORMATION; or the Marble Fawn. Two Parts.

HAZLITT (*W.*).—

TABLE-TALK: Essays on Men and Manners. Three Parts.

PLAIN SPEAKER: Opinions on Books, Men, and Things Three Parts.

LECTURES ON THE ENGLISH COMIC WRITERS.

LECTURES ON THE ENGLISH POETS.

HAZLITT (W.). *Continued.*

LECTURES ON THE CHARACTERS OF SHAKESPEARE'S PLAYS.

LECTURES ON THE LITERATURE OF THE AGE OF ELIZABETH, chiefly Dramatic.

IRVING (WASHINGTON).

LIFE OF MOHAMMED. With Portrait.

LIVES OF SUCCESSORS OF MOHAMMED.

LIFE OF GOLDSMITH.

SKETCH BOOK.

TALES OF A TRAVELLER.

TOUR ON THE PRAIRIES.

CONQUESTS OF GRANADA AND SPAIN. Two Parts.

LIFE AND VOYAGES OF COLUMBUS. Two Parts.

COMPANIONS OF COLUMBUS: Their Voyages and Discoveries.

ADVENTURES OF CAPTAIN BONNEVILLE in the Rocky Mountains and the Far West.

KNICKERBOCKER'S HISTORY OF NEW YORK, from the Beginning of the World to the End of the Dutch Dynasty.

TALES OF THE ALHAMBRA.

CONQUEST OF FLORIDA UNDER HERNANDO DE SOTO.

ABBOTSFORD AND NEWSTEAD ABBEY.

SALMAGUNDI; or, The Whim-Whams and Opinions of LAUNCELOT LANGSTAFF, Esq.

BRACEBRIDGE HALL; or, The Humourists.

ASTORIA; or, Anecdotes of an Enterprise beyond the Rocky Mountains.

WOLFERT'S ROOST, and Other Tales.

LAMB (CHARLES).—

ESSAYS OF ELIA. With a Portrait.

LAST ESSAYS OF ELIA.

ELIANA. With Biographical Sketch.

MARRYAT (CAPTAIN).

PIRATE AND THE THREE CUTTERS. With a Memoir of the Author.

The only authorised Edition; no others published in England contain the Derivations and Etymological Notes of Dr. Mahn, who devoted several years to this portion of the Work.

WEBSTER'S DICTIONARY

OF THE ENGLISH LANGUAGE.

Thoroughly revised and improved by Chauncey A. Goodrich, D.D., LL.D., and Noah Porter, D.D., of Yale College.

THE GUINEA DICTIONARY.

New Edition [1880], with a Supplement of upwards of 4600 New Words and Meanings.

1628 Pages. 3000 Illustrations.

The features of this volume, which render it perhaps the most useful Dictionary for general reference extant, as it is undoubtedly one of the cheapest books ever published, are as follows:—

1. Completeness.—It contains 114,000 words.
2. Accuracy of Definition.
3. Scientific and Technical Terms.
4. Etymology.
5. The Orthography is based, as far as possible, on Fixed Principles.
6. Pronunciation.
7. The Illustrative Citations.
8. The Synonyms.
9. The Illustrations, which exceed 3000.

Cloth, 21s.; half-bound in calf, 30s.; calf or half russia, 31s. 6d.; russia, 2l.

With New Biographical Appendix, containing over 9700 Names.

THE COMPLETE DICTIONARY

Contains, in addition to the above matter, several valuable Literary Appendices, and 70 extra pages of Illustrations, grouped and classified.

1 vol. 1919 pages, cloth, 31s. 6d.

'Certainly the best practical English Dictionary extant.'—*Quarterly Review*, 1873.

Prospectuses, with Specimen Pages, sent post free on application.

*** *To be obtained through all Booksellers.*

London: Printed by STRANGEWAYS & SONS, Tower Street, Cambridge Circus, W.C.

www.ingramcontent.com/pod-product-compliance
Lightning Source LLC
Chambersburg PA
CBHW031423020726
47499CB00005B/1576

* 9 7 8 3 3 3 7 3 9 9 4 3 6 *